for Jennie – 1959-2013
and Namira 1959 -
Two women who showed me how to live

Acknowledgements

I would like to thank Namira Williams for her multiple suggestions and careful proofreading and my family for their patience. For editorial advice I'm indebted to David Jack Fletcher. I would like to thank the staff at the Sydney Jewish Museum for their kind use of their library.
This book remembers Jennie Kerr who made it all possible.

The Formula of Memory

Two people
Three countries
One unspeakable crime

A Novel,
partly based on true events

Christopher M Williams

Traveler, there are no paths. Paths are made by walking.

— Antonio Machado

The increase of disorder or entropy is what distinguishes the past from the future, giving a direction to time.

— Stephen Hawking

Science, my lad, is made up of mistakes, but they are mistakes which are useful to make because they lead little by little to the truth.

— Jules Verne

Author's Note

Although The Formula of Memory is a work of fiction, some scenes are based on real events. The World Bike Ride toured Australia in 1982 and the author visited Hiroshima and Auschwitz as part of that bike ride. The names of the characters are invented to protect their identity.

ONE

1

The red-haired girl limped past the driveway of the cream-brick house, looked up and down the street, and rested a hand on the tin letterbox. Trusting only her gut, she rolled the dice one more time, hoping fate would take a different turn. One thought replayed, over and over, since that night three years ago when she'd lost her innocence, the young science teacher, the way he'd smiled at her. She yanked a small, blue object from her bag and stuffed it through the letterbox opening. Shuffling away, the hot, dusty wind hooked her hair, flaring it out like a spinnaker in a storm.

*

The life Daniel Cohen left behind melted in Winburn, population 16,500 and falling, 635km from nowhere. A beginning teacher's worse nightmare. He scanned the horizon from the top of the lookout, twelve kilometres from town, a jumble of metamorphics thrown up like a mocking rude finger. Glaring down at the Schwinn's punctured tyre, he stared back down the track for any sign of a vehicle, rising dust, a startled flock of crows, a distant thumping hum. Nothing. Dust spiralled up a willy willy carrying the stench of something dead. The wan light retreated with the sun, the bleached rocks, the colours blending into grey, the shrubs outlined in a shadow fading like a nebulous dream. *What the fuck am I doing here?* He shook his hand to relieve the throbbing pain of the three-cornered jack still in his rear tyre, as if he could shake away the throbbing pain and started the long walk back across the red corrugations towards town.

*

The next day, Daniel, just shy of 25, checked his diary for the day. *3:40 pm: Leave school; 3:45: doctor's appointment; 4:15: haircut; home by 5.* He sniffed the air, paying no attention to the letterbox as he left for school, a typical igneous February day in Winburn. Closest town was Bogan, 250 km to the east. Closest city, 450 km to the west. To the south, a mountain of tailings loomed over the train tracks. *Maybe they thought it'd make a nice windbreak?* He dumped two boxes of students' notebooks into the back of a purple '71 Corolla Skyla had loaned him last year and stopped at the bus stop opposite to collect a stranded Year 8 boy in mismatched socks.

'Miss the bus again, Will?'

'Slept in.'

'Had any breakfast?'

Will shook his head and wiped strands of black hair from his bloodshot eyes. Daniel offered a banana.

'No thanks, sir.'

They drove the three kilometres to Winburn High, past the hospital, the swimming pool and three unshaven men in tatty winter coats like actors in an Oliver Twist play. Waiting outside the Cricketeers' Arms Hotel. He nodded at Will, who stared out the window.

'Still there, in the same coats as last week.'

'Deros.'

He parked in the staff carpark on the cracked bitumen – solid now, oozing liquid by noon. Will slung his bag over his shoulder and walked away. The boy didn't look back. Daniel squinted at the blistering sky under a watchful black currawong perched on a branch hanging over the car park fence. He climbed the stairs to the Science staffroom, dumped his books on his desk, nodded and grunted a morning. Ben, the head teacher was discussing cricket with the Physics teacher Charles, whose hobby was betting equations and their application to horse racing. Other teachers chatted about a shopping trip to the city and what they would wear to a friend's wedding next week.

Four years out of college, the last three in the town that parodied the words wind and burn, Daniel had decided one morning last year he didn't much like teenagers and realised he didn't much like teaching. The lack of depth in the topics, the mechanical way he was supposed to teach-to-the-test method. His main problem was the students – their rudeness, lack of motivation, hideous mullets and poor taste in music. The other classes were mostly crowd control with frequent outbreaks of random dipshittery. Last week, Kayden in 8F, for a laugh, lit Jackson's farts with a match. He could still smell the burnt polyester.

Then Emma showed up. A tall park ranger he'd organised from the National Parks as a guest speaker. When she stood at his classroom door his jaw dropped and his breath caught in his chest. For an instance he was lost for words before his training kicked in. Welcome to our guest speaker, Emma. Introductions. Topic. Emma. Five ten, long auburn hair, gorgeous with a coquettish smile weak men found intimidating. The shape of her face, the distance of her mouth to her eyes, the way her khaki uniform hugged her body. All the details Daniel studied as if he was in class himself. She strode over in front of the bench, turned and faced the class. Daniel saw Casper and most of the other boys staring as if they seen aliens. After their second meeting, somehow accidental while walking his dog, she asked him what he wanted to do with his life. He paused and had said I honestly don't know. Jules, his housemate-come-boob-expert Maths teacher would say, 'Just learning my trade and marking time out here.' If he was honest, his only interest was moving back to the coast as soon as possible.

Then there was Skyla back in Randwick, they planned to get engaged when he returned. The parties, the beach, the nightlife. Doubts circled like a vinyl record – she'd not returned his calls of late. Three years in Winburn, the open country had begun to insinuate itself inside like scent on the wind.

Winburn? They can't even spell it.

She left before he could ask her out. A week later, as chance dressed up as fate might have it, he bumped into her at an art exhibition. They talked like they'd known each other since childhood, stringing diverse topics together without catching a breath. She was everything he dreamed of and couldn't wait to see her again. Skyla took a backseat.

*

In Year 11 Geology, the students examined crystals and minerals in four wooden boxes divided into twelve squares. Rose quartz from Victoria, zebra jasper from the Kimberley, blue calcite from Mexico, azurite/malachite from Areyonga. A student with thick glasses and forehead pimples picked up the azurite.

'Careful with that Casper.'

'Yes, sir. My mum has one of these on a necklace. It's mostly blue.'

'Then it's mostly azurite.'

'She reckons it's got healing powers. Said it cured her cancer.'

'Really?'

*

To relieve the monotony, he'd drive for hours out of town each weekend towards the hills taking the roughest dirt tracks the Corolla could handle. The setting sun, blood pulsing down his arms, the sky, like molten iron listening to the screech of the cockatoos wheeling overhead and the smell – petrichor after rain. The dusty land held no lasting attraction, nothing he'd hold onto, just a hundred different odours he couldn't name, bones bleached with the patina of time; carcasses picked clean by crows and dingos; the spear grass whistling as it waved in the dry westerly. *Wish Emma could see this.*

Later, he parked the car next to a blue-and-white '64 Valiant in the driveway of the cream, brick house he shared with Maths teacher Jules Jackson. The car came with history – the 60s, hotted up, a youth in a black leather jacket, sideburns way below his ears. Brylcreem-slicked hair.

Jules, a twenty-two-year-old Maths teacher with a habit of collecting female underwear, sipped a cup of mint tea in the kitchen. His auburn hair pinched at the neck in a ponytail wearing his favourite Pink Floyd T-shirt. His main interest outside of school – the application of formulae for 3D curves, mainly boobs.

'Dan, I found a great formula for you. $y = x^2 + x - 5$. Although if m stands for 'perfect', the formula is: $(y\text{-}y_1) = m(x\text{-}x_1)$.

'Go on. I know you want to,' Daniel said, one eyebrow raised.

'The shape of your perfect woman. What was her name? Anne?'

'Emma. And there's nothing intriguing about the formula. It's what's inside that's appealing, don't you think? Do you have a formula for that?' Daniel stared at Jules standing stock still, mouth ajar as if his internal gears had jammed.

'I'm still working on that. You know, there's gotta be a catch? A woman who looks that good, why hasn't she got a boyfriend?

'You tell me. She's never spoken of one.'

'Still, there's gotta be a catch.'

'You already said that. So, what's cooking?'

'You mean on the stove or in the letterbox?'

'What?'

'There's something in the letterbox for you.'

Something in his tone caught Daniel's attention. Growing up, he'd detect messages in his mother's unspoken words as she stood outside his bedroom door. Her sad smile, the colour draining from her eyes as she waited for his dad to come back. He sprinted to the letterbox, eyes wide and extracted a pair of teal underpants with frilly white lace stitching. A folded note fell out. He scanned the street. Deserted.

Daniel spread the underpants, smelling of cheap fabric softener, on the kitchen table. He unfolded the note and looked up as Jules leaned forward, mouth set in a grin.

'So that's what she left this morning,' Jules said.

'Who did?'

'The girl with the long red hair and the limp. Ruby something, she was in my Maths class last year for a while. Then she changed classes, don't know why. Do you know her?'

'Not sure. If it's the same one, I think I've seen her at school and the bus stop. Now that you mention it, I remember her hanging around my classroom a few times last year.'

'Well, Mr Popular, what does the letter say?'

Daniel held the note up to the light. The writing was small in left-slanted letters and parts of the ink smeared. Crab claw.

Dear Sir,

I've seen you give lifts to kids from school, so can I get a lift over town to my mum's house tomorrow after school? My nan doesn't have a car. She doesn't need to know. I'll be waiting down at the park after school.

I promise I won't tell.

Ruby

Daniel folded the letter and slipped it into his pocket. He left the underpants on the table. *Nan, huh?* he thought. *Promise she won't tell who?* Jules leaned in closer, mouth pinched, his voice tightening.

'Hell, you're not thinking of doing it, are you?'

'Probably not.' Daniel's voice softened. 'I'm throwing these in the bin. I don't want you adding them to your 'collection.''

'Hey, how do you know about that?' Jules said, palms open and extended.

'Mate, your wardrobe was open when I walked by. There must be thirty or more in there, hanging up like spray-painted bats. You might want to lock them up.'

'Thirty-eight, last count. I want to get forty.' He grinned. 'Yeah, I should lock them up, I guess. Not like it's hurting anyone, is it?'

Jules raised his eyebrows.

Daniel stared, conflicted. 'So why do you collect them? Like, the newsagent sells *Playboy* you know?'

'No, no, it's nothing like that. Well not quite.' He winced. 'I'm fascinated by who's worn them, where they have been and how many men, or women have taken them off.'

He gave a quick, high-pitched laugh.

Daniel thought: *Christ he's not taking this seriously. What am I going to do?*

Jules changed the topic. 'Hey, remember Smithy from Condo last year?'

'Of course. Run out of town after a Year Eight girl accused him of touching her.'

'She owned up later, said she'd made it up. Poor bastard. Teaching for twenty years, career ruined overnight. That's not going to happen to me.'

'Me either. All she's asking for is a lift.'

'And the panties? What about them?' Jules blinked and lowered his eyes.

'I told you. I don't want anything to do with them. They're going in the bin.'

Looking at the note, he was intrigued by the way the letters curved, how the love hearts bobbed above the 'i's'. *What was her story?* He thought. *Why me? It's probably a harmless prank. It'll go nowhere.*

Later, Daniel looked out of his open door and saw Jules tiptoe outside, open the bin, and pluck out the panties. They disappeared into his pocket.

2

She perched on the red-brick wall that bordered the park, a half-eaten Royal Gala in her hand. Her freckled, white legs flexed in and out as if set on perpetual motion. Cicadas hummed their ascending tune in a monotonous rhythm as the haze of the afternoon heat hung like a blanket of angry bees. It was around 2:30, she'd sneaked out the back gate during PE. From time to time, she gazed back up at the school.

*

Daniel took a chemistry extra, Year 11 last period and scanned Ben's lesson plan – *The Second Law of Thermodynamics.*

He sighed and read aloud, '*The energy available to any closed system is always less at the end of the process than the beginning.*'

He rolled his eyes around the room. Complete silence. A pen dropped and clattered to the floor.

'You guys get that? Energy is always lost.'

'Why, sir?' a boy with a ponytail asked.

'Well, James, it's because of this concept called entropy.'

'What's that, sir?'

'In general terms, it's the natural progression from order to disorder. I'll give you an example. Say your mother tidies up your room once a week. She folds up your clothes, puts them in their drawers, gives it order and reduces the entropy in there. Then you come along and day by day the mess gets worse. You increase the entropy.'

He looked out at a sea of blank faces – two guys stared out the window, another girl nodded her head, a girl with skull earrings studied her ebony hair like it was a Van Gogh. Daniel squirmed behind the Formica desk, sipped from a plastic water bottle and paced around the classroom.

"Entropy'. You now know it as chaos. Do you understand what chaos is?'

'Yeah. This fuckin' subject,' the girl with the silver skull earrings said.

Daniel tapped his fingers on the desk. 'Do you mind, Destiny? That language is not acceptable in this classroom.'

He looked up and heard a few snickers and grunts. It was like the classroom was closing in on him and all he could smell was the funk of chalk. *And the girl with the limp. Why risk it?*

The clock ticked. He closed the book. The 3 pm bell rang.

*

At 3:15, she climbed in, smiled and placed her bags under her legs. Daniel swallowed hard as she swung her feet over her bag. She leant over and removed a strawberry lollipop from the side pocket and bit through the plastic. Her skirt rode up her pale, closed thighs.

'Almost thought you weren't coming.' She twirled the lollipop between her lips, held it out and inspected it.

'Your note said you needed a lift to your mother's?'

'Didn't you read between the lines?'

'Where to?'

'Down Main Street, then left on Aerodrome Drive. She's out before the cemetery.' She spun the lollipop between her fingers and pursed her lips.

He glimpsed the tip of her tongue as it stabbed out an inch.

She gazed out the window, as they passed a pharmacy, newsagent and a café with empty tables and chairs outside on the footpath. Her long fingers opened one by one as if counting. A tension made him shift in his seat. *I shouldn't be here.*

At the first and only red traffic light, he studied her face, three freckles on her right cheek in a triangle that pointed to a curved scar next to her lips. She peeked across – two beads of sweat ran down Daniel's forehead.

'You want a tissue?' She held out the box.

He shook his head. 'How did you get your limp?'

She stared out the window, arched her back and pressed a fist to her lips. He looked across at her.

She nodded out the window. 'See that park up ahead? Pull over into the carpark.'

'I think we should go straight to your mother's place,' Daniel said and cleared his throat.

'I just want to talk.' She frowned, clasping her hands in her lap.

Daniel pursed his lips, sensing something wasn't right. First the panties, now this. She was a child and he only wanted to help. Despite his better judgement, he nodded and followed her directions. 'I'm happy to talk.'

They passed an empty child's playground with swings and an old metal merry-go-round set in sand under a bleached sunshade. The concrete path wove between beds of Queen Elizabeth roses. A middle-aged man in dark-green overalls stood stock-still as if meditating, a limp hose dribbled in his hands.

'Pull over here.'

Daniel parked under drooping leaves of a desiccated desert oak and switched off the motor. She turned, moved in closer, eyes switched from his face to the window and back again.

'You want to know how I got my limp?' she said through narrow lips. 'I'll tell you about Uncle fuckin' Kevin.'

Daniel's mouth opened as he stared at her face.

'When I was twelve, Uncle Kevin would come over and 'babysit' while Mum went to the club. He'd get me to sit on his lap and his hands would be all over me, you understand?'

Daniel nodded.

'After a few more visits, he held my hands and put his dick in them. When Mum came home, I told her. Do you know what she said?' She studied his face to make sure he heard. "I'll talk to him, ask him to stop'. Bullshit he did!'

Her face reddened as she wiped drops of spit from her lips with her sleeve. 'That's when I did it. One night he asked me to suck it. Told me to do it *enthusiastically*. So, I *enthusiastically* obliged. With my teeth. He screamed at the same time I tasted blood, then he punched my face with something hard.'

She pointed to the scar. 'I stumbled back and fell down the stairs, landed badly and broke my ankle. They tried to fix it. Did a shit job. I've got a shorter left leg, thanks to Uncle fuckin' Kevin.'

Daniel let out a long, low breath, wondering what he was doing here. He scanned out the windows, hoping no one was watching. The place was deserted. She put her hand on his leg. For a split-second time stopped. Sound vanished, his heart thumping in his chest.

'I'm so sorry, Ruby. Is there anything I can do? Where's the arsehole now?'

'Dead.' Her voice was hard. 'Killed himself about a year ago.'

'Suicide!' he said – it was not quite a question. His eyes widened. 'How?'

'He hung himself. Good riddance.' She bit her lower lip and searched his face. 'I know you're not like that. Do you know why I left those blue underpants?'

He shook his head, opened his mouth, the words froze at the back of his throat. She charged on. 'Because blue is the colour of trust. I know I can trust you. You're not like that Maths teacher. He's a perv.'

'Which Maths teacher?'

'Mr Jackson. Last year, said he'd *help me* after class. He liked to touch me, put his hand on my knee, squeeze my leg. I told him to stop but he kept doing it. So, I told the deputy I wanted to change classes.'

Daniel frowned. 'Did you report him?'

'No. He stopped when I threatened to. Then I changed class. Can we go to Mum's place now? I've got something to show you.'

'I think I need to speak with your mum. You should see someone, probably the counsellor about what happened to you.'

She turned her face towards the window. They drove in silence through a neglected part of the town unfamiliar to Daniel – like waking up drunk on a beach in Siberia. He wound the window down and a hot blast pushed her scent up his nose. From a distance, the rising crescendo of a Cessna 402C hammered as it geared up for take-off. A white brushstroke vapour trail of a passing jet drew a straight line across the sky. He squinted out the window as the houses passed and each dismal street floated by, weeds sprouting through dry, red soil.

'Stop here.' She nodded at a cream-coloured house with a rusted roof. The white window frames bled crusts of paint and the front gate hung obliquely on one rusty hinge. The cracks in the path so wide it looked like a plough had torn through. Opposite, a crinkle-skinned woman looked up, secateurs in hand. She stood behind a neat row of roses. Ruby walked around the car and yanked down the creases from her skirt that rode up her thighs. She leaned in the window, 'Are you coming?'

'Is your mother home?'

'Looks like she's not here. She's probably at her boyfriend's. Come on, I want to show you my new bikini.'

'Like, on you?' he asked, surprised.

'Duh,' she said as her mouth stretched wider.

He hesitated, not sure what to say. 'I'm curious. How old are you?'

'Why does it matter how old I am?' A puzzled look on her face changed to a wicked smile. 'Well,'– she tossed a braid over her shoulder – 'I'm sixteen, as of last week. So, are you coming in?'

He stared at her for a second. 'Look, I've dropped you home. I can't come in unless your mother's home. I'm happy to wait here while you go and check.'

He was torn between the thrill of the unknown, behind that door or doing the right thing and leaving. 'Dunno. Don't worry...you're not her type. She's into plumbers now.'

'I'm not coming in. Sorry. I've got to run. I've got exams to mark.'

'Then meet me day after tomorrow, same place. I've got something I need to ask you.'

'Why can't you ask me now?'

Her body stiffened and her eyes dropped. 'Just meet me the day after tomorrow or you'll be sorry.' She leaned in closer and perfume rushed up his nose. He blinked fast three times as she brought her face close to his and planted a soft kiss on his cheek. She smiled and turned her head and walked away.

Daniel drove off with the words *or you'll be sorry* echoing in his head. He pondered if he'd take Ruby's story to Bob Dunstan, the deputy principal. He couldn't decide. *Jules? I need to do something about him. I'll have to take that to Dunstan. Christ, why me?* He needed time to work out what he'd say, time to weigh up the consequences. Time wasn't on his side. The woman opposite stopped her pruning, removed a small notebook and pen from her apron pocket and started writing.

3

He tossed and turned that night as her story repeated in a continual loop. *Christ, sexual assault at twelve.* He had no idea about sixteen-year-old girls. He'd never discussed the subject with his sister, Rachel, who was three years older. *What if she wants me, like, as a boyfriend? That's ridiculous? I'm about to move on Emma. Should I tell Skyla?* His mind spun, too many unknown possibilities. *What about Jules? What's with the underpants?* He waited. Decided not to see her outside of school again.

The next day a note appeared folded and torn from an exercise book tucked under the front door. He saw his name and another love heart above the 'i'. He unfolded the note, its crinkled, torn edge crackling as if all moisture had leached from the paper. Jules poked his head in through the bedroom door.

'You cooking tonight?' Jules asked.

'Nope.'

'I'll do a salad then. Did you get a letter from Skyla?' Jules asked as his eyes dipped to Daniel's desk.

Daniel turned and folded the paper over fast. 'Er, yes. It came today.'

'No more underpants, love letters then?' Jules asked with a smile.

Daniel shook his head. When Jules left, Daniel closed the door. He unfolded the note and flattened it on his recycled wooden desk, which sat against the cream-coloured wall under a two-panel slider. He looked out on a patchy backyard full of dandelions, Cobbler's peg and rye grass going to seed. A rust-covered Victa mower lay abandoned under a clothesline that drooped at a dangerous angle. He'd placed the note next to his application for transfer.

Dear Sir,

Can I call you Daniel? I feel like I can, now that we are friends. And I'm relieved that I've told you my story. That makes you special, I've told no one else. I'm glad you know. When we meet tomorrow, I'll tell you what I need you to do. I need to ask you a favour, it's about when you leave this town for good. I know you'll be leaving soon. They all do after 3 or 4 years. All the nice ones. So, we'll go to our special place again and I know you'll say yes.

Ruby
PS: I love you X X

Shit. The love hearts burned a permanent pattern on his retina. *'Love,' 'Truth'? What do those words mean in this situation?* He blinked fast, then closed his eyes. *This has gone far enough.* A knock jolted his eyes open.

'Dinner's ready.'

He pushed his dilemma to the back of his mind and folded the letter into a tiny square and slid it into the desk drawer.

*

The following Saturday, he drove around the town's grid-like streets looking for Emma, inspecting every house for a sign, a clue. A car with the logo, a trailer with shovels, rakes and hoses, maybe a clothesline with khaki shirts.

Nothing. *I might try ringing her office on Monday.* Skyla wasn't returning his calls.

After school on Monday, he phoned the local NPWS office and asked for Emma. He explained he was a teacher and would like to book her for another 'guest talk,' the woman on the phone replied: 'Don't know when she'll be back from her honeymoon.' *Honeymoon?* A hot flush crawled up his neck. He stumbled back to his car. *How could I have been so stupid? Of course, she's married.* On the drive home, he smacked the steering wheel until his hands were numb. As soon as he walked in the front door, he rang Skyla. He got a recorded message and told her he'd be back next holiday break, in six weeks. Jules smiled, patted him on the back and said, 'Not the right formula, huh?' For the moment, he forgot about talking to Dunstan.

*

Two weeks went by. He pictured happily married Emma chatting with her new husband about the intense teacher who had a crush on her. He missed the meeting with Ruby and no more letters arrived. He focused more on teaching and what Skyla was up to. She became a fall-back position, an anchor he could rely on back home.

If only he knew...

On Friday in period four, a student handed him a note to come to the deputy's office at lunch break. Bob Dunstan was a short, Dany DeVito-esque man, 48, with dry, thin lips. The tea-tree garden outside was full of his Marlboro butts.

'Daniel, come in and close the door please,' he said as he stared at notes on his leather-lined desk, under the portraits of the prime minister and the queen.

'What's this about, Bob?' Daniel asked.

'I'll get straight to the point. We've received a complaint. A *serious* complaint. So, I'll be taking notes. You understand?'

A four-blade dusty fan squeaked in protest as the air was sucked from the room.

Daniel nodded, loosened his collar with his finger and squirmed a little further forward in his seat. 'Yes, but...'

'You drive a purple Corolla?' Bob's eyes widened as they drilled into Daniel's face.

'Yes. So?'

'Why don't you tell me what a fifteen-year-old schoolgirl was doing in your car?'

'Fifteen? She told me she was sixteen!'

'You bloody idiot. Her age makes no difference. She's made an accusation, said: *He touched my breasts, tried to kiss me.* Is that what happened?'

'Hell no! *She* tried to kiss *me.*'

'Well, sorry, but I've also got a witness statement. Your car, you and the girl, seen together.'

'So? That doesn't mean anything.'

'It does as far as this school and the department is concerned.'

'Fuck. She's lying!'

'Careful. Look. I like you Daniel, I've never had any doubts about you, not like some others here. But we must investigate.'

He fumbled in the drawer and opened a packet of Marlboros, pushing the packet towards Daniel. 'The department is sending out two specialists from Sydney. My hands are tied. This is what's going to happen. You are suspended – on full pay – until they can interview all concerned and make a decision. You must not contact the girl. You should remain in town until then, clear?'

Daniel saw his unflinching eyes and squirmed in his seat.

'Bob, this is bullshit. She's lying.'

'You've said that, but unless you have any witnesses to back up your story, I suggest you pack up here, go home and wait until they contact you. Maybe next week. Maybe. Do you have anyone who can back up your story?'

'No, I don't. She said she trusted me.'

This can't be happening.

'Well, sorry, but you'd better go home. If I can say anything, I hope you're right. I think you're a good teacher.'

Daniel stared out the window. *Hell, what would Skyla say if she found out?*

*

The following week, Daniel's nightmare gained momentum – strangers stared on the street as he passed by, colleagues avoided him, students huddled in groups that shrunk inwards like an amoeba as he approached. If he was honest, he only had two choices, stay and argue his case or run. It didn't take long to decide. That night, he packed Skyla's Corolla with his few possessions and left before daybreak, into the eastern glow. The garbage trucks shuttled from their depot. A slim woman in lycra jogged by with a trotting Afghan on a lead. The orange streetlights flicked off. He didn't look back. As he approached the town's limits and the highway stretched out before him, he switched on the local radio station, *Win2burn*. For a second all he heard was *You're so vain*, Rachel's favourite Carly Simon song. He listened: *You had me several years ago when I was still naïve...*

The town's skyline faded in the rear vision mirror. Saltbush, wattle and the occasional dead animal flashed by. He wound up the window and squirmed in his pocket for something to wipe away tears. A weathered grey kangaroo looked up from the edge of the cracked bitumen. The road arched in a long curve. A road-train roared by. Clouds of steam fizzed from the bonnet, the temperature gauge way past the red. The Corolla slowed and stopped. He opened the door, looked left and right. Nothing. Just the sound of hissing water and mist. He checked his water bottle, half empty. *Fuck! Hell, what's next?* He thought. *Fuck that song and Jules, his panties and weird equations. What else could go wrong?*

4

Renate

September 9, 1971

Kassel, West Germany, two blocks north of the Fulda River. A precocious eleven-year-old Renate Mayer stumbled on the last step before the Goethe Gymnasium, just as she'd stumbled on the first step moments before and hesitated for a second behind the queue. With a squint she'd gained from counting too many ants and beetles, her excitement multiplied like bacteria on agar, she was about to start her first day in high school. She gaped at the yellow brick walls. She checked through the chunky backpack: a lunch box, water bottle, six 148-page notebooks and a pencil case. Her stomach churned with anxiety as she counted the steps to the front door, the number of windows on each level, and hummed *Spring* by Vivaldi.

Two perfect rows lined up outside the classroom and the children stood erect before the teacher, Frau Vogel, who was 40-ish, wearing a sky-blue V-line dress. Frau Vogel mastered the space, adjusted a pair of uneven socks on a girl with angular legs, inspected shoes, bags, dress lengths. She darted around like a woodpecker. Renate took five deep breaths and felt her heart rate begin to slow.

'*Eintreten.*' Enter.

Renate, last to enter, sat at the front desk, middle row. She unpacked her books and pencil case and watched as Frau Vogel trotted around the room whispering to some students who straightened their backs, pens, rulers. Renate smiled and gazed at the map of the world on the front wall next to the poster of the solar system. At six, she knew the names of all the planets and local stars of the Milky Way. By six and a half she'd mastered the piano. At seven, the *Easter Sonata* by Mendelssohn. At seven and a half, she'd memorised the names of a hundred nearest stars; learned the Latin names of all the common birds of Hesse. *Picus canus,* the grey-headed woodpecker; *Picus viridid,* the green woodpecker; *Dryocopus martius,* a black woodpecker with a red crown, then onto the rambunctious birds of Australia. Renate expected to learn French and English, to be an explorer or a botanist or a concert pianist.

'Remember *mein Schatz,*' her mother said that morning, 'don't ask too many questions, it is not a competition.'

'But, Mama, isn't all life a competition? The stronger dominate the weak. Isn't that what Darwin proposed?' Renate asked with her hand on her tilted chin.

'If you say things like that at school, you might not make many friends. They might think you are being too smart.'

'Why, Mama? I don't want to be like the others. I want to be better.'

'You first need to find friends who like you for being you. Then worry about that later.'

During recess, she attempted to make friends by talking about music, stars and ants.

Two pairs of wide, blue eyes gaped at her, two girls with blonde curls and immaculate white socks shook their heads as though they were joined together. '*Sie ist komisch.*'

She's weird.

'She's funny,' a boy in dark socks and sandals replied as the others resumed their conversation as if she didn't exist.

At recess, she wandered off exploring the rear of the building. Outside a back room, off the school hall, she forced open a heavy door that gave with a squeal. She saw a dusty Bechstein piano. Tiptoeing over, she tried middle C. *Flat. Middle C, the starting point, a diving board all my fingers want to jump off from.* Slowly, she opened the lid. A yellow piece of frayed paper was stuffed between two taught wires.

A young German must be swift as a greyhound, as tough as leather and as hard as Krupp's steel.

'You're not allowed to be in here,' a clipped voice from the doorway boomed. Frau Vogel asked with a raised brow, 'Can you play?'

'Yes, Frau Vogel. I play all the time.'

'Well, show me. Play something. Now.'

Renate knew the middle C was flat. So, avoiding that note, she started on the exposition from the *Easter Sonata*. Frau Vogel stared wide eyed, mouth ajar. She ambled over, shoulders relaxed. 'That's...a clever way to avoid middle C, Renate. Would you like me to present you to the music teacher, Herr Schubert? He might have a place in his after-school class?'

'I'll have to ask Mama and Papa. Who does the piano belong to, Frau Vogel?'

'I believe it was left behind in the 40s by a Jewish family.'

'Where did they go?' Renate asked.

'Enough questions now. Back to class!'

After class, Renate caught the Route 3 bus to Sud and walked home the long way via Karlsaue Park. She weaved across the arched, white bridge that bisected a wide canal to the Siebenbergen island, ablaze in late snowdrops, corydalis and crocuses. She hummed the *Für Elise.* then stopped to collect cornflowers, chamomile and forget-me-nots. Time slowed and strangled like bradycardia and left her with a memory of a ghost, a forgotten piano and a dozen new questions needing answers.

5

The following year, Frau Vogel accompanied Renate's class to the *Naturkundemuseum*, the Natural History Museum known as the Ottoneum. Ten boys, nine girls and Renate, who had fast developed into a gangly teenager full of questions. Her classmates stock-standard response to her – *sie ist komische*.

Herr Schmitt, the guide, a portly 60-ish man in a tweed coat, carried a cane with a translucent amber tip. He tapped it on the cream marble floor and led the children past a mammoth skeleton to the herbarium. The girls held each other's hands while the boys snickered at a display of semi-naked Neanderthal females. Some students flipped through posters of extinct dinosaurs while others stared at cases full of giant moths from New Guinea. The guide showed them amber from Burma, malachite from Russia and azurite from Morocco. Renate had a piece of blue-green Azur malachite on a gold chain around her neck that her mother, Anne, had given her when she was ten. Anne called it the *Stone of Heaven,* said that it enhanced clairvoyant abilities. The guide stopped and stared at the stone.

'Let me see,' – through wafts of stale tobacco – 'colour looks stable. Still more blue than green. Lovely specimen,' he said, as if to himself. They walked out into the vast foyer and stood before a towering statue of a mammoth. A girl with powder-coated acne asked, 'How old is this giant elephant?'

'It's not an elephant. It's a mammoth and it's 21,000 years old,' the guide said. 'Mammoths lived here in the middle of the last Ice Age.'

'What happened to them?' a girl with a notebook asked, pencil poised at the ready.

Renate wanted to tell them but remembered her mother's warning from the previous year.

Herr Schmitt explained, 'When the climate changed, this area became forest and there was no grassland for food. Some scientists believed a few survived further west on the open fields of England.' He pointed with his cane and ushered them to the next exhibit. There was a glass case with a two-metre Narwhal tusk.

'Looks like a unicorn's horn. I didn't know they grew that long,' a boy from the back of the group said.

'It's a Narwhal's tusk,' the guide explained, 'the tusk is a spiral tooth, inside out with the nerves on the outside. If you look closely, you can see tiny holes.'

Renate said, 'Are they for measuring temperature and salinity of the water, Herr Schmitt? And doesn't '*monodon*' mean '*one tooth*?''

'That is correct.' He beamed a smile.

She let out a long whistle and a bumptious laugh. Renate Mayer, unsurprisingly, had few friends. The other students moaned.

'Show-off,' one boy with a crew cut said.

'Teacher's pet,' another whispered.

'The Inuit way up north still hunt them. Their skins are rich in Vitamin C,' Herr Schmitt said. 'In the Middle Ages, Narwhal tusks were traded as unicorn horns. If you're quiet, I'll tell you a story.'

Three boys sat at his feet. Renate straightened her back and strained her head forward.

'In Inuit lore, there's a tale of an evil woman who fed her daughter well but starved her blind son. The mother and daughter feasted on the meat of a polar bear the son had shot with his sister. The son didn't know he'd killed the bear, as his mother said it had fled. So, one day when his mother was out harvesting a pod of white whales, the son tied a harpoon rope around his mother's middle and harpooned a whale. The whale dragged the mother into the sea and she turned into a Narwhal when she twisted her hair. Her hair turned into the Narwhal's tusk.'

'Is that what you believe, Herr Schmitt?' Renate asked.

'It's not important what I think. What's important is whether you believe it?'

Renate wandered across the marble expanse. Frau Vogel and Herr Schmitt led the others to display cases filled with feathers, bones and pickled reptiles of all sizes. Renate pushed open a heavy door that read: *Zutritt verboten – Keep_out*. She tip-toed over to a stack of furniture covered in a blanket of dust. A silver trophy shaped like a rose bowl perched on a shelf in a dark-stained bookcase. Wiping the brass plaque with her handkerchief, she squinted to read the inscription. *Awarded to: Helena Rosenberg. First Place, Piano Recital. 1907. Mozart's Piano Concerto No. 5 in D Major. Could this be the same piano Helena Rosenberg played Mozart's Concerto on?* She bent over to get closer. A tingling spread at the base of her neck. For years she'd wondered about her roots and where her ancestors came from. Whenever she asked her mother, Anne had been evasive. Ulrich, her father, always changed the subject. *I'll just have to ask again.*

*

After the tour ended, the students lined up in two straight lines and were escorted to the bus back to school. Renate caught bus 23 home and sat at the front thinking about the trophy and Helena Rosenberg. She took a long route home through Schoenfeld park, frequently stopping to smell lavender flowers as she meandered, marvelling at the exquisite structure of the cacti from Bolivia, the yellow and orange nasturtiums. The paths wound around the lakes, the water lilies folded up for the night.

It was dusk when she reached her home and walked up the paved path bisecting the garden of pink and red roses, which lay in neat rows behind the white picket fence. She'd missed dinner – again – and was marched to her room by Ulrich, her papa. She wanted to ask if they knew who Helena Rosenberg was.

Later that night, she ate a cold dinner of pork knuckles, sauerkraut and cream. Papa sat in a brown velvet armchair and read the daily HNA newspaper in front of the *katchelofen* – the antique heater. Anne was in the kitchen washing the dishes. Renate looked up from the dining room table.

'I found an old trophy in the Ottoneum today,' Renate said. 'Do you know who Helena Rosenberg was?'

Ulrich folded the newspaper and placed it on the table, his neck muscles tensed, ears pink and flared. His vacant eyes stared past her. Anne frowned, clenched the dishcloth and inhaled sharply. She looked across at Ulrich, fists tight, the colour bleached from his face.

'She was your grandmother. Papa's mother.'

'When did she die?'

'She was taken by the Nazis during the war. We don't speak about that now.' Anne returned to face the sink. Her hands were fixed in position. Renate had a hundred questions and stared at Ulrich, saw tears in his eyes and down his face. He rose and plodded up the stairs. Anne came over, sat next to Renate and held her hands, her face softened as she told the tragic story. 'Papa gets distressed when he thinks about the past. He was not here when they were taken.'

'Why were they taken, Mama?'

'Even though they both converted to Christianity when they arrived from Kiev last century, that wasn't enough for the Nazis. They were still Jewish to them. Papa was away at boarding school in Berlin. He was training to join the motor corps. It was 1938. His papa, Gustav, was sent to a concentration camp. So, please be kind to your papa. He still feels guilty for what he didn't do back then.'

'But how could he, Mama? He was just a boy,' Renate said.

'They weren't like normal boys then, *mein Schatz,* they were more like robots.'

Later, in her room, Renate stared out the window at the lights and the pinpoints of shimmering stars. Something blinked far away. *A satellite maybe*? During the night, she tossed and turned in bed and heard Ulrich call out in his sleep, 'No No! Don't take her – take me! She's done nothing wrong!'

Outside a siren wailed. Rain pelted against the shutters. Renate shuddered as if trapped in a dream. *Who was the woman who did no wrong?*

6

Daniel
March, 1982

Three days later, back in his mother Helen's house in Randwick, Daniel called Skyla, again. He left an anxious message on the answering machine. *Where is she? She can't know why I'm back, not this soon. Can she?* He'd forgotten about Georgia, Skyla's best friend. Georgia, the meddler, who worked in the Department of Education's head office opposite Circular Quay. Georgia, everybody's confidant. *She couldn't have heard anything, could she?*

*

The first night back, he'd met his mates from uni and ended up on a pub crawl from Town Hall to the Cross. At 2 am, they dumped him from a taxi on his front lawn – minus his jeans and a few hundred bucks. The second night he met a group of airline stewards out on a night off. American, some English. He ended up in a dark corner with Clara from Scotland. Or it might have been Cora, he didn't pay too much attention as she shouted through the mucid background noise. She was tall and lean and when she unravelled her red hair it ran halfway down her back. By ten, she'd removed her tongue from inside his mouth long enough to call a taxi. He figured by eleven his mum would be asleep. He figured.

His mother surprised him as they crept in the back door. 'Evening. Your dinner's on the stove, luv. I'm going back to bed now,' she said, a sparkle in her eyes.

Daniel held Cora's shoes in his hand, called another taxi, promised to phone.

*

Two days later, he drove to Skyla's house in the Corolla with a new radiator. A tall, athletic guy walked out her gate and got into a red Datsun 240Z, tooted the horn and drove away. Daniel turned to watch him go, with a burning sensation in his stomach. He tapped the ends of his fingers on the door frame, knocked twice and waited. The door inched open and Skyla stared at Daniel for a second before she jerked straight, eyes narrowed.

'Hi. Did you get my messages? I'm back,' Daniel said and looked at her neck. There was a fresh bruise below her ear. Skyla raised her hand and flicked her blonde hair across her neck.

'I got your messages.' Her voice was flat, icy. She turned her head and looked out past Daniel. 'Thanks for returning my car.'

'Oh, no problem. It was...great.'

'Had no accidents, did you?' She said, one foot tapping up and down.

'Accidents? No. Why? Have you heard something?' he licked his lips and stared into her glacial eyes.

'Georgia told me. You remember Georgia, don't you? Head office Georgia.' Skyla's cheeks turned a darker shade of pink.

'You mean the story about the girl? How can she know about that?'

'So, it is true? I'm glad you've got the guts to come and tell me face to face, 'cause we're finished.'

'Hell, she's lying. I never touched her. She asked for a lift, I felt sorry for her because of her shitty home life. She tried to kiss me. C'mon.' He stared at her impassive face and thought *Why would she do that to me? I was only trying to be kind to her.* 'You believe me, don't you?' His words poured out like a puff of stale air. 'I wouldn't risk my job over a schoolgirl. When I ignored her, she must have turned angry and accused me.' His hand pushed on his belly to stop the flutters.

'Well, you ran and that makes you look guilty.' She looked away and then turned to him once more, her stare stabbing him. 'Anyway, you and I are finished. I'm seeing someone else.'

Daniel stared at her face. It was fixed like concrete. She stepped back as he reached out with the keys. Nodding in the direction of the Corolla, he said, 'Can you give me a lift back home?'

'Looks like...a nice day for a walk, 'cause I'm busy.' The door slammed. He stood, frozen to the spot, numbness sinking from his arms down through his stomach to his feet. He turned and began the long walk back to Randwick.

*

For two days he brooded in his bedroom scratching vague ideas on an A4 pad while a dusty overhead fan clanked apart the muggy March moisture. A lopsided pile of books beside his bed grew taller, hand-me-downs from his father, Ian, abandoned as either too complex, too vague, or too boring. *The Plague* by Camus; Tolstoy's *War and Peace*; *Heart of Darkness* by Conrad. He remembered the last time he saw him. Daniel was in Year 7. Ian walked out one night and slammed the door. Daniel had heard the argument from his room – *Do you love her more than me, is that it?* Helen pleaded. Ian's reply still stung; a voice devoid of emotion – *I don't love you anymore. Not sure if I ever did.* He hated Ian for that and promised himself that he'd never make the same mistake. *What am I going to do about the girl?*

*

Another week passed. On Saturday night, his mates left him outside a club on Bayswater Road just down from the Cross on midnight. Told them he'd *catch a bus home.* He walked down to Kellett Street to a two-story pink painted terrace and stopped, not sure why he was here. He told himself it was *scientific curiosity, or time to cross another experience off his bucket list.* By this time, he was adept at lying to himself. He honestly didn't know why, *just a whim,* he supposed. He walked in under a flashing pink neon sign and sat on a stool in front of a rose-coloured bar. The wooden stool – a carved elaborate penis with footrests set in a skin-coloured scrotum. He ordered a beer from a small man in a stained, white apron with mismatched pupils. Daniel scanned the room and counted eight women on couches in disparate skimpy clothes and lingerie. He stared at a woman smirking his way, she had long blonde hair in ringlets. He walked over and whispered in her ear. He thought she had a beguiling, hard face, both seductive and metallic. She nodded and pointed to a velvet-lined booth and an oversized 40-ish woman with large purple lips wearing a dark wig. A folded cardboard sign in front read: *Cashier.* Outside, a loud siren waxed and waned. The girl kicked off her high heels, climbed the narrow stairs and walked down the end of a hall to a room with a lopsided number 9 on the door. Daniel followed at a distance. She turned, smiled and waited inside the door. He walked in. There was a double bed, large mirror on the ceiling, a two-door wardrobe. She nodded at the wardrobe. 'That's where I keep my straps and chains. Wanna see them?'

He shook his head. She began to unbutton her blouse.

'You can stop doing that.' He shifted his weight, not sure how to proceed.

'Why? Do you want to fuck me with my top on?' A slow smile spread across her face.

'No, I don't. Can we just talk?' He sat down on the bed. She sat next to him.

'You've paid for a half, so you've got just under thirty minutes to thrill me with conversation. Don't tell me, you're a teacher, aren't you?'

'Wow. How can you tell?' He wanted to sound confident, in charge – the words were taut in his throat, his voice stuttering. 'Is it that easy for you, to, um, you know..'

She didn't wait for elaboration. 'You're all the same. Talk, talk, talk. But don't mind me, they call me a '*sarcastic bitch*' downstairs.'

She chuckled and sat close to him, close enough for her perfume to take effect. He took short, shallow breaths, unable to meet her gaze.

'How old are you?' he asked.

'Old enough to fuck you.'

'That's not what I meant. Are you twenty? Twenty-one?'

'Close enough. Why?'

'It's just...I'd like to tell you a story. Find out your reaction.'

'Okay, teach. You're paying, so I'm all ears.'

Daniel related the story about Ruby – her lies, deceit, how he was stood down. She stared ahead, nodded from time to time, examined her fingernails as if she'd heard the story before. Daniel finished and looked at her face. It was unreadable.

'So, you've come here to see if a hooker can give you some answers. That's pretty lame, don't you think? I'll tell you what. Here's my story. When I was sixteen, I fucked my English teacher. A few times. He was...I don't know, charming, needy.'

'What happened after?' Daniel blinked and leaned forward.

'I told him it was over. He cried like a baby. Told me not to tell anyone.'

'So, what did you do?'

'I told his wife, then the principal. She must have been pretty pissed about it.'

Daniel studied her face, lost for words. He nodded. 'What happened to him. Did you keep in contact?'

'Hell no. Why would I? Last I heard he was pushing trolleys at Woolies. Serves him right.'

'And you don't feel bad about that?'

'Not one bit. You can make good money doing this work. And it was a valuable lesson for a schoolgirl, don't you think?' She looked into his eyes, smiled and put her hand on his knee.

Daniel flinched under her penetrating stare. He blinked and for a second he saw Ruby sitting there.

'So, do you want to play with these? She reached for a blouse button. You've still got – she looked up at a clock on the wall – ten minutes.'

'No, but thanks for the story. It was...enlightening.' He was sorry he came.

'You don't have to worry about me, teach. There are a lot more suckers out there in this town to keep me busy.' Her face now had the complexion of lead. She buttoned her blouse. He got up to leave.

'Until next time hey? I'll do the talking.'

He walked down the steps and out the door. Outside, he turned left towards the streetlights and shook his head, as if his loneliness could be flung away. *Why should I feel guilty? I didn't do anything.* Somehow, it sounded hollow.

7

A week passed and he'd made up his mind. There was nothing for him in Sydney anymore. He phoned the department's head office three times without success. His case was *still being investigated*. He had one last person to try. Georgia. He'd tried Skyla but she wouldn't return his calls. He asked Rachel to ring her to find out where Georgia had moved to, but she said, 'I don't want to get involved. You need to move on, Daniel.'

He decided on a more direct approach: a visit to head office. But his other problem was he didn't know what to say. *I've got nothing to apologise for. Why can't they see that?* He paused as disparate thoughts blinked on and off – *I was just trying to help her... why did it backfire and turn into this chaos?* He knew one thing for sure – *I'm not going to teach teenagers again.* He needed space, to 'find himself'. His gut told him that was a cliché, but *how do I do that? Fuck.*

He rode his old ten-speed bike to the head office of the Department of Education as the ferries tooted their way into Circular Quay. Up three marble steps, he pushed open the doors and strode across the cavernous foyer. Arranged in no particular order were photos and displays of happy children seated in front of even happier-looking teachers. To the left, two polished, steel elevator doors; to the right, a stack of dusty wooden student desks. He marched to the oval desk where a 40-ish woman with pointy ears, long nose and narrow pupils stared at him through a pair of gold-rimmed glasses perched on the end of her nose. Daniel read her name badge. *Mrs A. Dankworth*. Outside, a train's whistle forced its way through the traffic that snarled up Bridge Street.

'Can I help you?' Dankworth said in a deep voice, as she peered down her long nose.

'I'm here to see Georgia Eastman, please.'

'Is that so? And you are?'

'My name is... It doesn't matter. Tell her I'm a friend.' Daniel tapped his fingers on the desk and licked his lips. The woman hesitated as she sucked in a breath.

'Do you know what department she's with?' Her pupils narrowed and bored into his.

'The gossip department. I suppose you'd call it 'personnel?''

'Excuse me?'

'Georgia Eastwood. Personnel. You, ring her now. Tell her Daniel is downstairs and wants to see her.' He drew back his shoulders. He knew he was being rude, but he was flustered, ready to explode. She stood motionless, mouth agape. He gave her a weak smile. He almost winked.

'I'm doing no such thing. I think you'd better leave, now, young man.' Her glasses inched further down her nose.

'I'm not going anywhere until I see her and her busybody face.' Daniel turned around, walked over to the elevators and sat in one of two navy sofas. Dankworth gripped her phone and whispered, then slammed down the hand piece. He clutched his trembling hands and stuffed them in his pockets. After a few minutes the elevator doors dinged. He stood and waited. Two burly men in navy caps and black suits – one at least one size too small – emerged and looked over at Dankworth, who nodded in Daniel's direction.

'I'll have to ask you to leave, sir,' the larger man said. Daniel gazed from one to the other. The smaller man clasped his hands tight.

'I'm waiting for a Miss Georgia Eastman.' Daniel said in a confident voice. 'I'm sure you've got more pressing business. Cars to park? Toilets to clean?'

'Look, sunshine. You ain't waiting for no one,' the large man said.

'We'll see about that.'

The big guy nodded to the smaller one, as they leaned down and grabbed Daniel's arms. He squirmed for a second in their harsh grip as they lifted him to his feet. One man held his arms behind his back as the other pushed him across the foyer and out the door.

'Ouch! Let go of me.'

They heaved him down the steps.

'Fuck you.' He pushed himself up and squinted at identical rows of windows. Four faces stared down at him, one woman pointed, another had her hand over her mouth. Daniel walked a few metres, turned around and gave them the finger.

'Fuck you all,' he whispered to no one.

*

That night, Rachel came over and brought chicken soup with mashed potato *kreplach*. 'James' favourite,' she said. She kissed their mum, who sat in a deep-green armchair, watching *Sale of the Century*. 'Don't get up, Mum, I'll turn it off,' Rachel said, nodded to Daniel and walked into the kitchen. She placed the pot on the bench, poured herself a chardonnay and looked at her brother. 'Was that really necessary – your visit downtown?' she said, sipping the wine.

Daniel tapped his fingers on the bench. He opened his mouth as if to reply but hesitated, not sure what to say.

'You know Skyla's new *boyfriend* just bought a house in Bondi. With views of the ocean. They're moving in next month,' Rachel said.

'I'm...happy for them. Is it red, like his car?'

'Don't tell me you're jealous, Daniel? Not even a little bit?' She stood back and watched him with an intense gaze.

'Couldn't care less,' he lied. 'So, where's James tonight? At the synagogue?'

'No, of course not. He's at home with Eva and Naomi.' She took another sip, traced a finger up and down the stem of the glass. 'Have they interviewed you yet about the charge?'

'What charge? What do you know?' Daniel's voice raised, his eyes flared open.

'Well, they will, you know. I've heard the girl's got a witness.'

'That's bullshit. She's got nothing, she's made it all up, fucking bitch. Her and that gossip, Georgia.'

'Daniel! Not in front of Mum, please. So, what are you planning to do?' she asked, her voice hollow.

'I'm going on a bike ride, travelling north, camping out. I bought a new bike. I'm leaving on Sunday.'

'What – what about the charges? Your job? Are you just going to run away from your responsibilities, like you've always done? And leave me to look after Mum?'

'Mum's okay here, aren't you, Mum?' Daniel turned around to Helen.

'Can you turn the tele back on?' Helen said.

'It's on, Mum.' Rachel lowered her voice, turned to her brother. 'She's *not* okay, Daniel. Can't you see she's losing it? Or don't you care?' Rachel marched around the bench, closer to Daniel. He walked away, sat in the chair next to Helen and stroked her arm. He looked up at the photos on the mantlepiece. Dad, Mum and the two children at the beach. Dad under a pile of sand, Dad and Mum pushing the kids on swings at a park. He thought, *can a life really be held together by memories and old photographs?* The muscles around his chest tightened. He looked across to his mum, face fixed on the screen, one tear rolling down her cheek. 'It'll be okay, Mum. I won't be gone for long. Rachel's still here,' he said and wiped the tear away with a tissue.

Rachel followed him into the lounge room and sat opposite him in a beige armchair. She placed her wine glass on the floor, inhaled deep and said,

'You doing a Henry Thoreau or something?'

'Don't know what you're talking about.'

'You know – go off into the wilderness – to find yourself?'

'I'm... not sure what I'll do. I just want to leave this place and...' he trailed off.

'Like I said,'– Rachel emphasised, drawing back her shoulders – 'you're being self-indulgent, as usual.'

'Really? It's my life, you know.'

Rachel rolled her eyes. 'Well jolly good fucking luck finding yourself.'

*

Later, in his inky bedroom, he felt a tedious monotony like an itch he couldn't scratch. The movies Helen watched – *Piranha* and *Attack of the Killer Tomatoes* – echoed down the hall and wormed under the bedsheets as a heavy darkness pressed him lower and lower into the mattress. He tried to jam his eyes closed – anything – to forget those memories: when he was twelve, under the glass-panelled front door, he'd waited for his dad to come home, then realised he wasn't coming back. Then for a split second, he was in a rainforest, birds wheeling silently in slow motion. He looked down and a woman lay motionless next to his feet. He sighed and watched the street-light flicker on and off. Then another sound, faint like breathing – a hum of a slight breeze, almost lost among the traffic rumble outside. The sound, almost inaudible, was no longer human but unique to the house itself, like slow, deliberate breaths of boredom. It was as if the house was trying to tell him, explain itself, how it waited, always waited for some violent action – a fight, a shouting match, a smashed glass or plate, even a death – something dramatic, a reason to hold your breath. If only his dad had the guts to do that, to fight it out – leave some kind of indelible mark to be remembered by. *I'm not like Dad, am I? I need new adventure, something I can control.* He got up and shut the door but the words still echoed in his head – *You're being self-indulgent, as usual.*

8

Renate

August 26, 1979

On her eighteenth birthday, Renate searched the attic. She opened boxes, some sealed since before she was born – for toys, photos and books from her childhood. She banged her head on a low rafter. The deep thud shot through her skull. She rubbed the top of her head, cursed and refused to let the incident spoil her mood. Outside, through the four-paned dormer, a neat lawn and garden hedge of roses separated the house from Frau Schiller, her nosy neighbour.

She flicked through Papa's old journals, papers, anything about her grandparents. Gustav Mayer, born 1890 in Kyiv, Ukraine and Helena Rosenberg, born 1895, in Dymer, a *shtetl,* twenty-five kilometres away. *Helena, the trophy winner of the cup in the museum. My grandmother.* There was an old leather suitcase, locks corroded, leather cracked and lined with age. Inside were letters written in beautiful script, faded, almost unreadable on yellowed paper, a pile of neatly folded newspaper clippings. Black and white photographs. One photo showed a smiling couple in formal clothes, the man in a long, black coat and tails, white gloves and a top hat. The lady in an elegant dress and trailing headdress of lace, linen or silk. A Rabbi stood with them. The caption read: *On our Wedding Day. Forever Happy. Kassel.*

1919. Renate studied the image of her grandmother and realised she held a missing piece of her family history. *That must be where I got my music skills from. I knew the trophy was important,* she thought. She took the photo and slipped it in her journal. *It's no good to them locked away.*

More photos: two smiling soldiers in spiked *pickelhaube* helmets with *Christmas, 1915, Papa, home on recuperation from the Western Front* handwritten on the back. Another with the smiling couple outside the *Orangerie* Palace in central Kassel. A happy baby on a picnic blanket with the caption – *Sholem bayes* – peace of the home. *Ulrich age one. 1921.* She was puzzled why these images were hidden, like memories abandoned in a suitcase. Newspaper clippings of men in swastikas smashing windows dated November 9, 1938, titled *Kristallnacht* – Night of broken glass. Five bearded men with their hands on their heads. No explanations. Renate needed to know the truth. Across the hall, she saw Ulrich on his bed, staring vacantly at his calloused hands. Her breathing shallowed. As she rose to leave, she tripped on the carpet edge. Anne called out *essen ist fertig* – dinner. Downstairs, a letter with an official stamp was on the edge of the table. Her mother's face, unreadable. 'Just came for you. From the university,' she said with a slight nod.

Renate stared at the letter as her eyes widened. 'I'll open it later when Papa comes down. It's from Göttingen University. I applied to three.' she said, excited.

Anne set the table. 'Papa is not happy about you leaving, Renate,' Anne said with a soft voice.

'It's my life. He can't stop me,' she snapped.

'Renate...' Anne stopped as Renate's mouth turned down.

'I found a suitcase in the attic. Why have you been hiding it from me?'

'We haven't hidden anything from you. Papa has problems with his memories. First, he lost his father, then his mother. That's why he doesn't want you to leave.' She looked at her more closely, then took a step forward.

'What happened to him in Berlin?' Renate asked with concern.

'Papa's never talked about it. He was in Berlin at the entrance examinations for the NSKK – the Motor Corps. That was 1938. When he came back, the Nazis had taken Gustav. He and Helena went to live with Onkel Rolf in Erfurt.'

Renate stared at the floor, then picked up the envelope. She ripped it open and unfolded the letter. She had been accepted into the Bachelor of Science course. Her orientation was in six weeks. Six weeks to organise everything: books, an apartment, a job. Emotions tore through her – excitement, uncertainty, anxiety.

'Tell me, Mama, how did you meet Papa?' she took her hand and sat down at the table.

'I worked at the library, two years before you were born. He'd come in every Saturday at ten, sit at the window and stare out, just stare as if he was looking for someone. Sometimes he'd get an atlas and open it, always on the map of Poland. I'd ask him if he needed any help, anything, he just shook his head. One day he asked for a coffee, I bought him one and we talked, well, I talked, he listened. He'd nod his head from time to time and slowly we became friends...' Anne's voice trailed off.

'After you became pregnant, what was he like?'

'He was a completely different man. Attentive, helpful, kind, but I knew he lacked an important part.' Her voice softened.

'What part?'

'How to love someone, unconditionally.'

They both looked up. Ulrich clomped down the stairs. He wheezed in short breaths, one fist closed, the other held a photograph. His dark-brown eyes glinted with determination.

'You can't go to Göttingen. I won't allow it,' he said, eyes boring into Renate's.

'It's my life, Papa. I'm eighteen now, you can't stop me.' Renate looked from his face to the photo he held. At that moment, she had no idea who this man in front of her was. 'I need a break from all this.' She waved her hand in a circle. 'There are too many secrets, I need to be free from all that. Why this, now? Why that photo?' Her breathing surged in her chest.

'This is all I have of them. I wasn't here to defend them, but I will defend you. I'm not going to lose anyone again,' he said as he wiped one cheek with a handkerchief.

'I don't need protecting, Papa. I can look after myself. Göttingen's only fifty kilometres away. I can come home every weekend.' She rose and stood stock-still aware that both fists were closed. She prodded him with her index finger. He was softer than she'd imagined. He didn't move. A lone tear squeezed out of the corner of his eye. Renate looked from Ulrich to Anne and back. Anne trembled, her hands shaking.

'And why won't you tell me what you did in the war? What did you do?' she shouted.

'I can't. That's all in the past, best left forgotten.'

'And that's just it, isn't it Papa. You haven't forgotten it. It's all buried inside. How can I respect you if you hide the truth from me. What terrible things did you do?'

'Please Renate,' Anne said, eyes rotating from Ulrich to Renate, 'He tried to do the right thing. You can't judge him, you weren't there. Can't you see? It broke him.'

'Stop defending him Mama, you weren't there either.'

Ulrich clenched his fists, opened his mouth, said nothing.

'Well, I'm taking this, it's no good to you anymore.' Renate snatched the photo from Ulrich's fingers. She turned and ran out the door into the night, the curled photograph in her fingers.

Renate fled into the dark, unsure where she was going. Claps of thunder rolled in from the east.

9

Daniel

March, 1982

Daniel kissed Helen on the cheek. 'Goodbye, Mum, I'll ring soon.' She said nothing, just stared and nodded her head. He staggered the overloaded bike down the front path, light-footed and found his legs on Alison Road, picking up the pace through Moore Park past toddlers on wobbling tricycles. He turned left into Oxford Street for the downhill run to Hyde Park. A constant hiss spurted from the back wheel and the bike seesawed. *Shit. Bloody flat. What else could go wrong?* He pulled his bike onto the footpath between a men's clothing shop and a bakery, unloaded the sleeping bag, tent, bedroll and panniers and upturned the bike. An unshaven man in a long, grey woollen coat and black motorcycle boots came and stood next to him, a bent cigarette in his yellowed fingers.

'Say, matey, you wouldn't have a light, would you?'

Daniel shook his head and looked up from the bike into a weathered grey face covered in white whiskers. His head turned from the man's outstretched arm to his bike and his gear lying in a pile. A crowd gathered.

'Anyone got a match?' he asked.

'What are you going to burn down now?' someone said from the back of the crowd.

'No, you idiot, Jacko. The old coot needs a light for his ciggie,' said a man in a white apron and baker's cap. Daniel looked up at the sign – Oxford Bakery.

'Whose calling me an old coot?'

Daniel gazed from face to face and smiled. The traffic hurried past.

Puncture fixed, he cycled past a poster nailed to a telegraph pole: *People for Nuclear Disarmament Rally. Hyde Park Fountain. Sunday 10.00 am,* then down to the War Memorial in Hyde Park awash with rainbow flags, women in bright, painted overalls, purple hair, kids in hand-painted strollers. A man in a black cape and mask like Darth Vader pushed a forty-four-gallon black drum in a wheelbarrow, a radiation symbol painted in yellow on the side. Daniel stared – a sea of humanity swarming north. *What the hell? Looks interesting, I'm in no hurry.*

Past the memorial pond he noticed a group of about twenty cyclists chanting: *one, two three, four, we don't want your....* They drifted north up a concrete walkway under the weeping Moreton Bay figs towards the Archibald fountain. He followed, pulled by their energy and parked his bike. Opposite, Saint Mary's Cathedral bells pealed ten. A tall girl with intense hazel eyes dressed in white overalls handed him a green leaflet. 'You interested in donating to the World Bike Ride?' she said and held out an open shoe box.

He fumbled in his pockets for a coin and said, 'How far are you riding?'

'To Darwin, then hop on a boat to Japan. Then China,' she said, waving the shoe box. 'We leave tomorrow. Do you want to join us?'

'Umm... It's not really my thing. I'm riding north for a while, not sure how far, but I'll take a leaflet.' He grinned and she started to move away. She turned around, smiled and said, 'Maybe we'll meet up on the road.'

'Maybe.' He sat on the fountain wall and toyed with the idea of cycling around the world. *How much would it cost? How long would it take*? While the idea jiggled around his head, he saw two wild-looking men with spiky hair and tattoos running down the path towards him. One waved a samurai sword above his head, a ray of sunlight reflected off the blade. A woman with purple hair screamed as they drew closer. Another woman with a baby in a backpack ran sideways across the lawn. The man with the sword ran closer, face contorted with rage. A swastika was tattooed on his arm.

'Let's get the commie bastards!' the man yelled. Daniel, in a split second, thrust out his leg and tripped him. The sword clattered away. Three guys jumped on the guy, now face down and another kicked the sword away. Another yelled, 'Go get the police!' Daniel breathed hard, his heart pounded. Someone said, 'Well done, mate. You're a hero!' Two mounted police came and escorted the pair away in handcuffs.

Daniel sat on his hands and trembled, people patted him and said, 'Good on you, mate'.

A man held a clipboard and wrote in a notebook, firing questions at him. 'What's your name for the record? What's your occupation? Where do you live?'

'Daniel. I live in Sydney. Thanks, but I'm leaving now.' He wheeled his bike past the small crowd of onlookers. A few clapped.

*

A few kilometres past Hornsby and just on dusk he was beat. He swerved into the car park outside the Kuring-Gai Motor Lodge while a red-orange radiance lit up the sky. The desk clerk, a middle-aged man in a dark toupee, took his $35 and handed him a key. Room six, one double bed with dark-blue bedspread and an air conditioner that rattled in the window. Daniel switched it to *fan low speed*, but it made no difference. What occupied his thoughts was conflict with Rachel at home, his teaching career, leaving Helen – the idea of cycling around the world bubbling away inside like shaking a can of soda. A nebulous, crazy idea. He opened the door, sniffed, then closed it to the sticky air. Traffic noise thinned on the Pacific Highway outside. The air con rattled unmolested in the worn-out aluminium window.

A car door slammed. A baby cried in a room nearby. The lightbulb above his head blinked out. Above his head, the arms of a wall clock were frozen at 8.16. *Hmmn, the exact time the bomb exploded over Hiroshima. Coincidence or omen?*

10

The road carved through tea-tree, scribbly gum and orange-bark angophora as it zig-zagged the noisy motorway nearby. Cramps gripped his thighs, sweat trickled down his back like a greedy leech. Every gust of wind carried a different smell that lingered in his nostrils – the subtle scent of scarlet banksia, lemon essence of the flowering gum, the hydrogen sulphide of the evaporating oil on the black tarmac. Cockatoos and galahs screeched under high cirrus clouds whizzing overhead. He already missed the sound of voices taken for granted – friends, family, lovers. This new life alone, on the open road, the only voices were inside his head. *Wasn't that the whole point of going on this journey? To eliminate those distracting voices and concentrate on my own, even if imaginary? What am I escaping from?* Endless questions without answers. The sun wound its way above as the blacktop slipped underneath. The responsibilities, memories, meetings, timetables flaked off like skin from an onion as each kilometre ticked by. He was free, an alien sensation mixed with loneliness. Daniel shook his head, embraced the change, always just around the next corner. Sooner or later, someone would enter his life.

A helicopter with a large number 9 thwock-thwocked overhead. A two-ton Avis removal van tooted as it whizzed by. Two magpies skimmed by and one pooped on his shoulder. The road dipped at the turnoff to Mt White.

He stopped outside a general store and parked his bike against the side of the building next to two rusting 1950s vintage cars. A man inside coughed, opened the screen door, spat and walked down the wooden steps. The screen door banged shut. Somewhere close, a wailing generator started. Daniel climbed the steps and pulled the door open with a piece of old rope that was tied to the cracked doorframe. He walked over to the counter and ordered a white coffee from a forty-something man with greasy stubble in a sleeveless dirty flannel shirt. The man looked Daniel up and down. Black grit spilled from his yellow fingernails.

'Got anything to eat?'

'Pies, sausage rolls, hot dogs. The pies are cold.'

'Got anything except meat?' Daniel stared at the opened packet of Marlboros on the counter. A cigarette was smouldering over the edge of an ashtray.

'Nope,' he said and hawked onto the floor.

'Yeah, I'll just take a coffee to go, thanks.' Outside, on a wobbly wooden bench, he sipped the lukewarm, watery coffee. Something black, motionless and insect-shaped floated on the surface. *Why would anyone want to live here?* He tipped the coffee over the handrail and scanned the surrounds, compounds of high barb-wire fences, metal poles and scaffolding that lay higgledy-piggledy, a large metal shed with a hand-painted sign: *Eggs for Sale.* As he was about to leave, an old Bedford van with 'No Nukes' painted down the side pulled up. A short, stubby man in his forties stepped out. He gazed at the shop, studied Daniel, then his mouth fell open.

'Hey you're the guy! The hero of Hyde Park, aren't you?'

'What are you talking about?' Daniel said in a surprised voice.

'It's on page bloody three in today's papers. You tripped that Nazi psycho with the sword. That's you, right?' he said as he walked over and extended his hand.

'I guess so. But I'm no hero.' Daniel rose and shook hands.

'Ben. Glad to meet you.'

'Daniel. Same.'

'That your bike? Which way you heading?' Ben's eyes darted from Daniel to his bike and back again.

'North, Byron, maybe Brisbane, then... I'm not sure.'

'Well, we've got forty riders just about to arrive. You'd be welcome to join us,' Ben said with a smile.

'Who are you with?'

'We're the World Bike Ride for Peace and Nuclear Disarmament and a few other things.'

'You guys in Hyde Park, yesterday? I met two women handing out pamphlets.'

'Yep, that was us. They'll be here soon. You can meet them.' Ben went inside. The door banged behind him. A Holden HK ute skidded and stopped in a cloud of dust and two teenagers jumped from the tray. They ran around the side of the shop and relieved themselves behind the wrecked cars. The driver – a clean-shaven guy of about thirty, in a white T-shirt – nodded to Daniel and went into the shop. A minute later he and Ben emerged, shook their heads, walked past and muttered, 'Redneck.' Daniel looked up as a battered red Falcon XL cruised by and slowed. The unshaven driver leaned out the window and yelled, 'Why don't you go back to Russia!' Ben gave him the finger. The car stopped and the man reached down and pointed a rifle out the window.

'Fuck, get down. He's got a gun!' Ben shouted.

The screen door banged open, the owner shouted, 'Put that thing away, Johnno, you dickhead!' He turned to Daniel and Ben now lying on the ground.

'Don't worry about him. It's not loaded. He's a harmless hothead.'

A dozen bike riders arrived, dismounted and walked inside the shop. They soon returned, all with looks of disbelief.

'I didn't think people like that existed anymore, hey?' a tall, skinny girl of about twenty said, wearing baggy grey pants that were cut off below her knees.

'I heard him say *vegos and lefties aren't welcome,*' a young guy said. 'I'm going to piss on his wall.'

Ben walked over to a woman with long brown hair in a 'Save the Whales' T-shirt. He whispered something in her ear and they walked over to Daniel.

'What a coincidence meeting you here. I thought we left you behind in Sydney. I'm Bexley,' she said, eyes sparkling as sunlight glinted through her hair. When she shook his hand and smiled his knees trembled. Bexley Harrison-Ross. When her mouth widened, she revealed possibly her one imperfection – there was a gap between her two front teeth – wide enough to park a bus in.

'Thanks. I'm Daniel.'

'So, would you like to ride with us? We're on our way to Darwin,' she said, as though it was just down the road.

'Look, it's not my thing. I'm just heading north, like. For a bit of peace and quiet.'

'Perfect, we ride for World Peace,' she said as if reciting from a script.

'Look, sounds great but I'm a bit of a loner, you know?' he lied.

'There's nothing stopping you riding with us.' Her smile was still fixed his way.

Hell, I'd ride anywhere with this woman. 'Where are you staying tonight?'

'Probably near Gosford.'

'Me too. Maybe I'll just tag along behind, my legs are still stiff.' Daniel looked down at his shoes and scratched the dirt.

'See you in Gosford, central park. We'll be busking.' She wheeled her bike away. Six riders cycled past. The van inched out onto the deserted road. He heard someone spit. The screen door opened, then banged shut. Daniel chuckled. *So, I'm riding for World Peace now? Sounds easy!*

11

Ulrich
August 26, 1980, 5:36 pm

Ulrich Mayer returned home from the Henschel Axle Factory, in North Kassel, a window grill tucked under his arm. He slipped off his backpack and removed a barrel lock. He left the grill outside, propped against the wall and carried the barrel lock upstairs to Renate's bedroom. At sixty, Ulrich's bushy eyebrows were turning grey. His eyes had aged with time – once light brown now darkened with guilt and trauma from the war. From what he'd seen and not done at Auschwitz. His hunched shoulders carried the history, and, in his face, his forever-tightened, thin red lips. He pushed thoughts of the war deep somewhere in his mind and focused on his task. His hands were rough and cracked from two decades of hard labour on engines, fireboxes and axles. He undressed and tossed the grey Henschel uniform into the dirty clothes basket. The house was deserted. Renate, home from uni, was out shopping with Anne at ALDI Hellenbohn. They had just celebrated her nineteenth birthday. The streets were busier than usual with shoppers rushing to beat the peak hour traffic. The only other sound, the repetitive ticking of the cuckoo clock on the mantlepiece next to the antique tiled, *Kachelofen*, in the lounge room.

Ulrich worked in quick, precise movements as he set the kettle on the stove to make tea. He flung open the windows, then dressed in clean overalls and descended the stairs that led to his only passion: model trains.

In the basement, a four-by-three metre table occupied most of the room. Set up with two model trains, towns, stations, mountains with mock snow. On one line, Ulrich rearranged the Airfix 54123-9 BR Black loco and attached a D778 Command car, POW 334 car and a R639 Sniper Car. On the second line, he placed his favourite, the Flying Scotsman Class A3, complete with coal wagon, three passenger wagons, a sleeping car and a dining car. Under the table was a locked drawer. He found the key in the coal wagon, inserted it and it opened with a click. Inside, was a grey HJ dagger about ten inches long, all that was left from forty years ago. He placed it on the table and polished the black swastika inside a red-and-white diamond pattern. Satisfied, he returned it to the drawer. He collected an AEG power drill, ten metre extension cord, screwdrivers and screw box and walked outside to the back shed for an extension ladder. He placed the ladder under Renate's window, stepped back inside, walked up the stairs to Renate's room and drilled a hole in the outside of the door jamb. He attached the barrel bolt and secured it with six screws, then checked the door. Locked and secure. Ulrich walked out the front door, climbed the ladder with the drill, the window grill and the screws and positioned the grill over Renate's window, marked twelve holes and drilled. The sound whined for a few seconds. He stared at the grill, the holes and shapes and patterns, Somehow, they reminded him of his cell in Block 11 at Auschwitz, 1944. He was afraid of closing his eyes, of the memory coming back again. It always did.

Moaning drifted under the door like snow piled in puffy pillows outside. The sound muffled the silence, he knew it was Sunday, they would be sleeping off their hangovers. No sound from the chemnitzer, just a steady drip drip drip of the snow melt seeping down the wall. Day or night? Even the temperature was below understanding. She was not here. Tomorrow, New Years Day, the scratch *on the wall said. He would be dead within a week. If they didn't hang him, to save bullets, the pain in his heart would kill him. He sat on the stool, placed his head in his hands and trickled the last of his water over them into the enamel bowl. He stared and imagined her eyes staring back...*He shook his head, blinked three times and the grill was back in his hands over Renate's window. He took a deep breath and attached the grill with heavy-gauge stainless steel screws. Checked for firmness. Satisfied, he replaced all the tools and returned to the dining room to wait for Anne and Renate to return.

In the kitchen, he made fennel tea. A cool breeze pushed the stale air as he sat down and scanned the *Hessisch Allegemeine* newspaper. There were articles about the bleak months expected for East Germany, job cuts in the Henschel factory – *Thank God, not my division* – and rising oil prices. He chewed slowly on a thick slice of kuchen left over from Renate's party.

At 6:30, they bustled in holding paper bags full of groceries. Renate dumped her bags of lentils, chickpeas and rice on the kitchen table. Ulrich looked up, eyes narrowed.

'I made your room more secure, *mein Engel*.'

Renate looked at Anne, turned and ran up the stairs. Seconds later, she shouted from the top floor, 'Why have you done this, Papa? I'm not a prisoner!'

'What have you done, Ulrich?' Anne said, eyes widening.

'Making sure she'll be safe in her room from now on.'

'Stop trying to control my life, Papa, I'm an adult now. Or have you forgotten?'

'I have never forgotten...'

'What are you talking about?' Renate looked across to Anne, then Ulrich and back again.

'Shush, both of you. Ulrich is your father, he's only trying to protect you. You should obey him,' Anne said, as if the steely conviction in her voice might convince them.

'No. I'm not letting him destroy me. I've had enough of him trying to control my life.' She started to stutter. 'I...can't live here anymore.'

A tense interval of silence surrounded them with laboured deep breaths. Renate clenched her jaw and her muscles quivered. She gaped back and forth for a sign, anything that might show they understood. Ulrich stood, scrunched a page of the newspaper, dropped it on the table and climbed the stairs. Anne remained motionless, her head turning back and forth from Ulrich's back to Renate. She couldn't look Renate in the face.

For Renate, all she had were questions waiting for answers – *Who is this man? Why don't I know his history? Why is his past an empty puzzle?*

12

Renate

August 26, 1981

Renate celebrated her twentieth birthday throwing up *Liebfraumilch* and bread dumplings into her apartment toilet from a night she was trying to forget. Her neighbour and best friend Ilse Liebig *tut-tutted* from the kitchen. While most students got around in jeans, T-shirts, halter tops and jackets, Ilse wore a black pleated skirt with a white blouse tucked in and done up severely to her stringy neck. By the time Renate had started uni, she'd grown a crust-like shell and a simulated confidence, but how she envied those girls who carried their sex appeal on their bare, tanned legs and slim waists. Ilse looked up from the kitchen and wiped crumbs from her Articles of Law folder.

'At least you came home with all your clothes on,' said Ilse with a half-smile.

'I was hoping you'd forgotten that.'

'What was his name? Werner or Heinz or…'

'Heinz. Don't worry, it's over. Can you bring me a new towel, please?' Renate showered and thought back to the first time she'd had sex with Heinz. In the Old Botanic Gardens, behind a row of giant bromeliads. The sound Heinz made, like a pig with asthma. He had pimples on his freckles and breath like dirty socks. For a prank, he had dared her to kiss the statue of Gänseliesel in the town square. The legend was if you kissed Gänseliesel before your PhD you'd get ten years bad luck. Like if you walk under a ladder. *Quatschen – piffle*, she thought. She knew she would leave Göttingen after her Bachelors. *But where? Berlin or Frankfurt?* Or somewhere exotic, further away. *The rainforests of Borneo? Brazil? Australia?*

She cleaned up and made a mental note to send some enquiry letters.

*

Next day in the auditorium, taking Research Techniques, she faced a red-faced Professor Henschel. His throat spilled out past a top button and covered the knot of his tie. Today's topic: Phyllotaxis – the arrangement of leaves on a stem. A guy edged past her and sat down. It was the smell she recognised – stale tobacco, cheap cologne, wet sneakers and dirty jeans.

Heinz.

She moved to the end of the row.

'Today I want to discuss phyllotaxis as proposed by Turing's theory of linear pattern formation, minus the mathematics. Any initial thoughts?' His voice boomed out across the cavernous theatre. 'I'll be more specific. How does the new theory of non-linear pattern formation add to our understanding of phyllotaxis?' The professor scanned the room, eyes darting as if seeking prey. They came to rest on Renate.

'Miss Meyer. Care to enlighten us?'

'If you are referring to Gierer and Meinhardt's theory of activator-inhibitor systems, the non-linear patterns are defined by their degree of randomness. Is that correct, professor?'

'Some examples might be helpful for the rest of the class. Please, Miss Meyer.'

'The patterns on pythons, giant puffer fish, zebra's stripes, leopard's spots. Do you want me to continue, Herr Professor?'

He moved to the front of the stage, head rotated around the room with a slight smirk on his face. Ideas revolved, crystallised and slotted together inside Renate like grand symphonies. Concepts expanded in ordered patterns like the petals of *primula farinosa* in the local botanic garden. Structure. Order. Beauty. That word again, *ordnung* – order. 'Would you like me to explain the mathematics that support the theory, professor?' she replied, over the muttering heads.

'That won't be necessary, Miss Meyer. Suffice it to say it's a bit more complicated than the Grimm brothers' tales. Yes?'

Some of her classmates stared between them in confusion. Renate flushed, her cheeks reddened. He referred to her last assignment when she included passages from *The House in the Woods* by Jacob Grimm. She folded up her books and left without looking back. As the heavy exit door snapped shut, the latch caught in her back-pack strap and jerked her sideways. *Damm.*

She walked briskly to Cheltenham Park, unaware that a figure followed from a distance. Along Judenstrasse and across the Wilhelmplatz, she took just a slight detour via the gravestones of magnetic measurement pioneer Carl Gauss, philosopher Herman Lotze and archaeologist Otto Jahn. Opposite the pond she watched the fountain spray symmetrical patterns on the mirror surface, the smell of the faint beech blossoms drift her way, the soft sound of the wind as it rustled through the Linden trees. She searched for skylark nests. One moment she was seated on the ground, the next her imagination soared above the trees. An unpleasant smell crept up behind her as hands covered over her eyes.

'That was rude, Renate, in class. I thought we had a connection,' Heinz whispered, voice tinged with menace.

'We had nothing, Heinz. It was a mistake. I'm sorry it happened.'

'I liked you, still do. I might have even asked you out again. Especially now I know about your father.'

'What are you talking about? What do you know?' She turned to face him.

'He was a Nazi, a patriot, Renate. Didn't you know that?'

'All I know is he was in the German *Wehrmacht* during the war. The Motor Corps. How did you find out?'

'Kurt knows someone who knows someone in the Stasi. They kept all the old records from the war. Didn't destroy them, just in case. Your father was in Poland. At Auschwitz. Like I said, he did his duty for the Fatherland. Why don't you ask him yourself?'

Renate's voice trembled. 'What are you going to do?'

'Well, that depends on you, Renate. All we want for our silence is a bit of fun. Tonight. At your place.'

'Who are '*we*?"

'Just me and Kurt. You know Kurt, the dean of science's son?'

'Wha... what do I have to do?'

'Meet us tonight outside the student lounge at eight. Then take us to your apartment.' He stroked her arm with his finger. 'Kurt and I will organise the activities.'

Renate clenched her fists, her body stiffened as his finger lifted slowly from her arm. *Family honour is all*, Ulrich had said, many times.

13

Renate cursed and turned her face away from an icy north wind wailing down Albrecht-von-Haller Strasse. *What will the consequences be if the dean of science discovers Papa is an ex-Nazi?* The student lounge, a dimly lit empty cavern on a Tuesday night, distant traffic a foreboding hum. She propped herself against the door jamb to deflect the icy current, illuminated by the single streetlight reflecting off the wet pavement. An orb spider swirled in a wide arc, helpless in battle with the wind and leaves. Somewhere a siren blared. She stamped both feet up and down and wished that Heinz and Kurt had changed their minds. Her body shivered in regular spasms. Three figures loomed from the swirling mist like slow-moving ghosts. Two swaggered, the third shuffled along crab-like swinging his arms as if impersonating Guy the Gorilla. They stopped in front of her.

'You said there would only be two, you and Kurt.'

'Hello. I'm Kurt.' He bowed a little. 'This is Willi, my brother. He only wants to watch.' Willi's large, red raw hands twitched, nails, chewed down to the quick. Willi grinned.

'Okay, let's get this straight. How do I know you'll keep your promise about my father?'

'One, we are honourable Germans,' Heinz replied. 'Two, we keep our promises.'

'And I keep my promises to my family. Ulrich is an honourable man.' Renate stared at Heinz who shuffled from foot to foot. Kurt stared at his watch.

'How can you be so sure about him?' Heinz said, taking one step forward, closer to Renate. She held her ground.

'We're wasting time here,' Kurt said.

'Yes, you are wasting your time, because I'm not going anywhere with you.' Renate crossed her arms tight around her body. Heinz glared back, eyes searching for weakness. Willi snorted and puffed. Heinz turned to go, stopped, swung around.

'You'll be sorry Renate.'

'I'll take my chances.'

*

Back in Ilse's apartment, Renate told the story about Ulrich's activities in wartime, the Motor Corps in Berlin, how her grandfather had been taken by the Nazis.

'What did your papa do in the war?'

'I don't know. He's never spoken about it. I don't think Mum knows.' They both sat in silence under the ticking wall clock. Renate related Kurt's threat to blackmail her and the part about Ulrich and Kurt's claim he was a Nazi. Ilse took her hand and nodded.

'That doesn't mean anything. He might not have joined them. You trust your father, don't you?' she said, sounding sincere. 'You know you can trust me, don't you?'

'Thanks. You're my closest friend. I trust Papa, I must, but...' She had her suspicions about Ulrich's version. *What is he hiding from me?* Ilse stroked Renate's hand. For the next thirty years Renate would regret confiding in her.

Outside, the wind abandoned its fury. A barn owl swooped and took the life of an orb spider. Three men hurried home through the sleet.

14

Daniel
March, 1982

Daniel settled into the group like yeast in a barrel of beer. The group, disparate riders, all accepted him as a fellow seeker on a journey to change the world, one person at a time. They were naïve, young adventurers with an idealism not yet dented by reality, with an unstoppable energy, an inexplicable momentum that drove them forward. Every action generated just enough results and donations to propel them to the next town, like following a script written in advance. They had one thing in common: a determination to do something about the threat of nuclear weapons.

Zoe, Zara and Cam led the feminist clique that dumped large and frequent doses of loathing on the white male patriarchy. They were often in a huddle spouting disdain, like prize cock fighters. The younger people under twenty instinctively avoided them as they struggled to stay on social security.

'Why do they make it so hard for us to stay on the dole?' two people moaned. 'We're riding for peace. The government should support us.'

There was nothing Daniel could add to their reasoning, as he'd worked continuously since leaving school. He gravitated to the group of six well-educated members over thirty, who held their nightly debating sessions complete with large dollops of cynicism. Most of them would be gone soon, driven away by chaos and the pointless arguments of conflicting egos. By weeks' end, during a rest day in Port Macquarie, Daniel learned two things that came out of the blue. Ben was leaving and Bexley had a boyfriend in Sydney. He found out from Zara, her best friend and, in a roundabout way, he asked her when the *boyfriend* would arrive.

'Don't know when, soon. I think.' she replied.

'Oh…that's a shame.'

'What, that Ben's leaving?' she said, with raised eyebrows.

He nodded his head. Bexley's voice and vision compelled others to listen. She argued her views in rich tones. Women in business suits or mothers with toddlers in prams stopped and nodded their heads as she explained what they were doing and they would then either thank her for the leaflet or give a donation. The men, especially those in suits, reacted differently. They were not sure where their eyes should be, on her vivacious face, the leaflet she held, or her chest. She performed her street theatre magic like she was born into the role. Daniel's role was rattling the donations tin. He gave it a shake.

*

The night before Ben left, Daniel helped transfer the bulk food and tents into Pete's ute. Ben called a spade a spade. Old school. A large journal sat open on the van's front seat.

'What are you writing?' Daniel nodded towards the open book.

'A book. It's called *How to Change the World by Arguing and not Washing.*'

'Doesn't sound like a best seller.' He smiled. 'I've never asked you why you joined the bike ride. Is there anything I can do to convince you to stay?' Daniel said, passing a large tent.

'Nah, it's a lot of things, probably joined for the same reasons you did, adventure, stop the nuclear beast, have fun. But there's no fun, especially from those two. When they're around spouting off, they spread chaos. I can live without that.' Ben nodded in the direction of Zara and Cam.

'And I'm sick of sneaking out for a burger and a beer. All that vego stuff they eat. Doesn't it bother you?' Ben waved his hands in their direction.

'I don't mind it, as long as I don't have to cook it.'

'The way they go on about it, like it's a religion...'

'Well, they do have strong ideas about most things. Isn't that why they're here?'

'For fuck's sake, there's no booze. No fun.' Ben huffed. 'It's all that feminist rubbish...' He trailed off. 'And they call all men liars. All men! Can you believe it?'

Ben banged his hand on the dashboard.

'Look, Ben. Maybe you need to try and walk in their shoes for a while, see what they feel like. So, you off in the morning?'

'You bet, boyo.'

'Shame. I'm going to miss you.'

*

Two days later, on the Pacific Highway about twenty-five kilometres north of Kempsey, Daniel, Bexley and Pete the ute-driver stood outside a locked gate. The rest of the riders cycled by towards Macksville and the CWA hall. Tied to the gate with black ribbon was a black-framed photo of a boy. *Reggie Morris, Aged 10. RIP.* Opposite, a farmer on a tractor ripped out a tree stump. They both stared at the silent buildings past an enormous Moreton Bay fig, red, black and yellow streamers fluttered in the breeze. Behind them a constant *ker-flap kerflap* hummed as cars and trucks hit the joins in the concrete highway.

'Wanna find out more about who this boy was and what happened to him?' Bexley asked.

'Sure. How?'

'Let's go back into Kempsey in the ute. Someone there will know.'

Twenty minutes later, parked on Belgrave Street opposite the post office, Bexley walked over to an Indigenous woman in a floral dress who sat on a bench. 'Hi. Mind if we sit here?'

'No, luv. It's a free country,' the woman said, staring straight ahead.

'I'm Bexley, this is Daniel. We rode through here yesterday with the world bike riders. Did you see us?'

'Name's Mavis. No, luv. I was in bed with the bronchitis. But I was told all about you. It's a good thing what you young people are doing. What are you doing back in town, if you don't mind me asking?'

'We saw a photo of a boy on a gate north of here near Kinchella. We wanted to know how he died,' Bexley said. Mavis sat up straighter, inhaled and said: 'Ah, yeah, poor bugger. That was Reggie. Died forty years ago today. Les's little brother. Les lives out at Green Hills. I'll tell you how he died. Can I get a lift home after?'

'Sure.'

She turned her head, slow like she was straining and took Bexley's hand. Her voice came out soft and gentle at first. Daniel recognised something painful gathering momentum, as the facts, the history unfolded like a shroud peeled back from a dead child. He closed his eyes, the words built the story, a story he was unaware of – *The Stolen Generation, herded onto the Mission, racist police,* and for a moment time stood still. Noises vanished – from traffic and the breeze and children laughing in the distance. Her words smashed against a world he thought he knew. They shattered something he'd fought hard against since his dad left. It was not complacency. Or ignorance. It was worse than that. More like a callous disregard for the truth.

When he escaped the second time, the manager, Frank Stanley, tied him to that big fig tree and flogged him with a horse whip...

He couldn't believe she was talking about a country he was born in. *How could this have happened only forty years ago?* Mavis' story advanced no answers, just etched a permanent space on Daniel's brain.

...After he escaped the third time, they tied him up in the lockup. Let him starve. When they checked on him, two days later, he was dead. Hung himself.

Daniel opened his eyes. Bexley stroked Mavis's arm. Tears ran down her cheeks. Daniel closed his fists and flexed his arms. He recalled Ruby's story – the part about how her uncle hanged himself. Daniel pondered the nature of shame, how the uncle might have felt as opposed to the hopelessness that little boy must have felt. He was resigned to accept how evil some people could be, had been to the Indigenous people. On the trip back out of town to find the others, Daniel stared out the window. *Why haven't I heard anything before about all this? Why has everyone been silent on these issues, this history?* A sudden urge to ring his mum was overwhelming.

He'll say: *I'm safe and learning lots, Mum.*

She'll say: *I miss you. When are you coming home?*

15

In Grafton, in a phone box under a gigantic jacaranda, he rang home. Rachel picked up on three. 'Hello?'

'Hi. Any letters arrived for me?'

'And how are you, Rachel? How are you coping with Mum full-time? Do you really want to know?' There was a pause while she waited for him to answer. He heard a deep sigh. 'There is a letter here, want me to open it?'

'Sure. And, sorry,' he said, twiddling the phone cord. He heard the envelope tear, and Rachel's unctuous breathing. *Dear Mr Cohen. This letter is to inform you that your employment with the NSW Department of Education has been terminated. Please be aware that the police have been instructed by another party to continue their investigations. If these...*blardy blah... It goes on about your rights and final settlement and other stuff. Do you want me to read the rest of it?'

'Don't bother. I'm not worried.' He searched his conscience for shreds of guilt, any pieces of dirty linen in need of tidying, found none.

'For your sake and Mum's, I hope you're right.'

They stopped for the night in a reserve on the outskirts of Grafton as rising Scorpio stung the crepuscular horizon. A herd of Hereford bellowed their presence. Light from the half-moon glittered like aluminium foil off a dam in a field. Daniel turned the pages of his journal, shining a torch on a blank page and wrote:

29th March

> *I'm beginning to understand the issues that most concern women, how they believe nuclear weapons are the most extreme product of male violence. They are determined to speak out about this to as many people that will listen. This time has given me the space to work out what I want, what I really need. And what about Ruby? What did she want? I don't know if she even knew what she wanted. Why is she still pursuing me? It's not fair, either for me or her being molested. I can't understand how people can do that. I'm not sure about this crazy bike ride either. I might as well leave. Probably in Brisbane.*

*

A large group of motorbikes roared up, pulled into the reserve and parked. Daniel saw 'Gypsy Jokers' on their black leather jackets. A few stood and stared back at the group, huddled around the campfire. Loud guffaws and the *pop pop pop* of cans pierced the night. Two bikies pointed. Pete and Daniel walked over to say hello. The women stood motionless, shoulder to shoulder around the fire.

'Hi. Where are you guys from?' Pete extended his hand. Their expressionless faces glared through the dim distance between them.

'Who wants to know?' a guy with a fresh scar across his nose said. The others stopped and stared.

'We're the World Bike Ride for Peace,' Daniel said.

'Well, *peace*, man, how about you share two of your women? You've got plenty.'

'That's not going to happen.' Daniel puffed his chest. 'Anyway, do you think you can scare us with your loud bikes, black jackets and tattoos?' Daniel crossed his arms.

'Yep, and who are you, tough guy, their dad?' They howled with laughter. Daniel didn't see the sudden movement beside him, just felt something heavy hit the side of his head. Then nothing.

*

He opened his eyes, aware of a vibration, a movement, the sound of an engine and the drone of tyres. And a smell – sudsy, like fresh clothes. His head was in Bexley's lap. She hummed and stroked his head. 'Am I in Heaven?' He sighed, loud enough that Bexley let out a laugh.

'No, Dan. You're in Pete's ute. We're taking you to the hospital.'

'Do they have a hospital in Heaven?' Daniel murmured.

'It's okay. Won't be long now. Just close your eyes.'

By noon the next day, the doctor in the white jacket and stethoscope announced that Daniel was cleared to leave. 'You may have a headache for a couple of days, Mr Cohen. If it gets worse, I'd advise you return.' The doctor scratched at a scruffy five-day growth and rubbed red eyes as he spoke. Some hope returned, something he needed more of since Mavis's story and the incident with the bikies. They drove past the campsite, deserted as if nothing ever happened. Beer cans rolled around in the breeze like empty barrels on an ocean liner's deck.

'Where are we going?' Daniel asked in a weak voice. 'And what happened with the bikies?'

'They didn't stick around too long after the cops came. And thanks for standing up to them,' Bexley said with a chuckle. 'The rest of our group should be halfway to Lismore. We'll meet up somewhere near Casino.'

His mind lingered on the letter he'd received from the education department, the way Ruby had framed him, that nobody was interested in his side of the story. 'Bexley, can you tell me a story about your time at school? Like, did you ever have a crush on a teacher?'

'That's a funny thing to ask.' She looked at him with wide eyes. Frowning, she answered, 'Not exactly, but I wasn't the most popular girl.'

'Why?'

'Most of my friends were boys, most girls my age avoided me.' She shrugged. 'I think because their boyfriends were always hanging with me. I don't know why…' She trailed off. Daniel cracked a smile as the tip of her tongue squeezed through the gap in her teeth. 'I never figured it out. Jealous of me? Why?' Her voice rose a note and her face widened. Daniel's brow furrowed, just a little. She had that combination of stunning looks, a one-in-a-million smile and an innocent presence. His only trouble was, she had a boyfriend.

'So, tell me about Tony?' he asked.

'Oh, why?' She turned and studied his face.

'Just…curious.'

'You'll meet him soon. You can find out yourself.'

*

Pete dropped Bexley at an old, two-storey house in South Lismore. They shopped for the basics: rice, vegetables, tofu. Tomorrow was a rest day and film night in Lismore before the short journey to Nimbin. The aspirin kicked in and the dull headache faded. Daniel looked forward to a long rest at the legendary town of Nimbin. When they returned to the house, Bexley and a new guy walked down the steps holding hands.

'Hey, who's the new guy with Bexley?'

'That's Tony. He arrived yesterday,' Pete said.

Fuck. So soon? Daniel's stomach froze as if he'd been dunked in ice water. He stared past the two, arm in arm, as they walked towards him, laughing. A policeman in a patrol car stared at him as it ambled by. Daniel felt the hair lift on the back of his neck.

16

Daniel

April 1, 1982

Nimbin. The fabled town in decline since the Aquarius Festival in 1973 and the battles to save Terania Creek rainforests. Long ago, the cedar cutters came. Then the banana farmers and dairy cattle. Now all gone. Around the creeks where the land had been raped and eroded, the camphor laurels, sucked on the lifeblood no longer there. The few stories Daniel had heard on the bike ride didn't prepare him for the reality of a hippie town in decline. The three hundred or so residents clung to the belief that society would change into a utopia – if the social security cheques arrived on time. Daniel had his own battles to face – what to do when he left the bike ride.

A multi-coloured station wagon painted with a peace sign tooted as it passed him. A young woman leaned out the window and waved a rainbow flag. Nimbin appeared through the haze like a cast set on an old Western movie. Old timers in blue overalls stopped and stared. Big-breasted women in multicoloured skirts carried toddlers on their hips. A brown cattle dog chased a family of mallards across the street. Daniel found most of the riders outside the Rainbow Information Centre where a street party was in full swing. Three shirtless blokes in flared pants played guitars. Kids and adults danced in the street. 'You okay, man?' a woman with spacious pupils wearing a purple sarong asked. She handed Daniel a bent joint. He shook his head.

By sunset, the community hall thumped with loud music and dancing. Joints, incense sticks and Coolabah Riesling casks were passed around as if they were lollies at a kids' party. Miss *dilated pupils* zeroed in on Daniel. 'I'm Summer, wanna dance?' Her body swayed like jelly from side to side. Daniel flopped his arms back and forth and jiggled his hips. She took no notice of him. The music switched from the Doobie brothers to Jethro Tull, The Who, then Bob Dylan. When *Like a Rolling Stone* belted out, the bike riders shouted out as one – *How does it feel?* He agreed, *like a rolling stone*. For the first time, he understood what the word *freedom* meant – without the boundaries of a school timetable or next month's rent – in all its flavours and applications. He was free to choose the next step, without worrying about the consequences. If only it was that simple. Momentarily, he'd forgotten about Ruby, out there plotting.

He turned around as Summer moved in closer on a slow song and flung her arms around him. She smelled of patchouli oil mixed with incense and herbs. She handed him a joint. When he inhaled, the smoke burnt his throat and he leaned back coughing. He ran outside, she followed.

'First time, hey?' She laughed and threw back her head. 'Hey, where have you been all my life?' She leaned in closer, closed her glazed eyes and kissed him.

*

They made love on a futon under a full canopy bed, with frankincense to enhance the mood. Afterwards, Summer hurried into the next bedroom, settled Aria, her seven-year-old daughter, and made tea. 'Her dad wanted to call her Autumn. No way! You know what comes after Autumn?'

Daniel nodded his head. Summer told him Aria was a bit of a princess, her dad wasn't around anymore. 'But who cares? There's lots of other dads here.'

'I wasn't cut out for teaching...'

'That's a strange thing to say. Why?'

'Not good at small talk.'

'So, when are you leaving on your crusade?' she asked fiddling with her bangles. There was something about that word *crusade* that irked him.

'Tomorrow. I like you. It was...nice,' Daniel said.

'Nice. Such an empty word.' Her smile fell away. 'Can you leave before she wakes up?'

He walked the two blocks back to the community hall under the night sky, a riot of sparkler speckles, with images of women scrolling inside his head – his mother, Rachel, Skyla, Ruby, Bexley. And what trust, loyalty and affection truly meant to him.

I love them all, in different ways. Not Ruby, though, I just feel sorry for her. In the short time he'd known Bexley, he'd come to respect her more and more. *If only.* A smouldering, gibbous moon reflected off the wet bitumen. A frogmouth or a barn owl – he couldn't tell which – hooted from a tall, twisted blackbutt in front of the hall. Daniel stepped through the open back door of the hall, over sleeping figures and around empty bottles to his bedroll on the stage.

A warm shower would be nice.

Snoring echoed around the cavernous space.

*

Shouts boomed around the hall in the pre-dawn twilight. Daniel, half asleep, tried to focus on the large figures – five police spread out, shining torches in faces. One held a black German Shepherd that strained on a silver leash. 'We're looking for Daniel Cohen. Where is he?' a sergeant shouted. He had a large gut hanging over his belt. 'We want Daniel Cohen! Hand him over and we'll leave the rest of you in peace!'

'Why? He hasn't done anything,' Bexley yelled back.

Daniel stood up, pulled up his pants and said, 'Yeah, I'm Daniel Cohen.' The sergeant and a constable walked over, turned Daniel around and handcuffed him. They pushed him outside and into a police wagon.

'Hey, that hurts.'

'Don't worry, fella. It's only a short trip back to Lismore.'

'But I haven't done anything wrong,' Daniel pleaded.

'You can tell that to the magistrate tomorrow.'

He passed through a small crowd outside. Pete leaned in as close as possible and said, 'Don't worry. We'll see you tomorrow. We won't leave you there alone.'

One hour later, Daniel sat, head in his hands in a cell with white walls, camp bed, a stainless-steel bucket and a stained wash sink. *Ruby? The Department of Education? Fuck. What else could it be?*

17

Daniel
April 2, 1982
Lismore

Daniel drifted in and out of sleep in a dirty cell in Lismore lockup, dreaming of drawing masterpieces on the blank cell wall. He jerked awake at every clanging bar, every thump and thud and whimpering cry from down the line of cells – *He hit me first. They planted the dope, it's not mine.* A dog howled somewhere.

'Hey you, next cell. What they get you on?'

'Dunno, mate,' Daniel replied.

'Seen a lawyer yet?'

'Nope.'

'You will. You'll get Hardwick or O'Connell.'

'You know them?' Daniel asked.

'Sure. Both staunch defenders of the status quo, the ordered system, the...' There was a pause as he coughed and spat. 'Break any of it down and *poof*! Out comes the chaos and before too long it's back to monkey time again.'

That's just great. A wacko giving me advice. He lay on his back and stared at the mould and stains on the ceiling, cobwebs hanging from a four-blade fan. *Speeding fine last year? I paid that. Tax bill? Paid that. Christ, what could it be?* He opened his eyes. A red glow reflected from the wall. The doors clanged and a balding corpulent man in a pin-stripe suit carrying a black battered briefcase shuffled in.

'You Daniel Cohen?'

'Yes.'

'I'm your assigned lawyer.'

'Do you have a name?'

'O'Connell. To get right to the point, you've been charged with indecent assault on a minor. How will you plead?'

'What? Who? When?' His chest tightened.

'It says here... February 7, 1982.'

'But I didn't do anything, I just sat there. She came on to me!'

'Says here she was fifteen. So, a minor. She couldn't give consent.'

'That's bullshit! I felt sorry for her, gave her a ride. That's all. She said she was sixteen.'

'So she lied. She was being...axiomatic. Did you check?'

'What, like ask for her birth certificate?' neither of them smiled.

'So, here's how it may go. At ten am you'll be in front of Magistrate Hardacre. He has a sixteen-year-old daughter. He doesn't like sex offenders. He may give you bail if your record is clean.' O'Connell droned on with some formalities. Daniel sat, frozen to the spot.

'Sign here. This allows me to act on your behalf. And tomorrow, go easy on the brio.'

'What's that?' Daniel raised his eyebrows.

'Enthusiastic elaboration. Don't bother.'

*

At 10:01 Daniel sat in the front pew facing a magistrate, who was dressed in a light grey suit. He gazed down like a cassowary over glasses perched on his nose. 'Mr Cohen. You are accused of indecently assaulting a fifteen-year-old girl on February 7, 1982. How do you plead?'

O'Connell elbowed Daniel's ribs. 'Not guilty. Sir.'

'Your hearing will be set for six weeks' time from today. I'm granting bail on the condition you report to a police station weekly and surrender your passport.'

Outside, in bright sunshine, Pete and Lexie waited next to the ute. 'What did they charge you with?' Pete asked.

Daniel hesitated, took Pete's elbow and whispered, 'Look, it's a setup, this schoolgirl back in Winburn is framing me. She told me she was sixteen when I rejected her, she must have gone to the cops.'

Pete took two steps back.

'Please, it's the truth. I didn't do anything. She's lying to get back at me.'

'What are you going to tell the others back in Murwillumbah?'

'I'll think of something. Just, promise me you won't say anything.'

'Okay. Don't worry. I believe you.'

The car looped back through Nimbin, past the community centre and on through the Nightcap Ranges. Lexie sat in the middle; Daniel stared out at a forest that Lexie said her mother fought for three years earlier.

'I was fourteen. We stayed for months in a tent near Terania Creek. It was scary, but fun.'

Daniel nodded and murmured something as the concept of truth ran a continual loop in his head. Truth, if it existed. *Or is it like some convenient tool kept in your back pocket that you drag out when needed?* He closed his eyes and for a second, he was twelve and sat before a glass-panelled front door, waiting for his dad to come home. He had lost his job, lost Skylar and now his self-confidence and his freedom.

What else could go wrong?

18

Renate

March 15, 1982

Frankfurt Airport

Renate waited for a Qantas 747-200 bound for Brisbane and clutched a pocketbook of Australian slang. She tried to memorise the unusual terms but was confused by the syntax. For her, there was a complete lack of order to the language. *Do they really talk like this?* She took a deep breath, sipped water from a plastic cup with a kangaroo logo on it. The last image of Ulrich still imprinted on her brain – his neck muscles bulging shouting, 'You're not going!' as she stomped out of the house. Anne had whimpered as she clasped and unclasped her hands. Two years since that night, Renate had no regrets. Her life so far, marked by order and chaos – mostly order, which she cherished – each waged a war for supremacy, the order, almost like a precondition of German society, one like the inside of a tight sleeping bag with a jammed zipper. The chaos, disorder of her previous world. Hushed secrets hidden in old suitcases in the attic.

*

She had completed her bachelor's with honours, researched courses in Australia and enrolled in a Master of Botany at the University of Queensland.

The only problem was her six-month visa. She decided she couldn't wait in Germany any longer. In her fist, clasped tight, was the Stone of Heaven – the Native Americans used similar stones to summon up their spirit guides and the Chinese, who believed the stone was captured moonbeams. She swore that no man would ever threaten her, ever lie to her, again. She tightened the seat belt, sitting in a window seat, 17C and rearranged the pamphlets in the seat holder. Some minutes later the plane charged into the night forcing her deep into the seat as the city's receding lights flashed by. Her breath fogged the window. The plane soared high over the battlefields of Europe, mountains of Turkey, the cradle of humanity. She nodded off.

When she opened her eyes, stewards with wide smiles and loud shirts were serving dinner on plastic trays. They skipped down the aisles passing out cups with a kangaroo logo. Female stewards in bright floral dresses – like they'd just walked in from a rainforest – leaned in close to answer questions with confident smiles. One child, about ten years old, sitting across the aisle, asked in rapid succession, 'How can you walk and not spill the drinks? What movie is coming on? How much do you get paid?' Young, attractive men in sky-blue jackets and dark-blue striped ties with name tags: Kevin, Murray, Peter.

The man next to her, mid-forties with a manicured beard in jeans and blue-checked shirt, snored like a slow ticking clock. Renate donned headphones to block out the sound. She closed her eyes before a voice next to her said, '*Wohin gehst du?*' *Where are you going?*

'English, please. I'm going to Brisbane. You?'

'Let me introduce myself. Dr Otto Bauer. I'm touring four Australian cities on a speaking tour.'

'What is your topic?' Renate asked, taking off the headphones.

'*Lebenmagnetismus.* Some call it 'animal magnetism' but I prefer mesmerism. Have you heard about it?'

'Sorry, no. It sounds vaguely scientific.'

'Oh, it is. Our clinic in Berlin is swamped with patients seeking help.'

'And what treatment do you offer, Herr Doctor?' she said with raised eyebrows.

'Well, why don't you take a pamphlet? It will explain the process. My lecture in Brisbane still has some tickets left, why don't you come along?'

'Maybe,' she said as she looked at the glossy leaflet with wild claims of all kinds of cures with no specific detail except 'channelling the magnetic force.' 'Pfft.' Renate dropped the leaflet and reached for the headphones. A *Givenchy* odour itched up her nose. She overheard two men from behind, having a conversation with an unusual modulation. She opened her Australian slang dictionary.

'Whadya think of the new Labor leader?'

'Pinko, mate.'

'Yair, too right. Better dead than red, hey?'

Renate flicked through her slang book. *A politician? Someone who died?* They resumed their oblivious staccato, back and forth. *'Twits'*, *'sheila'* and *'ding-dong'.* She turned around, perplexed. One had a Hawaiian shirt with a deep collar, top two buttons undone. They stopped talking as their mouths fell open.

'Excuse me. Sorry for interrupting. Are you speaking normal English?'

'It's Aussie-English luv.'

'Do you all talk like that?'

'Well, I can't speak for the prime minister, but all our friends talk like this. Why? You have a problem?'

'No. No problem. Thank you.' Renate turned back around. A few more hushed words reached her. 'Strewth mate. A bit of a looker.'

'Not wrong there, Brian.'

The knot in her stomach tightened.

19

Renate
Late March
Brisbane

Renate explored Brisbane from her on-campus room in the International House. Her room had a single bed, a double sofa, bathroom and a kitchenette, extras provided to post-graduate students. The first week she investigated the bus routes to the city, the ferry across the Brisbane River, the parks and the city library in Brisbane square. She spent most days in lectures or the campus library typing her notes on an IBM Selectric typewriter that the two librarians loaned to the *intense German girl*. She made friends with an Italian girl named Simone Lombardi who cooked often – lasagne, gnocchi, prosciutto di parma. She was an inch shy of Renate's shoulder, with milk chocolate skin, short hair, restless, with clear hazel eyes. She always wore an unusual earring in her right ear – a double-headed axe. In the neighbouring apartment, there was a fervent, slender girl Renate had seen twice. Each time they met, the woman had tried to give her a religious pamphlet about a Universal Life ('We Are One') Church. Simone called her '*That weird chick.*'

On Friday, after lectures, Simone dropped in with a bowl of steaming pasta. 'Just bumped into that weird chick again. She was carrying a bundle of those leaflets to hand out. She's a strange one.'

'I don't know her name,' Renate said and set the table. 'She doesn't smile much. Did you see Louis? That's his name, correct?'

'No, must have missed him. I'll see him later. But that weird chick… Never seen her smile either. Too busy passing out useless pamphlets with an excess of angst.'

They both laughed.

'Say, René, I know a couple of nice Aussie guys. Would you like to meet them?' Simone said as her mouth widened.

'I'm okay. But thanks anyway.'

'Don't tell me…you're gay?' Her eyes probed.

'Oh no…it's not that… Why?'

For a second, Simone's lips curved down before she burst out laughing. 'Oh, that's a shame,' she said.

'It's… It's just, I'm still finding my way here. I must study most of my spare time.'

Renate looked at Simone's face that said, 'Tell me more.'

'You need to lighten up René. Aussie guys can be fun, if not sexist and immature. You just gotta know how to play them.'

'Play? Like a musical instrument?' Lines creased Renate's brow.

'No, silly. Play, like tease… Manipulate, control.'

'Are you serious? I don't need to do that to like someone.'

'Well, good for you, girl.'

*

In the second week, her supervisor, Doctor Simon Green asked her to come to his office. He was a chubby man with a neat goatee and three chins. He plodded about his office, which was adorned with specimens in yellow mason jars and insects in clear perspex cubes. She looked at him closely, then took a step back. 'Miss Mayer. Your thesis title,' – he picked up a sheet of paper – '*Non-linear pattern formation in Australian Native Plants – a post-*

Turing analysis. I find the title just a bit...how would you say in German: *rätselhaft*. Enigmatic.'

'Enigmatic? I don't agree, doctor. I want to investigate if the patterns identified by Turing are replicated in Australia. I am keen to carry it further to a PhD.'

'Well, Miss Mayer, it's not too late to reconsider. My speciality is in genetics. Perhaps you'd like to submit a new title, something in current genetic research?'

'I'm not focusing on the genetics, doctor. I wish to continue with my original thesis.'

'Well, if that's the case,' – he paused to stroke his goatee – 'I know a professor who might be willing to take you on. His name is Beattie. Do you wish me to pass your name on?'

'As you wish. I'd be grateful.'

'Well, I'll see him this afternoon and give him this.' He held out Renate's synopsis. 'I'll ask him to contact you. It's been nice meeting you.' He held out his hand to shake. It was sweaty and warm.

That night, she planned her first field trip to Mt Warning National Park. In a deep sleep, she dreamt a black crow followed her through a dense forest. She stopped and watched as it pecked at a piece of rotting fruit. Suddenly she was riding a bicycle along a country road. A grey ute passed her, carrying a ghost who stared at her from the back tray.

*

On Thursday, students organised a protest rally against proposed increases to student fees. Renate caught the ferry across the river and rode Simone's bike through Dutton Park, along the south bank promenade and across the Victoria Bridge. She stopped a block away from King George Square, where a large police presence separated her from the rally. The police linked arms. Dogs snarled and strained on long leads. People who had begun to march were wrestled to the ground and led away into vans. Chaos erupted. Indigenous people held red, black and yellow signs and crude images of Premier Sven Johansen. Renate stared, mouth open, stomach tensed.

'Bloody animals they are,' a man in a black suit said.

'Pardon? Do you mean the police?'

'No. Those ratbags. How dare they insult our premier?'

A tremor passed through her body. She watched for a few more minutes, then pedalled back, as fast as she could. *Scheisse.* In two weeks, she already had second thoughts about coming.

*

A loud knocking came around midnight. Simone leant against the door frame, agitated, makeup smudged in lines down her cheeks. 'Bastards arrested Louis. They won't let him see a lawyer.'

'Is that normal?' Renate said.

'Sven's rules. And the police do what he says.'

'Are you okay? What are you going to do?'

'March down there tomorrow and stay until they let him out. A few of us are planning another rally next Wednesday. With the Black Protest Committee.'

'Maybe I'll come.'

'Thanks, Renate. And can I stay here tonight on your couch?'

'Sure.'

After dinner, they talked for hours – books, politics, history. Simone laughed when she told Renate how Louis gave her a bunch of roses last week and a card with a love heart inside. 'I'd better tell him soon.'

'Tell him what?'

'That I'm gay, of course!' She laughed at Renate's perplexed look. 'Sorry, I thought you knew?'

'No. but that's Okay. It doesn't change anything, our friendship.' Renate heard a bang nearby, a door slammed, then words like *...day of reckoning is coming.* She held Simone's hand just as one would pat dog. Simone stared into her eyes. Renate whispered, '*Ich glaube, er ist in dich verliebt.*' – I think he's in love with you. She thought, *what is your story, Simone?*

20

Saturday, April 3

Renate packed a backpack with enough clothes and food for three days, borrowed Simone's bicycle and caught a train to Coolangatta. At 3 pm the bus dropped her off on Tumbulgum Road, opposite the Murwillumbah YHA, an old house high on stilts with bright blue walls surrounded on three sides by fig trees. A grey Kingswood HT ute with a YHA sticker on the rear window was parked in the driveway. Renate unpacked her bike and walked down the dark hall to a desk. A bearded man in his mid-thirties sat with his feet up reading *Zen and the Art of Motorcycle Maintenance*. He looked up from behind thick glasses.

'Hi. And you are?'

'Hello. I'm Renate. From Brisbane. I have booked.'

'I'm Steve. The manager. Welcome to Murwillumbah, 'Renate-from-Brisbane'. That's a very strong accent. German?'

'Yes.'

'You don't mind sharing, do you? You'll be with Jane. She's English.' He removed his glasses, blinked three times and wiped his eyes.

'No problem. I love English people, they're just so good at...' she looked up at the ceiling and stroked her chin. 'Queueing.'

'Yes! Don't you love people who love... order?'

'Of course, don't we all?'

'Or you could try singing a bull to sleep. I've just read' – he held up the book – 'how the author explains the concept of *quality* by singing a bull to sleep. I'll quote: *One may attempt to sing the bull to sleep...* Page two hundred and twenty-four. I won't bore you with the details. Or maybe I will. Do you think the concept of 'quality' is subjective or objective?'

Renate stared for a second. 'I'll have to think on that, please. Is it possible?'

'What, to sing a bull to sleep or define quality?' He asked with a wry grin.

'How do you do that?' Renate asked, with her head tilted to one side.

'Maybe sing it lullabies in bull language?'

'Oh...do you think it works?' She hadn't detected his sarcasm.

He put the book down flat, looked at her through glazed eyes, smiled and said, 'Frankly, it's not possible, it's just a metaphor. Don't take it too seriously.'

She collected her key. *He's a strange one.*

He escorted her along a hall lined with walls of framed photos. Ancient men with thick moustaches and straight backs, axes and cross-cut saws next to massive logs. A logging truck rumbled past outside, its steel shackles rattling on the uneven road. The room had two single beds with a gap just wide enough to squeeze through. The window looked onto a Moreton Bay fig, whose shade reached down to a wide, silent river. She almost forgot Steve was standing behind her.

'That's the Tweed.'

'What is?'

'The river. Flooded eight years ago. Now we're going into a drought.'

'That's not good, right?' Renate expected another riddle.

'Only if you don't like water.'

'Right...' She turned to unpack her backpack. He stood there and stared out the window.

'She's in the kitchen.'

'Who?'

'Jane. Your roommate. Cooking an English meal. I can't wait.'

Again, she missed the sarcasm.

*

Downstairs, Jane and two men in their twenties stirred steaming pots on a gas stove. Jane had a small mountain of carrots and turnips on a massive breadboard. Renate waited a second then sat in a high-backed wooden chair. The table was a thick piece of maroon-coloured log, possibly cedar and polished like a mirror.

'I'm Simon. This is Liam. He's Irish,' a young man in white pants said. He wore a white T-shirt with a large Union Jack on it.

'I'm Renate,' she said, and held out her hand.

'Don't worry about him,' Liam said, 'he's just jealous.'

Renate turned and faced Simon. 'What are you jealous of?'

'He thinks the English own literature just because of Shakespeare.'

'Well, what have you got, boyo. Can you match Shakespeare?'

'Easy. How about Samuel Beckett. James Joyce. Brendan...'

'Okay. Okay. You don't have to rub it in.'

'Can't help it. I'm Irish. Say, Renate, you are...German?'

'Yes. I come from Kassel. It's in Hesse. Have you been there?' she raised her eyebrows and tilted her head to the left.

'Can't say I have. Simon looked at the others who as one shook their heads. 'Well, 'Renate-from-Kassel', what are you doing in bustling Murwillumbah?'

'I'm going to Mt Warning on a field trip.'

'Hey, so are we! Steve's giving us a lift tomorrow in his ute. At least that's what the weird geezer said. Wicked! Why don't we all go together?' Simon said.

'Do we have to queue?' she almost cracked a smile. Before they could answer, an icy chill tingled down her spine. She remembered the dream. Her hand closed around the stone in her pocket. 'Thanks for the offer but I want to ride my friend's bike. It's only fourteen kilometres.'

'No problem. We can give you a lift back if you like. Then after dinner, we're going to see a movie at the CWA hall about Aboriginals blockading mining on their land. A group of anti-nuclear bike riders is in town. You might like to see that.'

'Sure. Sounds interesting.'

*

The 6:30 morning light glittered through the black bean and fig trees. A slash of sunlight broke through the mist over the river and gilded the water surface yellow. Renate rode down Riverview Street and ducked as a magpie swooped and slapped her helmet. From 14km, Mt Warning reared up like a blackened wall of a sacked castle. A dust-covered logging truck blasted its horn as it tore past, flicking gravel from its chunky tyres. Out past the edge of town, she passed acres of abandoned sugar cane and crossed three narrow wooden bridges over eroded creeks. She cycled past rusted sheds and broken tractors, all shrouded in cobwebs. Glossy, black Angus cattle turned and looked up as the lone rider pedalled by and turned onto a narrow, signposted road that read: *Mt Warning NP 5km*. Hiding Simone's bike behind a massive, flooded gum at the edge of the carpark, her watch said 8.45. By 9 am, she was cocooned in rainforest canopy with towering Antarctic beech, booyongs and buttress roots of Moreton Bay figs large enough to sleep in. She tripped over a vine root and dropped the pocketbook Simone had lent her – *Rainforest Plants of Australia*. Red-headed brush turkeys scurried sideways, magpies wheeled and cried as time itself seemed to slow and drift. A chaotic diversity of trees, shrubs, vines, lichen and moss enthralled her – the lichen attached to rotting logs, the leaf arrangements, ample evidence of phyllotaxis. Taking a deep, long breath, she closed her eyes as whistles, trills and hoots assaulted her ears. It was an unknowable gestalt, more so than anything she had experienced. By 11 am, she stood before a wobbly steel ladder at the bottom of a vertical basalt monolith. An elderly couple descended out of the cloud, unaware Renate was there. She coughed.

'Oh, morning, luv. Beautiful view up there. Bit of cloud moved in. You going up?' the elderly man asked. 'You be careful on that ladder,' he nodded in the direction of a steel ladder. Renate nodded and smiled. She gave them a minute to leave. She placed her foot on the first rung and it slipped as she pressed down. *Vorsichtig. Careful.* Grabbing hold of the two sides she climbed, wiping away beads of sweat running into her eyes. Two point five metres up, one of the anchor bolts hidden in a crack had come loose. The ladder swayed to the right, the other anchor bolt popped out and her shoe slipped. As the ladder gave way, she lurched with an intense sensation of frisson and fell. A sharp pain shot up her leg. Then silence.

*

Twenty minutes and a half kilometre behind, Daniel stepped to the side and nodded at an elderly couple headed in the opposite direction. He ran his hand over moss like silk and for a second his mind wandered back to that girl and why she had accused him. *Did I read her wrong?* He thought. *I was sympathetic, why would she make up that rubbish?* It rattled him, like an unsolvable puzzle keeping him awake at night. The whole episode seemed so insignificant surrounded by this beauty, as the mephitic smell of something dead assaulted his nose. One metre behind Bexley, he checked his hand at the scintilla of light on her red-brown hair. Up ahead, Pete disappeared around a bend. He heard a shout. A flock of rosellas catapulted into the canopy.

'Hey, come quick. There's a woman injured here. She's not moving!'

Daniel, Cam and Bexley ran the last thirty metres. Daniel ran up to the figure and saw a sharp branch jutting from under her leg.

'Pete, run to the ranger station, call an ambulance. We'll need a stretcher,' Bexley said. She gently lifted the woman's head and slid her jacket under, checked for a pulse, then her breathing. 'Both okay. Daniel, can you stop the bleeding?'

Daniel took a clean T-shirt from his backpack, tore it into strips and removed his belt. He made a tourniquet above her knee and twisted it tight. The bleeding stopped. The woman stirred and moaned something. Daniel stroked her arm. 'Hey, you're going to be okay. Help is coming,' Bexley said.

The woman's eyes flickered open. 'I was clumsy again, wasn't I?'

'Pardon?'

'I can't feel my leg.'

'Don't worry. It's okay.' Daniel reassured her. 'I'll loosen the tourniquet.' Daniel blinked and felt time stretch as the woman murmured *gist* or *greenest. German?* Daniel held her soft, cold hand. There was a blue-speckled stone on a chain around her neck.

'I like your crystal.'

'*Verzeihung?* Excuse me?'

'Your stone. It's azurite, I think.'

The woman nodded her head as he passed her a bottle of water. He stared at her face, as colour began to return.

'Where are you from?'

'West Germany.'

'Oh, what's your name?'

'Renate.'

'I'm pleased to meet you, Renate. I'm Daniel.'

She gave a weak smile. Two park rangers arrived with a stretcher. Daniel helped them lift Renate. An hour later they loaded her into a waiting ambulance. The paramedics burst into action, removed the dirty bandages and checked her vitals. 'Sorry it took us so long. We had to come from Lismore,' the older paramedic said. 'The Murwillumbah crew are five k's down the road dealing with a car crash.'

'Any fatalities?' Daniel said.

'Could be. I'll have to stop and check on the way back. Think you'll be needing stitches and an X-ray, luv.'

Daniel held Renate's hand in the ambulance, as if it was fragile porcelain. Minutes later, they stopped on the main road next to an overturned ute. Two police cars held up a long line of traffic. Daniel looked out from the ambulance's window as a paramedic shook his head. On the ground next to him was a blue tarp covering a lump. A young woman stood next to the tarp, tears cascading down her face. Daniel let go of Renate's hand and made the sign of the cross.

21

Daniel and Renate sat outside the X-ray room discussing plants, music, favourite books. She told him of the strange manager with the weird sense of humour back at the hostel. He laughed when she told him the part about the bull. 'Really? A bull lullaby. I can't imagine that. He was pulling your leg.'

'Pardon?' Renate looked down at her leg, then up into his smiling face.

'It's just an idiom we use a lot. It means he was joking. Tell me, why are you here in Australia?'

'I am curious about the world. I want to get a different perspective from the German one. Germany has a very...rigid society.'

'Tell me about it.'

They swapped memories of childhood, growing up, school. She explained her research, her desire to understand the patterns in plant leaves. The way she explained it, with passion in her voice and eyes fascinated him. He'd never met anyone so intense and at the same time so comfortable to be around. He told her about being lost in the ghost train at Luna Park and hiding in a storeroom. She told the story of how she slipped on a jetty over the Fulda River and had to walk three kilometres home in wet clothes. Their conversation was like a pendulum – back and forth – as if they were close

100

friends catching up after years apart. Outside, a black hearse crept up the driveway and stopped around the back. After six stitches, a solid bandage around her ankle and a packet of paracetamol, a nurse said, 'You've got a nasty bump there.' She tapped her head. 'Doctor said you'll have to stay overnight.'

Daniel smiled and squeezed her hand. As he walked down the front steps, the melody from the Queen song *Crazy Little Thing Called Love* ran through his head. He had a new lively spring in his step, and a silly grin crept across his face.

Bexley was in the CWA hall marshalling the bike riders for the film night. She organised the tables with pamphlets, posters fixed on walls and the most important part, a large reel-to-reel 16mm film and a projector. He's seen the doco at least ten times and knew every line, every cop and the names of the Yungngora who defended their land at Noonkanbah in the Kimberleys, two years ago. Bexley was going over her speech. She looked up and smiled. 'You look happy. How is she?'

'Okay, considering. Said it could have been her wrapped in the body bag. Said she'd only met Liam the night before – and he seemed like a nice guy. Very sad.'

'Yes, a very lucky girl. You like her, don't you?' She beamed.

Daniel smiled and nodded. 'Sure. She's got a...cute accent. Anyway, she'll need friends around for a while.'

'Always welcome to join us. Did you say she's always safer on a bike?'

'Nope, but I'm sure you'll tell her.'

*

Next morning, Renate signed the release forms with Daniel beside her. She had a cut below her knee, a sprained ankle and a dull headache. Daniel waited outside as the nurse helped her dress and adjust the crutches. He carried her backpack and helped her to the waiting ute. Pete leaned out the window. 'All good? Are we going back to the hall?'

'No. Can we go back to the hostel, please?' she asked. 'I want to see how Jane and Simon are coping.'

They parked in the hostel driveway next to the patch of dead grass left by Steve's ute. Renate stared at the empty space, wishing she could have warned them. At the back of the building, Steve, Jane and Simon looked up from a table. Simon stared at his hands. Jane peered up, red rings around her eyes. Steve shook his head. Renate pulled out the chair close to Jane, sat down and put her arm around her shoulder.

'Fucking logging truck was in the middle of the road. I swerved and lost it on the gravel.'

'I phoned his parents in Dublin this morning,' Simon said, staring at the ground.

'Are they coming over?' Renate said.

'As soon as they can get a flight. Jane and I are staying here until they come. Steve's organising the funeral. Liam was a great mate. Loved his Irish poetry.'

'Can we do anything?' Pete asked.

'It's okay, mate, Steve's got it all covered. The police, the hospital, the funeral.'

Daniel collected Renate's bags from her room. Took a card with Steve's number and promised to ring from Brisbane. He packed her bike, crutches and bags into the ute and they drove back to the CWA hall. Bexley waited outside. She opened the door, crouched down and gave Renate a long hug. 'You okay going back to Brisbane with Pete and Daniel?' she said, as Lexie and Cam walked over with a basket of mangoes and homemade scones for the trip.

'Looks like we got a new member,' Pete said.

'See you in three days' time in Brisbane at the rally!' Bexley said, as they drove away.

In the car back to Brisbane, Renate sat close against Daniel. He was aware of her accent modulating as she asked questions about his life. During the silent gaps, his mind went through all the possibilities as if he were dissecting a science experiment. It was then she asked him why. 'Why are you on the bike ride?' Her knee touched his as she turned to face him. 'Apart from Bexley, I mean. She's lovely. I've noticed how you look at her. You like her, don't you?'

He paused for a long time before answering. 'Everyone does. And to answer your other question, it's the horizon.'

'The horizon? Which kind?' She scratched her head. 'In German, there are two meanings: *horizont*, meaning the line where the Earth's surface and the sky appear to meet and *gesichtskreis*, meaning field of vision.'

'Both, I guess... The second version. I want to... *need to* expand my field of vision.' Daniel said, turned and stared into her eyes. 'The other horizon, yeah, that's important too. You can see it, all of it on a bike. It opens your mind to possibilities you don't get in a car or a bus. I love it.'

'Oh, I never thought about it like that,' she said with a shy smile.

'You'll have to try it someday.'

'Someday...'

'What was your life like in Germany, growing up?'

She explained her school life, her lack of friends – *they couldn't understand me* – her one friend Ilse who accepted her. When he asked about her family she hesitated and said, 'It was difficult. My father, Ulrich, suffers from his time during the war.' Then she changed the topic. Once, he tried to squeeze her hand. Her body stiffened and she pulled away. Pete and Daniel talked about their old life. Pete used to be a submarine technician. 'I left when I discovered I was claustrophobic.' Daniel talked about his life as a teacher. He omitted his time in Winburn and the cloud hanging over him. He switched topics. 'I heard there are a lot of American bases in West Germany.'

'We discussed it often at uni,' Renate said. 'They say they are there to stop the Russians. They have cruise missiles there. Lots of them.'

Pete slowed, pointing at an amusement park. 'It's called Dreamworld. Some rich idiot opened it last year. Sven Johansen gave a speech,' Pete told them.

'Who's he?' Renate said.

'Premier of Queensland. A real nut job. He's trying to get a law passed through parliament banning lesbians.'

*

Renate made tea while Daniel flicked through her collection of books. Pete inserted a Pink Floyd tape into her cassette player. *Wish You Were Here* echoed around the room. Heavy texts covered the coffee table: *The Gem Kingdom* by Peter Desauetels, *Systematic Census of Australian Plants* by F. Mueller, *The Moss Flora of Britain and Ireland* by A.J. Smith. Daniel yawned. A paperback was next to the double sofa. *Sun Signs* by Linda Goodman. 'Astrology?' Daniel said, holding up the book. 'What gives?'

'It has some alternative perspectives on personality that science can't explain,' Renate replied, holding the teapot in mid-air. 'Guess what sign I am.' She smirked. 'Do you know *61 Virginis* has an exoplanet?'

'Really? And it's probably a hundred light years away. As if that could influence anything.'

'Twenty-seven point nine, actually,' she replied.

'Wow! How do you remember all that?' Daniel put the book down and stared at her face. She replied with a piercing stare. 'I've been practising all my life.'

'Okay, Virgo? *Mercurial charm and wit*,' he recited. 'So, tell me about your family?'

'My grandparents were Jewish when they came to Germany. They must have decided it was wiser to convert – Lutheran. They disappeared during the war...' Renate trailed off. She paused to stare at the teapot. Her eyes glazed over.

'And your parents?'

'Mum's Catholic. Dad doesn't talk about religion.'

'Hey, my mum's Catholic too. My dad was Jewish.'

'What happened to him?' she asked.

'He... left us one day. We don't talk about it.' Daniel lowered his eyes.

'Well, I guess we both have secrets, don't we?'

She served tea and *Wibele* vanilla biscuits. Pete excused himself to go check on the bikes. When the door closed, Renate sat close and put her hand on his. Daniel didn't flinch.

'I'm glad you're here,' she said.

There was a loud knock at the door. Pete walked back in, followed by a woman with milk chocolate skin and blazing hazel eyes which darted from Daniel to Renate and back to Daniel. Renate introduced her. Simone scowled at Daniel, then Renate. Her face changed, a darker colour.

'How long are you staying?' she asked Daniel. He glanced at Renate. She looked at both. There was a long uncomfortable silence. Renate frowned and shook her head.

'It's time to leave for our new house, Daniel,' Pete said. 'Just over the river.'

They said their goodbyes. The door closed behind them. Inside the room, the temperature dropped and the boundary – the unspoken rules of friendship – shifted between her and Simone.

'You can't have men stay here, Renate. It's against the rules,' she said, hands on hips.

'Rules? They were only visiting.'

'Good,' she said and slammed the door behind her. Renate stared at the door, rose and for the second time tripped on the edge of the carpet, at the same time thinking about what Simone had said. *What 'rules' did Simone mean? She's not the kind of person to bring that up. Why now?*

22

The five-bedroom group house was an original Queenslander, perched on a rise opposite a park in Highgate Hill. Maggie and Sandy, both in their twenties, two campaigners managing the Friends of the Earth office, opened their house to the bike riders as they prepared for an anti-Commonwealth Games protest. They painted banners, wrote newsletters and coordinated with other protest groups, including the Black Protest Committee. Daniel's focus was across the river. If he stood on the roof, he could see across the water and watch the ferry cross from Dutton Park to the university pier. On a clear night, he could see the lights in Renate's dorm. As the discussions meandered around who was marching, not marching, who was willing to get arrested, Daniel excused himself. He picked up his torch and walked to his tent, one of three set up in the backyard. He opened his diary and wrote: *She's intriguing, can't wait for tomorrow. It's great to have an intelligent female to talk to. I hope Simone's not coming. What's her problem?*

*

The sunlight stabbed through the trees in King George Square and beat down on Daniel's face. He kept a low profile on the edge of the crowd, ignoring the shouting, the monotonous slogans. He handed out newsletters, eyes flicked between Bexley, two policemen and Renate, who shuffled on her crutches with a worried frown. He sneezed again. The smell of horse shit, diesel and paperbark blossoms itched up his nose. He wandered over to Bexley, working her magic.

'We, the people, have right of assembly,' she said and passed the police a newsletter.

'You troublemakers don't have permission to march,' the older cop said, staring at the newsletter thrust into his hands. Their rigid bodies relaxed a little and their faces softened the more she talked. He looked around for Renate. She sat on a bench next to a young man who was barefoot, in dirty blue jeans and a torn Rolling Stones T-shirt. Daniel stood behind the bench and coughed. Renate looked up and her lips parted into a wide smile.

'Nature provides the hypothesis,' the barefoot man said.

'No, it doesn't,' Renate said. 'Nature provides experimental data. Do you agree, Daniel?' Before Daniel could reply, the barefoot man said:

'Christopher Columbus believed the Earth was flat. *A priori,* he was wrong,' the man said, looking at the newsletter in his hand. He crumpled it and dropped it at Renate's feet.

'Let's get out of here. This place is chockers,' Daniel said.

'Chocolates? Do they sell them here?' Renate replied with a frown. Daniel smiled. 'Not chocolates, *chockers*. It's just a term for *very crowded*.'

'Oh. That's not in my phrase book.' She tapped her bag.

'Don't worry, you'll get it. Eventually. I'll teach you some. Let's go and find some place quieter.' He matched her slow hop as they shuffled away from the noise down Albert Street to a small park. They sat on a bench under a flame tree and sipped water from her flask. 'Have you ever wondered what would have happened if we hadn't found you? There was nobody else out walking that day except an old couple going in the opposite direction.'

'Oh, I'm sure Steve and Simon from the hostel would have come, eventually, if I didn't return.'

'You sure about that?'

'Can you be sure about anything, Daniel? Or was it just a simple twist of fate?'

Daniel chuckled. 'And what's up with Simone? She didn't seem too glad to see me last night.'

'Strange, she's not usually like that.'

'Maybe she fancies you,' he said with a straight face.

'What? Do you mean...' She turned and stared as her eyes widened. 'I hope not... I mean... I'm *not like that*. Not that there's anything wrong with that.'

'No, I didn't think you were. I'm glad.' He looked back down the street. Bexley and an Indigenous man walked towards them. He had a long beard and a black Akubra covered in badges. Bexley introduced him as one of the organisers of the Black Protest Committee.

'What happened to your leg, luv?' He nodded down at Renate's bandaged ankle.

'I fell at the base of Mt Warning.'

'You didn't try to climb, did you?' he asked as his eyes narrowed.

Renate nodded. 'Didn't get very far.'

'Shouldn't have tried. Sacred place that Wollumbin. We Bundjalung people call it the Cloud Catcher. Only certain men can go up there. Not many left now,' he said and looked into the distance. 'People die up there.'

'I wish I'd met you earlier,' Renate said. 'Could have been worse. These nice people brought me to safety.'

'You are a lucky girl,' he said as he raised his black hat. 'I've gotta go now.

I don't want to be arrested, like last year for backchatting a cop. They bash us in the holding cells. Anything goes in this police state. Remember, don't go lookin' too hard for what you want. It might be standing right in front of you.'

He farewelled them with a tip of his hat.

*

Thursday, April 15

Daniel caught a bus to Tweed Heads for his weekly bail report. He mulled over his life – as a volunteer at the FOE office with Maggie and Sandy, selling T-shirts and books; how long could he keep this charade up, keeping his secret from the others? And Renate...

What does she really think of me? There's something about her... What is it? His eyes closed and he drifted to sleep, then jolted awake and looked around, disorientated.

'You okay, dear?' an elderly lady asked, wearing a red scarf and brown stockings. Daniel blinked twice, clenched his fists again, nodded and resumed his stare out the window. Dreamworld rolled by in a make-believe haze. The bus stopped outside the Tweed Heads Bowling Club. The doors hissed open. He walked back one block to the police station, up the stairs, through the open glass swing doors and across the faded-blue carpet. The same bored police officers sat behind the long, black-topped front desk: the sergeant with a stomach spilling out over his belt and the young constable with a 70s moustache and sideburns. Daniel walked up to the desk.

'Can we help you?' the sergeant said, looking up.

'Remember me? Daniel Cohen, reporting in again.' The sergeant approached the desk and rustled under the counter, extracting a thick clipboard.

'Let me see. Cohen, you say. Mmm. *Carr, Cartwright, Clark. Cohen, D.*'

'That's me.' Daniel stared at the scar above his left eye. 'I bet that hurt.'

'Sorry?' He paused with a vacant stare. 'Sign here. Can I see some ID?'

Daniel slid his driver's licence across the bench top. The sergeant looked down, yawned, then up at Daniel's face and nodded. 'That's all. See you next week.'

He tossed over all options at the bus stop. *Go back to Sydney – to what? Become a carer to Mum, a recluse? No, that life's over. But what? Re-join the bike ride?* He was not ready to leave Brisbane just yet, not ready to leave Renate. As the bus sped through Surfers Paradise, he looked up past the driver and out the front window. A large, grey bird, a cuckoo-shrike perhaps, swooped and hit the windscreen. A red stain dribbled down the glass in wavy patterns. The driver cursed, pulled the bus over and stopped. Daniel decided. He'd tell Renate the whole story about why he'd join the bike ride, why he'd left teaching. When the moment was right.

23

Simone knocked on the door and checked her bright mauve top. It hung off one revealing shoulder. A double-headed axe earring dangled from her right ear. She planned to loosen up Renate with a cask of rosé. Renate cooked *Käsespätzle* – egg noodles with cheese in a frypan. As she served up, Simone wrapped her arm around her shoulder and squeezed. Her eyes closed and she puckered her lips as if to kiss her. Renate blinked and jerked back. 'What are you doing?'

'C'mon Renate. We're more than just friends. I know you like me. I need to know I can trust you with my feelings. I'm just making the first move. I can tell you're not straight.'

'No... I'm not like that. Yes, I'm straight as Einstein's daydream.' She grabbed Simone's arm.

'What? You're not sleeping with that bike rider, are you?' Simone pulled back and stared.

'Daniel? No!' She spurted, 'We are just friends.'

'So, you haven't noticed?' Her lips cracked open. 'The way he looks at you with those needy eyes, the way his body goes limp when he's near you. He's just another sexist white Aussie male out for a good time. Most of them are.'

She held both of Renate's arms and squeezed.

'No! You don't mean? Oh no...' Renate stood still, mouth open.

'He's in love with you, silly.'

'*Scheisse.*' Renate backed over to the sofa and slumped down.

'So, why not, you and me? No one needs to know. I think you're sexy.'

'I told you. I'm not like that. Please leave.'

Simone glared at Renate, stuffed her purse in her bag and banged the door closed. After she left, Renate sat bewildered for a long time. *It's not possible to be lovers and just friends,* she thought. *I've only known the guy for three weeks. How could I be so stupid? Why isn't there a formula for this situation, something that I can use?* She sighed. She liked being with him, she admitted, but romantically? *How can I deal with his feelings? What about my feelings?* And now Simone. *I wish she could just like me as a friend. Maybe I need to move out?*

*

By the end of April, the bulk of the bike riders wound their way up the map, through Miriam Vale, Gladstone, Rockhampton. Daniel stood next to the ute, jacked up on ramps at the FOE house. Vix, a young woman who had joined the bike ride in Brisbane, handed him a wrench, which he passed down to the outstretched hand of Pete. 'Shit! Bloody diffs gone. I think.'

'Can you fix it?' Daniel asked.

'He can fix anything.' Vix smiled. 'If he can get the part.'

Daniel invented reasons for staying. *I'm working on a newsletter; I'm waiting for a money transfer; I'm helping Renate settle in.* He suspected Renate did not possess a talent for intimacy. *Or was that her German nature?* When she touched his hand it came with a question, like a gesture to see if he was listening.

The next day, Sunday, he rode through Dutton Park to the wharf and caught the wooden ferry, the *Pamela-Sue* across to the uni jetty. He climbed the stairs and knocked on her door. When it opened, she stared at him, gave a formal nod, walked over to the window and stopped. After a few long seconds, she turned and faced him. Vertical lines ran down between her eyes, her eyebrows arched up.

'Do you think I'm gay?' she asked.

'You? No way! Why?'

'It's Simone. She fancies me.'

'Can't say I'm surprised. You are beautiful, you know that, yes?'

'Daniel. You know... You and me... We're just friends, right?'

The words hit him in the pit of his stomach. 'Yes, but...'

'My other problem is my professor. He's a weird one. I often get the feeling he's hiding something. Strange, huh? Do you think I'm being *paranoid*? That's the correct word, yes?'

'Yes, but no. I don't know if you are being paranoid, but we all have secrets, Renate. Even me.'

'But...you'd tell me, yes, if it was important? I need to know I can trust you.'

'You can trust me. And yes, I'll tell you. That's what friends do, right?' he said.

'And Simone? I think I'll need to move out of here soon. Can you help me find a new place?'

'Sure. It so happens that Pete, Theo and Vix are leaving to re-join the bike ride on Wednesday. I'll ask Sandy and Maggie if you can move in with us. If you don't mind. It's a small room.'

She nodded as if everything was settled between them.

*

On Tuesday before leaving, she slipped a card under Simone's doorway.

Thanks for the loan of your bike. Your friend always, Renate.

Pete and Vix carried her two boxes of kitchenware, Daniel heaved her box of books. From the back of the ute, Pete gave her a women's bike with a flat tyre as a going away present. She climbed in without looking back. Theo, Sandy and Maggie – from Friends of the Earth – welcomed Renate into the house. 'I've always wanted to learn German,' Maggie said. Her room at the end of the hall had a small desk, mattress on the floor and one cupboard. A bookcase of boards on bricks. For dinner, she cooked vegetarian lasagne and a wonderful German strudel in the old gas oven.

'If you're looking for something to do, Renate, you're welcome at the FOE office. We could use the extra help,' Maggie said.

'Sorry. I've got a paper to complete this week for uni.'

'Any time you can spare. Thursdays are quiet. Daniel disappears then. So, where do you go Daniel?' Maggie asked, nonchalant.

'Um, all kinds of places. I go sightseeing... Maybe catch a bus to the Gold Coast and walk around.'

'Sounds boring.'

Renate's eyes drilled through him. She saw his eyes slip sideways. Her chest tightened.

24

Most Mondays and Tuesdays, Daniel worked in the Friends of the Earth office downtown. On Thursdays, he caught the bus to Tweed Heads Police Station. In the house, when Renate was around, he tip-toed as if on eggshells. At night after dinner, he'd smile and listen outside Renate's room to Maggie's German lesson.

'*Ich gehe...* Itch ghee.'

'*Wir gehen...* weir ga hen.'

'*Sie gehen...* see ga hen.'

'And again, Maggie. '*They go*'. Watch the pronunciation.'

He smiled, not quite sure why he was smiling.

*

Renate spent most days in the library on her research proposal for Professor Beattie, clacking away on the borrowed IBM *Selectric* typewriter. She chose a new title: *The Chemical Basis for Morphogenesis in water-limited environments*. The focus now diverged from Alan Turing's mathematical model to the biological aspects. The only references she found were two articles – a little-known publication in the *Journal of Mathematical Biology* (1978), a paper written by Alan Turing in 1952 and a critique by the Royal Society. Turing was not a biologist or chemist. He was a mathematician. It intrigued her how he could have known so much about the chemical reactions inside cells and how they determined the shape of the cells and therefore, the structure of the animal. She read: '*...irregularities arise from the molecular nature of matter and stationary wave pattern...*' She skipped over a page of complicated math: '*...the diffusion of a morphogen from a cell to a neighbour may be treated as if the passage of a molecule from one cell to another were a monomolecular reaction...*' She turned to the conclusion: '*The mathematical model (as proposed by Turing) is a simplification and an idealisation and consequently a falsification...*' Renate considered this. *So, his mathematical model must not have taken into consideration the other biological interactions, like how proteins diffuse through cells and the actions of genes. That's where I'll start*!

She flicked a pen over and over in her fingers, her mind focused on other problems. Her visa was soon to expire in three months. She'd left Germany in a hurry and had not filled out the extra paperwork. Not sure how to tackle that problem, her mind switched to Daniel and her growing feelings for him. *That's another distraction I don't need right now.* More than once, after dinner when the house had bedded down for the night, she'd walked by Daniel's room and pressed her ear to the door, imagining what he was up to. *Should I knock?* She hesitated, seconds too long, before returning to her room. She didn't need another complication.

*

Thursday, May 13

Daniel caught the 9am bus to Tweed Heads and sat next to the window. Opposite, a young boy sat next to a harassed-looking woman. She reminded him of his mother, the resigned look, the way her body slumped, her pinched expression months after Ian left. The bus stopped. He walked to the police station, up the steps, across the well-worn blue carpet to the front desk and rang the bell. Sergeant Watson looked up, nodded and walked back to a man in a dark-blue suit and tie with a Smith and Wesson .38 revolver strapped under his jacket. He looked at the papers, then at Daniel, nodded and left the room. The sergeant strolled over to the desk and pushed the papers in Daniel's direction.

'Ah, Mr Cohen. Must be your lucky day.'

'Why? What have I missed?'

'According to these papers, you are free to go.'

'What?'

'Free. To go. Says here' – looking down at the papers – '*complainant not proceeding.*'

'In English, please?'

'Looks like the charges have been dropped. As I said, sign here and you get your passport back. You are free to go.'

Daniel walked down the steps in a dreamlike trance. He stopped to consider his options and headed north towards Coolangatta, unaware his fists were clenched, the implications pounding around his head. *Fuck, I knew it. Little bitch. All this for nothing. I hope she pays for what she's put me through.* Along the beach, sharp sand soon covered his footprints as a few surfers braved the brisk southerly. He collected shells, picked them up, turned them over and dropped most of them. The *conidae* – Cone Snail – shells intrigued him most, their regular patterns in shades of brown reminded him of Renate and her theory. *She's onto something there. The patterns are everywhere.* He shook his head thinking about her. She'd made it clear, friendship only.

*

Later that night, as they washed up, Daniel turned and said he was leaving on Sunday. Her body stiffened. She put the tea towel down and turned to face him. The corners of her mouth drew down. 'I want to re-join the bike ride. They're leaving Townsville next week to cross Australia. I want to see the desert, always have.'

'Yes, to follow your horizon, but, Daniel, I'll...miss you. I really like being with you,' she said as her eyes glazed.

'I'll miss you too. But I can't stay here much longer, it's too hard.' He took both of her hands in his. 'You understand, don't you?'

She nodded and rested her head on his shoulder. They stood there, side by side, as the clock struck ten. As they went to their separate rooms he said, 'Saturday, let's go for a bike ride, I want to show you something.' She nodded and he kissed her on the cheek.

*

They rode to the Botanical Gardens, tied their bikes together behind a bench and walked in silence between the massive figs. They talked in bursts, often finishing each other's sentences, followed by lengthy pauses. The tension between them was almost tangible, the air thick with emotion. Daniel knew she only wanted to be friends and he respected that. But he knew, deep down, that he needed more. He just didn't know how to say it. He stopped and took her hand and pointed at the strange umbrella-shaped tree.

'It's called a dragon tree. Do you know why?'

She shook her head.

'Because of its dark, red sap. See the resin?'

She nodded again. 'Do you believe in dragons, Daniel?' she asked, as she squinted at the tree.

'No. Humans are scary enough.' He laughed. 'I want you to know I like the way you always appear so calm, so in control.'

'We Germans have a saying: *In der Ruhe liegt die Kraft.* Strength results from calm.' She tilted her head and frowned. 'What do you want in life, Dan? I mean, it's great you are seeking out horizons, but I think you haven't a clue what you really want.' She stared at him and leaned closer.

'C'mon. You are describing 99% of the human race...'

'I don't think so. I know what I want. Do you?' she closed her fists and studied his face. Before he could answer, she burst out: 'And I have another problem. It's my visa. It expires in three months.'

'What are you going to do?' he said.

'I'm not sure. I can't afford to leave the country and come back.'

He paused for a long time, then said, 'I've got an idea, it's crazy but how about this. We'd better sit down.' She gave him a puzzled frown. 'Why don't we get married?'

'What? Are you serious?' She burst into laughter.

'Sure. It's easy. Then you'll be able to stay indefinitely, no problem.'

'What do we have to do, I mean, do we have to sleep together?'

Daniel paused. He studied her wrinkled nose searching for the right words. 'No, of course not, it's just paperwork. Don't look so worried. People do it all the time to stay in the country.'

He saw a sceptical look cross her face. 'Can I think about it?'

'Sure. But I'll need to know soon. No pressure, hey?'

In the end, the decision was easy. She clutched the stone between her breasts and decided. Next morning before breakfast, she knocked on his door, walked over to Daniel and looked into his eyes.

'Let's get married.'

*

Monday morning, they stood hand in hand before the clerk in the Registry Office. A sixty-something man with a red, bulbous nose stooped forward. He stared at the photo in Renate's passport, then at her face and repeated the process with Daniel. His body became rigid, eyes narrowed. Before he stamped their papers, he took a deep breath. A heavy sigh escaped his lips. 'The marriage you are about to enter should not be taken lightly. It is a legally binding union. If I were a minister, I'd tell you it is a spiritual bond, but I'll spare you. I'm sure you'll take it seriously, as I take my official role in presiding. See you in four weeks from today. Bring these forms back, filled out and signed, plus two witnesses.'

*

On a crisp, clear Tuesday in the middle of June, they stood before a different magistrate – Maggie stood with Renate and Sandy next to Daniel. When the magistrate said to Daniel, 'You may kiss the bride,' Daniel turned, not sure how she'd react. Renate stumbled forward, almost tripped on the hem of her dress. Her eyes dropped to his mouth and hers parted a little. She slid her arms around him and pulled him close. When she kissed him, his heart raced. He released his grip. *Maybe she's just putting on a good show for the magistrate.* When they separated, he saw her run her fingers through her hair.

'You okay?'

She nodded and blinked rapidly. 'Let's go home.'

Later, while they washed up, she leaned in closer, eyebrows drawn.

'I've been thinking...'

'Yes?'

'Just after we kissed, you pulled away quickly. Why?'

'It's just...I..' he shuffled his feet. 'I guess I felt relieved it was over and I didn't want to embarrass you in front of the magistrate, I guess.' He stuttered.

'No other reason?' Fine wrinkles formed on her brow.

'It's just...I was surprised, that's all. Like, I didn't know how it would feel... it felt good.' He jerked his head back and turned to watch her face. A slow smile spread across her lips. 'Did you know most birds mate for life – galahs, Glossy black cockatoos, parrots.'

'Are they monogamous?' Daniel leaned forward and tilted his head.

'More just socially monogamous. Many females sneak away from the nest at daybreak seeking out stronger males.' She spoke as if reading from a text.

'That's smart – the females want tougher genes. But what's this got to do with us? Are you suggesting there's a formula for remembering who they mate with? I mean, it would help to know, don't you think.'

'Yep and no. Instinct, especially survival instinct has no formula. At least not one I know of.'

'Does that describe me? I'm leaving soon and may not come back.'

'It's okay, Daniel. We are not planning on starting a family. And, you are not a bird.' She gave a chuckle. 'I'm glad it's all over, that ceremony, I mean. And I don't have to worry about my visa anymore.' She closed her eyes and exhaled deeply. 'I really appreciate you doing this for me, Dan. And our friendship.' She sighed, put her hand on his shoulder.

'Just one more thing I want to ask. About us dating other people. Just because we are *married*, are you okay if I see other women? I don't mean right now, but sometime in the future?' He looked at her and took her hand in his.

'Of course, Daniel. You are leaving. And, who knows who will come into our lives? I would like that arrangement also for me.'

They both nodded, he squeezed her hand and walked to his room.

*

She returned to her thesis, finally given the green light by Beattie. Daniel roamed around Brisbane, worked in the FOE office, pretended his life was heading in a predictable, if not delayed, direction.

Renate smiled every time she passed him in the house, not sure how convinced she was about the status of their relationship. She decided she'd keep her own name, even if the papers read Mrs Renate Cohen. *I'm not giving up my identity or my independence for any man.*

*

In the library, working on her research at the back desk, she looked up, startled, as if her father's presence was lurking beside her, just out of vision. She shook her head, stretched and returned to her work. Her research, a puzzle, an unfinished work of a genius left behind by Alan Turing from a time when it was dangerous, even deadly, to be different.

TWO

25

Most days on the road, Daniel measured time and when it was meal time by position of the sun and saltbush shadows. They stopped for lunch when the sun was overhead riding strung out along the blacktop like runners in a Boston marathon. He slept in sandy clearings or dry riverbeds under wanton starlight, howling dingoes and the *flap flap flap* of the ghost bats for company. He spent two film nights in Aboriginal communities with a bed sheet as a screen entertained by boisterous barefoot children racing around, parents hooting and booing when the WA police moved in on the Nookanbah traditional owners. Daniel emptied his mind as if he could leave it all behind – the silly girl, teaching, his mum, Sydney. Every time he thought of Renate, warmth spread through his body, almost like an open fire on an icy night. Always there. And the horizon? It loomed and beckoned. The word she'd said – *gesichtskreis* – it reminded him of her, what he'd left behind, where he was headed, on the bike, inexorably towards the horizon and Darwin.

*

A day after returning from Kakadu National Park, Daniel walked to the phone box and dialled the number he'd written yesterday in his journal. It was printed on the back of an attractive tour guide's polo in Kakadu, outside of Ubirr Art Site. It rang five times.

'Hello. NT Outback Tours. Alice speaking.'

'Um, hi. I'm Daniel. You were out at Kakadu yesterday.'

'Yes. Do you want to book a tour?'

'Well, not exactly. Your group walked by the Rainbow Serpent cave and didn't stop. Are all your tours like that?'

'Not usually. We were running late so I cut that part out. Daniel, is it? What do you want?'

'Look, Alice. Darwin's pretty boring. Not much to do, hey? Here's an idea. We could meet up and discuss, um, tours or crocodiles or...'

'You're asking me out, like, on a date?'

'Sort of. How about tonight? The Top End Bar?'

'Let me think. I'm leaving for the Kimberleys in two days' time, so yes, it will have to be tonight.'

'Sounds perfect. See you there at seven? Will you be in uniform?'

'Always. Part of the job.'

*

Before leaving the squat, Daniel slipped the wedding ring into his wallet. *I'm a free man tonight. I'm sure Renate would understand.* The bar was quiet on a Tuesday night, a few locals and truckies in their blue singlets and thongs hovered around the buffet. Pizza, lasagne and three Chinese dishes in stainless steel bowls. Daniel's eyes glued to the door. Alice arrived in uniform, looked around and caught Daniel's eye, smiled and walked over.

'You must be Daniel. Pleased to meet you.'

'Hi Alice. Same.'

She sat opposite, placed a sizable red handbag on the circular tabletop. He noticed her hands, soft and delicate. *No dirt under those fingernails.* She scanned the room as if expecting someone.

'What are you drinking?'

'Bacardi and Coke please.'

Daniel's stomach rumbled while he looped around the buffet and brought drinks back. He made small talk. 'Still hot in here? Where is everyone?' Alice sucked her Bacardi and Coke through a straw.

'Been up here long?' he asked.

'Just a week with this tour. Finished today, thank God.'

'Why so relieved?'

'Try entertaining thirty retirees for a week?'

Daniel chuckled. He relaxed as the first beer drained from the glass.

'And I'll be glad to leave that crappy motel room they put me up in.'

'So, do you always go on a date in uniform?' His eyes slipped to the undone top of her shirt. She pulled her shoulders back.

'Have to. It's written in the contract.'

'So, how do you like Kakadu?'

'I don't. It's hot, lots of dust and shitty motel rooms. And you? What are you doing up here?'

Daniel hesitated, not sure what to say. 'I'm on my way to Japan. With a group of bike riders.'

'Wow.' She seemed genuinely intrigued. 'Adventurous, hey?'

A man with five-day stubble, dirty blue shorts and tatty boots towered next to Alice. He swayed back and forth as if he was on the top deck on an ocean liner in a storm. Frothy beer spilled from a schooner onto the carpet. Daniel smelled something strong. The man leered at Alice's chest.

'Hey, sweetheart. You wanna join my mates over there? Looks like you're not having much fun here?'

'No thanks.'

'What was that?'

'I said, *no thanks*. And my face is up here.'

Bloodshot eyes locked onto Daniel, staring straight through him as if he wasn't there.

'Aw, come on, luv. We won't bite.'

Daniel threw caution to the wind. 'She said *no*. Do you have a problem with English?' The man's eyes narrowed, breath hissing like escaping steam. A hand, almost as big as Daniel's head, grabbed his shirt and lifted him off the chair. Time stopped for a few seconds. Alice snatched her bag, opened it and rammed it under his red face. His mouth opened at the same time he dropped Daniel. Turning, he hurried backwards like a spider escaping from a scorpion. Daniel tucked his shirt in, stared at Alice with his mouth open.

'Wha-what's in your bag?'

'Just Snappy. My pet snake. He's harmless. A diamond python, not that that idiot would know.'

'Great trick. Thanks.'

'Welcome to the land of rednecks and creeps,' she replied. 'So, why are you going to Japan? Adventure? You're not part of that protest group, are you?'

'Yeah, that's us. We rode up here from Sydney.'

'Hell, how long did that take?'

'Five months. Some by train. I was delayed a few weeks in Brisbane.'

'Nothing serious, I hope, hey?'

'Not really.' He thought. *Just getting married.* 'You're from Queensland, aren't you?'

'How can you tell?'

'You end everything with a question.'

'Oh, that. Yes. Brisbane. Originally from Sydney, Pymble. Do you know it?'

They bantered back and forth, discussing favourite books and world politics before wandering across to the buffet. Alice stood close enough for her hips to touch his. She ordered the lasagne, Daniel the Chinese. The conversation headed in a different direction.

'Have you seen that big, ugly hole in the ground back in Kakadu?' he said.

'No, why should I? Tourists don't want to see that. As you say, it's ugly.'

'More than ugly. It's dangerous.'

'Oh, come on, Daniel. So's crossing the road! It has government approval. That's fine by me.'

'We'll just have to agree to disagree on that issue.' Daniel smiled and held up his drink. She clinked hers in response. After two more drinks, she leaned closer, her index finger making circles on the outside of her glass, then across her red lips.

'I'm getting tired. I'm going back to my room. Wanna escort me home?'

Daniel's breathing shallowed. He studied her face and nodded. It was a ten-minute walk back to the motel. She grabbed his hand. They reached the motel, a pale-blue, two-story job, iron handrails on the top floor, bougainvilleas in large pots, five cars and three utes parked outside. They climbed the concrete steps to the second floor, room 15. She opened the door, flicked on a dull neon light and dropped her bag on the table.

'Shitty, huh?'

'Well, you're not raising six kids here.'

She moved closer, switched off the light and in two seconds her tongue was down his throat. He could smell her scent, slick and sexed up like Lolita oozing from her skin and exploding up his nose, an artillery barrage in a Somme battle. Daniel's body stiffened, then fired up as gravity dumped them onto the double bed. They didn't bother with any prelims. When she climbed on top, Daniel whispered, 'You speak three languages? Is one German?'

'Are you being kinky?'

'No. Say something to me in German.'

'Sure. *Ich bin heiss!* I'm hot.'

'Nice.' Daniel ran his finger across her breast and over her nipple, which vibrated like a battery-run toy. Over the top of her moans, Daniel heard a gentle knock at the door.

'Hell, who's that?' Daniel whispered.

'Enter. Come in!'

A young woman with short spiky hair, slipped inside and closed the door.

'It's a bit early for housekeeping isn't it?' he said, unsure whether to cover up or not. The ghost of a smile crossed her face as the woman ignored Daniel and sat on the spare bed, pulled a face and reached for a glass of water.

'Oh, Monique. This is Daniel. We've almost finished.'

'We have?'

'Don't worry, Daniel. Monique is my friend. Sometimes she stays here. She's gay and there's a spare bed.' Wiping the sweat from his face with the sheet, he wrapped it around his body. Monique dumped her bag on the spare bed, walked to the bathroom and turned on the shower. Daniel drifted off to sleep with the sound of water dripping from the shower and Alice's snores next to him.

At daybreak, Daniel collected his clothes, wallet and shoes, found an Outback Tours pad and wrote: *Thanks for everything. I had a good time. Maybe I'll write sometime. Hope your next tour is better. Yours, Daniel.*

26

Seat 31C, JAL DC10 on the way to Tokyo, Daniel was quietly exhilarated by the striking contrasts of a world not his own. Theo Papadakis, ex-communist party organiser and women's hairdresser, sat next to him. They'd met in Brisbane and become instant friends. Behind were dark-suited chain-smoking Japanese men drinking an unlimited supply of *Asahi Super Dry*. A lean Aussie in a loud shirt ranted about *babes* and *chicks with dicks* in Bangkok. A beautiful female stewardess with flawless skin and a harmonic name – Tomoko – kept staring at him, her left hand often covering her mouth as if she was whispering a secret. He struck up a conversation, she would not tell him her phone number *–company policy* – only where she lived – *Hiroshima*.

*

The rancid, waterlogged air of Singapore airport assaulted him with every step across the tarmac as he zigzagged around the glassy puddles. He sat inside the terminal next to a sarcastic uranium salesman from ERA, who Daniel might have run into in Darwin. Daniel spied a name in glossy gold letters on a black notebook cover – Matt Savage – a name he recognised from a warning letter the group received in Darwin he'd almost forgotten but couldn't. They were all just passengers on a rollercoaster ride smashing into each other and bouncing off like rubber bumpers. He dozed off. The image of the flawless face and harmonic name remained behind his eyes, just out of reach.

27

Daniel and Theo spent an hour re-assembling their bikes, which they had checked in as luggage, part of their twenty-kilo allowance. When he wheeled the bike down the ramp at the exit of Narita International Airport, pressure built in the pit of his stomach. No one spoke English, the signs were all in kanji, he felt like head lice in a pack of jet-black hair. Daniel checked his compass and tried to match the street signs with the figures on his map. Two security guards in white gloves and helmets made comments about *jitensha* this *jitensha* that, before they got bored and left.

They cycled west on Route 51 until dusk and found a guesthouse for four thousand yen. The bathed before dinner in a traditional outhouse bath heated by wood.

After dinner, Theo said: 'So I was wondering where you disappeared to that last night in Darwin?' he asked.

'I met a someone, we went back to her house. Simple.'

'And what about the German woman?'

'Renate? What about her?' Daniel raised his eyebrow.

'You're married aren't you? Don't you think that's important?'

'I guess, sure, it's just... I was just helping her with her visa.'

'Well, Daniel, I think you're full of shit, it's not like testing different tyres on your bike to see which one lasts the longest, hey?'

'Kinda weird metaphor, isn't it? I don't agree.'

'Like some are hard, some are flexible and some last for a long time.'

'And some just go flat.'

Theo pulled a condescending smile, 'Sometimes.'

*

They cycled west towards Chiba and turned north onto Highway 51 towards Tokyo, recognising the bay on their left, then past a sign that said: 'Future Site of Disneyland'. Martin and Dazza said they'd wait each day outside the GPO opposite the train station until 5 pm. At 3 pm they were inside the post office at the Poste Restante desk collecting their mail. Daniel had one letter.

Guten tag Daniel,

How are things in Japan? I've been hectic these last three months now that the wooboras have left. It's been nice sharing the house with Sandy after Maggie decided to join them in Darwin. Did you meet up with her there?

I can study here okay but find the library much better for writing. I'm struggling, for two reasons. Alan Turing's work goes cold in the 50s. Then the poor man committed suicide. Such a waste! My favourite quote of his is: 'We can only see a short distance ahead, but we can see plenty there that needs to be done.'

The other issue I have now is my supervisor, Professor Beattie. Bah! Can't say I like him much. The other two girls who have him call him 'Sneaky Beattie'. I got a letter the other day from Mama who told me Papa is sick. She did not elaborate, just said he is in and out of hospital. I will ring home soon. Anyway, that's about all my news, mein Schatz. Met any nice girls yet?

Daniel blushed.

Do keep sending me all those interesting letters (ha ha) and watch out for those beautiful Japanese girls. Make sure you tell them you're married!

Yours,
Renate
PS: Did you remember to wish me Happy Birthday on the 21st?

Daniel carefully folded the letter back into its envelope and slid it into his chest pocket, tapped it twice.

At 4 pm, Martin and Dazza appeared with big smiles and hugs.

'When did you guys get here?' Martin asked.

'Like, about an hour ago.'

'We got food. You hungry?'

'Sure.'

'So, where are we crashing tonight?' Daniel asked.

'We contacted some Buddhist monks. They said we can stay with them if we join their meditation. You get to beat drums.'

'And at what time would that be exactly?'

'Early.'

'What about Hiroshima? It's only three days until the conference.'

'No worries. The monks said we could go with them on their bus. Even take our bikes.'

*

They heard the rhythmic beat before they arrived, outside a set of grey wooden doors leading to a courtyard with a dwarf pine bonsai in a round stone garden. A woman in her thirties in blue slacks and white blouse helped them park the bikes, gave them a drum and pointed to the back of the temple.

'I'm Masako. I'll be your interpreter.'

They listened to the chant and tried to copy the drumbeat. When the chanting finished at 6 pm, Masako led them to a small room to meet Rev Ueda, the monk in charge. He was an imposing man with a tanned, shiny bald head like polished teak. He bowed. Dazza and Daniel did the same.

'Thank you, reverend, for your hospitality,' Martin said.

'*Dono kurai taizai shite imasu ka?*' he replied. *How long are you staying?*

'Just two days, then we are going to Hiroshima.'

They ate miso soup with tofu, rice with vegetables and white bread toast at a long table with four monks and a wizened one-armed nun in a purple jumper. Theo helped clean up. Upstairs, four futons laid side by side in a long room next to a table and two chairs under an open window. Daniel sat at the table and re-read Renate's letter. He stared out the open window, the city throbbed with the hum of traffic and the drip of air-conditioners. He closed his eyes. The building swayed, another tremor rose through the ground. He'd had his chautauqua moment back on the road in central Australia before the seamless, infinite horizon. One, maybe two more pieces of the puzzle remained before he was ready to return. Hiroshima first, then maybe Auschwitz.

Outside, a distant drum boomed. Deep inside the crust, tension ground two plates together, energy multiplied. Chunks of rock, large as countries, jostled for supremacy. The floor oscillated. The girders moaned. A flock of bulbuls screeched as they bolted to the sky. *How's all this chanting and drumming supposed to help? And Alice? What's so bad about sleeping with her?*

28

The atmosphere mutated the next day when Zoe and Cam arrived. They took every opportunity to include the oppression of women in discussions. Daniel left the room bored of the same endless arguments. The group fractured. Daniel wondered if he too had been swept up in an idea, a dream coated in futility. They sat at a long table in the dining room. Toast and miso soup in steaming bowls. After breakfast, Daniel sat with Theo, Cam and Dazza opposite Rev Ueda and Sister Tanaka, the nun with one arm – she wore a purple jumper and a maroon woollen cap. Cam, ever direct, fired off questions, while Daniel studied the reverend's face. He spoke with such measure and humility his words hung over them like a giant bell, waiting to be struck.

'I entered this sect in 1946. I had been in the air force, zero fighters, you know them?' They nodded. 'When the war ended, many of my friends were lost, wandering around half-starved and desperate. Many took their own lives. Some became yakuza, you know, gangsters. I decided I needed to atone. One day I heard a monk beating the drum outside, so I joined him. He led me here, to inner peace.'

'And why do you beat the drums?' Daniel asked.

'The drums represent the Buddha. Before, it was a call to war, a way to rouse the soldiers, to give them courage for the battles ahead. Now it reminds us of the impermanent nature of the world. We all need to atone for our past mistakes. Some more than others.'

'And you, Sister Tanaka? How did you lose your arm?' Dazza asked. The old nun shifted in her seat. Her bones creaked like rusty hinges. 'Sorry, my English not so good. After the bombs stopped, I wandered alone near Shibuya station. The bombs, fire, all of Tokyo, a giant fireball. My parents were dead, the house fell on me. Crushed my arm. It got infected so' – she made a slicing motion with her hand – 'they cut off. I was twelve.' Her voice faded into silence.

The nature of war, life and death hung over the table, an uncomfortable silence. Daniel helped Theo clear away the dishes. As Theo stacked them, an idea struck Daniel: *Why am I here? Is it just a morbid fascination? It must be more than that. I must take something special back. If it's only a memory of the place, a memory of the death and destruction, so be it.*

'You good to go tomorrow? We are going with the monks on their bus,' Theo said.

Daniel cleared his throat. 'No, I've booked the bullet train. I need some time to think. After Hiroshima I might head back home.'

'That's sudden, mate. Is there anything I can help you with?' Theo stuttered as if struggling to find the right words.

'Probably not. I'm not so sure about all this protesting anymore, I've gotta decide where I'm going next. I think I'm ready for a 'normal' job again, back home. And I'm missing the beaches and my family. Cam and Zoe annoy me with their own agenda. I can't fight too many causes at once, I'm not like that. Anyway, what are our chances of achieving anything substantial here? Like, do you really think we are going to stop nuclear weapons or nuclear power?' He took a step backwards and crossed his arms.

'I get what you're saying. But maybe it's all just one cause, just a little more complicated than we think.'

'Maybe you're right.' He shrugged. 'But I still don't know if it's what I want to do for the rest of my life.'

'Well, if you want to know, me either.'

*

Much later, as they slept, downstairs Rev Ueda called out *karuma* in his sleep. *Hontou ni omen nasai – I am truly sorry.*

29

Daniel emerged from the bowels of Hiroshima train station into polite, noisy, ordered chaos. The atmosphere was electric, as if a thousand lightning bolts converged over the city and rolled towards him like bowling balls. People swarmed everywhere, a momentary episode of confusion before order sent them to their destination. To the right, a group of Buddhist monks chanted and drummed as if on continuous playback. To the left, three women sat in front of a larger group in tunics and headbands bearing slogans with lots of exclamation marks: *Stop Nuclear War!!*

Daniel wheeled his bike over. 'Hi. I'm Daniel Cohen from Australia. Are you with a group?'

A woman in her 30s in a neat blue dress stepped forward and bowed. A paper crane was pinned to her lapel.

'We are families of the *Hibakusha*. A-Bomb victims. This is my mother.'

Daniel bowed slightly as a woman looked up with a kind, disfigured face. 'Are you going to the ceremony at the Peace Park?' the woman asked.

'Yes, could we talk there later?' Daniel asked.

The woman nodded. Daniel pushed his bike out and crossed the road. He rode over the Enko river, shadowing a throng of humanity converging in one direction. He passed the reconstructed Hiroshima Castle and turned left on Aioi-dori Avenue. In the distance, the crowd telescoped on one spot, a place once illuminated by the light of billions of angry uranium atoms. He stopped opposite a grey forsaken building, the old Prefectural Industrial Promotional Hall. In a high-rise across the street, faces were outlined in double-glazed windows. Across the street in an office block, he saw two men in dark suits jerked sideways in a lift, they then resumed their ascent as if it was nothing out of the ordinary. *Shit, this is it. This is the place under the blast.* Across the Aioi bridge, he marvelled at how they'd look from a B-29's bombsight at 30,000 feet, just specks, no different from ants. His life flashed before him in an instant, everything from school years to family, lovers to work seemed insignificant here, apart from the crowd – no sense of urgency or passion to do something, only one thought *what am I doing here?* Doing something this insignificant, *how can it help?* He walked past the tolling bell as if it was an alive thing with a beating heart, the bell's echo held him rapt and strolled down to the arch that framed the Memorial Museum across a small lake. Everything – the physical, temporal, metaphorical – became soaked in a cacophony of jangles, chants and the sound of distant horns. In the middle distance, rows of monks sat cross-legged with heads so shiny they were like marbles in a sea of polished mirrors. Groups of school children in glossy, black shoes and perfect white socks walked in ordered rows. Seated businessmen ate their lunch as if it was just another day.

He parked his bicycle and walked over a bridge edged with rows of maples, cherry trees and azaleas so perfectly positioned as if placed there by the hand of God. Daniel's doubts vanished about why he was here. If anything, he was just *bearing witness,* a concept he'd never understood. Until now. These people were all doing the same. Like the crowd at Woodstock, only this crowd was bearing witness to a much more significant event. *If metaphors are one way of knowing, are memories a way of feeling?* The song lines triggered a memory of a feeling buried in his subconscious. *Song lines? Where have I come across that term before? Renate, under the dragon tree? In Kakadu. Across the desert.* He shook his head and looked up. Theo, Cam and

Zoe were chanting and drumming with monks in front of the monument. When he picked up a drum and sat down, the rhythm came more as an intuitive understanding of the sound, something primitive like the pulse of blood through his arteries.

A flock of black-tailed gulls flew over the Atom Bomb Dome. He looked sideways at a woman in her twenties in a white T and a green scarf. She was watching him. She looked familiar. When she smiled, he remembered.

Tomoko. 'Well, hi, I remember you from the plane. Tomoko, yes?'

'*Ohayo,*' – she bowed and smiled – 'you remembered?'

'Of course. How could I forget? You don't have to be so formal with me.'

'No? I'm just being polite.'

'Just like on the plane?'

'It's the training. So hard.' She flustered and her cheeks turned pink.

'Hey, so, what are you doing here?'

'Remember? I live in Hiroshima. It's my days off. And you?'

'I wanted to see this place. Peace, no nukes? You understand?'

'Of course. I am Japanese,' she said. 'I didn't know you were Buddhist?'

'I'm not.' He couldn't stop staring at her flawless face. His breath was so faint it was like he wasn't breathing at all. 'Wanna go for a walk? I'd like to see inside the museum.'

They wandered inside a vast cavern with photos, displays and statements of survivors. The group of *Hibakusha* he met at the train station were seated, resting. He touched Tomoko's hand. She didn't pull away.

'I'm going over to talk with them. Can you come in case I need a translator?'

'Of course.'

He walked up to the woman with the disfigured face, bowed and mumbled the words '*Ohayo goziamus.* I met you outside the train station. Can we talk now about what happened after the bombing?'

The woman in the blue dress whispered in Japanese to her mother, who nodded.

'This is Tomoko. She works at Japan Airlines.'

Tomoko bowed twice. The old lady spoke. Her pitch and tone were like a recording that never changed, as if she had done this before. Tomoko translated.

'There was a blinding light, then a roar like the sound of wind from Hell. Then the building collapsed. I tasted dust and something metallic. I crawled out from under the wall through a hole and stood up. I was nearly three kilometres from the hypocentre.' She took a moment to catch her breath, choking back tears. 'What I saw was like a horror movie in slow motion. People were walking step by step like they were hypnotised, some with their arms out in front, skin in strips, dangling down. One child held her eyeball. Many were crying *mizu, mizu, kudasai* – water, water please. There was no water. Everywhere there were cries, children trying to wake their dead mothers... And dust, dust everywhere and the sound of crashing buildings and the roaring of flames...'

Everything around him vanished, all that was left – this woman, tears running down her disfigured cheek. He bowed twice and felt Tomoko's hand squeeze his.

'Thank you very much for your story.' Daniel bowed again.

Tomoko translated and the woman nodded. There was nothing else to say. He smiled and thanked her again. Outside, Daniel and Tomoko walked back to the Aioi bridge and bought ramen noodles on Aioi-dori Avenue. She squeezed his hand.

'Let's walk to Central Park. There's something there I'd like to show you.'

He remembered Ruby, how she'd wanted to show him something, too. They walked side by side through the gardens as if Hiroshima was a backdrop to a stage play and he was watching from the audience. At the park, Tomoko walked up to a twisted eucalypt. Daniel stopped and stared at a metal sign. 'What does it say?'

'*This eucalypt tree from Australia was planted in 1921. It survived the atom bomb blast.* Trees have magical powers, Daniel.' She looked at him, searched his eyes. 'Do you believe that Daniel?'

'I guess it's the perfect survivor story.'

Tomoko's eyebrows squished together. Daniel's heart skipped a beat.

'I must go back home and get changed. I start work in Osaka on Monday.'

'Can I walk you home?'

'Just to the bus stop, it's not far.'

'Can I see you tomorrow? Maybe you can show me another place like this?'

Tomoko hesitated for an instant before shaking her head. 'Not possible. I have a boyfriend. He would... not be happy.' She frowned.

'That's a shame...I'd like to get to know you better. I'm thinking about returning home soon. I was hoping you'd help me change my decision.' He paused to study her reaction. 'How can I convince you to change your mind?' Daniel stared at her for just a glimmer of hope.

'Again, not possible. Sorry. My boyfriend wants to marry me. I don't think this is a good idea, being here with you.' She looked up at him.

'Do you love him?' Daniel's body stiffened, hands trembling.

'I honour him. Respect him.'

'Is that enough? Love, takes time to grow.' Daniel looked into her eyes. They were unreadable. The bus approached, time stretched, then snapped back. The western sky turned an alluring nirvana. She looked up and squeezed his hands. 'Goodbye Daniel. I hope you find what you're looking for.'

He watched, fixed to the spot, as the rear of the bus merged into traffic on Jonan dori Avenue. *Why am I drawn to the exotic?* He thought. *Is it because it is unreachable? Renate, Tomoko, what is it about them? Renate, could I love her? I respect her, love being with her. Love? Maybe I need to go home and find out.* He stared at the twisted eucalypt. *A survivor.* For the first time that day, a smile creased his lips.

30

Two months passed. Daniel cycled with the group to Nagasaki, sat in the Peace Park and beat drums under the atom bomb memorial statue, staying with monks who shared unlimited hospitality. They rode across Kyushu, past active volcanoes, slept in quiet gardens or accommodated by supporters. They caught a ferry across to Shikoku Island and cycled to Fukuoka's Farm from *the One Straw Revolution*. Daniel knew his time with the group was over. He spent most of the time trying to forget Tomoko. Some people occupy your memory like permanent residents. Some are ephemeral. Tomoko was such a person.

As winter approached, the arguments increased, the group split into two camps – men versus women. The extreme and inflexible views of Zoe and Cam corroded Daniel's resolve. By the first week of December, he'd decided to return to Australia. It was an emotional time, he'd miss Theo, Martin and Dazza. They had bonded as brothers on Fukuoka's citrus farm with its simple way of life and their intense philosophical discussions. Each morning, he waited for the sound of the mailman's toot. Two days before he caught the ferry from Matsuyama to Hiroshima, a letter from Alice arrived. She was moving to Blackheath in the Blue Mountains, west of Sydney.

Hey you!

What a surprise to get your letter! Next week I'm moving. My dad's opened another branch in the Blue Mountains. I'll be the office manager. Cool, hey?

How's your little bike ride going? Broken any girl's hearts yet? I don't want to know.

She rambled about her life, how she hated her old job, how much she was looking forward to living in the mountains.

So, if you are ever in Katoomba, look me up. Here's the office address.

He folded the letter and put it inside his passport, just in case. *What might I find in the Blue Mountains? Another Tomoko?*

31

Next day, he caught the Shinkansen train to Tokyo, booked a flight to Sydney and phoned the temple from the station. In four days he'd leave, clueless as to what it all had meant, like waking from a vivid dream. He'd seen Hiroshima, witnessed suffering up close and fallen for a woman he could never have.

After prayers and supper, he told his story to Rev Ueda. 'So, that's why I've decided to leave the group and return to Australia.'

'Everyone must decide how they will live their life. I am just a simple monk, now at peace with my life.' He let out a long sigh.

'Do you have any advice you can share before I leave?' Daniel inched forward in his chair.

'I can only tell you what I think. Only through love will you find acceptance of yourself.' He gazed across at Daniel. The discussion was over.

He passed the days strolling the extensive gardens of Tokyo lost in thought about his plans, what he'd do when he returned. His visa and passport were in order, so he packed and re-packed his backpack multiple times. Once, Alice's letter fell out and he scoffed over her line – *Broken any girl's hearts yet*?

Four days later, he gazed out the window at the distant snow-capped Mt Fuji, on the airport train for the last time. Outside the speeding window, the beige stubble of rice stalks poked clumps of dirty ice through the thin dusting of snow.

The plane climbed through cloud to 30,000 feet and levelled off. Daniel strained to see out the window for one last view of the twisted coastline and the curve of Osaka Bay. In his pocket was the gold wedding ring, a token of the past. He fished it out, the warm metal itchy in his palm, rolling it between his fingers. Outside, plane wings hissed through the thin air. *Are memories just memories or are they more like a formula, imprinted on your brain, or just random visions from your subconscious? And azurite? It's just the sea, distilled into stone.* That blue-green stone she had worn reminded him of what he'd left behind. The more important question was not could he find her again but what would she be like, when he found her?

THREE

32

Renate
Brisbane,
September, 1982

In the mid-semester break, Renate approached David Barillaro, the manager of the student union bar, for a job. A thick-set man with long, black sideburns in a light-blue sweat-stained shirt. Clutching her resumé, she stood in the doorway of the drab office with its grey-stained carpet under a fluorescent bulb. Boxes of cups, plates and beer coasters covered the floor. Sarah Johnston, a student in the Masters by Coursework with Prof Beattie, had said to ask for David. 'He's the President of the Student Council. I know him, he'll help.' He flicked through her resumé and gave her a trial – one week, two shifts, no pay, lunch and drinks provided. On her final shift, he said, 'So, Renate. Max told me you're a hard worker if a little on the *intense* side. *She doesn't joke around much.* You're German, yes?' he asked, inching closer.

'Yes, I am.'

'Figures.'

'But he said I was a good worker, so,' she said, as she tilted her head, 'have I got the job?'

'Depends if you'll have a drink with me.'

'Are you asking me on a date?'

'Sort of. How about in ten minutes, when your shift ends?'

'Okay.' Renate's eyes narrowed and her skin flushed. 'Where would you like to go?'

He nodded slightly. 'See that table over by the window? Nice and quiet. In ten minutes, okay?'

She turned, nodded, knocked her knee on the table leg and cursed.

*

They sat at a table near the vast curve of glass and looked out on the concrete forecourt. Thursday afternoon, they had the place to themselves. Renate removed her apron, still crisp and spotless, brushed her long dark hair behind her ear and squinted over at David. He'd changed into a blue polo, a mismatched tweed coat and tapped a cheap Bic pen on the table. His head pivoted as if waiting to see someone. Manly funk inched up her twitching nose.

'So, Max told me he gave you three shifts next week. That's good, yes?'

Renate nodded her head.

'Are you always this quiet on a first date?'

'This is not a date. I take a bit longer to trust new people. Sorry, it's just me.'

'Are you always this blunt?' He stared at her waiting for an answer. She didn't respond, just stared at his sideburns. 'So, what part of Germany do you come from?'

'Kassel, it's in Hessen.'

'You with Prof Green in Bio?'

'Actually, he passed me on to Prof Beattie.'

'Oh. Watch that one.'

'How do you mean?' Renate arched her eyebrows.

'Just some rumours at this stage. Overheard some girls talking last week. I'll have to investigate if I hear more, part of my role as the President of the

Student Council, you understand?'

'Okay. I'll, um,' – Renate cupped her hand under her chin – 'what's the expression in English?'

'*Keep your eyes wide open.*' David smiled. 'So, what do your parents do in Kassel?'

'Mum volunteers at the kindergarten and Dad works at the Henschel factory.'

'Henschel?' His voiced raised and his eyes narrowed. 'They made fighters and bombers during the last war, didn't they?'

'Most factories were made to produce weapons. But that has nothing to do with me. That was before I was born.' She returned his piercing glare.

'Fair comment.'

Renate squirmed in her seat as if it was on fire and changed the topic. 'So, David. What are you studying?'

'Law. I'm in my final year. Hope to move into international law next year.'

'Any particular field you want to work in?'

'Trials of the Nazi War Criminals. Do you know they are still tracking them down?'

'We don't talk about it much back home.' Renate stared at his piercing eyes and fidgeted with her purse zipper.

'Well, seeing your Saturday shift ends at three, how about coming to a party for the new union committee?' He twirled the pen between two fingers. 'Sounds like fun?'

'Maybe. Let me think about it?'

'No problem. It's here in the back room. 6 pm. Okay?'

*

The next day, she sat in the front row of a pale green seminar room with Sarah Johnston and Aimee Murphy. Professor Alan Beattie, sweating in a white shirt with a pink bowtie, swiped the whiteboard with a rag, complaining about *lack of consideration* by other lecturers. He turned to the lectern and fumbled with a folder. A glossy magazine flopped to the floor. A near-naked *Penthouse* pet on the cover. Beattie looked down, face flushed and scooped it up. Aimee nudged Sarah who nudged Renate. 'Told you so.' She whispered.

'Yes, um, where was I?' he said, fumbling with his notes, 'and I do wish those noisy protests would stop. Never worked a day between them, I suspect, complaining about how we treat the Aborigines and those slogans they chant. *Queenslanders racist*? How preposterous! So, todays topic...'

After the lecture on the genetic foundations of evolutionary patterns, Beattie called her over. Aimee and Sarah had left, it was just the two of them. Alone. She pushed aside David's warning.

'Miss Mayer. I've talked with a colleague in evolution and genetics, Professor Dalton. He would like to discuss your thesis with you. He has some ideas he wishes to share. Are you free tomorrow at ten?'

'Yes, thank you, Professor.' She froze as he touched her arm just a second too long, stepped back, turned and left.

Later, in the union café, Renate, Sarah and Aimee discussed over coffee how Beattie gave them the creeps, the way he stood too close, the magazine. 'He even put his arm around Sarah's waist last week.' Sarah said.

Aimee gasped, her nose wrinkled.

'He's a perv, you know. Watch him if you're alone,' Aimee said.

*

The next morning, Renate sat in Beattie's office opposite Professor Dalton, a balding man in his mid-fifties in brown corduroy pants and a polka-dot bowtie. He sucked a brown pipe with a curved, black mouthpiece. 'Um... Miss Mayer.'

'Please, call me Renate.'

She sat, transfixed by the pipe, expecting a mouse or a small puff of smoke might pop out.

'Well then, Renate, Alan has given me a synopsis of your thesis.' He shuffled a pile of papers and looked down: *An alternative perspective on Phyllotaxis – Post-Turing theory of Linear Pattern Formation.* I must say, I'm intrigued,' he said, wrinkles appearing horizontal on his forehead. 'However, it sounds terribly dry to me, don't you think?'

'I don't think so, Professor. In this country there is no other current or published research on this important topic. That's why I chose it.'

'Important? How so, Miss, er, Renate. Do elaborate.' He struck a match and puffed three times on his pipe.

'I'm looking at how patterns in nature are defined by their degree of randomness.'

'You mean '*randomness*' as in entropy? Would you also agree that randomness is the same as disorder?'

'No, Professor. The two concepts are related but not synonymous. *Randomness* can exist within a system that is otherwise orderly, while *disorderliness* implies a lack of both randomness and order. '*Disorder*' is only a metaphor for entropy.'

'Something you Germans know a lot about, eh?' he said, puffing hard.

Renate took a deep breath. Her eyes narrowed. 'What do you mean, Professor?'

'The Third Reich. Order, loyalty, obedience. You could even hypothesise that entropy was the reason the Third Reich was defeated?' He puffed vigorously and stared at her. Renate inhaled, when she opened her mouth to respond, he pressed on. 'And how does *randomness* express itself in nature?'

Her breathing slowed, she tried to stay focused. 'Random arrangement of genes on chromosomes, the random decay of radioisotopes, do you mean?'

'That's part of it, Miss Mayer. Are you familiar with the second law of thermodynamics?'

'Yes, it defines entropy, am I correct?'

'Yes, but only in closed systems. Steam engines being a prime example,' he said, wrinkling his nose, 'and gas chambers, they were sealed tight, yes?' He tapped the side of his pipe. 'Did they follow this law Miss Mayer, or is it Mrs Cohen?'

Renate gasped, her body tensed. She gazed down her nose at the bald spot on his head. *They know.*

'But what has this got to do with my research, Professor?' Renate frowned, puzzled by his tone.

'Oh, just a little analogy, just came to my mind as we were speaking,' he said with a smug look. Renate stared. She realised in this small office her work and research could be crushed as one might crush an insect. She changed tact. 'Well, thank you for the interesting analogy, Professor, but I think you are wasting your time giving me, a German, a history lesson. I think I'll just focus on the science behind my thesis,' she said through her clenched jaw.

'Jolly well said. I'm always looking for talented PhD students and I think you have the qualities to exceed.'

She nodded and left the room. A smell, like burning plastic followed her out the door. A knot of anxiety, like rubber bands, coiled and twisted around her chest as the memories of the past bubbled up. *Why do they keep bringing up the past? They are not history professors.* The memories flooded back – When Ulrich locked her door, Heinz's threats. She needed a drink. *Why?*

With a bottle of Southern Comfort in her bag, she detoured via Tower J and climbed the stairs to Simone's room. *How long has it been? Almost three months.* She knocked twice and heard soft footsteps on the carpet. When the door opened, Simone stared hard at the bottle, then at Renate's face and a wry smile edged across her face.

'So, the mystery girl returns. Need a drink, huh?'

'And some company.'

33

'So...what have you been up to all this time?' Simone said from the kitchen. She shuffled bowls of snacks, chips, dips onto a tray and clutched a steel ladle, waving it around like a conductor's baton. She bantered in a non-stop monologue while arranging gnocci fritto, cute-looking panzerotti, cheddar cubes, taralli biscuits, like mini donuts on an entrée – *her painting, her hair, how hard it is to meet girls like her.* The words washed over Renate like a waterfall. She checked over Simone's book collection jumbled on the floor. All female authors: *Desperate Characters* by Paula Fox was on the top of the pile. Looking for clues, anything to explain the inside workings of her friend, her motives, what made her gay. *Was it genes? Something drastic in the past? Or did she just like the smell of other women? Probably a mixture of all but it would be a hard experiment to control, impossible?* She shook her head, unaware she'd been mumbling.

'What?' Simone gave a startled look.

'Oh...nothing. I was just thinking of an impossible experiment.' Renate stared at the plate and picked a cheese cube and two biscuits.

'That's what I like about you René, you're not afraid to try the impossible.'

Renate thought about what Dalton had said, *Miss Mayer or is it Mrs Cohen? How is it any of his business?* Cohen, Mayer and Rosenberg – all Jewish. *Why didn't Mum or Dad ever talk about it?*

'It's been three months, you realise?' Simone said, tapping her right foot.

'Where have you been?'

'Oh, you know, busy with my course and adjusting to my new supervisor, Professor Beattie.'

'Have you heard from that bike rider, what's his name?' she said, tilting her head.

'Daniel. He's written two letters, one from Darwin and the other from Japan.'

'Sounds adventurous. Do you miss him?'

Renate considered the question a second too long. 'You know we got married? Had to, my visa was almost up.'

'What? Oh, you devil!' She grabbed Renate's arm.

'No, nothing like that, he helped me out so I can stay for good.'

'Sounds like a nice guy. So, what should I call you now? Mrs...'

'Just Renate. I'm not changing my name,' she said as she stared at Simone's face.

'Good for you, girl.'

They laughed at the same time and something indiscernible passed between them.

'He doesn't identify as Jewish, neither do I, if you were wondering.'

'Still, you can't ignore your roots, *amore mio*. Without roots, you are nothing.' Simone moved from the kitchen and sat on the couch. Renate smelled musk and lavender, gazed at the sheen of her dark hair, her bronze skin reflecting in the kitchen light. She blinked and drained the first glass.

'So, how about you, Simone, what's happening in your life? Before you answer, can I ask you a question?'

'Sure.'

'Why do you wear that earring on your right ear?'

'Because... I thought you'd know? It's a symbol of who I am. And so I can identify other women like me quickly. Without speaking.'

'When did you realise you were gay?'

Simone inhaled deeply and stared at something past Renate. Her body sagged. 'Growing up, I always felt attracted to girls, never boys. I felt uncomfortable being alone with a boy. Dad had left by then, so there was just Mum, my sister Cara and brother Marco. When I was sixteen, I went to a party with a straight girlfriend and as soon as we got there, she disappeared with a boy and left me alone.' Her nostrils flared and vertical wrinkles creased her brow. 'So, I went exploring the big house. Upstairs, I walked into a bedroom and my friend was lying on her back, pants around her ankles. A white bum on top was going up and down.'

Simone paused, lifted her glass and downed two gulps.

'So, I went to the next door and put my ear up close and heard voices and someone sobbing, like a distressed child. I opened the door and stood half inside. Four older guys stood over a girl about my age. Her mascara had run down her face and there was blood on her legs. The boys looked at me for a second and one said, '*Get her*'. Then someone grabbed me.' She trailed off. Simone's face clouded over, eyes clenched tight. She reached for a tissue and dabbed the wet corners of her eyes. 'Two guys held me down while another raped me. All I remember is the smell, beer and vomit mixed with tobacco. I'll spare you the rest of the details. That was five years ago. No man has touched me since.'

'Why didn't you report it to the police?'

'I was scared. I didn't think they'd believe me. Men, they're all bastards.'

Renate put her arm around Simone, drew her close and squeezed her hand. Simone kissed her on the neck and let out a long sigh. 'Maybe some are not bastards.' Renate said and looked into her eyes.

'You're the only one I've told.' Simone said. She wiped a tear away and smiled, her body was still tense. She took a deep breath and turned to Renate. 'Now it's your turn. Can you tell me a story from Germany?'

Renate paused, closing her eyes. She told her about her day in the museum and when she found her grandmother's trophy, her first day at school. When she finished one story Simone asked for another, then another, as if trying to stack them like Lego bricks and build walls of intimacy around them, seal them up together.

'Please...stay with me tonight... I-I...don't want to be...alone,' she stuttered. 'I need some company, that's all.'

*

Renate woke on the couch with the memory of Simone's story scrolling in her head. She remembered the emotion – shocked by Simone's story, it had shackled them together. Renate came up short, she wasn't ready, just yet, to reveal all her secrets. In her confusion and indecision, she knew they were now bound, as only suffering can bind two people.

Is this what love is like, she pondered, *a wound opening and closing and staying open, defying any attempt to heal? And Daniel? Was he just a traveller, helping me out, passing through to somewhere else, maybe nothing more?* Something else bothered her as she dressed and wrote a letter to Simone.

Thank you for a wonderful night and sharing your story. I will make time in my schedule to see you more frequently.

Your good friend,
Renate

An old memory was on her mind as she cycled back to her house. The story of her grandparents and how they vanished one cold day in 1938. If there was an answer, it was back in Germany, a place she thought she had left forever.

34

Friday, September 24

Renate sat with Aimee and Sarah in the union café, intrigued over the latest news. They'd just learned from the dean that Professor Beattie was no longer their supervisor. A temporary replacement was being organised. No explanation was given.

On the six o'clock news, she saw a chubby, sweaty, hand-cuffed man in a white, torn shirt, man-handled into the back of a police wagon. The news reporter announced, '*The man was seen lurking around the girl's toilets in a city park the day before and two girls had declared he'd exposed himself to them. The man, a local university professor, was reported to police by two teenage girls...*' the news reporter said with a straight face.

'Told you he was a perv.' Sarah gasped, narrowing her eyes. 'What about us? Have you met the new guy yet?'

'Not yet, but the dean said it was only temporary,' Renate said.

'So, we just plough on. We can work together, help each other out. Where are you up to, Renate?'

'I've just started outlining my thesis up to the methodology.'

'I'm almost finished my last core subject, Statistical Methods in Biological Research. God, it's boring,' Aimee said and lightly touched Renate's arm.

'Amen to that,' Sarah said, closing her folder. 'So, Aimee, tell us what happened after the party?'

'Oh, you know... I was pretty wasted, met a guy who didn't have zits or hair on the back of his hands, so we went back to my place.'

'And?' they both said together.

'I let him think he could do it – he almost begged for it – some guys, you know, are hopeless. They're pathetic, really.'

'And? Did you?'

'Hell no, I was smashed, not stupid. He just came on my tits then cried when I told him to leave,' she said with a wrinkled nose.

Renate stared at Sarah's face, eyes wide, mouth fixed.

'So, Renate. You seeing anybody?' Sarah tilted her head.

She shook her head and blinked. 'No. Not exactly. You know I'm married, don't you?'

Aimee laughed that helium laugh of hers and said, 'Yeah. But he's not here anymore. I know a cute guy, want me to hook you up with a date?'

'I'll think about it.' Renate nodded, just to be polite. She didn't need any more complication in her life. Everything was on track to finish her master's by the middle of next year. Then apply for a PhD. In her world, she was single-minded about her study.

'So, Sarah, you going to the rally on Sunday?' Renate asked.

'No, not my thing. It's those Aboriginals again, trying to stir up trouble, always complaining about something. Most of them are on welfare, *pffft*,' she said with her head tilted back.

'How, exactly, do you know that?' Renate asked.

'It's common knowledge, my parents say.'

Renate turned to Aimee. 'And you? Are you going?'

'Nah. I'll probably be loaded after the party on Saturday night. You coming Renate, should be fun?'

Renate shook her head. She remembered she'd promised to help Maggie and Sandy paint banners for the rally.

By 9 pm, she was sitting on the lounge room floor, next to a three-metre strip of white calico, paintbrush poised above a can of black paint. *What had Sarah said about the Aboriginals? Always complaining about something.* The conversation with Daniel and the others before they left Brisbane, about the massacres and genocide in the nineteenth century and the Stolen Generation. *Was it really genocide? I might investigate further.* She didn't fancy being trapped in a noisy crowd. Her role was supporting Sandy, so she sat on the floor and painted. Painted the last 'e' on the banner in black paint – *No Games in a Racist State.* Only five days to go before the opening ceremony of the Commonwealth Games. Tomorrow, at the rally, she'd stand away from the crowd and observe.

*

Sunday, 10 am

Renate stood on the corner of Anne and Albert streets, opposite King George Square. Sandy moved over to the crowd and clutched the banner. An anxious tingle crept up her spine, her heart thumped, her palms sweated. It was riotous, chaotic, overwhelming. About 2000 people in all colours jostled amidst a sea of signs: *'Feminists for Peace', 'Communist Party of Australia', 'People for Nuclear Disarmament', 'Land Rights Now'.* One guy, dressed as the grim reaper, stood on top of black-painted drums. A large, noisy group of Indigenous Australians were out in front. Two men stood next to her talking about the Games' opening ceremony's dance performance. She overheard, 'Just a hand-picked group of painted actors in red lap-laps blowing didgeridoos.' She didn't know what they meant. Opposite them, lines of police wielded shields and batons. Her breathing shallowed, her chest tightened, she turned right and walked down Anne Street to George Street to the East Wind Bookshop, took a deep breath and opened the door. A small, brass bell tinkled twice through the musty ink smell mixed with coffee and tobacco. A man in his fifties dressed in a cream cashmere cardigan and navy-blue bowtie stood behind a cluttered table and an antique cash register. She spied the cover of the book he was reading – *The Complete Works of Charles Dickens*.

He looked up. 'Can I help you, Miss?'

'Just browsing, thank you. Do you have any books on Australian Aboriginal history?'

'Yes, a few, depends on what part of their history you're interested in. We have the classic non-fiction texts by Broome, Isaacs and Elkin, all rather dry and outdated now, I think. Times have changed with all the protests, don't you think?'

'Do you mean the protests about the Games?'

'In a nutshell, yes. Maybe you'd be more interested in this book released last year.' He held up a book titled *Baal Belbora* by Geoffrey Blomfield. 'I'm afraid I know nothing about the author, some gent from Armidale, I believe. It's a disturbing read if you can believe it,' he said, as the corners of his mouth drew downwards.

'Thank you. You don't mind if I flick through a copy?'

'Here, take mine. You're welcome to sit anywhere. Take your time.'

Renate sat on a stool between two rows of books stacked almost to the ceiling. A single light on a brass chain hung from an ornate, white Art Deco holder. She flicked through the book, stopping at rough drawings of dark-skinned men in lines with long spears, men crouched down in hats holding rifles, a family, all females, gathered outside a primitive tent. Near the front of the book, she was drawn to a map titled *THE FALLS*, with nine arrows labelled *INVASION* and the dates: 1828, 1832, 1836. On the opposite page a map titled *Map of the Massacres*. Either map would be about the same size as southern Poland. *Invasion and massacres.* These words bounced around Renate's head until they moved lower and settled in the pit of her stomach. *It did happen here.* She bought a copy and left.

In her room, on her bed, was a letter from Germany. She recognised her mother's neat script, made a herbal tea and sat at the kitchen table.

Mein liebes Renate,

I'm writing to you in English as I need to practice more if you are staying any longer in Australia. I'm writing to tell you that Ulrich is in hospital having treatment for cancer. It was picked up in his lungs on X-ray. He's been asking about you lately. Asking when you are coming home? When are you?

I've lived with him for over twenty years and he's still a mystery about some things. Especially the war. There was a girl here last week named Ilse asking about you. She said she was a friend from uni. I said I'd give her your address if you wish. Well, if you can come home, even for a week or two, I'll send you the airfare. Ulrich needs all the love and support right now. He's a fighter, but I think he's finally admitted that he's only human and he misses you. Of course, I miss you and it would be wonderful to see you.

Your loving mother,
Anne

Renate folded the letter and placed it back in the envelope. *Do I want to go back home now?* She wrote:

Dear Mama,

Thanks for your letter. I have a long break at Christmas and I can come home then on one condition. Papa has to tell me everything about Oma and Opa. He has to tell me what he did in the war. Please ask

him this for me. When he agrees, write to me again and I'll tell you
when I'm coming. And yes, please give my address to Ilse.

I miss you! Love, Renate

Renate flicked through her new book; the stories were disturbing bedtime reading. Towards the back, two lines stood out. '*But the shock suffered by modern man is minor compared with the Holocaust, which enveloped the Aboriginal people.*' She wrestled with the word before switching off the light. *Holocaust? I thought that word only applied to the Jews?* She tried to scratch an uncomfortable itch in the middle of her back. In the gloom when she closed her eyes, the pile of headless bodies remained. And a date – 10th June, 1838.

35

The library in the Biological Science building had rows of study hutches, some with graffiti – *I wuz here* – and phone numbers for a *good time*, faded from the failed scrubbing of frazzled librarians. Renate sat against the far wall and mulled over Simone's story while trying to focus on her thesis. The library's normal hum: the crisp cacophony, pages turning, slumped students sighing and the clack and ding of typewriters. She had her three regular desks, arranged in a U-shape with her back to the wall. When she closed her eyes and tried to visualise the concepts, an image of the group of Aboriginal women from the book she'd read last night remained. She opened her eyes and shook her head – *C'mon schmoe, focus!* She looked down at the journals, books arranged to the left and right on separate tables and a typewriter in front. Texts on phyllotaxis were on her left and those about morphogenesis, including Turing's on her right.

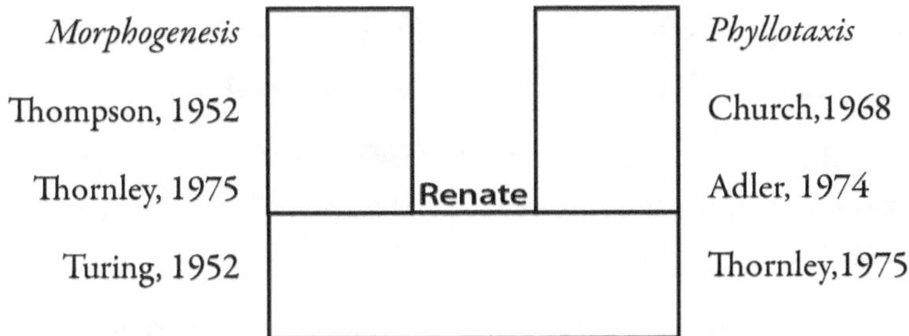

Alan Turing. *Why did this gifted mathematician and code breaker switch to studying biology, specifically phyllotaxis?* That fundamental property of all living things that included the arrangement of leaves on plant stems. The question bothered her not because of Turing's struggle with his personal life – arrested due to his homosexuality and forced to undergo oestrogen therapy – but why was he so careless with the gold and cyanide experiments that eventually killed him?

She never believed the poison apple theory. *C'mon, he wasn't Snow White.* The questions multiplied inversely to progress on her thesis. Turing had discovered a chemical basis for morphogenesis which was the biological process that causes a cell, tissue or organism to develop its shape. *Okay, well that's pretty basic.* All this while struggling to organise her outline. Her body stiffened, her arms dead weights on the table. She stood up, stretched, walked to the toilet and splashed her face. *How could he have known all this one year before the discovery of DNA?* She knew about genes and chromosomes, how genes coded for proteins and enzymes to make reactions happen, so, she deduced, *they must control morphogenesis and ultimately evolution. How had a gifted mathematician pre-empted this discovery?* What troubled her most was the exponential explosion of information she needed to organise. And morphogens? Those chemicals that controlled the process? Nobody had discovered them yet. She was reluctant to branch out too far from her neat, little plant phyllotaxis topic to encompass more of Turing's work, but she felt she had no choice now. She also wanted to include a section on cancer-cell development, after Anne's letter about Ulrich's cancer. *It is another example of a process, a highly abnormal pathological tissue morphogenesis.* She looked at the ordered texts arranged around and tried to relax.

She didn't hear the soft footsteps on the carpet.

'Hi. Fancy finding you here.'

Renate looked up into Simone's face hovering above her desk.

'Oh, hi.'

'What happened to your *'frequent visits'*?'

'Sorry, I've been busy.' She scanned the papers, stood up and shuffled her feet. 'I'm trying to organise my thesis. I want to prepare for a PhD. I'm stuck with how much to include.'

'Don't you think it's a little early for that, *non credi*?'

Renate dipped her head and stared at the table.

'You look... snowed under. How about some fun to distract you on Saturday?'

'Fun? Where?' Renate's neck locked in position.

'My flat. I'm inviting two other friends over for drinks and dinner. I'm cooking something special. Come on, it'll be fun. A foursome would be nice, *non*?' She came closer and placed her warm hand on Renate's arm.

'What exactly do you mean?'

'You know me, Renate, adventurous.' She huffed a little laugh. Renate did not get the joke.

'I'll see. Can't make any promises. What time?'

'For you, exactly seven pm. You're always punctual, I like that. Come for drinks if you like.'

'I'll think about it. Thanks.' Renate, eager to get back to work, stared down at the typewriter and shuffled her pens on the desk.

'Okay then. *Ciao*!'

She squirmed in her seat at the images of gossiping strangers in Simone's flat. Then the Fibonacci sequence flashed before her eyes, 1, 1, 2, 3, 5, 8, 13... and the formula: $F_n = F_{n-1} + F_{n-2}$

Hell, where did that come from? Why now? How am I going to fit all this into forty thousand words? Damn typewriter, gotta swap the alphabet ball for the special symbol one. She threw her hands up, packed up her reference texts and returned the typewriter to the front desk. Just thirty minutes before her shift started at the café.

*

Four hours later, wiping cups and glasses in the café, the problem still flustered her. *How much to include? Phyllotaxis of plants or morphogenesis and entropy, evolution and cancer development?*

'You look distracted, Renate,' David said, as she mumbled a reply to his question. The problem consumed her, swallowed her like something wild, chaotic, something cursed. She ran her hands through her hair. A prickle ran along the back of her neck. She flung the apron in the back room and slammed the door shut with the words echoing in her head, *'you look distracted'. If only he knew.* If it was a defining moment in her career, she would be mistaken – but then again – what frustrated her the most was her inability to find a formula to predict the future.

36

October 7

Renate returned to an empty house with Simone's allegation that 'orderly people are very judgemental' playing on her mind. *Am I judgemental? I suppose I am, if it's a fault, I don't think I can overcome it. I was born this way, can't see myself changing anytime soon.* About that time, downtown, over one hundred protestors were arrested by police and charged with unlawful assembly, including Simone.

After dinner, she opened her journal, the title clear in bold letters in her mind: *Morphogenesis and Phyllotaxis: The hunt for morphogens.* Morphogens – those substances Turing proposed to be the cause of the patterning of cells during the embryonic development stage. *The morphogen signals must be controlled by feedback loops, but how does that work, exactly?* There was no current research on this problem and she wondered, *how do you say it – zu viel zuzumuten, womit sies ich selbst – I've bitten off more that I can chew?* The phone rang out in the hall.

'Hello. I'm calling from the Royal. I'm the night supervisor. Is this Miss Mayer?'

'Speaking.'

'I'm ringing on behalf of Simone Lombardi. Are you a friend, or...'

'Yes, good friend, why? What's happened?'

'There's been an accident. Miss Lombardi was struck by a car and is in surgery. Do you know where her parents live?'

'I think they're in Italy.'

'Well, you might like to come in.'

'Okay. I'll be there.' An icy chill spread through her body. She hung up the phone and closed her eyes. A flashback – *a wobbly ladder, falling, Liam, a car accident, a hospital.*

At 9 pm, Renate tightened the hood of her jacket and waited for the bus in patchy drizzle. Above, the streetlights flashed orange. The bus dropped her outside the red *'Emergency'* sign. Once inside, she waited before the Triage window scanning the room. There was a row of chairs around a pale-blue wall that matched the nurses' uniforms. The receptionist, a bored-looking woman in her forties, took her details and disappeared through the back door. Renate sat down in the corner with the smell of disinfectant and sweat, like an unwanted guest refusing to leave. As the wall clock ticked 10 pm, a dishevelled woman walked in holding a sniffling child of about three. She pushed against the sliding window. It didn't budge.

'Mummy, I'm thirsty.'

'I know, luv.'

'Mummy it hurts.'

'I know luv.'

'Mummy, I want to go home.'

'I know luv, they won't be long.'

A doctor in a long, white coat, stethoscope around his neck stood before the woman and cleared his throat as if about to give a speech. His eyes narrowed as he stared at the child. 'Can you come this way please?'

'Excuse me. Do you know when I can see my friend?' Renate asked another lady in a white, starched uniform. The woman looked up, removed her glasses and studied Renate's face. 'Shouldn't be long now. They're still in theatre.'

Renate clenched her fists and folded them in her lap, clamped her feet together and sat perfectly still, just as she remembered Anne doing when she was a little girl. She counted her breaths and remembered what Anne had said: 'Renate, the best way to get through life is don't ask too many questions.' *Pfft. That's not helpful.* Ulrich had said that to her when she asked him about his past. Simone had said it. *Am I 'judgemental'?* She had no close friends to gauge how others perceived her. *At least Sandy accepts me as I am.* It was unpredictable chaos she feared the most. Her love of order seemed to be in her blood. *What if it's all pre-set? Genetic? Is that possible?'* She shook her head. A different nurse marched over to Renate.

'You here to see Miss Lombardi?'

'Yes.'

'Come this way.'

She followed the white apron down a pale-blue corridor, through plastic doors that swished open into a large recovery ward with twenty beds lined up, all full. At the far end, the nurse parted the bed curtains and ushered Renate in, closed the curtains behind her. Simone was fully wrapped like an Egyptian mummy in bandages and plaster. Tubes were going in three different directions, one carried a yellow liquid to a bag hooked on the side of the bed. A monitor was beeping in time to the second-hand clock above the bed. A ventilator hissed. Renate sat next to the bed and held Simone's cold, limp hand. The black hands of the clock marked off the seconds. A different doctor approached – bags under his eyes.

'Miss, are you, a relative?'

'Renate. No, just a good friend.'

'Do you know how we can contact her family?'

'Not exactly. I think they are in Italy.'

'Do you have any way of finding out?' he asked, tilting his head. 'If you find anything, can you ring me back? Ask for Doctor Harris. I'm the staff neurosurgeon.' He came over and sat next to her and sighed. His body slumped. He turned towards her. 'You might as well go home and get some sleep. I don't think there's going to be much change tonight. Sorry.' It was the tone of his voice. Renate knew.

'How did it happen?'

'I believe she was hit by a car. The driver didn't stop.'

'*Schweinehund!*' Renate clenched her fists.

'Pardon?'

'Look, I want to stay a bit longer. I'm her closest friend.'

'All right. Just one hour.'

Renate's fingers trembled; she pushed them under Simone's pillows. Her head drooped. Her eyes closed. She jerked awake. The hour hand crept past twelve. She questioned every aspect of her life – her friendship with Simone and Daniel – her family, how friendship sometimes turns into love. *Is there a formula for that? Or is there a separate formula for platonic love and another for romantic? Something with a checklist you could tick off and tally up each time, but how would you control all the variables?*

Outside, a shiny slick of water covered the road. A quarter moon dangled overhead, a dog howled in the distance. She caught the last bus back to the uni, climbed the stairs and found Simone's hidden key. Inside, she combed the rooms – scattered clothes made a trail from the bedroom, books and papers spilt from her desk, a pile of paperbacks in a leaning stack next to her bed. Renate searched through the bedroom and found a letter inside the novel *Desperate Characters*. She opened the letter and read:

Giuseppe and Maria Lombardi
4/20 Via GiovAnnei Pastorelli
Navigli. Milan. Italy.

And a phone number. Renate dialled the number. She wanted to be the first to tell them.

'Hello? Is this Mrs Lombardi?'

Through a noisy conversation Renate heard a '*Sì.*'

'Do you speak English?'

'Excusi, Marco! Come! English!'

'Hello? Who is this?'

'Hi, my name is Renate Mayer. I'm a good friend of Simone's. Is she your, um...'

'Sister, yes? Why? What's happened?'

'She's been in an accident. She's in hospital.'

Pause.

'What kind of accident?'

'She was hit by a car.'

'How bad is she, she's going to be alright, yes?'

'I can't say right now, it's the middle of the night here. I'll find out more tomorrow. Do you want me to pass on your number to the hospital?'

'Yes of course. Thank you. Grazie.'

Renate folded the clothes and stacked the books in two piles, washed the dishes and packed them away. She undressed, showered and climbed into Simone's bed, clutching Simone's favourite toy puppy in one hand and the Stone of Heaven in the other. The words '*the driver didn't stop*' repeated, over and over. Unfamiliar emotions burned in her head and sadness boiled under her skin. She thought of praying, *But what?* The only words that came to her was *please. And please help her.*

37

Doctor Harris joined her the next day at Simone's bedside – she had not regained consciousness.

'I spoke with her parents this morning, they are waiting to catch a flight tonight.' He looked at Renate and sighed. 'They'll have a difficult decision to make when they get here.'

'You mean about the machine?' she didn't need any elaboration. He nodded. 'You may stay here if you wish, but I don't think it'll register with her.' She stayed all day and returned home at dusk, kept her routine, routine for sanity's sake. Her studies put on hold.

The next day she tried to keep to a schedule – shower at 6:30, breakfast by 7, bus to uni by 8:30. She sat in the library surrounded by her desks and her reference journals arranged in meticulous order. And waited for time to pass. Waited for the Lombardis.

They arrived the following morning, she met them at the hospital. Maria in a long black full mourning dress, Giuseppe in a dark suit, Marco in slacks and a white shirt. Renate excused herself when Dr Harris asked to speak with them in private. 'I'll wait outside.' In about twenty minutes Marco came out and sat beside her.

'Thank you for being here and calling us. Have you known Simone long?' Renate told him that she'd only known her since this year, but they were very close.

'Have they caught the driver?' Marco's eyes bulged, his nostrils flared.

'I don't think so. If they do it'll be on the news. Where are you staying?' she asked.

'It's called the Crest International downtown. Here is their number. Please ring me if you hear anything. The doctor said we'll have to decide about turning off the machine soon.' He shook his head. 'He doesn't think there's much hope. Meanwhile, we pray.' He stared at his feet. When he looked up his eyes were harder. He cracked his knuckles. 'Of course we'll want justice, retribution, you understand? When they find him. Our relatives are coming to help.'

'I'm sure the police will deal with him when they...'

'Fuck police, exscusi... we'll deal with him our way, Italian way.' Marco flexed his fingers and made a fist. Renate's nod was wooden.

*

After seven days, Simone had not regained consciousness. Her parents made the decision. Endless arrangements began – pine casket, flowers, red and white roses, the funeral home, the burial plot at Toowong Cemetery, the reception after at the uni bar. David volunteered to organise Italian food, Aimee and Sarah volunteered to serve. Still, *keep working,* she told herself, just managing to type a word, a sentence followed by full stops trailing off the page while she dealt with anger, bewilderment, loss, revenge even. Emotions unfamiliar to her.

She avoided lectures, avoided Aimee and Sarah, couldn't avoid the necessary responsibilities of the preparation. No one understood what she was going through. Her feelings for Simone came unforeseen – in the shower, cooking dinner, on the bus. They defied all attempts at analysis. It was like how a lab rat might feel – frightened in a disembodied, visceral way – stuck inside a cage.

And revenge? *Do I want revenge or retribution?* She knew revenge was normal in some cultures: payback, honour-killing, to satisfy the relatives. She wanted retribution at the least, if and when the person was found.

She coped by throwing herself into simple organising tasks. The uni helped with the reception, the state government donated a burial plot while they searched for the driver. Simone's relatives, those that could come on short notice, would arrive just before the service at the Sacred Heart Church in Rosalie.

*

Thursday

Two days before the funeral, Sandy designed the condolence cards and Renate wrote her speech, with the constant drone of the evening news in the background. They froze as they heard: *Police have arrested a man at Gold Coast airport in connection with the hit-and-run death of a university student last week. The man, identified as Matthew Savage, 39, of Brisbane, was stopped as he tried to board a flight to Sydney, police stated. He is currently being questioned at Police Headquarters in Brisbane.'* They turned and saw police escorting a balding man of about 40, face covered in black stubble, to a police van.

'Glad they caught the bastard,' Sandy said.

Renate's breathing shallowed. Her eyes locked onto the man with the black stubble. *I wonder if Marco knows and is enjoying the schadenfreude with me? Now he's been caught, order can return and retribution follow.*

38

The church service and wake passed as if they'd happened on Mars. Giuseppe and Maria, stoic on the couch, Marco stiff with the word *revenge* on his lips like poison. When she asked him why he was so quiet he looked up and replied: *I più gran doloro sono muti* –very great griefs are silent. She nodded and watched two cousins from Griffith lurking in the corner in deep conversation.

When they left, she sat on her bed with her head in her hands and Simone's laugh echoing inside her head, her mischievous eyes sparkling and her silky, bronze skin. More and more, Daniel occupied her thoughts – *why did I keep Ulrich's past from Daniel? I couldn't tell him what I don't know, what would he think if he knew that Ulrich participated in the holocaust? Was he? How can I find out?* She carried a sense of cultural shame for what had happened and was determined to find out what her father had done in the war. *If only Daniel was here. Where was he? Who was he with? Is he happy?* For her, happiness was fleeting, like a line drawn in the sand that vanishes when the next tide comes in. The trick, she realised, is to not wait for another person to draw the line, however long, short or deep, but to draw the line yourself. She was not waiting for others, the crazy things they do, like dying and leaving you. From now on, she was going to harden up, thicken her skin, struggle through the unhappiness and grief and continue out the other side not the same, but a stronger person. *I'm strong enough now to face Ulrich and demand the truth. Is there time? What will I do if he was involved in the holocaust?*

39

The next day, the hit and run driver was again on the news: *'The man identified as Matthew Savage, arrested for the hit-and-run accident that tragically resulted in the death of Simone Lombardi, was released on bail today. Energy Resources of Australia posted security and he was released and taken to an unknown location accompanied by the company's lawyer. He is due back in court...'*

She looked at her books, her hands, the pens all lined up neatly as if waiting for an order to start and hated herself for it. *Why is everything grey?* – the clothing, the language, all leaden. She equally feared colour and order never returning. Her *Weltanschauung*, her view of the world around her, had changed forever since Simone's death.

What has happened to my black-and-white world? Did it ever exist? And the Nazi's obsession with blood. She jumped up and ran to the bathroom, scrubbing her hands over and over as if some of that blood was on her and she had to wash it off. Blood. Jewish blood. *Yes, that was it! That was why Germany was defeated. An unstoppable descent into chaos caused by one man. What am I doing? This is not helping. I'm getting further away from my thesis. Schiesse. I need to return to Turing's rabbit hole.* She flexed her fingers, caught her breath and when she exhaled the air rushed around the room, over her papers and joined the disjointed thoughts into something larger, something beyond the simple concept of order. She grabbed her pen and wrote as the house, the streets outside, the city beyond fell silent, the ideas in her head became words that leaped across the page. She wrote and wrote and only stopped when her fingers cramped. She prowled the room, pulled her hair, squeezed the Stone of Heaven until her hand throbbed. Raided the refrigerator and drank from random bottles – juice, wine, spirits, vodka – her throat burned and her body blazed. More ideas bubbled to the surface, roared inside her, sparked like lightning between the pen in one hand and the Stone in the other. Inside the stone, less than the width of a human hair, the electric blue changed. Was it the heat of her palm or the pressure of her fist? The copper atoms and the carbonate molecules broke from each other in a mutual separation and fled into the crystal matrix. The azure colour morphed into green – a green like the shallow waters of a warm sea – a mad rush of change swept neighbours alike in the metamorphosis, a sea of caterpillars in a cocoon of butterflies. On the surface it was a subtle, inevitable change, almost like the spreading of a green fungus. But the change was inexorable, irrevocable. It was the stone's destiny, to break into smaller pieces of sand and attack other stones on the shoreline of that emerald-coloured sea...

Towards 5 am, she was done, just a flaccid emptiness remained. Never had she been so empty, so drained. Her master's now seemed irrelevant compared to the loss of Simone. She hunched over and stared at the pages – intrigued or entranced by the script that was the culmination of her life so far. She breathed hard, gathered her books and dumped them on the table, swallowed two paracetamols, gulped two glasses of water. She collapsed on the bed, blind to the envelope that had been there all day, on her pillow, not feeling the layers of paper crunch under her head. Little did she realise that the letter, like any unexpected harbinger, would determine the direction of the rest of her life.

40

L ater that morning she read:

Mein liebes Renate

Papa is back in hospital; the cancer has spread to his bones. The doctors say they have run out of treatment options. They have given him weeks to live. But you know Papa, he's a fighter! He's asking for you constantly. So, I'm sending you an open ticket for any airline you choose. Just come home soon, please. He has promised to tell you everything he can remember.

Deine liebe mutter,
Anne

A week passed. The suspect's house was firebombed. The police questioned anyone with even a vague connection with anti-uranium activities. Renate kept quiet – not out of honour to Marco, now back in Milan, but with a tinge of satisfaction that the driver had suffered burns in the firebombing and his house was destroyed.

She had a decision to make, though deep down the decision was already made. In a flurry of activity, Renate organised the flight to Germany, her permission to postpone her studies, packed up her books, spare clothes and offered Sandy six weeks rent, which she refused.

'Your room will be waiting when you return.'

At the airport, she was unaware of a balding man in a dark-grey suit behind her in the queue. She rose to board, dropped her passport and bumped into the passenger behind. When she stooped to pick it up, the balding man already had it and offered it to her. He transfixed her with a penetrating stare as if looking right through her. *Why do I feel like he can read my mind?*

FOUR

41

Daniel
January 1983

Daniel's eyes roamed the room and settled on a photo of a young soldier in a lieutenant's uniform with neat-cut dark hair and piercing eyes. *A distant cousin or uncle perhaps*? Daniel sat at the dining room table in the house where he grew up, a 1920s brick four-bedroom bungalow in a quiet street off Alison Road, Randwick, just over a kilometre from Centennial Park. With high ceilings and plaster light roses, cream walls with cedar-stained, full length picture rails in the lounge room. His mother, Helen, cooked breakfast. She hummed and made small talk, how helpful Rachel had been, even mentioned Skyla.

He'd been home three weeks, back to his familiar haunts, sometimes with Steve, his old flatmate. Their relationship had shifted, Daniel couldn't tolerate his remarks about women anymore. Every second sentence contained stories about tits or babes. Within minutes, Daniel made excuses to leave. Once he tried to check in with the Friends of the Earth office. Those he missed the most had either moved on or were still overseas.

A couple of times he'd brought a girl back from a nightclub, tiptoeing in the back door, glancing uncomfortably down the hall. When Helen asked him if he was going to catch up with Skyla, he changed the subject. Helen sat down, crossed one leg over the other and pulled her pale-blue dressing gown tight. Between chews and swallows he looked up at the photo above her head.

'Who's that in the photo?'

'That's Uncle David, Dad's older brother.'

'Can't say I remember the guy. What happened to him?'

'Well, don't you remember the story? He went to fight in Greece in 1941 with the Sixth Division. Never came back.'

'Nah, don't remember that one,' he said, chewing an egg on toast.

'He led a platoon in one of the first engagements with the Germans at Brallos Pass. Captured and sent to Germany as a POW. That's all we know. Dad's mum tried to get him to change his name to Cullen before he left but he wouldn't. He was proud of his Jewish ancestry.'

'Did they know then what the Germans were doing to the Jews?'

'Oh yes, it was common knowledge, especially after November 1938.'

'*Kristallnacht.* Did they find out what happened to him?'

'After the war, one of his comrades came by to tell Ian that David was sent to a camp in Germany. Then, nothing.'

'Why didn't Dad enlist?'

She looked down at his empty plate, picked it up and carried it to the kitchen. 'They needed engineers back here to upgrade the bridges. Ian was one of the best. But he always missed David, they were inseparable as kids.'

'If I ever go to Germany I'll try and find out what happened to him. So why wasn't I brought up Jewish?'

'Your father was not practising when we met. I was a Catholic, he converted so we could marry. We brought you up Catholic.'

'Well, that explains the nuns at school.'

'So,' she said, putting on an apron, 'are you going back teaching, back to Winburn?'

'No, Mum, not going back there.'

'Why? There were rumours after you left, gossip, that kind of thing. Not that I took any notice.'

'It was nothing Mum, just a mixed-up girl who tried to get me. Vindictive, you understand?' Daniel caught his breath and swallowed. He rose to leave.

'Don't go yet. I bumped into Skyla a few weeks ago. She asked after you.'
'What did she say?'

'How were you getting on. What were you doing, she seemed curious. Are you going to look her up?'

'I'm thinking about it.' The words came out just a second too fast.

'She looked nice. She was alone if you are wondering.'

'I'm not.' Daniel looked away, he closed his eyes. Some things just were.

*

He met Skyla on a bench next to the bike path in Centennial Park. She was in floral dress in blues and yellows, shiny brown boots. She chatted non-stop – her new job at the hospital, how she hated night duty, her new car. Away in the distance, ducks quacked in clanging crescendos. A few families rode bikes, toddlers swayed on their training wheels, bells rang, mothers barked out warnings, couples walked hand in hand. A 747 passed across the sun, its shadow slowed as engines wound down for landing. He was aware of her smell, the powder, her clothes, always spotless and fresh, the smell of eucalyptus. They used to ride here years ago. Said she was seeing someone sporty. 'He loves surfing, plays football.'

'Sounds just like me, hey?'

She made a face as her eyes narrowed. 'So, tell me about Japan. How was it?'

'Intense. Great cycling, Lots of beer. Nice girls.' He smirked.

'Did you get close to anyone?' she said, with a gleam in her eyes.

'Once. It didn't work out.'

'You must tell me everything, please.' Her eyes widened as she turned to look at him.

Everything. That word. Even if he found the words, she would not understand. 'Not right now...' The words trailed off.

'Okay then, tell me, what stands out most?'

'The temples, the chanting. The tolling of the Hiroshima bell.'

'Well, that's fascinating, really. What are you going to do now, Daniel? Any other causes need saving?'

The questions lingered and hung in the air like Chinese sky lanterns.

'Not sure. I want to, need to leave Sydney. Mum seems okay, Rachel can pop in and check on her. I don't think I'll go as far this time. I'd like to check out the Blue Mountains.'

'Nice and cold!'

'That'll complement how I'm feeling.' He let out a long sigh.

'Oh Daniel, c'mon, you always were so... melodramatic.'

'How so?'

'You're not serious? Don't you remember? You were always so intense, I often didn't know where you were. And that music you played when I was out, who was it again? Leonard something?'

'No, Jackson Browne.'

'Yes, him. God, Daniel, you needed to lighten up.' She laughed and tossed her head back.

Daniel inhaled. *Maybe she's right?* 'Anyway, I don't think you ever really tried to understand me, you were always too busy, running around doing stuff.'

'And you were doing what, exactly?'

'Well, I've changed.'

'Have you?' She stood up, checked her watch and walked around behind him.

Have I changed? In less than a minute, the gulf widened between them.

Skyla looked up as a car horn sounded.

'Well, there's my ride. It's been great catching up. I do hope you find what you're looking for, I really mean that.' She pecked him faintly on the cheek. She stood.

He nodded as she turned and left.

*

One week before Christmas in his room, he flicked through the employment columns of the *Weekend Herald* while Helen watched *Four Corners*. He stopped and read: 'Biology/Science Secondary Full-Time – Temporary. Blue Mountains Grammar. Post resumé to...'

He snipped out the ad and stuck it next to the phone. That night, he mulled over teaching a class of adolescents again, if he still had the confidence.

What the hell. Might be fun.

42

Daniel
February 1986

Daniel braced on the end of a 38 mm Class H fire hose, training with the Rural Bushfire Service in Katoomba. The call came in. 'Time to go.' He jumped in the truck, already suited up in his orange overalls, helmet and gloves on the seat next to him.

After three years, the beauty of the wilderness kept him there. Still enthralled by the quaint villages, the vastness of the view, the dense mist over the valleys in winter. The air had a quality, a purity like no other – a crisp, European-like chill in winter. Diverse groups of quirky alternatives: single mums with rugged-up toddlers, astrologers, vegans and Buddhists of all flavours. Then there were the others like him – those with jobs who commuted to work each day, came home to watch *Home and Away* or *Sale of the Century*. Two different species oblivious to each other. As of last month, his Saturday job gave him a foot in both camps.

From the back seat he yelled, 'Where're we off to?'

'Govett's Leap. A fire's coming up from the Blue Gum Forest. We're on watch and wait, hosing down spot fires.'

They roared past the Hydro Majestic, down the straight through Medlow Bath and slowed going over the railway bridge, past another crew folding

192

hoses. They cranked up the speed down Govett's Leap Road, passing a frantic woman grabbing people willy-nilly, pointing up and down the road. Something about her looked familiar. On impulse he shouted, 'Hey, stop the truck. I gotta get out and check if that woman needs help!'

As one, they turned and looked. The Deputy Captain, Michael smiled. 'Take the radio and let us know when you're finished.' The others chuckled. Daniel kept an eye on the young woman as he walked back. She had long, blonde hair, dressed in a baggy tee that hung loose over pyjama pants. Her face had that worried, lost-something-important look.

When he approached, her eyes wandered over his face for a second. 'You! I know you!'

He smiled and remembered. 'Alice from Darwin. Well, hi again!'

'David?'

'It's Daniel.'

'Shit. I mean, yes. What are you doing here?' her eyes widened.

'On bushfire watch-and-wait duty. What about you?'

'Snuffy, my naughty terrier. He's escaped again. He's scared of the smoke. Wanna help me find him?' She grabbed his hand as if he might run away.

'I think I saw a dog like that, up towards the shops.'

They walked back the two blocks to the shops. She chatted non-stop the whole way as if making up for lost time. *Her work, her house, her life.* They saw the dog waiting outside the post office.

'Snuffy! Why did you run off, you naughty boy!' She ran up and picked him up and buried her face in its white curls. The two-way crackled 'All clear here Daniel now. Over.'

They walked back to Alice's house, and at the gate, she motioned for him to come in. He nodded as she opened the front door. Snuffy ignored Daniel and trotted inside to the kitchen. Daniel stood, arms by his side, eyes scanning the rooms. There was an old black-and-white gas stove set in wooden cupboards, a polished wooden benchtop, walls painted in lilac. In the lounge room, a black, cast-iron fireplace set in a column of bricks. Three rows of brown tiles merged with the floorboards.

'What can I get you to drink? Beer?' She opened the refrigerator and pulled out a can of Coke.

'Water's fine. I'm still on duty. I gotta call in soon'

'Well look at you then, big, handsome firefighter. I could use someone like you around here. Gavin is, well, so much focused on his car. He loves that BMW.'

'Gavin?' He raised an eyebrow.

'My boyfriend. He's an accountant. Lives in Chatswood.' she said with a shrug and bent down to give Scruffy a scratch, walked to the kitchen, filled the kettle and lit the gas.

'Hang on a sec,' – he reached for his radio – 'I've got to radio in. Okay. Won't be long. Over.' he smiled. 'Boss said to call back later.'

She poured water into two identical glasses. He nodded at a photo on the window frame. 'Nice car. Is that Gavin's latest?'

'That's the BMW. Says he wants to move up here, become a teacher like you, isn't that exciting? Though I don't see him leaving Sydney any time soon. He likes the night life and his job. 'But, Daniel, tell me about you? What are you doing? Who are you seeing? Maybe I know her?'

'I'm teaching at the Grammar. No, I'm not seeing anyone right now.'

'Seriously, I can't believe it's been over three years? God, remember Darwin? What a dump. It's so much nicer here, I'm the manager at Daddy's shop in Katoomba – *Mountain Tours* – maybe you've seen it. Anyway, it's good, don't have to put up with too many boring old retirees and I've just moved in here. It's delightful, don't you think?' She was talking a mile a minute while spreading butter on a plate of croissants.

'Sure, glad you're happy.'

'Anyway, Gavin takes me out to fabulous places, Jenolan Caves, Bathurst, our favourite place is just up the road. The Hydro.' She turned to check her hair in the mirror.

'Really? Sounds like fun.' He tried to sound convincing.

'So, where were you going again? China? Japan? Did you save them from that terrible uranium thing? Don't tell me. I'm more interested in your love life. What's her name?'

'Oh no…remember? I'm having a break from that.' His jaw tensed at the way she dismissed the bike ride and that *terrible uranium thing*.

'Daniel. You're missing out. You know the mountains are crawling with single women. Sure, some with kids. Probably just makes them more desperate.'

'I'm not that desperate.' He fidgeted with the volume dial. It crackled and a voice echoed: *Daniel, you're needed now. Be out the front ASAP.* 'Sorry, Alice I have to go.'

'Well, you'll have to tell me all about your travels. How about next Saturday for dinner? I'm asking a couple of friends over. It should be fun. Do you like lasagne?'

'Can't, sorry. I've got to go and stay with mum in Randwick. She's coming off chemo and my sister needs help. Another time?' Outside, a truck roared up, stopped and tooted.

'Well, here's my number if your plans change.' She handed him a slip of paper with a border of pink love hearts.

Daniel stood in the swirling smoke, hose pointed at the base of a smouldering angophora. He was comfortable in his room at Ray and Angie's share house. He could afford to rent his own place but liked the company. Angie was a chef and cooked great vegetarian meals, Ray played an old, battered guitar. They liked the same music. He even enjoyed teaching again, they were mostly well-behaved students, some who even pushed him intellectually. He had one History class each cycle to cover and they were on the Second World War. His Biology class was almost all girls, chatty and curious. He volunteered at the Food Co-op in Katoomba every second weekend, mainly to meet the dozens of single women who shopped there. He'd met Bec, a tall, blonde woman with two kids and was captivated by the way she swished her skirts in time with her long ponytail. Like that song swirling around his head – *You can't start a fire without a spark...*

Her wicked laugh had him hooked from the start.

43

On the second Saturday in March, Daniel waited behind the till at the Co-op until Bec had finished shopping and offered to carry a twenty-kilo bag of rice to her battered, yellow 1972 Kingswood. He asked about her kids, Amber and Lennon, about their dad – 'Is their dad around?' – 'Down in Sydney.' She replied.

Then he spurted: 'Do you want to have dinner on Friday?'

'Can't, but I can do Saturday,' she replied. 'Come over to my place.'

*

Saturday

They talked in the small kitchen after Amber and Lennon settled for the night. Outside, a clammy mist drooped and settled on the pencil pines in the backyard. Four garden plots were covered in weeds. She followed his gaze out the window.

'No time for gardening.'

He nodded. They talked about music and life in the mountains and made polite conversation as new couples do. What she was doing: astrology, childcare, conservation. 'You know, *important stuff*. The conversation ebbed and flowed. He'd just flicked through a book on astrology he'd borrowed from the local library, just for these occasions. They ate rice and curry, sat in front of a dusty open fire and discussed music. She put on a Dire Straits album. *Where you think you're going? Don't you know it's dark outside...* He was a small insect she was winding her web around.

When she kissed him, the trap slammed shut.

*

Two weeks later he was sleeping over. One night, out of the blue she asked,

'Do you have other girlfriends?'

'A few.' Pause. She didn't react. He cleared his throat. 'No, just joking. You're plenty enough for me.'

Another month passed. He was still hooked on the idea he was in love. The way she laughed abruptly at his jokes, the intense, passionate way she'd kiss him, the mysterious way she'd know what to talk about. She never talked about the kids' dad, just that he *'lived in Sydney'*. He even enjoyed Amber and Lennon's company. Amber was fun, nice to be with, chatty. Bec never discussed the most important topic for him: the future. The other thing that played on his mind was their lovemaking. *Why was she so emotional? So mysterious? I hope she's using protection.* She assured him she had that covered. He formed a plan to move in with her. *Just another month, when the time is right.*

*

In class, he taught with new-found energy. In Year 11 Biology, Celeste, red hair hanging straight on her shoulders and Crystal, eyes like heavy-duty searchlights, elbowed each other and giggled. They'd seen him and Bec last Sunday on Katoomba Street, holding hands.

'You look happy today, sir,' Crystal said with a cool smile.

During lunch, John Black the Science Master moved across the staffroom slowly, like a tiger ready to pounce. There were deep furrows chiselled in his forehead by years of teaching impervious to modern perspectives. He stopped next to Daniel and cleared his throat. Up close, he smelled of bleach. 'Just want to ask you a favour, Daniel.'

'Yes.'

'It's about that boy Michael, in your Year 11. You know, the effeminate one. I heard he was being bullied. Just some of those boys in P.E. Probably nothing much to it.'

'Yes, I can talk with him.' To be honest, he hadn't paid too much attention to the quiet, serious student.

'Good man. He might make a good waiter or nurse one day, like a lot of the girls in your class, no doubt.'

'That sounds very judgemental, John.' His eyes narrowed.

'Not a bit. If they were smarter, they'd be taking Physics and Chemistry with me. But they are only girls. Make good mothers one day. Here's hoping.' He turned to walk away but stopped when Daniel shot back: 'And how do you explain Marie Curie winning the Nobel Prize for Chemistry?'

'That radium woman? Just an anomaly.' He tut-tutted as he walked away. Daniel shook his head as Black disappeared down the hall. *Pompous prick. What century does he think this is? Some of my Biology girls will become doctors and mothers. And 'effeminate'? Michael is a nice, gentle boy. He has every right to express his identity and sexuality any way he likes. I'll see what support he'd like from me.* He realised then that, maybe, some things in life were unteachable.

*

On the playground, Michael sat in the girls' section next to a Year 10 girl. As Daniel approached, he noticed Crystal held his hand. Michael looked up with red eyes.

'How's it going, Michael? Mind if I sit down?'

'No, sir. It's a free country.'

The girl let go of his hand, stood and walked away.

'Rumours are that you're being bullied. Is that the case?'

'They're just ignorant blockheads. They don't like anyone who's different,' he said, as the corners of his lips drew down.

'We're all different, Michael.' Daniel searched the playground for likely culprits, saw them everywhere he looked. He sighed. 'You'll need to stand up for yourself, not just at school, right? I can talk to them, give them a warning, but it's still largely up to you. If there's any other way I can help you, please let me know.'

'Don't worry, sir. I'll be okay.' He looked at the ground in front of his shoes. His face sagged, his eyebrows lowered and pulled together.

'Have you told your parents?'

'Mum's mostly on her own. Dads in Canberra most of the time. I think he's got a girlfriend there. *Bastard.*' He spat out the word.

'Do they tease you because you're...different or...'

Michael shrugged. 'I don't like football or any of their mean talk, the way they go on about girls. They're sexist. I like drama and writing poetry.'

'If I can ask,' Daniel said, 'are you... Are you gay?'

Michael shot him a look, defiance crossed his face. 'Who said that? Just because I like drama? Anyway, I don't want people to know. It's difficult enough for me now, without that label attached.'

'Okay, I won't mention it again.'

Daniel put a hand on Michael's shoulder and smiled. 'It's okay if you are, seriously...' He paused, studied the kid's face. 'But your mum would be supportive, right? Don't bottle it up, Michael. Some of the nicest people I know are gay.'

'Really?' He turned and faced Daniel as his mouth hung open.

Daniel bent the truth just a little. It was worth it to see Michael's face soften.

'Thanks, sir. I'll try.'

*

Winter came early in June, with a silent frost and a sprinkle of snow. He'd not seen Bec for a couple of weeks before he walked in her front door for dinner on Saturday night. There was a different atmosphere, foreign, unfamiliar. She offered a perfunctory kiss. He sat at the usual spot by the window and read the room. He didn't like what it said. Amber and Lennon played outside among the weeds on a second-hand swing set with one swing missing. Bec prepared dinner as usual, minus her bouncy flair. She had avoided him the past two weeks, making up new excuses not to see him. The way she leaned against the bench with her back straight, minus the usual chatter unsettled him. She sighed, turned, knife in hand.

'There's something I need to tell you.' She paused and took a deep breath. 'I'm getting back with their dad. I'm moving back down to Sydney.'

Daniel dropped his fork. It clattered on the table.

'Like, when?' His body tensed.

'Next week. So, this will be goodbye.' She wiped her face with the back of her hand. 'Don't take it personally, you're a nice guy. But this is what the stars are telling me.'

'But I think I'm in love with you. Doesn't that mean anything?' The words stuttered from his dry lips. His eyes watered.

'No, it can't. We had fun. Pure and simple. Now it's over.' The knife slapped through the carrot. 'I made my mind up a few days ago. You're the first to know. Look on the bright side' – she stopped cutting – 'at least I'm not pregnant.'

'But *us*? I could move in, help look after Amber and Lennon.' He swallowed. His throat was a desert. He was wishing he'd stayed in Brisbane and worked on his marriage with Renate.

'There is no 'us' now.' She indicated that the conversation was over.

201

'Shit. Shitshitshit!' He felt like punching something. His hand came down on the table. Her body stiffened, the knife motionless in her hand. He kissed her cheek lightly and left. He found Ray and Angie in the kitchen and unloaded: what Bec had said, how it shouldn't concern him, *the stars told her,* what the fuck was the matter with her, what the hell was wrong with him? 'What am I missing? I love her, isn't that enough?' They both looked at each other and gave him that look people give when they don't know what else to do, which always makes it worse.

If he was being honest with himself, he knew what he was missing – the close companionship with Renate. *At least she was always honest with me, wasn't she?*

44

6:30 am, Monday

The alarm clock rang. He splashed ice-cold water on his face, showered, donned a dressing gown and checked his daybook. First period: *Genetics and reproduction.* He gulped down toast and tea, flicked through the textbook, packed his bag and left. He crossed over Katoomba Street and walked up the hill. A couple of noisy miners squabbled in the gutter over a mouldy bread roll. In the newsagent window, the daily headlines – *Iran invades Iraq... Mir goes into Earth Orbit.* The traffic slowed, tyres squished and squealed on the wet road. It started to rain, not that full-blown tropical deluge, just silent, clammy, misty drizzle. He paused under the wide awning outside Katoomba Health Foods. A blue bicycle leant against the concrete pot plant caught his eye. It had four faded panniers with stickers and badges that were popular with the alternative crowd: *Land Rights Now! Stop Rainforest logging! Stop Uranium Mining!* A guy carried bread loaves past him into the shop. He checked his watch, ten minutes to spare. He waited until he returned. There was grease under the guy's fingernails and his face was lined and aged from the wind. He looked up with denim-blue eyes as Daniel stared at his bike.

'Nice bike,' Daniel said. 'Do you deliver to the Co-op?'

'My next stop, why?'

'Just curious. I work there every second Saturday.'

'Oh... If you don't mind me asking' – the guy fiddled with the strap on his pannier – 'you don't look like the type who'd work there. They're mostly alternatives, astrologers, you know the type?' He frowned and tilted his head.

'Looks can be deceiving, hey? Just want to connect with the alternatives, makes a welcome change from teaching at the Grammar.'

'Hell, what you teach?' he said, eyes lifting a little further.

'Science.'

'Gosh, I couldn't even imagine doing that. What, like, in front of teenagers? That's scary.' He grimaced, drawing his cheeks low like thin elastic.

'They're not like that. They're mostly well-behaved.'

'Okay, if you say so.' The guy began to untie the straps on his rack.

Daniel checked his watch again. 'Hey, I'm curious about your bike. Have you cycled overseas?'

'Just to Europe in '82. Mostly Germany.' The guy said.

'You didn't happen to visit Auschwitz in Poland, did you?'

'Actually, yes. Why?'

'Oh, I'd like to go there one day, vested interest, you understand?' Daniel checked his watch – 'I think my uncle might have been sent there.'

'You're not Jewish, are you?' he said, peering intently at Daniel.

'On my dad's side. You?'

'Nah. Buddhist.'

'That figures. Well, I gotta go and catch my train. See you around.'

'If you see Bec, say hello to her for me, will you?'

'Bec? Blonde Bec?' Daniel's eyes widened.

'That's the one.'

'Do you know her?'

'Sure. Everyone does... Bit of a minx, hey?' Daniel didn't like the smirk on his face. The feelings he had for her were still raw. *I'm glad Renate didn't leave me with those feelings. Anyway, I left her, so it was all on me.*

On the corner of Lovel Street, a group of people stood outside the Mountains Adventure Shop in a semi-circle. In the middle he recognised Alice. Dressed in dark-grey slacks and a white blouse with a loose red and blue scarf, she didn't see him creep up. He caught her eye in mid-sentence.

'Excuse me Miss, can I book a tour here?' he said, smiling.

'I'll be with you in a second, sir.' When the crowd went inside, she pecked him on the cheek. 'Hey Mr Fireman. Where have you been? I've been waiting for your call.'

'Oh, you know, busy working.'

'Okay. What's her name this time?' she said with an uncanny, disarming smile.

'Oh, no it's not like that.' He lied.

'Well then, I'm free this Friday night. You interested?'

He paused for a second. 'Yes, that'd be great.'

*

During recess he sat in the HSIE – Geography/History staffroom and went over a lesson on the Holocaust for his history lesson. The phone rang. He picked up.

'I've got a Jules Jackson for Daniel.' Karen from front office said.

'Put him through'.

'Hey, Daniel. Remember me? Winburn? Finally tracked you down. Still teaching Science? I'm at Shore now.'

They exchanged pleasantries. Daniel was tempted to ask if he's had any luck with his curve formulas. Jules seemed eager to speak. 'Guess who I bumped into last Friday? Made me think of you. That red head girl, you know, the one that caused all the trouble for you. Well, she's cut her hair real short, working in a bar in Pitt St and going to uni. I tried to hit on her, guess what she said? *I remember you Mr Jackson, my maths teacher in year 9. Still touching girls up?* What a hide, especially after what she did to you. Can you believe it?'

The air escaped slowly from his lungs. He didn't know what to believe. Still, he was glad she'd turned her life around. 'Thanks for the info, Jules, but that's all in the past. I have a new life up here.' He thought about getting the address of the bar, then had second thoughts. 'Did you ask what she was doing at Uni?'

'Psychology. Imagine that, hey? Maybe we can catch up next time you're in Sydney?' Jules said.

'Maybe.' Daniel hung up, wondered why Jules had contacted him after so long, and the girl, studying psychology, how she'd changed her life and his. Only after their conversation, he realised he'd forgiven her. No consequences can ever camouflage the memories she'd live with.

The bell went. Martin, the History Master sat next to him.

'You know, Daniel, I've got some advice for you.'

'Okay, fire away,' he said without looking up.

'About history. It's all history, really. The important thing is how you explain it, what language you use. I'll explain – Metaphors are just a way of knowing, memories are just a way of feeling, but history... History is a combination of both told through broken glasses.' Daniel blinked. *Well, that's... profound. God knows what it means.* Martin saw the confused look on Daniel's face. 'It's about the story of both the living and the dead.'

'Well, thanks for that.' Daniel walked out the door, confident in his delusion he'd left the past behind.

*

In History class, he taught as if he lived it, role played it, fought in it, conspired with the Bolsheviks, fought with the French partisans against the Germans, ran with the Kuomintang to Formosa. He started with a quote: '*Those that fail to learn from history are doomed to repeat it.*' Does anyone know who said that?' He waited five heartbeats. Silence.

'It was Winston Churchill.' He scanned the room.

'What's it mean, sir?' a girl from the back asked.

'It means the terrible things that have happened in the past can occur again, unless we all become active and stop it.' He looked around. Most faces were perplexed, some were bored. This lesson was on WWII, the Nazi's occupation of Poland and the Holocaust. He lurched into facts, how many murdered, how many Jews, Gypsies, homosexuals, Soviet prisoners, the gas chambers, the crematoriums.

'My dad works in a crematorium,'– one boy volunteered – 'he's a funeral director.'

'Thanks for that, um, sorry, what's your name?' Daniel studied the boy.

'Thomas, sir. Everyone calls me Tom.' The boy smiled and looked around the room.

'Do you like that job your father does, Tom?'

'Nah, don't go there. Don't like the smell. It stinks when they burn.' He turned his nose up. Daniel scanned the room. The message was lost on the blank faces.

'Does anyone have personal stories about the war they'd like to share?'

A boy with greasy dark hair and piercing eyes raised his hand. His shirt, tie and shiny black shoes were immaculate, as if he'd just come out of a shop display window.

'Yes, Isaac. Go ahead.'

'My Grandad's Polish cousin, Jacob, was sent to Auschwitz. He was a mechanic before the war, so he was sent to work in the motor pool.'

'Go on.'

'He became friends with a German sergeant named Mayer. He survived the war and tried to keep in contact with the man.'

'Why would he want to do that?' Daniel said and tilted his head.

'Well, this guy – Mayer – helped him escape in a truck January 1945 after they left Auschwitz. They were on one of those death marches. Do you know about them, sir?'

'Yes, thousands were forced to march west towards Germany before the Russians arrived. Many died,' he said as his eyebrows lowered.

'Well, Jacob – my Grandad's cousin – was in the truck Sergeant Mayer was driving. As a mechanic, you know, to help if there was a breakdown. When they stopped the third night outside of Breslau, this Mayer guy hatched a plan to let Jacob escape. In the morning, he told his lieutenant that his truck was backfiring and he needed Jacob to look at it. Then he let him escape.'

'He sounds like a brave man.'

'After the war, Dad said Jacob tried to find Mayer's address to thank him but couldn't.' Kurt shrugged.

'What was his name again, this German sergeant?'

'Mayer, sir. Ulrich Mayer.'

Where have I heard that name? He thought. *Didn't Renate mention her father's name was Ulrich in the car back to Brisbane? It couldn't be the same person, could it? That would be an almost impossible coincidence.* He searched the faces looking for any sign of understanding or emotion. One girl dabbed her eyes with a white hanky. Two boys squirmed in their seats, one gazed at his wristwatch. Daniel's eyes rested on the face of a girl in the second row. She packed up her pens into her striped pencil case, picked up her bag and smiled as she left as if he'd just told a funny story.

45

Three weeks later he quit his job at the Co-op. He'd grown tired of the constant parade of single mums with restless toddlers and love-struck boyfriends in tow. Bec was not returning his calls, he couldn't believe it was over. Once he'd driven by her house. A different car was parked out front. Another week rolled by. After listening to endless songs about love and loss, Seals and Crofts, the Beatles, Chicago, he called Alice.

'Hello, this is Daniel, the fireman.'

*

He sat at the round, polished kitchen table with the white lace tablecloth. A present from a satisfied Japanese group, she'd told him. The photo of Gavin was gone, in its place, a picture of Alice in the middle of a group of Japanese with Australian and Japanese flags shouting something like *Banzai!* She cooked shepherd's pie and pasta. He opened a bottle of Margaret River Cabernet and poured two glasses. She downed hers in three gulps.

'Keep 'em coming, boyo, I need some more of that after today. Changed a flat tyre while the retirees complained in the bus.'

'What's happened to Gavin?' he asked nonchalantly.

She shook her head. 'Found some bimbo more into cars than me. Hmph. His loss.' She chatted incessantly, flitting from one frantic anecdote to another, the tourists who wanted her to explain who the three sisters were. 'Some Aboriginal myth or something,' she said, with a quizzical look. The Chinese who paid up-front with cash. 'Cash! Can you believe it?' The pushy Americans, lost without their 'sidearms' and asking directions to the nearest Walmart. And, of course, the neat Japanese with their order and politeness. Always on time. Daniel nodded and opened his mouth to reply as she lurched into the next topic. How the single mums lived arcadian-style on welfare, crowding the cafés on pension days with their *unruly brats*. 'Some even have terrible mohawks. Can you believe it?'

'They can't all be like that, surely?' He looked at her puzzled frown.

'Why? Do you know any that are not?' She stopped talking and looked at him. 'And where are their fathers? Probably working real jobs in Sydney, paying them child support. It's not right.'

'What part of it is 'not right', Alice?'

'You're not serious, are you? You pay taxes, I don't think we should support their lifestyle choices!' She grabbed the bottle and poured herself another. She looked across at Daniel, who shook his head.

She glared as if to say *drop it*. 'So, Daniel, tell me about your work, are your classes full of beautiful young women?'

He stared at her, lost for words. 'Mostly, yes, and all spoilt rotten with their privileged upbringing.'

'Do any of the girls try to hit on you?' She smiled, that little knowing smile, as his face turned red.

'No, it's mostly the boys, ha ha.' He chuckled.

She gave him a penetrating stare. 'Come on, Daniel, you're not like that, I can tell.'

'Can you? Is it that easy?'

'Of course. Don't you remember our last night in Darwin?'

'You can tell by that?'

'Of course! I am a woman, duh.' She gave another light chuckle and continued with certain gestalt that drove her relentlessly forward and woe to anything that stood in her way. 'But don't tell me you're not tempted, just a smidgen?'

'Look, I'm thirty-two. They're sixteen, seventeen, still children. I'd lose my job in an instant if I touched one of them the wrong way. You get that, don't you?' He wondered why it was so hard finding women with both intelligence and good looks. *They must exist?*

'If they complained,' she said. 'What if they want it?'

'What?' *Where's she going with this?* he thought. 'We all want it, but they're not going to get *it* from me.' Daniel laughed at Alice's scrunched up face.

She nodded. 'I'm glad that's settled.'

They moved to the dark-brown velvet couch in the lounge and bantered on as wine fired up their bodies. She excused herself to the loo and returned braless. Her hand crept up his arm in slow cat-like moves.

'Am I moving too fast for you, fireman?'

'I'll tell you after I kiss you. Before that, I need to know if you're safe. I don't want to get you pregnant.' He held her at arm's length.

She studied his face and smiled, 'Well don't you worry, fire boy, I've got that covered.' Her tongue darted in and out of his mouth like a honeyeater on heat. He slipped his hand under her blouse, ran his thumb and index finger over her nipple. Rubbed his palm over it, back and forth. He squeezed her breasts and tensed as her hand touched his erection.

'Wait here. I won't be long.'

*

She hastened into the bedroom and closed the door. In her mind, he was a rare catch – thoughtful, funny, a hard worker. *At least he's different from most of the other creeps I've met. I just have to convince him I'm on the pill.* She looked down at her wedding finger and imagined diamonds, lots of them there. In a minute, she stood silhouetted in the half open door, the golden light of the bedside lamp shining through her white lingerie. He panted, a fast, shallow breath that gripped his chest and increased the pressure in his pants. She turned side-on for effect. The light pierced the transparent material as if it wasn't there. Her finger signalled *come here*.

'Are you going to put my fire out?'

'Mmmm. I'll try.' He was beyond thinking as she sunk between his legs.

'Careful, I don't want to come in your mouth.' He panted.

'If you do, I own you.'

'What?' It perplexed him, what she meant. He couldn't compare it with making love with Bec. Alice was a machine. A wild animal. A snapping live wire. He didn't last long.

'That was quick, cowboy!'

'Sorry. Truly, must have been the wine.'

'Not my hot body? Daniel, I'm offended.' She feigned a look of hurt, laughed, then cupped his frowning face in her hands. Her hair dangled ribbons of gold on the blue pillowcase, shimmering and sparkling in the glow of the bedside lamp. He studied her face. Soft tiny hairs covered her cheeks, her eyes glimmered like pool surface reflections on a hardness, not like steel but a steadfastness of will. He wished this moment would last forever, suspended in time. Still, something bothered him. *Who's pulling the strings here? Have I already passed the point of no return? I don't want to be an add-on to this beautiful woman's cozy and predictable life. What the heck. I could do with the company.* He looked down at her breasts, a narrow space with a shadowed track of servitude between them.

'When can you go again?' she asked, with eyebrows raised.

'How about tomorrow morning?'

'See you then, cowboy. Don't worry, I'll wake you up.'

'How?' his smile widened.

'Wait and see.'

As his body relaxed and he closed his eyes, she whispered close to his ear, 'You're mine now.'

He dreamed he was giving a eulogy at a funeral. The girl was in an open coffin, one white rose resting on her chest. He couldn't remember her name as he stood over and studied her face. There were implants beneath the skin, in the mouth, to keep things in place. Suddenly the girl's eyes opened. She said, '*I expect you to do this now…*' Then: '*You will not betray me.*' He sat up straight in bed, breathing hard and fast. Alice jerked awake with a smile on her face. 'Glad you're awake. Let me help you get started.' Their lovemaking was businesslike, efficient, mechanical. Just before Alice came, he blinked and her face morphed into Renate's. He shook his head and closed his eyes. When he opened them, Alice stared at him, her mouth hung open loosely, eyes wide with excitement and pleasure. Afterwards, as she rested her head on his chest and twisted his pubic hairs with a detached insouciance, he wondered, *where did she come from?* But the question that nagged him was: *Where did she go?*

46

December 3, 1986

Two weeks before the end of the school year, the headmaster, Dr Rogers, called the staff to a meeting in the hall. 'What's up?' Daniel whispered to Jim Martin, standing beside him against the back wall.

'Shush. Something important.'

'I'll get straight to the point. On Sunday, police were alerted to a body below the Conservation Hut, just off the walking track to Empress Falls. The body has been identified as Michael Robinson, one of our Year 11 students. It appears that he committed suicide, but that is yet to be confirmed by the coroner.' He paused as a sharp gasp echoed around the hall. 'The police have asked me to provide them with the names of relevant staff who taught Michael who might be available for interviews. This will be voluntary.' His voice, a pallid monotony, devoid of emotion or sincerity, a cold steel file rasping away at the boy's sweet memory. 'I am awaiting instructions from the family as to the funeral arrangements and you will be notified in due course.'

Daniel stood there, incredulous, after the news filtered through the audience.

'I taught him in Year 7. He was such a quiet, lovely boy,' Jennifer, a casual, said, blowing her nose. 'And he wasn't like that, you know, 'deviant.' I heard some PE staff saying the other day.'

'I'll remember him differently – a sensitive, gentle soul.' Daniel said.

'What would cause him to take his own life, especially like that?'

'Intolerance? Being misunderstood? I guess now we'll never know.'

He waited until lunch to discuss the interviews with John Black, who just said, 'Don't worry yourself too much about it. Rogers is taking care of it.'

'I think I'll just call into Katoomba Police on my way home and give them a statement.' Daniel tapped his fingers on the desk.

'I wouldn't do that, if I were you, Daniel. You'd be wasting your time. Anyway, I heard that he had AIDS. So, I don't think the Police will be wasting their time either.' Black's face scrunched up. '

'That's just a nasty rumour, John. I'm still going to give them my statement.'

Daniel dwelled on the tragedy in class all afternoon. He wrote notes on the board, made the students write to take their minds off the fact that one of them was missing. He avoided John. The man gave him chills and an almost uncontrollable desire to throw his fists into something. He planned to take a few days off, sick leave. He couldn't stop thinking about his one and only decent conversation with Michael and the advice he'd given him. *It wasn't enough.* On the train home, he removed his coat, loosened his tie and stared out the window at shades of olive flashing by. He heard the screech and squeal of the train wheels. Smelled the acrid tang of brake pads. The sound of French fries crunched by a man across the aisle. When the train stopped at Leura, creosote from the sleepers wafted through the open doors. He looked up. A young woman pushed a toddler inside. She leaned against the glass divider, two dark eyes set in an entrancing face. He couldn't help but smile and when she looked at him, she blushed. He stood up and offered his seat. She pushed the stroller over and sat down. 'Where do I know you from?' Daniel said.

'That's a bit weak. Can't you do better than that?' She frowned and tilted her head.

'No, really, I've seen you somewhere. At the Food Co-op?'

'Yes, um, oh, you're that guy. I remember, you had some trouble with my order.' Her eyes sparkled.

'That was just my way of keeping you chatting longer.' He tried to smile, then held back remembering the news about Michael.

'Well, cats got your tongue? You don't look to happy to see me again?'

'No, sorry, its… not you. I heard some bad news today about a boy I knew.'

'Do you want to tell me about it?' she asked, looking up.

He looked away. 'Maybe some other time, if that's okay.' He didn't feel like sharing sad news with someone he just met. He looked away.

He looked at the child in the stroller and said, 'Here's my stop. Nice meeting you again.'

*

The police station had polished wooden floorboards, a short, black counter and a sliding glass window. The counter had a silver bell that was glued in place.

'Can I help you?' Squeaked a hoarse voice in a tight sergeant's uniform.

'Excuse me?' Daniel's forehead wrinkled as he licked his lips.

'Laryngitis,' – the sergeant reached for a glass of water – 'what's your problem?'

'Okay, look… I just want to give a statement about the boy who committed suicide.'

The oversized sergeant scrunched his eyes, trying to decide what to do next. 'Wait over there. I'll see who's available.' He walked through a back door, which banged shut. Daniel sat on a blue plastic chair against the wall, painted periwinkle, with police and NSW government logos in shades of lavender. The vinyl floor was in ultramarine except for the middle where boots trailed scuff marks across to the counter. A tall, dark-haired man in a dark-blue suit emerged from a side door and as he turned, his jacket opened.

A S&W Model 10 revolver in a brown leather holster was strapped under his armpit.

'You want to give a statement about the suicide,' he said, opening a blue note pad.

'Yes.'

'Come with me, please.' The detective was polite, nodded occasionally and jotted a couple of notes. Daniel told him about the bullying, how he'd warned Craig and Ivan and added: 'I didn't think Michael would take his own life.'

'Well, that's very helpful, Mr Cohen.' The detective closed his notepad and checked his wristwatch. He sighed, yawned and looked around the room. 'I'll pass on your details to Homicide. They'll add it to the list, I expect.' He fidgeted with his pen.

'Homicide? What list?' Daniel looked perplexed.

'They're handling the case now... They have experience in these sorts of crimes.'

'So, you're telling me it was *not* suicide?' Daniel said, jaw tight with rage.

'I can't give you any more details, Mr Cohen, except that in Sydney they have more pressing concerns than what happens to these kinds of people. As I said, Homicide is in charge. But I wouldn't waste my time trying to follow up with their investigation. They have more important cases to work on. Thanks for coming in.'

Daniel rang Alice as soon as he got home.

'Hey. I just found out that the police are treating Michael's death as a homicide.'

'Wow and *how are you, Alice?*'

'Oh, sorry, yes, I guess I'm worked up by the news,' Daniel said and fiddled with the phone cord.

'Do you want to come over and eat? I'm cooking a roast,' she said.

'Not sure if I can make it tonight, I've got lessons to prepare. Can I ring you back later?'

'Okay.' She sounded miffed.

He looked around his room at the books that defined who he was: *Biology, The Web of Life, Mila 18, Child of God.* On the wall above his desk, photos of a group hug on a mountain top in Townsville, Tomoko smiling outside the Peace Park Museum, Mum, Rachel and Daniel when he was about three at the beach, photographer unknown. *Was it Dad?* He tidied his room, made his bed. His mind drifted back – a straight road in central Australia, wind slipstreaming past his face, the open country laid out like flat corn bread and the sound of tyres swishing on the bitumen, galahs in swooping flocks and cackling black cockatoos. Laughing conversations that ebbed and flowed, the campfires and the bubbling stews in blackened pots. *Maybe there's a formula for those memories, are they just chemicals arranged in different ways, the pleasant ones feel warm, the sad ones, a cold, lingering ache?* The happy childhood he thought he'd had was just an illusion, a fleeting glimpse of innocence. There could be no formula for anything involving human interaction – *we are too complicated, it's not like finding the right formula for a calculus derivative problem, not even close.* He ran cold water over his face and stared at the books on the floor, texts opened, pictures spilling out, empty chip packets.

Can my life be described like this, a collection of photos fading on a wall, a list of memories that come and go like cars passing by outside? What did Renate say about birds? That they mate for life, like turtle doves. And what did Renate say about memories? Daniel struggled to remember. The thought was buried deep in there somewhere. He looked around and had a feeling that the empty house was listening, waiting for his next move. *Maybe Alice has the answer?* As he rose, he tripped over an opened textbook and kicked *The History of the Third Reich* under the bed.

He waited at the train station in the warm December air, western sky lit up like raw egg yolk, trying to make up his mind. He knew a night with

Alice was just three or four Bob Dylan songs away. *How did that song go? Relationships of ownership they whisper... something? What makes her think she owns me?* He traipsed back home, streets empty of tourists, café's closing down for the day, girls in white aprons moving stacks of chairs inside. He dragged the phone to his room.

'Hi Alice. Look, I'm still snowed under, sorry. How about I make it up to you on the weekend?'

'Let's go out to celebrate.'

'What are we celebrating?'

'Don't you remember? One year since we met, well, the second time. Or have you forgotten, ya doofus.'

'Oh no, of course not. How could I forget that?' he said twirling and untwirling the cord.

'Well, I'll take you to someplace special, you deserve that.'

'Okay. See you! I miss you,' he said.

'Love you!' she replied.

47

February, 1987

The Hydro Majestic loomed like a bizarre out-of-place spaceship. Daniel gawked at the dome, built in Chicago and shipped to Australia. *I bet they had fun getting that thing up here.* The building, a quirky eccentricity, was a cross between an Indian Palace and an English castle. Alice parked the car. They walked under the arched entrance and through the casino lobby.

'Why are we here, again?'

'It's our one-year anniversary. Remember? Paper.'

'Just *paper*? No words?'

'I'm waiting for those.'

Oops, the card.

They walked arm in arm under the Art Deco architecture to the Belgravia lounge past lush sofas and deep armchairs. All vacant. The place was almost empty, a far cry from the thronging partygoers of the 20s and 30s. Into a long, claret-coloured passage called Cat's Alley, the walls were adorned with violent images of Roman centurions impaling lions with bloody spears, charging goats and gladiators wielding head-chopping swords.

What sadist chose these? he said to himself.

She squeezed his hand and giggled. A huge, open fireplace dominated one wall of the Belgravia. An enormous window framed the Megalong

Valley below like a panorama painting.

'Incredible, isn't it?' she said.

He nodded.

'You can close your mouth now.'

A girl in a white apron carrying a note pad approached.

'Is Kate Campbell working tonight?'

'Sorry, I think she's on days off.'

'Okay thanks,' she turned to Daniel. 'She's the day manager here. My best friend.'

'Eating tonight? Can I suggest the baked duck breast? It's our speciality.'

'Thanks, but we'll just order drinks first. I'll have a beer.' said Daniel.

'I'll have a fire engine.'

'Fire engine, of course. With vodka?'

'Of course.' She guided them to a window table. Alice's lips tightened through a plastered-on smile.

'Why do you do that?' she asked, nodding at the departing girl.

'What?'

'I saw you checking her out.'

'Curious, just wondering what school she might be at.'

'Why? Do I need to be concerned?'

'Of course not, Alice. It's not always about you, it's just...' He tapped his fingers as the memory of Michael confiding in him at school came back. 'And what was so important you wanted to talk about?' he said.

'I've been thinking... I live by myself, so do you.'

'I share, actually.' He held his glass to his mouth, looked across at her face then put the glass down without drinking.

'Okay, share then. But I've got a big, old house, it needs plenty of work done, gardens, renovations, it would be nice to share it with someone I get along with.' She leaned forward in her chair.

'You mean me?'

'Yes, of course I mean you, silly. Why don't you move in? You can do maintenance and gardening in lieu of board. Isn't that a great idea?'

Daniel stared out the window, toying with the idea. He avoided her piercing eyes. For a split second her voice became an echo. In a backroom, perhaps the kitchen, a glass shattered.

'Look, Alice. I'm happy where I am right now. I'm no handyman, but I'll give it some serious thought, okay? Give me a week or two to think it over?' He looked at her intense gaze. She pressed her lips together and nodded. 'Okay?'

She took a deep breath. 'Then it'll be fun together, won't it?' Another deep breath. 'Renovating together. You've got one week.'

Outside, the blue-green coloured bush faded and crept into the distance. The valley blazed in an apricot haze. A bell tinkled.

'This place gives me the creeps. Can we eat somewhere else?' he said.

She drove back to Blackheath and parked the car outside her cottage. He turned around to face her.

'Where are we eating?'

'Let's walk up to Glenella. It's on the corner,' she opened her door and stepped out. 'I know the owner, James. He'll squeeze us in.' They walked hand in hand. She chatted about the first thing that popped into her head. He hummed, nodded and squeezed her hand. *I guess it's decision time. Am I ready for this? She must be serious.* He needed a drink.

'I'll stop and get a bottle of Cab Merlot. You okay with that?'

She nodded.

As they rang the doorbell, a tall man in his 40s grinned. 'Alice! You've come at last!'

'James!' They brushed cheeks. 'It's only been six months. I'd like you to meet my friend, Daniel.'

They shook hands. He waited on them personally, poured their wine, made them feel at home, talking with Alice like she was family. Daniel ordered something, didn't care what, more interested in drinking his mood away. She downed her first glass and poured herself another. Daniel sipped. They chatted back and forth. He liked the way they were interested in the same things, bush walking, history and travel. When he raised the issue of land rights and what he'd learned travelling to Darwin, she replied, 'Why can't they work for their houses like we have to?' He tried to explain the history, the dispossession, the Stolen Generation.

'Stolen what? How can you steal a generation?' She looked across at Daniel.

'The term has been around for a few years. It was an attempt by state governments to assimilate the Aboriginal race. Genocide, some believe.'

She stopped reading the menu and studied his face.

'They took Aboriginal children – mainly those of mixed race – from their families and sent them to training camps, separate ones for boys and girls – to train them as domestics for white families. Brothers and sisters were separated. Families broken up. The governments believed the Aboriginal race would then be assimilated and die out. They were wrong.' He tightened his grip on the glass and looked across. Her face had that look he remembered from kids in his class. She grimaced and tugged her right ear.

'That...doesn't concern me. Why should it? I'm not Aboriginal. And I don't see why it concerns you. Let me tell you about growing up. My big sister Sarah was the favourite one – top swimmer, great netballer and always first in class in most subjects at Loreto. Dad adored her. Then when she went to uni, she changed. Discovered she wasn't into boys. Dropped out. Went bumming around the bars doing odd jobs. Does that sound like me?' She was breathing hard now, hands became fists. 'So, I worked hard, did a tourism course, then business. Worked my way up through Daddy's company. And here I am. So, I don't have a 'bleeding heart' for those so-called less privileged than me. Does that clear things up about the *poor Aboriginals*? I mean...what's it got to do with us?' she glared across the table and took a large gulp of wine.

'You mean 'us' as a couple? Are we a couple?' Daniel searched her face. It was fixed with resolve.

'We could be. Just say the word.'

He thought about their differences. *Is it something I can live with?* 'Let's agree to disagree, okay?

'Okay. I can live with that. What are you going to order?' She smiled for the first time and held up her glass. The chink that followed sounded hollow. She looked down at the menu, hummed and looked back to his face. He blinked and she returned a puzzled frown.

'What?'

He was halfway gone as they walked back to her house.

48

They showered together, splashing water like they were kids sticking their tongues down each other's throats to see whose was the longest, wrapped an oversized beach towel around them and ran into the bedroom, dripping wet. Alice surprised him by combing his wet hair, then giving the brush to him. After, she fell asleep, curled up against his sweaty back. She'd stopped murmuring *you're mine now*. She expected it to be so. *He's like … what's that saying… an open book? So easy to read. I'm everything he needs.*

*

In the morning, after they'd exhausted themselves again and mulling over her offer to move in, the words of a song Rachel used to listen to in the 70s popped up, about making love until their strength is gone.

'Hey, do you remember a song from the seventies about making love,' he called out as he dressed, 'I think it's called *The Pretender*?'

'Nope, before my time,' she said, humming in the kitchen. 'I'm free today. How about we go for a walk?'

'Only if it's easy. I'm afraid you've worn me out.' He rolled out of bed and smiled.

'Again? No! I never! Pope's Glen is a nice easy one.'

'Something else I've been wondering. You are using protection, right?'

'Like sunscreen?' She froze, egg flipper in mid-air. Her eyebrows scrunched together.

'No, silly, you know what I mean.'

'Contraception? I thought we discussed this. Of course, I'm not stupid, Daniel. The last thing I need is to end up like all those other single mums up here.' She huffed as she emphasised *other single mums.*

'Happy, now that that's settled?' Her lips tightened as she threw eggs onto the second plate.

'Okay. Look Alice. I'm sorry, I guess I don't want any surprises, you know...'

'No surprises? Hell, I'm full of surprises? Maybe I'm the wrong woman for you?' She turned, the flipper clanged as it fell into the pan.

'No, no, it's just that...' He started with a small voice. He began to tap.

'What? You don't trust me?' she said, her mouth frozen open.

'Trust? Is that what you call it?'

'Well, what do *you* call it *Mr Science Teacher*?' She winced. Her hand trembled.

He was silent for a while. 'Come here. Of course, I trust you. Always. And you know you can trust me. Just one other thing – what do you want to do with your life?' he asked.

'Like now, or tomorrow?' She tilted her head at him and pulled the chair out. It squealed on the timber floor.

'I mean for the next ten years or so.'

'You know, more of this.' She made a wide sweep with her arm. 'Take over the business, buy another house, have two kids. How about you?' She held the fork in front of her mouth and gazed into his eyes. Daniel stared back past Alice, eyes focused on the garden outside. He sighed and said, 'I'm... not sure... I haven't yet figured that out.'

She clenched her jaw. 'So I won't bother holding my breath?'

That night, at his desk in his room, his books were open, the bed unmade, when there came a quiet knock on his door. He kicks a textbook out of the way. The door creaked open.

'Look, mate. Real estate just told me that the owners are putting the house up for sale,' Ray says.

'Oh, like when?' Daniel looks up.

'Now. They've given us six weeks. Angie and I are looking at a smaller flat in Lurline Street but it's just for the two of us.'

'Oh… I like living here with you guys.' He gave a sad smile and rests his chin on a hand. Thanks for the notice. I'll start looking soon.'

Daniel flopped down in his chair, toying with the idea of moving in with Alice. He closed his eyes. Images flicked by – Alice's long hair on the pillow, her laugh, her quick wit. Then another. A different woman, one with eyes he could fall into like magnetic iron filings. His body softened. He shook his head and sighed.

The phone rang.

'Daniel, it's for you.'

'Mum's in hospital. They suspect a stroke. She's been asking for you.' Rachel paused – 'when can you come?'

'I'll be there tomorrow.'

49

Daniel tried the door handle. It turned and he pushed his way out of the thick February air. He called out, 'You there, Rach?'

'In the kitchen.'

She cooked eggs in a black skillet for breakfast. 'You want bacon? Too bad, there's none.' She slammed the eggbeater down on the bench and hefted the skillet off the stove. 'Why didn't you come back home when you found out Mum was sick?'

'I... I couldn't. Remember, I was just about to get on a plane to Japan,' he stammered.

She gave him a withering look. 'And that crusade you were on? Was it more important than your own mother?' She flicked two pieces of toast on two plates.

'You have no idea, Rach, your life has always been so... perfect, so predictable.' He sat down at the table and leaned forward. Her face reddened.

'Don't talk to me about perfect. Skyla was perfect, until you hooked up with that schoolgirl.'

'Hey, I never! Nothing happened! Nothing. She came on to me. I was just trying to help her. Anyway, I was vindicated.'

'Well, why did you run?' she said, walking to the table and pulling out a chair. 'Made you look guilty.'

'I needed some space, to find out what's important to me in life. I think I found it in Brisbane.' He was thinking about Renate, and the time they had together.

'Well, why aren't you there?' – Rachel rolled her eyes – 'don't tell me, she dropped you, whoever she was?' She grabbed her plate and walked out the side door to the patio. He stared at the yolk on the plate. He had no appetite for this. *Shit, not even my sister believes me.* He swallowed and yelled out, 'I'm seeing someone. I'm thinking of moving in with her.'

'Great. Fucking fantastic. I can't wait. Just don't fuck her life up like Dad did ours.'

'Dad had problems, he...'

'And don't bother trying to defend him. You're wasting your time. You always were his favourite. Now I'm left to pick up the pieces of Mum's broken life.'

'I can help. I can...'

'No. You can't, Daniel. You have your own precious life to live in your idyllic Blue Mountains.' She looked down at her watch. 'Anyway, we can't go until ten. You've got two hours to read a book or do whatever you do to pass the time.' She slammed the door.

*

A stout nurse in an over-starched white uniform ushered them down pale-blue labyrinthine passageways. At every turn, the smell of pungent disinfectant itched his nose. They reached a private room with a label '*Mrs Cohen*' attached to the door.

A figure lay stick-like, skinny arms punctured with IVs full of amber-coloured liquids. An oxygen mask hissed. Rachel covered her mouth with her hand. Daniel grabbed the chair next to the bed and gave his mum a gentle hug.

'Be careful of those tubes,' Rachel said. Helen had dyed her hair purple, except for a broad stripe that was bright yellow. Her skin was ashen, face lopsided and palsied.

'What's with the hair, Mum?' Rachel asked.

'If I'm going out, I'm going in style. I've always wanted to look like a unicorn. Doctors said I can go home soon.'

Daniel looked across at Rachel who shook her head faintly.

'Great news, Mum.'

'Will you be there, Dan?'

He hesitated for a second, avoiding Rachel's eyes. 'Can't Mum. I'm teaching in the Blue Mountains. Did you forget? I can come see you on the weekends, Rachel will be here.'

Rachel held his gaze, unable to hide the anger smouldering there. She pulled over a blue armchair and sat at the end of the bed. He shrugged, picked up Helen's hand and closed his fingers.

'Tell me about Dad again, Mum. Why did he leave?' he said.

'Daniel!' Rachel made a strangled noise. He ignored her. Helen's eyes flicked from Daniel to Rachel, not knowing where to rest. She coughed a feeble noise and reached across for the oxygen mask sucking in three shallow puffs.

'It's all a bit foggy now, sorry. I'll tell you what I can remember' – her eyes sunk as if she was looking for a piece of paper or a book – 'Ian was unhappy. At me, your education by the nuns, Catholics. He hated the bishop, said it was all '*hypocrisy*'. When he started coming home later and later, I knew then. He wouldn't tell me her name. I could always handle the truth, but he denied me that. It all just built up until one day he was gone.'

'How could he just leave us like that, Mum? You never explained why.'

Helen frowned for a moment at Daniel's remark, then continued. 'In other ways he was honourable. You know he supported you through uni. He was always generous. He just... He just needed to be free of us. I guess he just stopped loving us.'

The word consumed him – *love – is it possible to love someone at first sight? I don't think so, not until time has confirmed the initial attraction* – love, a concept that binds couples together – *is it just an illusion projected on a transparent screen that is your day-to-day life*? 'I've found a girl I think I love, Mum. She's asked me to move in with her.'

'That's nice, Dan. Is she Catholic?'

'Yes Mum.'

'That's nice.' Helen looked at him intently and coughed into a tissue. Daniel looked away, not wanting to see the red stain spreading.

'Mum, tell me a story.'

'That's a strange thing to ask.' She coughed again, a hacking, bitter sound, like gears grinding and reached for the oxygen mask. It clattered off the trolley. 'A story. About a magic unicorn. The Inuit of northern Canada used to trade the narwhale tusks as unicorn horns. Said they were magic. You know I've always wanted to be a unicorn.' She ran her free hand through her hair, stopped and stared up at Daniel.

'So I see. I do like your hair, Mum. I've heard that story a few years back when I was on the bike ride.'

'Who told you?'

'A German girl in Brisbane. We were...close.'

'Was she Catholic?'

'I don't think it matters now, Mum, she was just a very nice person.'

'I'm a bit tired now. Can you find a magic cure for me, Danny?'

'I'll try, Mum.' Daniel looked over at Rachel, who nodded. *Time to go.* He kissed his mum on the cheek and whispered, 'Goodbye. Love you Mum.'

He walked out the door. It was like he'd walked into a vacuum that swallowed him and sucked away all the love he'd known. He stopped and tilted his head, listening to notes on a violin. It was only the sound of crockery clattering on the lunch trolley as it rumbled down the corridor.

50

Alice returned from the hairdressers wearing the heart-shaped earrings her sister Sarah had given her on her last birthday. Her hair – an elegant updo that Krystal, her hairdresser, had suggested. She spent the next hour doing her makeup in front of the dresser mirror, *lipstick? Cherry red? Not modern enough. Burgundy? Yes!* She studied herself in the mirror, pouted her lips, lifted and dropped her breasts. She tried on three pairs of jeans, chose the pair least faded, a crisp white Levi's T-shirt and considered the lace bra or the uplift. *Better uplift.* She laced on her white Reeboks.

Kate and Ben arrived in his fancy company car. When Kate stepped out, she looked around as if expecting someone. She was tall, confident, braless in a tight white top that revealed a tanned midriff. Her eyes – flirty, slip-sliding, calculating. She owned the adjective *vivacious.* Ben, more of your jejune type, wore pressed bone slacks over brown RM Williams boots, beaming his natural *trust me* look. As they walked in, Alice whispered to Kate, 'Sarah and Ebony are inside. Be nice to them.'

They tiptoed through the hall into the lounge room past Sarah and Ebony, who were locked in an embrace, oblivious to the rest of the universe.

'Hi, you two,' Kate said.

Alice opened a bottle of Great Western Champagne and poured three glasses.

'What are we celebrating?' Kate asked, studying the bubbles surging in her glass.

'Come outside and I'll tell you.' Alice held open the back screen door to a deep green veranda. A thin concrete path led up to a Hills Hoist, leaning at angle as if bracing against a ferocious storm. Alice complained about how little time she had to spruce the place up, Ben nodded and said, 'I can give you some names if you're ever thinking of selling?'

'Thanks for doing the cooking, Ben. Kate and I have some girl business to discuss.' She handed him a bucket of tools, rags, sprays and sponges nodding at the dusty BBQ. He stared with an open mouth. It was a rare moment when he was lost for words.

They wandered up the path to a wooden settee that squeaked each time it rocked.

'Well, where is he?' Kate asked. 'I'm dying to meet him.'

'He's down in Sydney. His mum is sick in hospital.'

'So, what's he like?' Kate said, taking a long sip from her frosty glass.

'He's a teacher at the Grammar. We met in Darwin when he was on some protest bike ride, something to do with uranium. We only had one night together, if you know what I mean.'

'Alice, that doesn't sound like you,' she said, wrinkling her forehead.

'Seriously, I think he's the one.' Alice took a hurried gulp. She walked back inside, grabbed the champagne bottle, peeked at Sarah and Ebony, still locked together on the couch and returned to the swing seat. Kate held out her glass.

'Alice. Wow... Really? How can you be so sure he's *the one*? He doesn't sound like your type.'

'I've changed him. Though he still thinks the Aboriginals are hard done by. I mean, really?'

Kate held her breath, mouth frozen open.

'And he's great in bed, does anything I ask.'

'Anything?' Kate's mouth let out a fugacious squeak.

'He's a good worker, reliable, without the hang-ups he had when I met him.'

'Like what *hang-ups*?' Kate tilted her head at a sharp angle.

'He wouldn't stop talking about a chick called Bec. You know the type? Single mum with two kids. One of them came into the office last week pushing a brat with a mohawk, can you believe it?'

'What did she want?' Kate stared, eyes widened.

'Wanted to know if there were any 'easy walks' around Katoomba. I told her go over the road to the café, that's an easy walk.'

'Yikes! Why would he want to get hung up over a single mum with two kids?' she said, her mouth still hanging open. 'Maybe he's ready to settle down? Or she's hot in bed. Did he elaborate?'

'C'mon, he's not that vulgar. He's...decent.' Alice drew out the last word.

'Do you trust him?' Kate inched her body around to face Alice and watched her intently.

'Absolutely. He's mine.' Alice's mouth widened and her eyes sparkled.

Sarah yelled out from the veranda. 'You got any Tab or Tarino?'

'No. Only lemonade. If you want anything fancy, the bottle shop is open.'

'Hey before you go, can we talk about Mum and Dad?' Alice said, watching as Ebony hung back behind the screen door. 'What about them?'

'I've invited them up for Easter Sunday dinner. You coming?'

'Oh, I don't know, Alice,' Sarah said, her face fell. 'You know they don't approve of us.' Her lips pouted down.

'Maybe that's telling you something, Sarah. Your lifestyle, your butch haircut, your clubbing,' Alice replied in her big sister voice.

'Stuff them. It's my life. If they don't approve of who I'm seeing, too bad. I won't see them.'

'Well, you can't ignore them forever. They are buying a new place in Pymble, did you know? They'll want us all to see it. They expect us to come and gush over it.'

'Don't talk to me about Dad and his houses. You know we don't like rich people, do we, Eb?'

Ebony shrugged and nodded.

'Well, at least think about it. Mum's a bit softer about these things than Dad. She misses you, Sarah.'

'They should have thought about that before they snubbed my last partner.'

Alice's lips tightened. *That one. She didn't last long. At least I don't have to worry.* Alice locked the door. She closed her eyes. A vague unease like a chill swept across her chest and down her arms, strong enough to make her shake out her fingers. *Where did that come from? It couldn't have anything to do with Daniel, could it?*

51

Two weeks later, at his desk in the staffroom, John handed him a note: *Ring your sister urgently.* He already knew before he dialled the number.

'Rachel, it's me.'

'Mum's gone, Dan. This morning at ten. I was there. The last thing she whispered was '*Where's my boy?*''

He paused, unsure of what to say. 'I'm sorry I wasn't there. I'll come down now, give me an hour to pack.'

'You don't need to hurry anymore.'

He heard a click down the line.

The westerly picked up as he plodded down Falls Road towards his new house in Wentworth Falls. The noise of the wind whistled through the pines, the black cockatoos screeched and cackled, the occasional pinecone thumped. There was something melancholic about the place, it nurtured an atmosphere of loneliness like an abandoned haunted house holds onto it's past – his mood amplified by the loss of his mother. Daydreaming over past childhood memories as if they were comfort blankets – his mother, and how he'd miss her, even Renate, how at times like these he'd love to be with her sharing his feelings. *That's all in the past now. This is my life now.* He went straight to his room, packed pjs, a toothbrush, spare clothes and a book he'd recently bought at Mr Pickwicks, *The Bluest Eye* by Toni Morrison. He boiled the jug and rang Alice at work.

'Hi Alice. It's me.'

'Hi. What's up? I'm with someone right now. Can I ring you back in ten?'

'Sure. But it's Mum. She died today.'

Silence, then: 'Oh, hell, I'll call you back in five.'

He sat on the bed next to the phone, staring at the faded cream walls, then out the window across the lawn to a row of pencil pines. Next to his bed was a photo of him and Rachel as kids with their smiling mother. The background blurred. He held the photo between his fingers and rubbed as if it was Aladdin's Lamp, wanting it to release a formula to bring the happy memory back to life. He closed his eyes, lost track of time. *The bike ride. What was that? A pointless adventure? Just what did I achieve? Renate. I met Renate. And now? Am I ready to settle down with someone like Alice and her small-minded views about Aboriginal history? Am I in too deep? Well, at least I'm free to decide.*

The phone rang. Alice.

'Daniel. Are you okay? What's happened?'

'Rachel just told me Mum died at ten this morning. I'm catching the four pm train down.'

'Can I help? Do you know when the funeral is?'

'No, but I'll be in touch. I promise.'

'Love you.'

'You, too.'

He started reading *The Bluest Eye* by Toni Morrison as the train wound its way down the mountain. After skipping the opening jumble of words heaped together like a child's poor grammar, he went back to the start and read again to see if he'd missed anything significant. He stopped at two lines that had been underlined in pencil: *morning glory blue eyes,* followed by, *each night, without fail, she prayed for blue eyes.* He closed the book. *Why would a poor black girl pray for blue eyes? Why pray for something impossible? Maybe that's it, isn't it?* It was like he was speaking to a friend sitting next to him. *Is that what makes this all worthwhile? The freedom to choose, even if it is impossible?*

*

Daniel saw Rachel's red eyes vacant over a cup of coffee. He stood in the doorway for a second, walked over and hugged her as she erupted into sobs. 'Sorry, I'm sorry I couldn't be there when she passed.' It took a while holding her for her grip to slacken and her breathing returned to normal. She held him at arm's length and said: 'How long can you stay?'

'Not all week. Maybe till Tuesday if you need me. They'll let me take more time if I ask.'

'Of course I need you. You owe me at least that time. James is away doing his prac. He's hoping to make it to the funeral.'

'Do you know when it might be?' Daniel squeezed her hand then let go and studied Rachel's face.

'They're trying for Friday. We won't know for sure until tomorrow.'

'So, we can talk now. How have things been for you these last couple of years? I'm sorry I haven't been more involved in your life lately.' He took a step back. Rachel talked about James and his service at the synagogue, how devout he was – how much the girls love him – how she's studying the faith and is considering converting. 'It'll make it easier as the girls grow up if we are all Jewish.' Daniel nodded. 'Tell me about Mum and Dad.'

They ordered pizza and searched the pantry for anything alcoholic. Daniel found two bottles of ancient cider and a half bottle of sweet sherry which he tipped down the sink. They sat there sipping raspberry cordials and chatted like long-lost friends. And for the first time in years, he thought there was hope, hope she'd see him like a brother again, not as a child sex offender.

Later, sometime after midnight when the traffic's snarl had withered, he lay on his bed listening to the empty silence. Another soul had departed and left him behind, contemplating his life. In the kitchen, the wall clock counted down with each drip from the leaking tap. He thought about faith, why some people took it seriously and why he couldn't. *I have faith that everything will work out for the best. That's all I can hope for. If I was to pray for something impossible, what would that be?*

52

On Thursday afternoon, the day before the funeral, Alice and Daniel drove down to Randwick, collected Rachel and shopped for the wake. Ian, Daniel's dad, was overseas somewhere out of contact.

'I'm glad he won't be here tomorrow,' Rachel said.

'I wish he was here, so I could look him in the eye.' he said.

'Wouldn't change anything. That's all in the past. I feel like he doesn't exist anymore.' She tensed her jaw and tightened her lips. Alice, lost for words, stared at Daniel, then Rachel, then back at Daniel, and said, 'I've never been to a funeral before. What am I supposed to wear?'

Outside the church, the funeral directors handed out programs as Father Chris's orthodox black chasuble gathered between his legs. James and Daniel shook hands while Skyla hugged Rachel. Skyla's partner, Matt, stood apart, tugging at his pinched-tight collar.

They sat in the front pew while Father Chris shuffled his notes and adjusted his prayer book. Rachel held Daniel's left hand so tight that the tips of his fingers turned white. A tall man in the dark-blue suit sat at the back of the church, alone.

After the funeral, the tall man slipped outside and stood apart from the emerging crowd. He walked over to Daniel.

'Hi. You must be Daniel.'

He nodded. 'And you are?'

'I'm Jim Sanderson. I was a good friend of your father.' He held out his arm and Daniel gripped his hand.' His head jerked back.

'Was? What do you mean?'

'He died four months ago. The doctors at Whittington hospital said he'd had a massive aneurysm. He said he was feeling breathless for a while. He must have known his time was up because before he died he asked me to give you this.'

Daniel stared as the man handed over a white envelope. The mourners were standing around in groups. Rachel, Alice and Skyla huddled in a group on the other side of the church.

'What's this?' He looked down at the thick envelope and turned it over in his hands.

'The Cohen family ancestry. At least your side of the Cohen's. Ian wanted you to know where Henry Cohen's family came from. That's your...'

'Yes, I know. My great, great, great grandfather,' Daniel said abruptly.

'Ian asked me to come and give you this. He said Helen would not be interested.'

'She was Catholic,' – Daniel looked around – 'as you can see.'

'Ian was very determined to rediscover his Jewish ancestors. Tracked Henry's grandparents down to Germany. Then he just...ran out of time.' Jim pulled a packet of Camels from his pocket and offered Daniel one. Daniel shook his head and said, 'Don't we always.'

'Pardon?'

'Run out of time. Sorry, I was being...sarcastic.' Daniel tapped the envelope in his hand.

'Why do you say that?' Jim tilted his head.

'He was never here for us kids. Never practiced his faith, as far as I know, didn't support Mum either. But I thank you, Mr Sanderson, for bothering to come to the funeral.'

'I'm sorry I was late. Did you know he planned to come back at Easter?'

'That's too bad.' Daniel's eyes slid down to his shoes then peered over to Alice, who had broken away from Rachel's group. Alice wandered over, awkwardly pulling at her tight black dress, a size too small. Her high heels dug into the soft soil. She smiled, gave Daniel a quizzical look and grabbed his hand.

'Alice, meet Jim, he was a friend of Dad's.'

Alice offered a deferential smile.

'Well, I'll be going,' Jim said. 'Do you think I should introduce myself to Rachel?'

'No. Talking about dad now isn't the right time. I'll explain everything. But before you go, where is Dad buried?'

'In Highgate Cemetery, London. Jewish section.'

'Okay. Thanks again for...this.' Daniel shook his hand and walked over to Rachel. 'Time to clean up.'

As they tidied up in the back room, Rachel turned to Daniel. 'Who was that man you were talking to outside the church?'

'A Mr Jim Sanderson. Ever heard of him?'

'No, why? Should I?'

'He was a close friend of Dad's, apparently. He told me that Dad died a few months ago in England. He gave me this.'

'What is it?' Rachel said, more interested in the note than in her dead father.

'Cohen family history?'

Rachel stiffened, her arms hung straight at her side. She looked at the envelope and crunched her eyes. She turned and walked away. 'I'm not interested,' she said through tight lips.

'Well, I'm interested in Dad's side of the family. This,' – holding out the envelope – 'has come from London and I'm keen to see what it says,' Daniel said.

'It'll take some time before I'm ready for that. I still haven't forgiven him for what he did to us. I'm surprised you have.' He saw a tightness in her eyes before she turned and walked away.

*

Around 9 pm, Alice dropped Daniel back at his house in Wentworth Falls. She planted a soft kiss on his lips and looked back and forth between him and the dark house, silhouetted in the half-moon. 'Looks a bit bleak. Are you sure you want to live here?'

'It's...convenient.'

'Well, the offer at my place is still open, you know that, right?' She opened the door and walked around to his side.

'Thanks. Give me a few days to get over this and I'll let you know.'

Later, he lay on his bed staring at the ceiling. *Dad, why didn't you contact us? Why did you leave it till the end to seek out your Jewish past? And our German ancestors? How important is that?*

53

Two weeks later, a month out from Easter, Daniel packed his clothes, sheets and books and moved to Alice's. It was time he committed. *I'm tired of drifting through life as if it was only a series of events and contributing nothing of value.* It was time for more order – predictable, substantial, romantic order. In his mind, he'd planned it all out. He'd come home from work, clean up the house, wash the dishes from breakfast, take Snuffy for a walk, prepare dinner. She'd come home, storm through the house like a tornado. She'd talk non-stop about her day, the tourists, the single mums with their strollers, *the terrible clothes they wore.* Daniel would nod and agree, because it was easier than arguing.

Friday – the regular drinks with Ben and Kate. Ben's news about house prices on the way up and terrible renters *'They left the place in such a pigsty.'* Kate's gossip from the Hydro (*'Did you know so and so was gay?'* – *'No, I never!'* – *'Yes, I saw a young male sneaking out of his room this morning holding his shoes.'* – *'No!'* – *'Yes. Tiptoeing.'* – *'Wicked! Really?'*) On cue, Kate and Alice pulled faces and laughed.

Is it any of your business? He thought. And Michael, the suicide – *was it homicide?* He hadn't heard any updates on the investigation, which confirmed what the police had told him in the police station. Still, those events were a million miles from his life now. Daniel was submerged in Alice's world – and

Kate, he noticed the way she tossed her head back and how her face exploded in laughter, how she ended most sentences with *wicked* as if she thought they might misunderstand her. The way she pursed her lips. *She must know how good that looks on her.* In that way, she was just like Bec.

'I bet you get that all the time, Kate. Got any other juicy ones?' he said.

Kate smiled and mouthed *wicked* as she excused herself. 'We won't be long boys.' Outside, Kate pulled Alice in close and looked around. 'So, have you fixed the date?'

'Oh, that. He hasn't said anything yet,' Alice replied, topping up Snuffy's water bowl.

'Why don't you, like, persuade him?'

'How?' Alice studied the wry smile creeping across Kate's lips. 'You don't mean...no! I couldn't do that.'

'Why not? He won't know. Anyway, what's his problem?'

'He's just got stuff to work through, family stuff. He doesn't like to talk about it.'

'That's a worry. Are you sure you trust him? You're not getting any younger, you know.' Kate touched Alice's hand. 'Whatever you do, I'd be careful with him.' There was an edge in her voice, no mistaking the warning, blunt as a broken bottle. Alice walked back to Daniel and squeezed his hand.

'Watch out for Kate,' she whispered.

'Why?'

'I think she fancies you.' She grimaced.

'Oh, that's...*wicked*, but don't worry. She's not my type.' Daniel smiled.

Alice had a ready-made answer for everything. Why they only made love on the weekends. *'I like taking my time and waking up on lazy Sundays and doing it all again.'* How she wanted two kids, a boy and a girl: *'One for me and one for you, I'll take time off, Daddy won't mind.'* How she'd be ready next year. *'When I'm thirty, in spring, it'll be perfect.'*

Daniel smiled and nodded.

'Remember next weekend, Ben and Kate are coming over for lunch. Dad and Mum said they'd come up too.'

Smile. Nod. 'Are they staying here?'

'No, silly. Glenella, of course. Dad's looking forward to meeting you at last.'

*

Next Saturday, they lingered in bed, Alice's arm limp across Daniel's chest, the sunlight streamed under the blind, laser-like on their faces.

'God that's bright. Any brighter and I might need my sunglasses.' Daniel edged to the side of the bed and stood up.

Alice propped herself up on one elbow. 'Wait... You were calling her name out again last night.'

'Whose name?' He turned around fast to see her face. It was glowing in the sunlight.

'Bec. Twice. I counted.' Her nostrils flared.

'Oh. Can't say I remember,' he said, licking his lips.

'What's with that woman? Was she better in bed? What did she do that I don't?'

'No, nothing like that, it's just, I guess she must have gotten into my head.'

'Well, I suggest you get her out of your head and soon, if you want this,' – Alice swept the room with her arm – 'to work.' She stared long enough to make her point, slipped on her light-blue dressing gown and stormed into the kitchen. She placed her hands on the benchtop, searching for a word that strangled somewhere between shallow and vacuous. The word was 'one-dimensional'.

*

Left alone in peace, Daniel touched the cover of a new book *A Brief History of Time* but didn't open it. Alice showed him a predictable world, comfortable, ordered. *I'd be a fool not to want that. Wouldn't I? And my marriage to Renate? How am I going to explain that little complication?*

54

Easter Saturday, 1987

Ben and Kate arrived promptly at twelve, Ben in a Wallabies jersey, Kate in long, dark slacks and a tight white tee. She tossed her head back, pecked Alice on the cheek. Daniel was outside, scrubbing the BBQ.

'What time will I start cooking, hon?' he said.

'When Mum and Dad get here.'

Kate and Alice gossiped, Daniel and Ben nodded in time. Daniel's eyes glazed over when Ben started on golf. He was aware of Kate's pheromones as just another nuclear weapon coming Ben's way, mouth frozen open. *He's got no chance.* Alice elbowed him in the ribs. Kate broke into tinkling laughter.

'Why, Daniel, I can see you're licking your lips. Have you tasted something nice?'

He smiled and replied, 'Not yet.'

'Wicked!'

Kate wore her tight white tee for effect, an effortless sexual abandon. Daniel watched as she played Ben like modelling clay – her voice, the timbre, smoky and smooth, the pitch and inflections, how she alternated her words between brittle and soft, running loops around him. She turned her face a little to see his reaction, his doe eyes, his head slumped like warm butter. The way she arched her shoulders back, taut muscles boosting her breasts. *Did she practice at night in front of a mirror, before she went to bed, or did it just come naturally?* It was a question without an answer, a rhetorical conundrum. By now, he was almost jealous of their lives, the predictable way they followed the script. It was, he now understood, a fake jealousy, a jealousy that circled at the periphery. An outsider's perspective for players who did not understand the rules. He'd caught Alice practising sometimes, surreptitiously, up on one elbow in bed, neck arched, studying her pose in the dresser mirror. He was almost hypnotised by her. In the end, it was easier just to surrender. He heard a voice call out 'Hello?' through the open door.

'Out the back, Dad.'

Daniel and Ben rose and shook hands with Bill, Alice's father. He was sixtyish, neat, grey hair swept back. Her mum, Margaret, face lined with experience, hovered behind him.

'Glad to finally meet you, Daniel.' Bill pumped his hand in a vice-like grip.

'And you, Mr Taylor.'

'Oh no, please call me Bill.'

Daniel excused himself to the BBQ. Bill and Ben followed him outside. He overheard some of their conversation – the latest trends in real estate and golf clubs. 'Might be a good place to invest in,' Ben said. 'This area hasn't taken off yet.'

'I think I'll stick to Sydney. We're about to move into a new place in West Pymble, did you know? Almost an acre of green, plenty of room for the grandkids to run around.'

Daniel heard snippets of the conversation, aware that Alice and Margaret were discussing something in hushed tones. They nodded, Alice said, 'Well, I'm sorry to disappoint you, Mum. I'm stopping at two.'

Over lunch, Daniel's eyes wandered from face to face – the intense, calculating Bill, the quiet, thoughtful Margaret, carefree Alice, scandalous Kate. Bill sat directly opposite Daniel. He stopped chewing a corned beef sandwich, cleared his throat and looked at Daniel.

'So, Daniel. Tell me about the Grammar.'

'Oh, it's a good school, kids are well-behaved.' Daniel morphed into teacher mode.

'Do you see your future there, or would you like to branch out?' Bill's eyes bored into Daniel.

'How do you mean?'

'Well, teacher's renumeration's a bit thin, don't you think?'

'It's...reasonable.'

'And Alice tells me you have another job on Saturdays?'

'Oh that, no... I quit a few months ago.'

'Why?'

'I moved on.' Daniel tilted his glass as if inspecting a priceless Château Lafite Rothschild. He excused himself and walked to the kitchen. Alice poured two wines. She swayed on her feet.

'You okay?'

'Yes, why?' She clinked the glasses together.

'You're a bit unsteady there. Your father, he's a bit intense.'

'He's always like that. That's how he got to be where he is. You have a problem with that?'

Daniel stared and said nothing. He made polite small talk for the rest of the afternoon and counted down the minutes on the wall clock. He overheard parts of conversation: 'That know-it-all Hawke.' – 'That smart alec Keating.'

He'd had enough. "This is the one that brings home the bacon." he said.

Alice and Bill turned and stared at him.

'Keating said that last week in parliament. I like a politician who speaks in metaphors.' The joke fell flat on ears. 'Well, I might start the washing up. If you would excuse me.'

*

After the guests had left, Alice and Daniel sat on the couch in the lounge room and finished off a bottle of Riesling. Snuffy slept under Alice's feet, Daniel studied the TV guide. Outside lightning flashed and thunder boomed.

'Sounds like a big one coming.'

'We'd better go check the windows.' She grew unusually quiet.

'I'll do it.' He returned and said: 'What do you want to watch?'

'*Home and Away.*'

'Do we have to?'

'No, not if you don't want to. Mum and Dad like you.'

'Did they say anything?'

'Mum likes how you know your way around the kitchen. Dad said your comments about Keating were strange,' she said, dropping the TV guide on the table. 'He's always voted Liberal, so have I.'

'Why? I think Keating's a very capable politician. Hard working, speaks his mind, even uses humour to effect.'

'I've never really been interested in that, you know.'

'What about your Mum? How does she vote?'

'She doesn't talk about that.'

'Okay. Well, I like her. She's got a very calm nature.' He took her hand and stroked her knuckles. She turned up the volume.

'Do you think she'll have blonde hair?' she asked, staring at the screen.

'Who?'

'Our daughter, silly.'

Daniel licked his lips. *She's keen to have children... I hope my marriage of convenience to Renate won't be a problem. Why is it so difficult telling her?*

'Probably, just like you.'

She smiled, satisfied with his answer and switched to *Home and Away.*

Daniel retreated to the bedroom to read his new book, *A Brief History of Time*. Daniel was curious if Hawking had any clues about the future. *'The increase of disorder or entropy is what distinguishes the past from the future, giving direction to time.'* Right now, Daniel had no idea how much entropy was waiting, just around the corner.

55

Christmas, 1987

Alice set a table for ten, individual name cards, champagne coupes, wine glasses, fresh mountain natives in crystal vases. Eight family and friends to celebrate Christmas. They arrived at 5, bottles clinking in cooler bags. Marcus, Alice's boss, still in his dark suit with blue striped tie, and his wife Grace. Marcus was the manager of *Mountain Adventure* company. Alice was boss of the Blue Mountains operations, everything from hiring staff (*'Must be neat, polite and adventurous!'*) to running the day-to-day tours. Kate and Ben arrived with the latest gossip from the Hydro.

'Elton John and his boyfriend stayed with us last Saturday,' Kate said.

'Did anybody recognise them?' Alice asked.

'Are you kidding? He found a piano. Then...'

'Don't tell me. Wicked?'

Sarah, Alice's older sister, arrived with Ebony, who she introduced as *'my partner'*. Ebony's buzz-cut hair was dyed purple on one side and a stud beneath her lower lip had an immediate effect, like a planetary vacuum – silence sucked the sound from the room then sprung back. Weight transferred from one uncomfortable position to another. Daniel smiled at Ebony, Alice gave them a cursory embrace. 'So glad you could make it. How's life in, um, Newtown? How's the live music scene?' Alice said.

'No idea. We usually go to The Exchange on Oxford Street.'

'Or Patch's. They've got a better DJ,' Ebony added. At the table, the other guests ignored them and resumed their conversations. Sarah and Ebony held hands and completed each other's sentences.

Margaret and Bill were the last to arrive. He complained about the terrible traffic leaving Sydney, the dangerous, winding roads. Alice positioned them at the opposite end of the table from Sarah and Ebony. Bill ignored them and sauntered over to the couch, removed his tweed jacket and ordered a scotch, two cubes as if he was in a private gentleman's club. Alice, the dutiful daughter, looked at Daniel, who nodded and repeated the pantomime. He poured himself a Guinness, a Johnnie Walker for Bill.

'Thanks. How's teaching? You still at the Grammar?'

'Yes, still there.'

'That's Anglican, isn't it?'

'Yes, in name only. Why?' Daniel grimaced and bit his lip.

Bill swirled the brown liquid three times and took a measured sip from his glass. He looked up at Daniel.

'You know Alice went to Loreto. Good school that. Taught her the right Catholic values.' He looked up at Daniel to see if he understood.

Lines crept across Daniel's brow. 'And just how are Catholic values different from other Christian values?'

'Don't be naïve, Dan. Do you realise the Anglicans are only in it for the money?'

'And the Catholics are in it for what, exactly?' Daniel clenched his jaw.

'It's something you can't understand unless you were raised one.'

Daniel opened his mouth, about to challenge. Bill continued. 'So, Daniel, have you popped the question yet?'

'No. We are fine, but thanks for asking.' His hand tightened around the glass.

'She'll be wanting children soon, son. The clock's ticking.'

Daniel stared, not sure how to reply. Alice stood and rang a small brass bell.

If he was honest, the gloss was wearing thin from the routine – train to work, drinks on Friday night, parties on Saturday. They made love once, sometimes twice a week if Alice's hectic schedule allowed it. She'd hinted a few times about marriage, he'd said that financially, they were better off not married. She ranted on, dropping hints, he replied '*Why?*' With all the trappings a comfortable routine offered, he pretended he was unaware of how things really were.

*

After dinner, they joined Sarah and Ebony on the back porch.

'We've got a surprise to tell you,' Sarah said with a wide-eyed smile. 'We're having a baby!'

Alice's mouth froze open and the skin around her eyes stretched. She stared at Sarah, then at Daniel. 'Christ. How is that even possible, you know, with Ebony?'

'You know what a turkey baster is?'

'I think so. You use them to baste chickens and turkeys, why?'

'That's not all they're good for. Ebony's brother slipped us a sample. Then I just, you know, do I need to explain?' Sarah eyes lit up. 'It didn't work the first time, we just kept trying.'

'Just like that?' Alice stared, incredulous, hands fixed by her side. 'That's disgusting. And it worked?'

'Must have. Although it's taken four months – that's fast apparently, the clinic doctor said. The baby's due in July.'

Daniel nudged Alice. She backed away. An intense silence followed.

'Congratulations. I'm happy for you,' he said.

He watched Sarah and Ebony kiss and hug. Alice stormed back inside.

After the guests had left, Alice tidied up and Daniel washed the dishes.

When she brought the last of the plates over and handed him a tray of glasses he said, 'I miss it you know, out there on the empty road, sleeping under the stars, our endless discussions about...everything.'

Alice said nothing. He stared out the window, a wet plate in his hand and when she handed him the next wine glass it fell and smashed to floor. She glanced back and forth from his frozen face to the shattered shards as he searched in the cupboard for the dustpan. 'Sorrysorrrysorry.'

She cleared her throat and sighed and handed him the dustpan. He bit his lip. 'Sorry...'

'I've been thinking hon, you know, I've always wanted to start a family before I'm thirty. Let's make this permanent. Let's get married.'

'Look, we've discussed this. We don't need to be married, you know, to have kids.'

'You're not taking me seriously. I want to get married before we have kids.' Her back stiffened and she clenched her jaw.

'Well, it's not that simple, I....' He tapped his fingers on the benchtop and licked his lips.

'Why not? We love each other and that's what people who love each other do...' She continued to stare at him as if the power of her resolve would solve the impasse or at least get the truth from him.

He couldn't lick his lips, his mouth felt like the inside of a clothes dryer. *I only married her to help her out so why should it be a problem? I'm not sure Alice will see it that way.* 'It's...it's complicated. I'm already married.' He stared at her face, her crinkled forehead. Her eyes narrowed and she stepped back hard against the bench. Daniel dragged his eyes over her face, lit up like a firecracker, ready to explode.

'What? What are you saying? Who? Where? When? And you're telling me this now, you, you...'

'I just did it for a friend, you know to help her out, stay in Australia. I can fix it.'

'Was it that German girl?' She crossed her arms around her chest.

'Yes.'

'So, did you love her?' Her eyes pierced the short distance between them.

'No, of course not. We were just good friends. I love you, Alice. You know that.' He tried to stroke her shoulders. She pulled away.

'So how can you fix it, exactly?'

'Look, I'll go and find her and get the marriage annulled.'

'Just like that, huh? Do you even know where she is?' She twirled a necklace with her index finger. *Kate was right. I should have listened.*

'Somewhere in Germany, from her last letter. She sent me the address of her closest friend in Göttingen. That was two years ago.' Alice sat down while Daniel walked around the table and stood next to her. She looked up. 'I guess you'll have to get it sorted, and soon. And don't bother staying here till you have.' Her anger wrapped the words around and froze him to the spot.

'Okay. Let me organise it for the New Year. I'll have six weeks holidays. That should be plenty enough time.'

He tried to hug her, but Alice moved away, and he was left there staring at her back with the silence booming over him like so many exploding cannons. He left, stumbling into the black air outside and turned left towards the shops. He walked, head bowed and repeated over and over, 'Go back and get it done,' like he was going out to buy milk.

The door slammed behind him. He'd always had a buffer, a little slack in his life for moments like these, moments that made the tautness bearable. Now that had snapped clean, like two frayed ends of film winding down on separate reels. *And Renate? Where was she?* Was she the one to splice the two frayed ends of the tape together? Now the wait, the worse kind of existence, a kind of hell, a kind of pause in normal life, a button with two parallel bars that Alice had pressed hard on the tape deck of his life.

Much later, he stumbled back to her house. A bulging backpack was on the path just inside the front gate next to his random possessions in an open cardboard box. She'd tossed his crumpled duffle coat on top. He hefted the bag and banged the gate closed.

*

Two weeks later, with the sweat finally dry on the back of his clingy shirt, he sits in the departure lounge clutching a small backpack and a large yellow envelope containing the divorce papers. He opens it, pulls out Renate's gold ring from his pocket and slips it inside, sealing the envelope with tape, having no idea how unnecessary the documents inside would become.

FIVE

56

Renate

Late October, 1982.

Renate sliced through the train's hissing doors into the warm air, oblivious to a man in a black homberg following her. She sat next to the window and peered out at the blanched fields, fallow and flat as a runway. Opposite her were two school-skipping teenagers, mouths glued together, seemingly oblivious to the world around them. The man placed his Homberg on the seat, unfolded a newspaper and stared at the woman in the fur-lined grey coat. *She's no threat, he has no need to carry a weapon.* An announcer's clipped voice droned from the speakers.

Landmarks flashed by through the wide window: the Hausberg Tower in Butzbach, the church tower of St. Pankratius in Giessen, the Naumburger Dom Cathedral in Naumburg, each jolting vague memories from her childhood. The waiting passengers with masklike faces and stiff backs on passing stations reminded her she was back in Germany. Outside, rain jerked down the windows in sleety waves like traditional Chinese calligraphy. She lost track of time, her still hands folded in her lap. She had two hours and thirty-six minutes to think about Ulrich, what information he'd share. Could she live with the knowledge that he'd been a mass murderer? *How could he be?* She shook her head and looked down at her hands, wishing Daniel was here. *I... I can't be held responsible.* She remembered a saying from Australia: *She'll be right, mate.* She knew, deep down, that it wouldn't. A heavy sigh escaped her lips and fell to the floor.

The man adjusted the collar on his thick jacket and followed Renate to bus station Sud, hopped on last and walked down the aisle to the end seat. Renate's head lolled back and forward as Karlsaue Park rolled past in the fading, grey afternoon light. Sleet turned to early wet snow and covered the cornflower and chamomile beds where she played as a child. She stopped the bus halfway down Bergshauser Str., paying no attention to the man, who followed at a distance. He walked to the bus shelter opposite, pulled out a notepad and jotted down the address. Across the empty street, she aimed for a glowing light in a glass inlay front door. A path bisected the rose gardens, now just sharp stick skeletons. She shouted, 'Hallo Mama!' and walked inside.

'Renate!' Anne lunged into Renate's open arms, almost knocked her off her feet. The atmosphere was different – something had lifted and dispersed. 'I've missed you so much, you've been gone so long,' Anne said and held her tight, 'are you hungry? Thirsty? Are you...' Anne held her at arm's length and studied her from head to foot.

'Mama, I'm tired. I need to go to my room and lie down.'

'It's exactly as you left it.'

'If I sleep, wake me for dinner please?'

'Of course.'

Renate fluffed the quilt, collapsed on the bed and checked the thermometer on her window. *Tomorrow I'll search the attic.* She fell into a deep sleep and dreamed she was a prisoner in a room with no windows, shouting to be released. Prof Beattie loomed close and whispered in her ear: *Mrs Cohen? Can you smell their fear?* She jerked awake, steadying her breathing. How long had she slept? It was two degrees on the thermometer. Smells drifted up the stairs, rye bread, smoke from the *katchelofen*, the steamy, closed-up dank of late autumn. In the shower, the last scent of eucalyptus washed from her hair. She tiptoed down the stars.

'*Das essen ist fertig.*' Dinner is ready.

Anne served on her best China, chatting non-stop. 'They've just opened a new Aldi that's closer, the price of fresh fruit is so expensive, I might be starting a new job soon.'

Renate picked at her *sauerbraten* and nodded, adding a few *ahs* and *mmms*. The elephant in the room expanded. She dropped her knife – it clattered on the ceramic plate – and gripped her teacup. She stared at Anne's face, at the secrets hidden by years of silence as if they could be laid out on the table and counted, then scrunched up and thrown away. If only it was that easy. 'You want to know about Papa?'

Renate nodded.

'His cancer has spread to his liver. The doctors say he's got weeks, maybe a month. Are you going to see him?'

'Of course, I'll go tomorrow morning. Then I'll catch the train to Göttingen and stay with Ilse.'

'Oh... How long will you be away?' Anne blinked. Her eyebrows drew together.

'I don't know, Mama.'

'I'd like you to stay here with me.'

'I'm not sure if I can. I want to go back to Göttingen and finish my Masters.'

Anne stared at her teacup and changed the topic. 'I think Papa has some important things to tell you.'

'I hope so. I'm tired of secrets. Why didn't you tell me about Opa Gustav and Oma Helena? What happened to them?'

Anne's face blanched and sagged, her eyes dropped to the table. Her hands opened and closed around the cup as if it was alive and she wanted it dead. 'It was not my story to tell. They were Papa's mother and father. He felt guilty he could not save them. He was in the thrall of the Nazis. Many were.'

'That doesn't excuse anything.'

'What would you know?' She glared at Renate. 'Everything was different then. Most of us believed everything Hitler said.'

'And look where that ended. What did Papa do in the war?' Renate's eyes tightened, searching for answers.

'You'll have to ask him. He's only told me snippets, not much. After we married, Ulrich insisted I erase all memories of the war. He said: "It's all in the past now". We live in a different world.' Anne folded her napkin and reached across the table to hold Renate's hand.

'Or you won't say.' Renate pulled her hand away and squinted her eyes. She watched as Anne's face turned pink. It was enough.

'Did you know they were Jewish?'

'Yes, he told me.'

'And you couldn't help them?'

'How Renate? I was a girl myself. I was not even here. You must understand.' Anne looked away, slowly shaking her head.

'I've come back and want Papa to explain. Everything. You understand?'

Anne nodded. The silence hung like an anchor. 'What did you do in Australia? How was your Masters?'

'I got married, Mama.'

Anne jerked her head back. 'What? Why didn't you tell me...'

'It's nothing, just a nice guy helped me out with my visa. It means I can go back anytime.'

'Tell me about this 'nice man." Anne leaned forward on her chair.

Renate spoke in hushed, rapid words of the time she met Daniel in the rainforest, in hospital, in Brisbane, picnics under a dragon tree. How he loved the Stone of Heaven. She omitted the part about Simone, the funeral, Marco. That was the past too. Gone.

'His father was Jewish, you know. His name is Cohen.'

'Did he die?'

'Yes and no. He just left.'

'Does he practice his faith?'

'No, he was raised a Catholic, just like you.' Renate stared hard at Anne's expressionless face. They drifted into an understanding, an acceptance that some things just are. Renate compared her life to Anne's, the years she put up with Ulrich, wondering if it were possible she still loved him. She'd decided, by then, that her life would be different. It was not grief they shared, it was more a growing sense of sympathy for Anne and the twenty years she lived with Ulrich. All Renate could offer was a hand, a touch, a weak smile. Anne stared down at a dwindling supply of chamomile tea. Memories stacked up like bricks on the table, randomly, without a formula. They sat there in silence as the wall clock ticked and chimed ten times.

She pushed the chair back. '*Gute Nacht.*'

Anne nodded. Renate left her sitting there still holding the cup, a frail object in danger of breaking.

*

In her room, she tossed around the idea of searching through the attic for more clues to the past. Instead, she collapsed on the bed. Above the bedhead a photo – an image of a little girl on her first day of school. She weighed it in her hand, as if memories had a substance, a mass you could measure. Could she measure guilt, not a cynical guilt, but a collective guilt, there, just under her skin? Her chest tightened, she let out a deep sigh. *How can I understand the past without the context of the people who lived in it?* Instead, she tiptoed down the stairs, opened the small door to the cellar, flicked on the light and walked down more stairs. Ulrich's train set sat silent, motionless, trains at stations, miniature figures in caps leaning out of engines. An image – the boxcars disgorging hundreds of frantic figures, rugged-up skeletons, some on their final journey on Earth.

Where were you, Papa, when this was happening? What were you shouting in your nightmares, all those years ago?

57

Inside room 207, curtains thrown open against the dull autumn sun, Renate blinked hard. Ulrich lay before her, an unrecognisable figure like a skeleton in bed clothes. She smelt the sweet, musty odour of sickness and stared for some time as if she'd lost something. He was right there, invalid, feeble, dependent. His face like polished saffron, in blue pyjamas as if dressed up in a Ukrainian flag. She placed the Stone of Heaven in Ulrich's hand, closed his fingers and hurried back, pushed away by the smell of rotten eggs.

'Tell me, Papa, what happened to you in the war?'

When Ulrich opened his eyes, something quivered behind his wet corneas. He parted his ashen lips and tombstone-like teeth protruded from bog-coloured gums. His chest rose with a wheeze like fire bellows. Every sentence was spaced with a pause so long she wondered if each was the last. He was only 63.

He sucked in some air. 'It was Christmas, 1938. I returned from Berlin-Spandau. Whole streets were boarded up where the Jewish shops had traded. Broken glass was still on the footpaths. I was at the NSKK training school, the Motor Corps run by Adolf Huhnlen. I trained for two years as a driver and mechanic. I loved the machines, the precision of the working parts, how each one had a purpose.' He stopped and wheezed, fighting to suck in air. 'They always got me to listen to the motors, I was the only one who could hear if something was wrong.'

'Tell me about your papa and mama.'

Ulrich paused and stared at a spot on the wall. He shuffled up the bed and propped his tube-covered arm on a pillow. Renate followed the drips, mesmerised as they cascaded down the cannula.

'Papa disappeared in November 1938. After the night of broken glass, *Kristallnacht*. The neighbours said he was taken away in a truck. Mama didn't know what to do. I had to be back in Berlin. When I had my interview, I had to prove I was not Jewish, I was lucky Mama and Papa did not have me circumcised. In Berlin, I passed my exams in August 1939 and entered the Motor Corps with the rank of Section Leader.'

Ulrich coughed green slime on a white napkin and dropped it in a bin with a dozen others. 'I was stationed in Warsaw as a mechanic and driver. One day I drove Oberfuhrer-Senior Leader Alfred Funk to Lublin for a meeting with General Odilo Globocnik the SS Police Chief. They were setting up a Ghetto to force all Jews from Germany and towns around Lublin together. When we returned, Funk was laughing to his aide about the plan for the final solution of the Jews. 'Odilo's got a plan for an extermination camp near Belzec'. Then he said, '*They must be killed to fulfil our dream*'. I never forgot that. I was a young man caught in a sinister plan of extermination.'

Ulrich paused, blinked twice and closed his eyes. 'That was a long time ago, *mein Schatz*. I remember like it was yesterday.'

'What did you think about all that, Papa?' She inched her chair closer.

'It did not matter what you thought, as long as you obeyed. For two years that's what I did. Then they promoted me to sergeant and sent me to a place called Chelmo in December 1941. You know what that place was?'

'No, Papa.'

'It was an extermination camp, *Vernichtungslager*. Like Auschwitz.'

Renate's arms stiffened. Her fingers tightened.

'Chelmo was nothing like Auschwitz. I was the relief driver for a sadist named Walter Burmeister. He was often drunk, so I drove the *einsatzwagon*, the mobile gas van – we collected them straight off the trains and stuffed them forty or fifty inside and sealed it tight. By the time we arrived back at the crematorium they were dead. Occasionally, I had to drive bodies out to the forest where they buried them. That's what I did, Renate, I drove them to their deaths. One day, the truck broke down on the highway. They were screaming inside. I couldn't fix it for over two hours. They blamed me and sent me to Auschwitz. That was February 1943. I was 23.'

'What happened to you there, Papa?'

At precisely noon, a lady in a starched blue uniform and white apron wheeled a trolley with trays into the room. She stopped, looked at Renate and said, 'Lunch time. Visiting hours are over.'

Renate looked at Ulrich and squeezed his hand. 'See you tomorrow, Papa, I'd like to hear more of your story.'

He raised his hand an inch and where Renate's fingers had held his marks remained, ivory on an orange background next to the Stone of Heaven. 'Can I keep this tonight?' He held up the Stone.

'Of course, Papa.' She waited for the bus outside the hospital and mulled over Ulrich's story, Daniel and her marriage, what she would do. She rode home on the bus, overcome with anger. Anne was in the kitchen. It was time for the truth. She marched over, tripped on a chair leg, jerked it aside. Anne stiffened.

'What did he tell you exactly?' Anne said.

'How his papa disappeared. About his job at the Chelmo extermination camp.'

'Did he mention what happened at Auschwitz?'

'Not yet. I'm going back tomorrow. I want to know everything.'

'Ask him about Eva.'

'Eva?' Renate stared, her stomach fluttering.

'Eva Blumenthal. He met her at Auschwitz. And be careful. I got a phone call today from a police detective asking questions about Ulrich. His role in the war. I said he was in hospital with cancer.'

'Who was Eva Blumenthal?'

'Let Papa tell you, you owe him that much.' Anne spun around and began to wash the dishes. Renate walked up the stairs and paused on the landing. *Why are the police asking questions about him now? What other secrets is he hiding?*

58

Next morning at ten, Renate walked into Ulrich's room. Two men in dark suits – one holding a black homburg – took notes next to Ulrich's bed. She heard the words '...and exactly what was your position at Auschwitz?' They stopped when she walked in.

'Who are you? What's going on here? she said, knocking over a cup of water on the trolley.

'Excuse me, miss, you are?'

'Renate, I'm his daughter.' She crossed her arms and stared at the younger man's face, unreadable as a whiteboard message under water. He turned his head and nodded at his partner.

'We are from the Federal Crime Police Office. We're investigating your father's involvement in the war.'

'Can't you just leave him alone,' she dropped her backpack on the chair, 'he's dying. He was a driver and a mechanic. Nothing more. You're wasting your time.'

'We'd like to ask him. We can come back later if you prefer?'

Renate stared from one to the other and nodded her head. They closed their note pads and left. She sat next to Ulrich and gripped his hand. He held the Stone and the orange skin on his face slumped.

'I'm feeling better today. This helped.' He opened his fingers. The stone left a white cavity in his palm. 'Those men, I'd hoped they'd forgotten about me. They mentioned Richard Boch. He must have told them about me.'

'Who is Richard Boch, Papa?' She refilled the cup from a jug on the trolley.

'He was a guard, a corporal working in the motor pool in Auschwitz when I arrived. A good man, loved music, played the chemnitzer concertina. One day he told me he was ordered to drive four Jews who couldn't walk to the gas chambers. When he got there, he said he could hear the screaming from inside. Told his superior officer he wouldn't do it again, so they sent him to the motor pool. He wasn't wooden like most of them. Bend them a little and they'd snap.'

'Who was Eva Blumenthal?' she spurted.

Ulrich's face hardened at the same instant that Renate heard a long, onerous sigh. 'She was a young, Jewish woman from Hamburg. She worked in the laundry. Because she was German, Baer – the Commandant – kept her as his personal servant. If his gabardine suits were not perfect, he'd beat her. One day early in October 1944 she came to the motor pool to check on his car, his Mercedes-Benz 770k. She had a bruise on the left side of her face under her eye. I smiled and something passed between us, do you understand?'

She nodded.

'She had the most beautiful, luminous eyes, and spoke German with a lovely northern accent. I whispered, *Meet me outside on Sunday at noon.* Sunday was our day off. She told me about her life in Hamburg before the Nazis arrested her family. As I listened, I knew I loved her. You could say we fell in love in a hopeless place.' He paused.

She added – 'Maybe one day someone will write a song about it.'

He continued as if she hadn't spoken. 'On Saturday nights, when most of the guards would get drunk and sing, Boch played the concertina, I'd sneak out to meet her. I had a key to Block 26, the darkroom and a photographic studio. We did things there that lovers do.'

Ulrich's voice trailed off. He sighed and squeezed Renate's hand tighter.

'What happened to her, Papa?'

'Someone must have reported us. It was just after Christmas 1944. It was minus twenty-five or more. They held me in the cellar of Block 11. Then after about a week I heard explosions. They were blowing up the crematoriums before the Russians came. On January fourteen, they let me out, most of the prisoners had left, forced to march west towards Germany. When she was marched away, I realised it was because of me. I was just a cog in the machine of death. Have you heard of the death marches?'

Renate nodded.

'On the eighteenth a lieutenant told me they needed a driver and qualified mechanic to drive Richard Baer, the commandant, away to safety. I drove while a Polish mechanic named Jacob sat in the passenger seat. Twenty soldiers piled into the back of the Opel Blitz. A man dressed in gardener's overalls and wellingtons was the last to climb in. Commandant Baer.' Ulrich hawked green sputum into the bucket, slurped water from a cup, swirled it around and spat it out. He looked up at her attentive face and continued. 'We passed columns of prisoners, many lying still on the side of the road. I never saw her again.' Tears ran down Ulrich's face in wavy lines.

She squeezed his hand like old leather and whispered, 'Love isn't something you find, Papa. Love finds you.'

'Before I go, remember this. Remember what happened at Auschwitz. You must tell your children. We can never undo what happened but in remembering, we can honour their deaths. Do you promise me?' he pleaded.

'Yes Papa. I promise.' She stayed there for some time and held his hand. Her body softened, she wasn't sure if it was from relief or love of a dying man she never really knew. A weight, more constant than gravity, lifted from her shoulders.

*

As the night nurse was walking past room 207, she heard a shout. Her right foot froze in mid-air. She cocked her head to block out the beeps and hisses. She thought she heard two men arguing inside.

'Don't hurt her. I'm not a *Rassenschander*, a race polluter. Take me!'

She opened the door a fraction. A pile of blankets was jumbled on the floor as if flung away by a mighty hand. She shut the door behind her, but that word, that she'd only once read about, still echoed in her head.

59

Renate walked past her old flat in Göttingen to number 22 and knocked. When it swung open, Ilse beamed and hugged her like family.

'You've cut your hair.'

'Do you like the colour? Couldn't stay boring and single forever. Are you coming in?' She waved her hand. Renate's shoe caught on the edge of the carpet. 'Still as clumsy as ever.' Ilse smiled. They walked over to the kitchen.

Renate dropped her backpack on the floor and sat on a stool. 'I want to know everything about him. It's Max, right? Is he studying Law too?'

'No, Medicine. I'm his anatomy dummy,' Ilse said with a wide grin. They both laughed. Renate smiled up from the green sofa as Ilse filled the pot with water and put it on the stove.

'Tea? Tell me all about Australia.'

Renate talked in rapid bursts, Brisbane, the Commonwealth Games protests, the wild rainforests and amazing birds, how everything burst with life. The open and friendly people. She omitted the part about Simone. 'I got married.'

'No! You devil! What's he like?' Ilse's eyes widened as the water hissed on the stove.

'His name's Daniel. He's a teacher, or was, until he joined a protest bike ride.'

'What was he protesting about?'

'Uranium, nuclear stuff. I think he's in Japan now.' Renate's forehead wrinkled, her stomach tensed.

'He sounds interesting. Why did you get married? Did you sleep with him? Do you love him?'

Renate paused, frowned and shuffled her feet. 'No and no, silly. My visa was about to expire.'

Ilse nodded and studied her friend, making up for lost time. 'So, did you finish your Masters?'

'No. I've got to write up my thesis. I was hoping to finish it here.'

'Why not? Get them to send over your results and then you can apply. You can stay here until you find a place.' Ilse bustled about making tea, the silence hanging in the air. Renate looked up.

'Do you still observe your Jewish practices?' she said, tilting her head to the side.

'Only the major ones. Mum and Dad still do. Hey, they've invited you to Passover in April.'

'Thanks. I'll see. Got any plans for tomorrow?' she asked, sipping her tea.

'Why don't we go for a walk out through the Stadtwald forest? We could walk up to the Bismarck tower like before?'

'I'd like that. I need to clear my head. I've spent time with Ulrich. He's told me stuff about the war. Its…distressing.'

'Do you want to tell me about it?' Ilse tilted her head to the side.

'Maybe later.'

They talked until Renate's eyes drooped. Ilse showed her the spare bed and hugged her goodnight. Outside, a black car inched into traffic. A flare from a cigarette glowed orange. The driver removed a homburg and placed it on the passenger seat.

*

275

The east bus on *Kreuzbergring* dropped them under a crystal-clear blue sky outside the Tennis and Ski club. A path led through a neat carpark and into leafless trees. Ilse walked and chatted to Renate's *ums* and *ahs*. 'Let's go this way, it's longer but more interesting.'

Frost thickened the edged of the path as it wound through beech, maples and birch, silent in the frozen morning air, distant, sharp sounds amplified: the thwack of tennis balls, a rumbling bus, a dog with a tiny bark in the distance. Her mind slipped back to the stark contrast of the Mt Warning rainforest – here, just the neat, ordered trunks, the lack of screeching birds, the absent, whistling wind. Beside her, Ilse's voice battered against her ears like an unlatched gate in a gale.

'You go on. I'll catch up soon,' Renate said.

Ilse made a face but took the hint and left, crunching over a pool of ice.

Renate looked for signs of wildcats, woodpeckers, wryneck nests. Prints of a lone deer or a wild boar crossed the path at an angle. She stooped to inspect closely, *deer*. A middle-aged woman in a white fur-lined coat approached, holding a poodle on a chain. The dog was dressed in a pink woollen jacket that matched its leather booties. Renate breathed in and sighed as the woman passed. In the distance, a dog barked. She reached the Bismarck Tower. Ilse looked up from a bench. 'It's closed until April. Shoulda known. Did you know Bismarck studied Law here?'

'No, but he was a warmonger. Started three wars in less than twenty years.'

'And re-unified Germany.'

'Look where that's got us.'

'Do you remember coming here in first year? You were so innocent then, that was before you met Heinz.'

'Don't mention him. I've forgotten. He doesn't exist anymore.'

'So, how is your dad?' Ilse slid closer and leaned forward.

'He's dying of terminal cancer. It's in his liver, bones, probably everywhere.'

'Gosh, I'm so sorry. Has he told you any...secrets...about what he did in the war?' She struggled to find the right words.

'Secrets? What secrets?' Renate's voice rose, her body stiffened.

'You know... What he did at Auschwitz.'

'How do you know he was at Auschwitz?' Her voice became a whisper as if a crowd was listening. Her heart thumped.

'I asked your mum before you came home. You don't mind, do you? She didn't say much.'

'No...she wouldn't. Anyway, he was a driver, a mechanic. Worked in the motor pool, that's all.'

'He didn't work on the gas chambers?'

'No. Of course not. Why do you want to know?' Renate stared at Ilse and narrowed her eyes. A cold chill ran down her back.

'Sorry. I don't want to be nosy but...'

'That was forty years ago. He's trying to forget. We all are.' Renate clenched her jaw as she shook her head.

'Some people never forget, Renate.'

That night as Renate lay awake, an interior voice whispered, *why would Ilse want to know about that?* Something niggled away inside. *Was Ulrich telling the whole truth? How would I know if he was?*

60

At 10 am next morning, on a wooden bench, she waited outside Professor Merkel's office, the dean of Biology. A plump receptionist with a severe bob gathered papers and placed them in a folder.

'Have you completed Ecology 1 and 2?' the woman said without looking up.

'No.'

'Then you'll have to wait and see him.'

Renate stared at the qualifications on either side of the framed photograph of the new Chancellor Helmut Kohl. The plump woman hummed something annoying and ignored her. The woman stiffened her back every time the phone rang and answered, 'Professor Merkel's office,' in an overzealous whine. The minute hand on the wall clock reached six, Renate coughed and stared at the woman.

'He knows you're here. Shouldn't be long now.'

A shadow appeared behind the translucent glass square inlay and the door opened. A large man with a red, egg-shaped nose in a waistcoat and bow tie stared across the room. 'Miss Mayer? Please come in.' He pointed to an ornate wooden chair with red plush leather padding and a window that looked out onto a green quadrangle. The wall was covered in plaques and citations. He read from her open folder: 'Research Techniques – High

Distinction; Plant Biology – High Distinction. Year award for outstanding student. Very impressive, Miss Mayer.'

'Thank you, Professor.'

'So, you wish to complete your Masters here. We'll have to send away to your Australian university to get a copy of your transcript. That may take time. Have you completed Ecology 1 and 2?'

'No, Professor.'

'Well, you'll have to complete both. Ecology 1 has started, you'll have to catch up. Will that be a problem? He raised his eyebrows.

'No, thank you Professor.'

*

Renate joined the student union and put her name down for work in the café after inspecting three apartments close to Ilse's. She chose a one-bedroom place in Blumenbach Strasse just around the corner.

'Hey, we're almost neighbours.'

'When are you going home?'

'Tomorrow. My course starts in three weeks. I'll move in just before then.'

Ilse made a phone call while Renate was out ordering pizza. 'Ilse Engelman reporting in as ordered, Herr Schiller.'

'Miss Engelman. What news to do have?'

'She said no. He wasn't involved with the gas chambers.'

'Are you sure? What else did she say?'

'Look, I don't know if she knows anything else. She said he was dying.'

'We know that. It doesn't get the Israelis off our backs. They want a conviction. That's all they want.' He sounded frustrated. 'Ask her again. You know there's a job waiting for you here when you finish your studies. We need good lawyers, especially Jewish ones.'

Her fingers trembled as she gripped the phone. Her intuition said, *don't alarm Renate.* If Ulrich was lying, she needed to know. She never forgot what her parents had said when she was growing up – *Find those responsible.* She had someone now, just how responsible remained to be seen. It was uncomfortable, what she was doing, but in memory of all those millions who had been murdered, she decided one friendship was worth the price.

'I'll keep that in mind, Herr Schiller.' She squeezed the phone with thumb and forefinger. On the other end, Herr Schiller placed the homburg on his bald head and closed the door to his office.

61

Renate sat in the lecture hall with forty other freshmen facing the lecturer, Dr Roth, as he shook his curly brown hair and dropped his notes. She sighed as he began to explain the most complex of ideas in far too simple terms. He outlined the problems as if they were a shopping list of dinner ingredients. Renate's hand shot up for the third time. He ignored her. After about fifteen minutes, she couldn't stop squirming in the plastic chair. For the past four weeks she'd attended most lectures and had made a name for herself as the classes' most unpopular student. When she raised her hand to ask a question, Dr Roth would stop mid-sentence and freeze. 'What does a healthy population actually look like?', 'How many 'future generations' are you talking about doctor? 30? 3000?', 'What happens when the population in your neat box labelled 'marine' breaks out?' Later, she was requested to attend the dean's office for a 'chat' about her progress.

She stopped attending classes. She wrote her assignments alone in the library on their new Compaq computers and started every session with a prayer of thanks to Alan Turing. Her work was above high distinction grade. Dr Roth, in spite, stamped the front pages with a large blue 'C'. That only made her question why she was there. She crossed off another week on her calendar.

Once every week or two, she rode to the Stadtwald and walked a different path to study the changes from winter to spring. She searched for owls and the footprints of feral animals, recording it all in a leather-covered notebook. Late in March, as winter ebbed, she sat in the sun on a bench under her favourite beech tree and remembered how Daniel had laughed when she tripped on the carpet in Brisbane, a joke they shared together. She opened her pad and wrote:

Dear Daniel,

I don't know where you are or who you're with now. Your face has faded over time from the photo I still have that day in the Brisbane Registry Office. So, I'll tell you what I have been doing...

She stopped writing. She wanted to tell him her news, but the writing process triggered memories of Simone – the meals they shared, the laughter, the bike rides she and Daniel went on, the dragon tree. She had Anne to think of now. They spent the days walking or visiting Ulrich. He slipped further and further away each time they came and shared no more stories of the past. The same two policemen who questioned her last month stalked around the hospital, nodding at her when she walked by. With Anne, Renate had reached an understanding, a comfortable acceptance. Anne's life expanded proportional to Ulrich's contracting as she spent more time with old friends, started a book club at the library and joined the local bird watching group. They went on tours – Frankfurt, Hannover, Dortmund. A new step appeared in her walk. Renate used this time to reflect on her future, her Masters thesis, her life. What bewildered her most: the avalanche of choices, where to live, the old problem of what to include or exclude from her thesis. There was nothing left for her in Kassel except a tired old house full of memories and faded photographs.

The conversations with Anne were perfunctory, superficial. Except one day while they were eating dinner.

'What do you want to do with your life, Renate?' Anne said.

Renate looked up. 'I just don't want to spend my life apologising for anything.'

Anne stared, nodded once and resumed eating.

*

March 28, 1983

Ilse invited Renate to her parents' house to celebrate the first night of Passover. Ilse's mum, Hannah, greeted Renate with a hug as if she was one of the family. She pointed to the *tzedakah* box. Renate nodded and slipped a ten Deutsche Mark note through the slot. She watched Hannah light the Shabbot candles and Ilse showed her the table set for a traditional Passover feast. The challah covered over the matzah, the divided plate of food with eggs, bitter herbs, parsley and haroset sauce. There were seven silver kiddush cups for the wine which Samuel, Ilse's dad, poured. They sat and Samuel opened a leather-bound book and read the story of the Israelites fleeing from Egypt.

'That's the *Haggadah*. Only Dad reads from that.'

The meal was simple and Renate found herself relaxing in the lively conversations that went back and forth around the room. Ben, Ilse's older brother, spoke about his time in East Berlin as a businessman and his dealing with the corrupt officials. 'If we could take the best from the DDR and combine it with the best from our section, we'd have a better Germany.' Then he spoke about the anarchists and squatters in Kreuzberg, the riots. 'Sometimes it's like a war on the streets.'

As she helped Hannah and Ilse clear up the table, Ilse said, 'How's your dad?'

'Not good. Sometimes when we visit, he says nothing. Other times, like last weekend, he raved about the war again.'

'What did he say? Did he say anything about Auschwitz?'

'No...you've asked me that before. What's so important?'

Just for a second, hesitation swept across Ilse's blank face. 'We all carry it with us, don't we Renate.' Ilse drove Renate back to her apartment. They talked about their studies, student politics. The conversation drifted back and forth, what mattered most remained buried. Renate wondered, *why does Ilse keep asking about Ulrich?*

62

April, 1983

Four weeks before Renate's final examination in Ecology 1, the phone in the hallway outside her apartment rang.

'He's gone.' Anne's voice sounded hollow. 'They're taking him to the mortuary. I'm still at the hospital waiting for the paperwork.'

'I'll come home tomorrow.' Renate stumbled, almost fell as she closed the door. She packed her bag with enough clothes for a week, booked her ticket and switched on the kettle. It was not until she heard the whistling that she realised where she was and what had happened. *He's gone.* An icy shiver crept over her as she reached for a dressing gown. Small things, tidying up the sofa, making tea, passed the time. Much later, she remembered the tea still sitting cold on the bench.

When the morning light broke through the slit in the curtain, she woke as if she'd been in a deep coma.

*

Anne sat in the loungeroom staring at the wall, teacup in hand. She looked up, eyes vacant and red. Renate sat and put her arm around her, not knowing what to say. Anne put her head on Renate's shoulder and sighed. It was so unfamiliar that Renate didn't know what else to do. Later, Anne stiffened enough to sit up. Ingrid and Heike, two of Anne's friends from book club, prepared food in the kitchen. Ingrid had that well-aged slim figure, Heike, in contrast, had a nose that constantly twitched and a *zaftig* figure. She poked her head out of the kitchen door.

'Can we make you any tea?'

They chatted in low whispers. The slow ticking of time was unfamiliar, the strangers in the shadows. At night, she swore the darkness protracted and stretched as if afraid of letting go.

'Where have they taken Dad?'

Anne raised an eyebrow and studied Renate's face. 'To the Holzapfel funeral home. Ulrich said he wanted to be cremated and his ashes scattered. What do you think?'

'Simple. Bury them here with one of his favourite toy engines,' she said, touching Anne's shoulder lightly, 'that's what he loved the most, didn't he?' Anne looked away, unable to reply. Renate opened the door to the basement, descended the stairs and turned the light on. The vast table with its model trains and stations like a small town asleep on a public holiday. She plucked the Flying Scotsman loco from the tracks, carried it upstairs and handed it to Anne. 'This was his favourite.'

*

She spent the next week in her room memorising the ecology text and coming to terms with her feelings about Ulrich. It was a different kind of grief than Simone's – a less personal sadness – as if sadness could be measured. She'd miss her dad, but felt lighter, buoyant even, as if the past might be buried or burned with his body. Her exams loomed. *What if I know too much? What if I answer with what I know, not what they want?* Every time the phone rang, she ran down the stairs to be told by a distant relative of Ulrich, whom she'd probably never meet, 'We're so sorry to hear the news'. Anne was away most days organising the funeral and the dinner after at

Ulrich's favourite restaurant, Lohmann's. Renate nodded, agreeing with everything Anne decided. Ingrid offered her a spare black dress, almost a perfect fit.

*

Renate drove Anne to the chapel inside the entrance to the Bettenhausen Cemetery. A silver hearse crawled up, Anne stepped out and stumbled. Renate held her up. There were five couples there including Ingrid and Heike, three others who said later they knew Ulrich from the Henschel factory and two men about sixty whom Renate didn't recognise. As soon as the coffin was in place, the priest chanted the Agnus Dei in a practiced falsetto. Without a pause to catch his breath, he turned the pages and continued with the *Requiem aeternam.* He walked around the coffin three times and flicked water that reached over Renate's head to the second row, nodded to the funeral director and walked back to the altar. One of the funeral directors pressed a button and the coffin glided into the flames. Renate blinked. The still door expanded, then expanded again. She closed her eyes. Cadaverous, stick-like figures were being thrown off a cart into flames by rough hands in striped shirts. She shook her head, and when her eyes opened, a curtain covered the door. Tears ran down Anne's face. Renate held her trembling body tight.

They drove in silence to Lohmann's, Renate clutching photos in her hand: when she was a toddler, a picnic outside the Orangerie, a happy family together besides Lake Buga, Renate about seven. She placed the photos on the table next to Anne, who stared at them with a weak smile. It was enough. Renate sipped her wine and noticed the two elderly gentlemen drinking ale. After she finished eating, one of the men approached her.

'You must be Renate. Ulrich spoke fondly of you.' He reached out, bowed a little and took her hand.

'How did you know my father?' Renate tilted her head to the side.

'Sorry, I'm Richard Boch. We were in the army together.'

Renate studied his nodding face, the way he fumbled his words, his trembling hands as if they held a great secret. He quickly shoved them in his pockets.

'Where did you serve with him?'

'I met him at that terrible place in Poland, in the motor workshop.'

'Do you mean at Auschwitz?'

Richard froze for an instant, looked left and right and leaned in closer, close enough for Renate to smell the wine. 'Can we talk privately?' he whispered.

She nodded and they walked over to a quiet part of the bar. He offered her a seat. 'I'll stand, thank you. Tell me about Auschwitz.'

'We were both in the motor pool in 1944. Did he tell you?'

'Yes. Go on.'

'He was a kind man. Honest. Hated the SS and what they were doing. There was no way out for any of us. We had sworn an oath. The eastern front had collapsed. They were gassing the arrivals as quickly as possible. Ulrich was a haunted man.'

'How so?'

'He fell for a Jewish woman. They'd sneak off on Sundays. Told me to keep quiet. Of course I did, but around Christmas they were seen going in to Block 26. He was thrown in Block 11 – the punishment block – and left there. I thought they'd shoot him but Baer, the Commandant, had other plans for him.'

'He told me some of this.' The back of her neck tingled.

'So, after New Year when the Russians were getting closer, Baer was very agitated and needed a driver to take him back to Germany. Ulrich was the only one he trusted. After they had left, I didn't see Ulrich again until 1963.'

'What happened then?'

'I was living in Frankfurt. They held the Auschwitz trials there. I was called up as a witness and told them I was just a driver. They asked me about Ulrich. I said the same thing. The German prosecutors were not keen to prosecute because of the Holocaust deniers. I thought it was all over until two men came last year asking questions again. They wanted to know more about Ulrich.'

'Did one man carry a homburg?'

Richard arched his eyebrows. 'Yes, he did. Have you seen him?'

'Yes, in the hospital when I first arrived.'

'Well, you shouldn't have to worry about that now.'

'Did my father say any more about the woman he was in love with?'

'I wouldn't call it 'love'. I don't think that was possible in a place like Auschwitz. But who am I to judge? Love keeps you going through *schlechte Zeiten* – the bad times.'

Renate stared at the man for a long time, trying to decide what she'd do with the information. She touched his arm and nodded, breathing deeper now that Ulrich's story was confirmed. *One day I think I'll go there, see for myself.*

*

The next day, as Anne prepared to go shopping, Renate heard a soft knocking at the door. The man with the homburg stood there, flexing the brim in his fingers.

'Miss Mayer. May I offer my condolences.'

'Why? As if you care. My dad's dead. What do you want?'

'I'm here to inform you that our investigation of your father is officially closed.'

'Naturally. Is there anything else you'd like to enlighten me with?' she said, her nostrils flared.

'Not exactly. Your story and your father's version of events at Auschwitz have been confirmed by a third party.'

'Who, exactly?' Any chance it was a Miss Engelman?' Renate had her suspicions. His face reddened. 'I can't tell you that. We always seek out independent evidence.'

'You mean 'informers?'' she knew, somehow, it was true.

'You should be thankful, Miss Mayer, that it's all over.'

'Please go away. Now.' Renate slammed the door. She paced around the house breathing rapidly, swinging her arms.

Anne looked up alarmed. 'Who was that?'

'That bastard policeman. Please wait for me here. I won't be long.' Renate stomped outside through the back yard to the garden shed and flung open the door and picked up four flat packing boxes. In the basement, she dropped the boxes, scanned the room, the dusty table, the towns, tracks and trains. With one movement, she swept the trains into a box. A brass key fell to the floor. Bending down to pick it up, she looked under the table and saw a white-painted drawer. *Interesting.* Searching inside, something pricked her index finger. *Ouch!* A blob of blood welled out. She wiped off the blood with a clean cloth and looked inside. Ulrich's dagger. When she saw the swastika, she dropped it as if a wasp had bitten her. In one movement, she kicked it across the floor. All that it represented – the past, the pain, the powerless panic – distilled into a piece of metal. Wrapped tightly in an old rag, she carried it as you would carry a dead rat to the backyard, dug a hole and dropped it in. *Let it rust.* She packed away the rest of the trains, shut off the light and returned, up the stairs.

Anne stared with lips pursed. 'What have you done?'

'Don't worry, Mama, I just buried the past.'

63

Christmas, 1986

Renate struggled with the decrepit coal heater in her room as the temperature dropped below freezing. She'd moved in six months earlier, a room on the first floor in the *Rauchhaus* squat on Bethaniendamm five hundred metres from the wall in Kreuzberg, Berlin. She's made the room semi-comfortable, furniture and material scrounged from every derelict house in Kreuzberg, even a bed from the old nurses' storeroom abandoned since the end of the war. The walls were covered with protest banners and a 'Stop Uranium Mining' poster she'd brought from Australia.

For most of the year, she'd worked in the Free University's café – the *Mensa* – in Dahlem and saved up to start her PhD. She dissected every text on genetics in the library and harassed every professor and post-doc in the biology department to be her supervisor. Eventually, Dr Maria Volhard, a post-doc, agreed to supervise on two conditions: Renate maintained a strict attendance schedule and submit work every month. Her new title: *Morphogenesis – genetic or chemical control of embryology.*

Günter's footsteps plodded up the stairs.

'Did you get the coal?' she asked, kneeling with a dustpan full of black clinkers.

'What's left of it. Just one bucket. Got anything else that can burn?'

'How about that old box of yours? What's in it that's so precious?' Wrinkling her nose and tilting her head in the direction of a padlocked, wooden box under the table.

'Just some sensitive papers I'm keeping secure. That's not a problem, is it?' he said, with a slight stutter.

'Only if the cops raid us. They did four months ago. Evicted us for a day. Found nothing.'

'So, what did you do?' He moved over and stood in front of the box, gave it a sudden glance, then looked away.

'We came back and started over again. It was routine, apparently.'

Next day, the box disappeared.

They'd met five months earlier when the lingering summer light brought all the alternatives, peace activists, squatters and anti-nuclear protestors onto the streets and cafés of West Berlin. Wild hair, brown eyes and timbred voice pierced through what others called *Schwachsinn* – 'bullshit'. Günter's job as administrator for the German Red Cross Tracing Service took him all over Eastern Europe. He was nearly twelve years older than her. Later, when she asked him about their age difference, he said, 'I like younger women,' with a half-smile. He handed her a pamphlet for the Alternative Liste party. She took the bait. Two hours later, over cold coffee, they were still discussing politics and the value of her research.

'Morphogenesis? Who gives a shit?' he said with a blank stare.

'My supervisor does. So do I. You got a problem with that?' She tapped her feet rapidly.

'Shouldn't you be more concerned with the division of Germany?'

'Shouldn't you be more concerned about not trying to tell me what to think?' She crossed her arms.

'Isn't that a man's right?'

'No, it's not 'your right,' not anymore.' He opened his satchel, reached in and removed a stack of A4 papers and a book. Renate saw the cover, *Lolita* by Nabokov. When he saw the curious look on her face, he stuffed it back in his satchel. He blushed and changed the topic.

'My fear is that if the wall comes down, we'll be swamped by Easties.'

'At least they'll be our refugees.'

She explained she needed a doctorate to travel, to study overseas and return one day to Australia. He sat there, staring into the distance.

'You just want a better meal ticket.'

'Günter, don't be so...cynical.'

He stuck his tongue out in reply.

It had been a long time since she'd laughed with another man. She thought back to Ilse's betrayal, how much it hurt. She was cautious with him, often thinking, *I can trust him, can't I?* Günter lived across town in Mitte and his work took him out of the country. He tolerated the Americans and their 'abundance of money,' hated the Russians – 'Most of them are pigs. It'll come down one day you know?' he said, matter-of-factly, as he stared into his empty coffee cup.

'I can't see that happening until there's a change in the Kremlin.'

'The new guy, Gorbachev sounds positive.'

'If he is, he won't last long.'

'Why are you so cynical?'

'Just because.' She stood up and stared at his face.

By December, Günter was staying over most nights when he was back in Berlin. At first it was surreptitious lovemaking under the wraps and layers of clothes they wore to keep warm. She surrendered to the feel of another man's skin on hers, another balmy breath tickling her ear as it passed. She remembered the time she had kissed Daniel and their wedding day. The memory was crisp – like it was only yesterday – something she held onto, even if it was faint. She and Günter drew lots to see who would get up to put coal in the fireplace. Next morning after he had left for work, Renate chatted with Asha from the adjoining room about Australia while they washed the dishes.

'What did you do there?' Asha said, handing her a chipped plate to wipe.

'Started my Masters. Went to a few protests about Aboriginal rights. Met a man. Got married.'

'Hell, all that in six months?' Asha turned and stared, wide eyed.

'It was great. They are very friendly people.'

'I met a few Australians about three years ago,' Asha said, handing Renate another plate. 'They were staying in a squat down the street.'

'What were they doing here?'

'One of the women, who had an amazing smile I'll never forget, said they were going to the Nuclear Disarmament Convention. They were riding bikes.'

Renate stopped wiping, looked around and said, 'Did you meet a guy on a blue bike, tall with brown eyes?'

'Can't say I did. I was only looking at the women, Renate.'

Asha smiled. Renate knew. *I wonder, could Daniel have been here?*

64

January came with glacial winds from the east and icy, treacherous footpaths. Renate woke up most mornings, jumped out of bed and ran to the toilet, vomiting. *Was it the soup, or the leftover curry, what else could it be?* After two weeks she decided it was time to get 'the test.' A nurse in a blue and white uniform at the St Joseph's clinic told her the news. *Positive.* She nodded, like she was hypnotised. She turned left, not sure where to go. Walked around the block, jumped on a bus back to the old hospital on Marriannenplatz and walked, thinking about Günter and the Red Cross conference in Bonn. That gave her some time to analyse her new situation. There was a creche at uni. They had childcare at the squat, she'd volunteered twice. Günter said he wanted to have kids 'in the future'. *But now? What about my thesis?* Seeing Asha's door open, she walked in and burst out crying. Over the next two hours and lots of mint tea, she decided she'd have the baby. *When should I tell Anne? Maybe after the baby.* And Dr Volhard. *What will be her reaction?*

One week later, when Günter arrived holding a bunch of tulips, she looked at him and burst out crying.

'What's wrong? Don't you like them?'

'No, it's just... I'm having a baby!'

'What...'

'Your baby.'

Günter froze. Renate watched as his face switched from astonishment to apprehension. 'But weren't you using protection? I'm not sure I'm ready to be a father right now. When's it due?'

'September.' Renate bit her bottom lip.

'I suppose you'll want to get married now?' he said.

'Hell no,' she said in a flash. 'Anyway, I can't marry you. At least not right now.'

'Why?'

'It's...complicated.'

'Enlighten me, please.' He started to pace around the room, stared at the floor then back at her face.

'I'm already married to a guy in Australia.'

'And you were going to tell me, when?' He crossed his arms and narrowed his eyes.

'It's not like that. He just helped me get a resident's visa. That's all.'

'I hope you don't have any more secrets I need to know about?' He tapped his foot.

'No. Günter. I'm having the baby. That's my decision.' She felt a hot flush spread up her neck into her face. He turned and walked away.

On Saturday, Renate caught the train to Kassel and stayed with Anne for the weekend. She didn't mention anything about the baby.

'You must be eating well in Berlin,' Anne commented, eyes wandering down to Renate's waist.

'Yes Mum. You know I love my food.'

*

Five months passed. On Friday, June 12, she stood in a crowd opposite the Brandenberg gate with Asha and others from the squat. She listened as Mr Reagan, the president of the United States, gave a speech and heard '*Mr Gor-*

bachev, tear down this wall.' How could that happen, she thought. *At least I can dream.* She ran her hand over her belly wishing that Günter was here. In the past few months, she'd grown used to him being absent most of the time.

Her studies slipped further behind. Günter, when he was there, made some effort to help with cleaning and cooking. He offered vague answers when she asked him where he was going and when he would be back. She was anxious, sick and tired of wanting to throw up most mornings. Her legs ached. Dr Volhard did not relax her expectations. 'Don't fall behind Renate, you'll find it impossible to catch up with a baby. Why don't you complete as much as you can before September, then apply for a year's leave? I will support your application.'

'Thank you, Dr Volhard. I'll think it over.'

*

Helena came two weeks early on September 2, penetrating hazel eyes, an ear-piercing wail and curly black hair like Günter's. He was away for the week, she expected he would be thrilled when he saw his daughter for the first time.

'Are you thinking of moving in with him?' Asha said.

'No. I want to get to know Helena first. Spend time with her while it's still warm. Then I'll decide.'

'We'd all hate to see you leave the squat.' Asha said with a sigh. 'You know... We could be lovers, you and me... I can see it in your eyes.' Asha's face softened and she drew closer.

Renate froze, then jerked back. 'That...would destroy our friendship.'

'We can have both, can't we?' Asha touched Renate's arm and stroked down to her fingers. Renate froze.

'No. They are different. I was fond of someone once and lost her. It nearly destroyed me. Now I have Helena to love.' Renate stared into Asha's glistening eyes.

'Lucky you. I'm happy for you... I hope it lasts.' Asha took a step backwards. 'What's Günter going to do?'

'Don't know. He seems happy where he is.'

'You can't be serious?' Asha scoffed, tilting her head.

'We'll see... We're good.' She smiled up at Asha and she squeezed her hand, thinking she had it all planned out.

Five days later, Günter was not back yet. Renate wasn't too concerned. That night she woke to feed Helena twice. Candles flickered through the murky twilight. She placed the Stone in Helena's hand and wrapped her fingers around it. Outside, thunder boomed and the first drops of rain hammered on the roof.

65

2:30 am, 2 months later

Light rain pattered on the windowsill. Helena wailed on the pillow beside her. Renate couldn't decide if it was hunger or colic. Too wet to go outside. She picked her up, put her on her breast and walked around the room to get her back asleep. Some mornings Renate didn't bother getting out of bed. *Thank God I deferred my PhD.* Nappies hung everywhere inside on a long, slow dry. For the first month, Günter would visit on most nights, then his visits grew less frequent. When she mentioned it, he said he was either in meetings or away on refugee business. By December, after leaving five messages on his phone, she decided to visit him. It wasn't like him not to return her calls.

Towards midday, she strapped Helena – asleep across her chest – with a homemade sling, walked down the cracked path to the bus stop, past old hand-painted vans on one side and three drab-blue tents on the other. A mongrel dog sniffed at a crusty smear of feathers in the gutter. A van door clattered open and a shock of curly long hair and hollow eyes watched her walk down the path. He yelled out, 'Remember to bring back some blonde hair dye for dinner.' She'd grown used to it over the months. Some would stay for a few weeks, others longer. A police van crawled by at least once a day looking for a reason to drag someone away. She'd adapted to surviving on the government 115 DM child support. Everyone in the squat help provide for food. Almost like the FOE share house in Brisbane. People looked out for each other. With Gunter showing less interest, a new distance grew between them. He dropped his idea for her to move in and never again mentioned marriage.

*

The bus shelter was directly opposite Günter's apartment. Helena squirmed, crying to be fed. Günter's building had four stone steps, a set of oak wood doors with two narrow glass panels. As she looked across, the doors swung out, Günter walked down the steps with a blonde girl about sixteen or seventeen in clothes more suited for a warm summer's day. The tight, pink tank top and white shorts looked incongruous in the cold December gloom. Her face looked much older that the rest of her body. She stopped, turned around. Günter placed his hands on her shoulders, one slipped down on her bum and stayed there a second too long. He gave her a playful push just like an owner might give a frisky pony. He did not see Renate with Helena. She was welded to the seat, frozen in position, unsure what to do. After a few minutes, she strapped Helena back in and marched across the road, climbed the steps, pushed through the entrance and banged on Günter's door.

'Renate! What a surprise! I was just about to call you,' he said, a little too fast.

A red flush spread up his neck to his face.

'Really?' Her heartbeat pounded and she leant in closer.

'Yes, of course. Why? Is anything wrong?' He gave her a surprised look.

'You tell me who that blonde girl was who just left?' she said, raising her voice.

'Oh, Liselle? She's Inge's daughter. You know Inge, my boss at work?'

'No...you've never mentioned her,' she said, jaw set tight.

300

'Well, she was just dropping off a parcel from work. I'm on my lunch break. Why don't we stop off for a coffee before I go back?'

'That's all it was?' She let out a long, deep breath.

'Yes, I swear. Don't you trust me?'

'I do... I can, can't I?' Renate peered into his eyes. Deep down her stomach pinched as if gripped in a clamp.

'Of course you can. Here, let me take Helena.'

As they walked, his rapid, innocuous words somewhat settled her. Günter insisted on holding Helena and assured Renate everything was fine. She started to doubt herself.

'I'm going to visit Mama. I'll be gone three or four weeks. Mama can look after Helena so I can work on my thesis. Can you come down and visit? She would like to meet you.'

'I don't think so. Christmas is very busy for us. Refugees need our help even more in winter,' he said, touching his face while shaking his head.

'Not even for a couple of days?'

'I'll see. No promises though.' His eyes dropped to his watch. 'Sorry, I've gotta go.' He pecked her on the cheek. She nodded a weak smile.

That night Renate tossed and turned. She couldn't get the image of that girl out of her mind and the way he'd touched her. *Might give the girl's mother, Inge, a call soon.*

66

Two days after Christmas, Renate returned alone to Berlin to collect her folders, books, clothes and Helena's toys. It was time to say goodbye. She stared into Asha's long face. 'I wasn't expecting that... What am I going to do without you?' Renate held her at arm's length and thrust out a handkerchief. Asha gave her a hug, sniffled and wiped her eyes.

'Where's that wild child?'

'I left her with Mama. I'm catching the 2 pm train back.'

'We'll miss you... Don't be a stranger.'

'Here's my address in Kassel. Visit me. Promise?'

As she waited for the train, the image of the blonde girl played over in her head. How Günter had touched her. She wanted to believe him. *Just a gut feeling?* Signs kept adding up she couldn't ignore: he'd never once disclosed what he did when he was away, the messages she left at his office were not returned, how difficult it was contacting him.

The intercity train crawled into Potsdamer Platz out of damp, eerie and grey winter gloom. It stopped for a minute while six East German inspectors got on. Their dark-green uniforms and green cuff stripes identified them as *Grenztruppen*-border guards. Later, as the train sped through East Germany towards Braunschweig, she checked her papers. The border guards, always in pairs, issued so called 'transit visas' after checking everyone's identification papers. Everything was in order. In about an hour the train crossed into West Germany. Passengers resumed smiling and moved around the carriage. She kept her head down until the train crossed the 'border.'

She cinched her jacket hood tight and carried her suitcase and two backpacks from the bus stop down the front path to the front door. She opened the door, hoping Anne had not put Helena to sleep and tiptoed through the lounge to the kitchen. Anne looked up, held her arms wide and embraced her. 'She missed you.'

'She asleep?'

'Why don't you go and check?' Anne folded Helena's clothes and stacked them in a straw basket. Renate crept up the stairs and looked in through the bedroom door past the nightlight at the end of Helena's cot. She padded over and gave her a kiss. Renate removed her shoes, laid on her bed and closed her eyes. That's all she remembered until Anne prodded her and whispered, 'Come down for dinner.'

She walked down the stairs and sat at the table. *I wish it could be so easy. This is just like being a child again.*

'Go ahead. I ate at seven,' Anne said from the sofa, turning the volume down on the TV.

'What am I going to do Mum? I couldn't even talk to him.' Renate threw her arms up.

'Did you try?'

'I called, twice. Got his damn answer machine.' Renate crossed her arms tight, to calm the pressure in her chest.

'I'll tell you what. If he wants to see you and Helena, he can come here.'

'Thanks Mama, but somehow I don't think that's going to happen.'

She looked down at her plate, pushed it away as tears ran down her cheeks.

'If he's worth it, he'll work it out,' Anne said, sitting still. 'What are you going to do while you're here? Ilse called in a few weeks ago asking about you.' Anne gazed up intensely.

'I don't want to see her. She lied to me about the police.' Renate flexed her fingers. The knuckles cracked.

'I have forgiven her for that. Can't you?' Anne gave a half-hearted shrug.

'No.'

Anne watched Renate poke at her roast chicken in silence. It wasn't an uncomfortable silence or even an unusual one given the time and space that had grown between them. Anne sighed as she washed up, it was more like an escape of air bottled up since Ulrich passed, waiting for this moment. Renate thought, *I will never end up alone in a house in Germany wishing I was someplace else.* 'Tomorrow I'm going to see about childcare. Though I might have to wait until Helena's one.' Renate said, pushing her plate aside.

'Let's worry about that tomorrow. I'm putting on the late news. Join me if you wish.'

Renate nodded, cleaned up her plate and joined Anne on the couch. A female presenter with glued-down blonde hair introduced the lead story. A police car and four police outside the entrance to an apartment block. Renate's eyes narrowed as two police manhandled a struggling man from the entrance and bundle him into a police car. Other police held back a small crowd. *'Today, police in Mitte have arrested a Günter Schreiber, a West German national and taken him to police headquarters. A police spokesman said he was being questioned into the underground trafficking in women and girls from the East.'*

A picture of eight faces appeared on the screen. One of the girls was the girl Günter said was Liselle. Renate gasped. Anne looked back at Renate, then back to the TV and back to Renate again like she was a puppet doll.

'What's wrong? Looks like you've seen a ghost.'

'That fucking ghost is Helena's father.' Her stomach lurched as if she were about to be sick.

'What...' Anne turned her head from Renate to the TV then back again. 'Are you sure?'

'That's him! That's Günter.'

'How is that possible?' Anne said, mouth gaping open.

Renate stared at the TV as if it was a dangerous animal. She jumped up, opened the front door and walked out into a blast of arctic air. She turned left and walked, just walked until she lost feeling in her fingers and toes.

*

The next day two men in dark suits questioned Renate in Anne's lounge-room. They identified themselves as federal police. She stood, erect, with a deep, pained look, eyebrows drawn.

'No, he never told me what he was doing.'

'Didn't you get suspicious when he was away so often?' The older man asked. The other man jotted in a small notepad.

'No. I thought it was his refugee work... Yes, he is the father of my child... No, I won't be visiting him in Berlin.' She responded without emotion, mind split between answering the questions and the more immediate issue: the future as a single mum living with her mother in the house she'd hated as a child. Her arms hung by her waist as if attached to weights. A stark reality scratched and clawed its way to the surface. *How am I going to respond to the inquisitive, judgemental stares on the bus to town?* She had no answer, no ready formula for the next phase of her life as a single mum.

67

Two weeks later, despite the bitter cold, she took Helena to the parks and gardens wrapped snuggly in a pouch tied to her front. At five months, Renate's days were ruled by Helena's sleeps. Renate joined a mother's club, left soon after hearing gossip about *single mums*. Anne supported her but Renate couldn't accept some of her old ideas about children. There was one memory she held onto – her time in Brisbane and the man she married there. Günter became a knot in the pit of her stomach, someone she knew she'd have to deal with when he came out of prison. One day in Ulrich's basement, she cleaned out the mess and carried the broken pieces of wood to the backyard. There, she danced around the burning smoke and flames, Helena babbling with 'mama' and blowing raspberries. A new neighbour stared motionless from a high window next door.

Deep down, she knew this would not last. The mundane necessities of raising a child were beginning to suffocate. Her sleep was spasmodic with disturbing dreams, most she couldn't remember. Except the most recent one.

A vice tightened around her chest sometime after 3 am. She dreamed of a distorted landscape. It wasn't rainforest or pasture or desert or city she floated above but a blend of all these, a passive observer. There was a girl with blonde hair of about sixteen. She struggled with a beast who had the body of a man with the head of a bull, the Minotaur of Crete. His face switched back and forth from Ulrich to Günter and back again. The monster ripped the clothes from the girl. From a different perspective, another man appeared in a loin cloth with leather straps around his thighs and bulging biceps carrying a net and a short, shiny sword. He cast the net over the Minotaur and pulled it away. The half-naked girl ran away. Her vision zoomed in to study the man's face. She thought she recognised the face but couldn't identify the man.

It was after sunrise Helena woke her for a feed. The tight bands around Renate's chest were gone, her breathing returned to normal.

*

She was eager to return to her thesis. Anne helped with childcare and Renate applied for a job at a café on Friedrichplatz just around the corner from the Orangerie, offered to volunteer at the planetarium but they were closed until March. She resumed typing her thesis in her spare time after Helena went to sleep – Anne somehow wasn't disturbed by the clatter of the typewriter pounding through her bedroom wall, like morse code. At times she felt she was hammering away at her demons, turning those memories into words. Christmas became another new year. Ordered, family life returned, a fall-back formula she now appreciated at last.

68

Daniel

January 8, 1988

The white intercity carriage flashed through the German countryside. Daniel clutched the divorce papers and small gift for Renate in a black backpack that had taken a week to find in Sydney – a *Minties*-sized piece of Azur malachite on a gold chain. He'd had a lot of thinking time since leaving Sydney, thirty hours of scrolling through endless 'what if' scenarios, about Alice, what she'd said, *'Don't bother coming back without the papers signed.'* *What if I can't?* He unfolded the phone number of Ilse, an old friend of Renate's and her address in Göttingen. He'd ring her tonight from his hotel.

*

Next morning at ten, he fidgeted before the door knocker on a two-story, white-painted house in a quiet suburb of Göttingen. He doubled-checked the address before he knocked. The door opened and a woman with shoulder-length dark hair stared back with piercing eyes like full stops pressed into her face. He smelled ginger and sweet almond wafting out the door. A tabby cat weaved in and out through her generous skirt like an eel in a barrel of oil. 'Baking sweets?' he asked with quizzical inflection.

'*Verzeihung* – Excuse me? You are?'

'I'm Daniel from Australia.' He studied her drawn face, her neat shoulder-length hair.

'The Daniel, the bike man? Is this about Renate?'

'Sure is.'

'You'd better come in.'

She swept the flour from her apron with a flick of the wrist. Daniel followed, past a small wooden *tzedakah* box on the shelf above a framed picture of a couple in black formal suits. He stopped and stared at the photo.

'My grandparents. That's all we have of them.' He nodded as she continued. 'So, you are Daniel Cohen. What can I do for you?'

'I'm trying to find Renate. It's about our marriage.'

'Well, you better sit down, Daniel Cohen. Excuse me for a minute while I get the biscuits out of the oven. Would you like tea or coffee?' He stared and nodded. She brought out both and sat down opposite in a velvet-lined brown sofa. The smell of the warm biscuits weaved its way through the lounge. 'I can't tell you much. We are no longer friends. It's sad, but that's the way things go sometimes, even with friends you consider part of your *mishpokhe*.' Daniel's eyebrows raised. 'Sorry, I meant 'family.''

'You must have been close?' Daniel wrinkled his nose.

Her pin-point eyes contracted as she nodded. She stared down at her hands.

'I thought Renate and I had a *Verwandtschaft* – a closeness, propinquity. It was my fault. I trusted a police officer with some information about her father. She found out. That was four years ago. We haven't talked since.'

'Do you know where she lives?'

Ilse paused for a second. 'As an old friend, I don't know if I can tell you that.'

'Please. I need to see her. I have some important papers she needs to sign,' he said in a shaky voice.

'What kind of papers?'

'Divorce papers.'

'Oh...' Ilse stared at her cup and raised it to her lips without drinking. 'I'll have to think about it.' She paused and stared into her cup. 'Ring me tomorrow and I'll give you my answer.'

*

Daniel passed the time in the old marketplace staring at the Gänseliesel statue. Around the old city wall and into the ice-covered Botanical Gardens, snow banked up on either side until his feet were freezing and he couldn't feel his fingers. He walked past a lone tree stump, an ancient beech or oak poking it's jagged edges through a hill of fresh snow. Inside, one perfect blue egg, its speckled spots frozen in place. Noise vanished and for a split-second human shadows surrounded him dressed in pin-striped rags shuffling forward down the path, some on blackened stumps. A susurrus rose – not a wail, more of a moan, he turned around and blinked, only the stump was there, nothing else. *Must be the cold.* His breathing returned to normal, he stamped his feet four or five times, blew some warmth back into his closed fist and tightened the cord on his hoodie. Suddenly homesick, he missed the shrill screech of the rainforest, meeting Renate and the petrichor smell on the straight, flat road out of Tennant Creek. *Bugger this cold! If I find her tomorrow and get it done, I might be home in a week.*

Back in his room, he removed his wet socks, spread them on top of the heater fans, turned the dial to max and opened his battered copy of *Zen and the Art of Motorcycle Maintenance* at the last page, looking for inspiration. A line caught his eye – *...and what is 'quality' Robert?* He read. *The echo replied: 'Quality is the common ground of art and technology.' I guess I'll have to think about that. What if Ilse doesn't come through with Renate's address, I'll have to find another way. If not, I'm screwed.*

He phoned Alice.

'Hi. I'm here. It's 8:30 Friday night. What time is it there?'

'Have you seen her yet?' he heard a frosty, austere voice.

'No. I'm in the wrong town. Tomorrow I'm hoping to go to her house in Kassel.'

'Good. Get the papers signed. You can ring me then.'

'How have you been?'

'I can't talk now. Mum and Dad just arrived. Good luck tomorrow.'

Daniel, dumbfounded, drifted closer to sleep, stuck between the past and the present, glued between two different women on opposite sides of the world. *Is this what you have to do to love somebody completely?*

Next morning he rang Ilse.

'I'm giving you her address because I owe her for our past friendship and I want her life to be less complicated. You're here, now. That's reason enough.'

'Thank you.' He breathed a sigh of relief.

'And there's one other thing you need to know. She has a daughter.'

*

The Göttingen-Kassel train doors hissed open. Daniel found a seat next to a foggy window with a panorama of grey buildings, some with steaming chimneys. Roads glistened under morning mist. Snow-covered fields flashed by. About twenty passengers shared his carriage, clumped together like clotted cream. A mother was feeding her baby, two men in dark suits were reading newspapers, the others stared out the window. They ignored him. *One step closer to 'less complicated'? Is that what this is called?*

Just before 1 pm, he stood stock-still before the door of Renate's house, twisting his head, taking in the layout. A woman in her fifties stared down at him from the house next door, then moved away. He raised his gloved hand to knock. It froze in mid-air.

69

Anne ushered Daniel inside with surprise tinged with formality when he introduced himself as Renate's 'husband'. She took his backpack and coat, hung them in the hall and showed him the lounge room. 'I'm sorry, my English not so good.' She made tea. He studied the room, the furnishing, the statues, cuckoo clock, ornate gas heater. Spaces Renate grew up in.

'Never seen one of those before,' he said, pointing to the heater.

'*Katchelofen.* Traditional in German house.'

'Oh... Is Renate here?'

She turned and paused just for a second before answering. 'Nein... No. She's, uh,' – she shut her eyes, thinking hard – 'at *work* in café. Finish at 3.' She smiled.

Daniel checked his watch. 'Where is her daughter?'

'Upstairs... Asleep,' she said, nodding upwards. She placed eight marzipan and hazelnut cookies in a perfect octagon on a platter.

'Can you give me the address? I might surprise her.'

Anne looked at him and nodded. She brought out the biscuits and tea, cleared her throat and returned to the kitchen.

*

He parked the rental on Friedrichplatz with a clear view of Café Bella across the road, leaving his backpack on the backseat. Striding across the road to the café, the knot growing in the pit of his stomach, he prayed the door had no tinkling bell. Daniel opened the door and sat in the booth closest to the entrance. Picking up a menu, he held it in front of his face just below his eyes and surveyed the room – two staff behind the bar, two empty booths, hushed conversations. A young woman in white tennis shoes and an apron was clearing plates from a booth at the far end. A smile cracked his lips as she stumbled on a chair leg and almost dropped the tray. A spoon clattered to the floor. *She hasn't changed much, nice.* She looked down in Daniel's direction, picked the spoon off the floor and removed the order pad from the pocket in her apron. Daniel lowered his eyes as she approached.

'*Was kanne ich Ihnen bringen?*' Are you ready to order?

Daniel raised his eyes. A smile stretched across his face.

For a split second, an invisible bubble stretched around them.

'Daniel!' Her face froze as her eyes fixed on him. She fumbled with the pad and dropped her pen.

'Renate. You haven't changed much. It's...been a long time.'

'What...are you doing here?' she sputtered.

'Came to see you, of course.'

'But how did you find me?' Her eyes were like plates, her body, stiff and still.

'Your mum told me. Are you still wearing that blue stone?'

'Of course.' She pulled down the top of her apron. The Stone of Heaven nestled below her throat.

'So, are you happy to see me?' He spread his arms wide, palms facing up.

She stood stock-still, a smile spread across her nodding face.

'Wow, nice to see you too. When do you finish?'

'In ten minutes.'

'Any chance of a coffee?'

She slipped into the passenger seat of the Volkswagen Golf and gave directions to the vast car park outside the *Orangerie*. 'I'm going to volunteer in the planetarium when they open in March. The grounds are beautiful in summer.' He realised he'd missed her English pronunciation. Past the lake and her old school – 'Needs a new coat of paint' – then she showed him the Ottoneum where she would like to work. 'They said come back in spring.' All chit-chat. He nodded back, happy hearing her voice. By 4 pm in the fading gloom, they were parked outside Renate's house.

'Of course, you're coming in for dinner?' She moved closer and grabbed his arm.

'Sure, but, before we go in, I've got something for you. Go on, close your eyes.'

Daniel reached over and unzipped the backpack. His hand brushed past a yellow envelope and pulled out a small, square box wrapped in lilac paper tied with a red bow. He placed it in her hand with a little squeeze.

'Go on, open it.'

She gaped at the box. Inside, a blue crystal sparkled with veins of green radiating the whole length. Holding it up to the light, her eyes stretched wide. Daniel's pulse quickened.

'It's Azur malachite. I was told it's a very rare specimen.'

'It's beautiful! Where did you get it?' her mouth fell open, her eyebrows raised.

'Back home. Took me nearly a week to find it.'

She leaned over and kissed him on the cheek. He hesitated, not sure what to do. *The divorce papers – they can wait.*

'I'm putting it on. I want to surprise Anne and Helena. Helena won't go to sleep unless she's holding the stone.'

'Sounds just like you.'

She wanted to know everything, starting with the obvious. 'How was your trip over?'

He studied her face, the curve of her nose, the way she cocked her head, her intense smile. 'Quick,' was all he said. Just so he could watch her face as she took that word in, studied it in her logical, rational way. She replied with a smile, less intense but just as beautiful, that contained, in its essence, all he needed to know.

'Was it too quick or not quick enough?'

Touché! There it was. He strolled over to her, held both her arms just below the shoulders, smiled into her face and drew her to him. She collapsed onto his chest and sighed.

'It's been a long time.'

*

They sat close on the sofa as he told her about Japan, Hiroshima, Kakadu, the panorama of the Blue Mountains, like a painting you can touch. She told him about squatting in Berlin, her PhD, raising Helena.

He paused, blinking twice. 'Where's ... um ... Helena's father?'

'Günter's in jail, I think. I don't really know. We don't talk anymore.'

'Oh...'

The seconds stretched. Her face sagged, her eyes sunk. 'I don't talk about him in front of Helena. As far as I'm concerned, he doesn't exist.' The cuckoo clock on the mantle ticked down the evening, Renate excused herself to put Helena to sleep. 'Come up and say goodnight if you like.'

In the bedroom, Anne finished reading *Hansel and Gretel* and left them.

He smiled at Helena, her eyes were half closed. 'Good night.'

They tiptoed down the stairs, he sat in the sofa and reached for the backpack, unzipped it and pulled out the yellow envelope. When Renate returned with two peppermint teas he hesitated, searching for a way to tell her.

'Look, there's something else I have with me.'

'Wow, must be my lucky night! Why the long face?' she said, as her eyes widened.

'I need you to look through these.' He handed over the envelope. *Why isn't this easy? It should be easy. Don't make this difficult for me. It's hard enough being this close to you again.* She pulled out the papers, read the title, looked back and forth. Her face froze.

'Divorce?'

'Yes.'

'But Daniel, we have been separated for more than five years. This is not necessary.'

'Please Renate. I have a girl back home, a very *insistent* woman who wants to marry me. Can you do this one thing for me?'

'Wait, you said 'wants to marry me.' First, I need to know if you want to marry her?'

'I think so. At least I did three weeks ago.'

'And now?' She straightened her back as she studied his face.

Daniel blushed and fumbled with a napkin. 'I...'

'Hold on,' she spurted, 'I will, I still owe you for your kindness in Brisbane and helping me out there, but I want you to help me with something first, before I decide. I need someone to come with me to Auschwitz, someone I can trust. I can't trust Ilse anymore. Would you? It could be like a short holiday. We can discuss this... these divorce papers then. What do you think?'

'When were you thinking of going? I need to visit there too before I return home, so I don't have much time,' he said, turning to face her.

'I need to find any evidence to support my father's story. Why do you need to go?'

'I'm also searching for the past. I think my uncle David was sent there. I want to find out if they have any records of him.'

'How about in two days?'

'Sounds perfect. I can drive.' The words rushed out. He moved to the edge of the sofa.

'Do you want to go the most direct route?'

'Of course.'

'It'll take us through Prague. We can spend a day sightseeing the old town.'

'Fantastic.' He let his head fall back on the sofa and placed the papers back in the envelope.

Renate placed her hand on his. 'After we return. I'll sign them.'

He smiled. 'Agreed. You have a deal.'

70

They travelled south-east in the Golf rental towards the Czechoslovakia border, skirting Fulda and the hidden American nukes buried in bunkers in the surrounding hills. There were acres of barb-wire fences, Daniel counted ten 'No Trespassing' signs.

'How do you know about them?' he asked, giving the sign a nod.

'They were on a map of nuke locations we had in Berlin. Günter had a copy.'

They drew close to Schweinfurt passing lines of US military trucks parked on the sides of the road. Then the three spires of Bamberg Cathedral next to the Main River – 'Rebuilt three times over six hundred years.' Renate did a running commentary as though giving Daniel a history lesson.

'Really?' he replied and: 'That's interesting.'

'Do you want to see some old castles?' she asked.

'Nope. I'm hungry.'

'Me too. Let's stop in Bayreuth. You must try the *spätzle.*'

They parked near the Franz-Liszt Museum, stretching their legs through the *Hofgarten.* She held his hand like a guide showing a friend around her hometown. Strolling past the front of the old *Stadthalle* government office, they found an open café. '*Spätzle's* on the menu!' A waiter in a white chef's cap brought out strudel and coffee and apologised to Renate in German.

'The cook is *sick today* so, no spätzle.' Daniel chuckled at Renate's down-turned face.

Renate drove while Daniel squinted at the map on his lap. 'About thirty kilometres to the border. Can you get your passport out? How much money do we need to exchange?' he said.

'30DM each day.'

'That should buy us a lot of beer.'

*

At the boom gate, a border guard in a white hat, with a face flat like a bowl of water asked for their passports. He studied Renate's photo, looked at her face and back again to the passport. He handed it back without speaking.

Daniel offered his passport.

'You are Australian?' he asked, shuffling back two steps.

'Yes.'

'INXS good, yes?'

'Sorry, what?' Daniel turned to Renate who shrugged her shoulders.

'INXS. *Mechel Huchnence.*'

'Oh... Yes, now I get it. INXS, the band. Michael Hutchence.' Daniel chuckled.

'I help them in Prague last year. They made video.' The guard thrust out his chest.

'Did they? Very good. What was the video about?' Daniel tilted his head as a slow smile spread across his lips.

'New song. *Never tear us apart.*'

'Really? Sounds nice.' Daniel held out his hand and the guard returned his passport.

'Nice. Great saxophone.' The guard laughed and his face softened. 'Have a pleasant stay in Czechoslovakia.'

They drove off slowly around a curve in the road. Daniel started laughing so hard Renate had to pull off and stop.

'What's so funny?'

'INXS. *Never tear us apart.* Get it?'

'Not really. Is this an Australian joke?' she said, perplexed.

Daniel shook his head and thought about Alice, her inflexible views, the way she giggled with Kate, her body. His skin itched with something just out of reach. Something annoying, like a lost set of car keys. As the light faded, they rounded a bend next to the Ohre river and reached the outskirts of Karlovy Vary.

'Let's find a place to sleep. I'm tired,' she said.

At a Benzina gas station on the outskirts, she asked directions in German. The man pumping petrol kept looking back the way they had come before pointing down the road. 'Two kilometres. Cross the bridge. Look for a blue sign.'

As they turned off and crossed the river, a yellow and white GAZ24 *Volga* Czech police car followed them, at a safe distance, to the guest house.

71

The furnishings were sparse – two single beds, a table covered with fine grey ash, two chairs and a coal fireplace that spewed more smoke than heat. The beds, first world war vintage. Downstairs, they sat at a table for two covered with a white-frilled tablecloth. She didn't ask about Alice, he didn't mention Günter. The waiter, in a white apron, served a meal that Renate pronounced as *moravský vrabec* – dumplings in a pork sauce. Pilsner was served in half-litre glasses. Renate barely touched hers – 'Lost the taste for it after Helena' – they finished their meal and retired to their room.

Later, Daniel, tossing and turning in the squeaky bed, stole a peek over at Renate. His mind wouldn't switch off – what he was doing, what would happen after Auschwitz, when they returned. He wished he had some strong sleeping tablets. Around two he drifted off.

When he woke, she was sitting at the window in jeans and a thick, blue jumper.

'Come over, you can see the mist rising on the river.'

He struggled under the bedclothes to pull up his jeans and two shirts and blew into his hands. She looked across, smiled and said, 'Are you cold?'

'Bloody freezing.'

'You're just not used to it. C'mon. Come see the view.'

A police car crawled by as they stared through the window.

'That's the second time in fifteen minutes,' she said, rubbing the back of her neck.

'Let's get breakfast. I'm keen to get moving.'

*

By eleven they were in Prague, walking across the Charles Bridge to the statue of St John of Nepomuk.

'It says here *touch the statue to give you good luck.*" Daniel turned and grinned. 'At least you don't have to kiss it.'

They crossed the bridge and explored the old Jewish Quarter and the cemetery.

'Looks like they built it on a hill?' Daniel said, looking up through the fence. The street was almost deserted.

'No. It's custom never to remove a grave or headstone. They just kept piling soil on top. Let's get going. It'll be dark by the time we reach Oswiecim.'

'Maybe we should stop in Brno. It's about halfway.'

By two they were halfway to Brno. Renate chatted about Helena, how she was missing her, how fast she was growing up. How she was unsure now about her PhD.

'It'd be a pity to give it up after all the work you've put in,' Daniel said, brushing her arm.

'I know, Daniel. But Helena is my priority now.'

'I think you'll regret it later if you stop.' His voice was firm.

Her face half turned as if she was studying his profile, she opened her mouth, closed it, then said, 'Maybe you're right. I'll give it more thought when we return home.'

'Tell me a story about your father?' he asked.

She hesitated for a second and took a deep breath. 'There used to be a suitcase in our attic with pictures and letters from before the war. There was one of a little boy about one, sitting on a picnic blanket. It was Ulrich in

322

1921. The suitcase had not been opened for years. One night about the same time, I heard him calling out in his sleep. He was shouting, 'Don't take her! Take me, she's done nothing wrong!' When I mentioned this to Mama the next day, she said, 'We don't talk about that. Forget it.' That's just it, I never have.'

'Who do you think he was dreaming about?'

'I don't know. Might have been the woman he loved in Auschwitz. Hopefully I'll find out some more there.'

*

In Brno, they signed into Apartmany Brno on Francouzska Street as Mr and Mrs Cohen and were shown to a spacious bedroom with a double bed. For a second Renate stared at Daniel, who burst out laughing.

'I'll go and get the swag.'

'You don't have to do that. It's a big bed, I won't bite,' she said, a tight smile crept across her lips.

*

They had lunch at a highway café on the outskirts of Ostrava and tried to spend the rest of their Czech money. Renate was keen to get going. She rang Anne to check on Helena.

'Everything's okay. I'm keen to get there now and get back.'

At the border, a Polish guard stopped them to check their passports.

'Going to Oswiecim?' he asked.

They nodded. 'How does he know that?' Daniel whispered.

'Do you have any Czech money with you?' he asked, head swivelling from Daniel to Renate. Daniel showed him a ten Koruna note. The guard looked back from the note to Daniel's face and back at the note.

'Just give him the money, Daniel.'

72

They pulled up in the carpark outside the main gate of Auschwitz 1, late in the decaying afternoon light. They looked up at the sign: '*ARBEIT MACHT FREI* – Work Will Set You Free'. He grabbed her hand and felt a tremor run down Renate's arm. He tightened his grip.

'Now to find the truth.'

'If you wander off, meet me back here in an hour,' she said, at the entrance to the museum.

She veered off towards the archive section. Daniel walked trance-like from display to display. The glass partitions contained thousands of jumbled-up shoes, combs, purses, glasses and handbags in mountainous piles. He walked to a large table with a miniature display of the camp as it was in the war. The dusty model looked abandoned, its tiny structures a pastiche of the suffering inside. One building was enlarged, a '*Block*' with an open door. Daniel squatted down at eye level and peered through the door, expecting to see stick figures in pinstripes lying on the floor.

Renate was in a small room with a door marked '*Archives*'. He walked in. The heavy wooden door banged shut. A woman with grey hair in a tight bun and glasses perched halfway down her nose looked up.

'Can I help you? We are closing in fifteen minutes.'

'Yes, please. Do you have any prisoner records from 1943? I'm looking for my uncle, his name was David Cohen.'

'What nationality?'

'Australian.'

She raised her eyebrows and the skin between her eyes pinched.

'Not many Australians were sent here unless he was Jewish.'

'He was.'

'Wait then, I'll check.'

She turned and trotted through a back door. While she was gone, Daniel studied the room – a vast wooden desk covered in stacks of papers, a mountain of folders, large boxes in piles on the floor. The lady returned, stared at his face for a second and shook her head.

'Sorry. No records of a David Cohen in 1943.'

Daniel sat on the bench outside next to Renate. 'Any luck? I struck out on my uncle.'

'She said they had no records of any German soldiers anymore. The Russians took them all after the war. She also said there was a tour at nine tomorrow.'

'Let's do that. I've seen enough here.'

73

Daniel tossed and turned in the guesthouse bed in Oswiecim, conscious of Renate's muttering and snuffles. At 2 am he'd had enough, got up, dressed in two pairs of socks, two jumpers and a thick coat. Round the back of the storeroom, he selected the cleanest guest bicycle, with just enough air in the tyres.

He cycled back to the gate outside Auschwitz II/ Birkenau under a mid-winter's full moon, the bike wobbling and slipping on the frozen road. He stopped to blow some warmth into the woollen mittens. The metal handlebars were blocks of ice in his grip. At the main gate, he stopped and cocked his head to the sound of a distant train's whistle. For a split second the moon darkened. *Where are those sounds coming from? It sounds like a violin, if that's possible?* A wave of garbled voices washed through his ears. It sounded like two or three different languages reading a script from the afterlife. He shook his head again and trotted along the fence line. Deep down, he knew behind the fence, it was empty, devoid of the millions who had lived and died here. The smell – drifting fumes of coal from a smouldering chimney mixed with the tang of some bitter herb. Stumbling over a branch poking from the ground, he stooped to pick it up. It was white, straight, polished dull in the moonlight. He gasped and dropped it in one movement. It was a femur. *What else lies below, covered by forty years of dirt?* There was no sensation in his feet and fingers – he turned back, exhausted from the effort.

*

During breakfast of crepes, apple pancakes and coffee, Renate leaned in close with one eyebrow raised. 'Where did you go last night?'

'Oh, just out for a walk. Couldn't sleep. Thought I'd check out the scenery.'

'Are you being serious?' she said, frowning.

'Deadly.' He looked at her. The joke fell flat.

'I wondered where those bags under your eyes came from. Did you find anything?'

'Just a cold, bleached femur. And a bloody long fence.'

She studied his face for a second, nodded and checked the time. 'It's 8:45. There's the bus.'

They were the last to board after a group of four Canadians, a French couple and a Polish middle-aged lady. Mr Jaworski, the guide, was mid-thirties in faded-blue jeans with a strong jaw covered with a black stubble. He sat behind the driver, translating from Polish to French and finally English, clutching a microphone with one hand he gripped a cup of coffee with the other.

'It is pleasant day, no? Not raining. We can walk. Please notice the donation box next to the door,' he said, glancing down the bus aisle.

Daniel gave Renate a wry grin as the bus lurched to a stop outside the 'Commandant's former villa, the bakery, the staff accommodation building', a vast brick complex now divided into apartments. They trotted off, with polite *ahhs and umms,* then back on the bus. Next, the bus jerked to a halt outside the main gate of Birkenau. Daniel looked down at fresh boot marks from last night.

'Come. Follow please. We go to the last block standing.'

327

The building stood in the middle of a vast wasteland, twenty metres from train tracks, incongruous like a single incisor in a sea of decay, covered in fresh powder snow that crunched under their boots. Inside, they stared at the long row of holes in wooden benches running down the middle. 'Toilets, you may look inside.' The rows of wooden sleeping benches stacked to the ceiling, bunk-bases of pine slats. 'Very uncomfortable. Top bunk is best. No one can shit on you.' Daniel peeked at the Canadians. The woman had a handkerchief over her nose as if the past could smell. The man's face was fixed, his colour drained away. They shuffled to the end of the railway tracks. 'Selection was here. To the right, you go to gas chamber. To the left, tattoo and live.'

'How many got to live?' the Frenchman asked.

The guide shook his head. 'Not many. Only those useful for work.'

Daniel turned and faced him. 'Why do people still come here, I mean there is nothing here except piles of shoes, glasses, photos and empty buildings?'

The guide scratched the stubble on his chin in deep thought. When he spoke his face had changed from confident to clouded, unsure, even haunted. 'Why don't you ask the ghosts here that question and ask them why they don't leave?' He waved his arm around in a circle. 'No one can answer your question. Just remember, we must stop this from happening again. That's why you've come, no?' Daniel nodded and realised there were no answers here. No formula, no solution.

They walked to a large pile of concrete rubble shaped like a building. There were steps leading down to a grimy concrete floor.

'Come please. Gas Chamber.'

The Canadians remained behind. Daniel clutched Renate's hand tight as they descended the steps.

'You okay?' he said.

'Just.'

Daniel descended into a broken hall, walls splotched with faded Prussian blue acid stains. It was one of those moments when time itself seemed to split and splutter backwards. He heard the guide's words echo as if they were coming from a long tube. *Poison gas stains. Zyklon-B.* The French couple were transfixed in front of the memorials. Renate ducked over to speak with the guide.

'I would like to ask you if there is anyone who might remember a German driver who was here in 1944. His name was Ulrich Mayer?'

'You're German? Why do you ask?'

'He was my father. He died a short time ago. I'm looking for anyone who may have known him?'

Jaworski studied her face for a long time, like he was staring at an alien from another planet. His eyes clouded over, a puzzlement deep in them that narrowed as his lips pinched.

'Anyone? What you mean? Are you crazy? They've all gone, up those.' He pointed to the last two remaining chimney stacks, rising above broken red bricks, rusting metal doors and dirty snow. His face, a sadness mixed with anger. The light faded from his eyes. Daniel wandered over and looked up at the two remaining chimneys, washed clean by decades of rain, sleet and neglect like a painful memory refusing to be forgotten.

'I lost uncles, my father lost his brother, father. All murdered by the Nazis. *Mishpokhe,* all gone. There are only ghosts and memories here. Where did all that madness go? The Russians took it through Germany to Berlin and raped thousands of women and girls. Where did the truth go, you ask me? You're walking on it. And you come here asking if I can help you? No. This is how you help me. Go back to Germany and tell as many who will listen what happened here.' He stared at her with black billiard balls eyes. She nodded and clasped her hands tight together through the woollen gloves. As he glared at her with a mixture of anger and pity, she was surrounded by a maelstrom, it enveloped her like smoke from an explosion, freezing her to the spot. Daniel came closer and put his arm around her shoulder. Her hands were still shaking. She leaned into him as you would in a gale until the shaking stopped.

'Did he tell you anything useful?'

'No. And yes. Strange. He said the same thing Ulrich said, just before he died. '*Tell them what happened here.*''

'Do you want to see anything else?'

'Only Helena's smile. Let's go home.'

74

Renate stared out the car window as the dreary landscape flashed by, trying to make sense of it all, what the guide had said: 'Tell them what happened here.' *But tell them what? Anyway, who would listen? How can I speak for the dead?* A story of more than a million murdered innocents, or a few brave survivors? *Why couldn't Ulrich have lived longer to explain what happened?* Maybe some memories are just that painful. What Günter had done to her didn't come close. *I have Helena, that's all I need.*

But was it? *What about Daniel and those blasted divorce papers? If he insists, I'll sign.* Something deep inside her said, *Forget the past, you have a child, move on.* If it was that simple. Just one day at Auschwitz and her life would never be the same again. She thought about the young woman Ulrich had loved there. *Maybe that was it! Love and kindness gave them something to live for. Even in Hell.*

*

He stared at the road, the sleet washing back and forth across the windshield, slowed to eighty on the frozen surface, having said three words to Renate in the past hour – 'Looks like snow.' She'd barely nodded a reply. The barren gloom he'd seen would stay with him forever. It was the nature of the emptiness that fascinated his scientific mind. The essence of empty space, once filled with humans, coming, going, dying, surviving in a chaotic yet ordered way. Of the few artefacts – glasses, hair, buildings that remained, most were overshadowed by the vast void of desolation as if that place was reserved on the surface of the earth to honour those who had died. A physical place, immortal, a reminder that this should never happen again. He understood, deep down, that memories can only illuminate the past in a fuzzy, imprecise way, and there was no ready-made formula to help understand it. Again, he had to remind himself of the reason he was here – *To get the divorce papers signed*. Somehow all that seemed insignificant now after everything they'd experienced together. It had bonded them like glue bonds timber, alive, like a final, futile embrace in the gas chambers. It left them relieved that they could walk outside into the sunshine and feel wind on their faces. His thoughts about the divorce papers tumbled around like wet clothes in a tumble dryer as the lights of Prague shone in the distance.

'Let's stop and get dinner. I'm exhausted.'

Towards 10 pm, they both collapsed on the double bed.

'I just want you close tonight, nothing else,' she said, taking his hand.

'Yeah, me too. What did you make of Auschwitz?'

'I'm still trying to work that out. You?'

'Sadness. Emptiness. Nothingness. Just rubble and faded symbols. The destruction said it all,' he said, staring at the ceiling.

'Like a lack of entropy?'

'More like time, frozen in place.'

'If you say so.'

75

Two days after they returned home, the divorce papers still untouched in his backpack, Daniel suggested they go for a bike ride while Helena was in day care. 'It'll get us out of the house. We need the exercise.'

They crossed the bridge over the Fulda River on Damaschkes Str and turned left onto Am Sportzentrum. Renate laughed for the first time in days as Daniel wobbled on Ulrich's bike. They had three hours in sparse sunshine until they collected Helena from childcare. Renate showed Daniel the sights around Kassel. Daniel showed off by racing ahead around a slippery curve, hooting like a kid, only slowing down when he almost lost it on an icy patch. He stopped to catch his breath, looked back as a car skidded out of control and slammed into Renate. The car spun twice before stopping awry in the middle of the road. Flinging Ulrich's bike aside, he ran down to see Renate lying crumpled on the road, blood oozing from a wound behind her left ear and her left leg bent at an obscene angle. He propped his jacket under her head and pressed his sleeve onto the bleeding wound. Her breathing was sputtering on and off like a boat motor starved of fuel. The stunned driver came over, his hands shaking and pointed to the road.

'Don't just stand there, go call a fucking ambulance!' Daniel shouted.

'*Nicht verstehen.*'

'Ambulance! Get an ambulance!'

A woman in a passing car stopped and said, 'I'll go and call the *Krankenwagen*, the ambulance.'

Fifteen minutes later he was in the back of a Mercedes-Benz ambulance, holding Renate's clammy hand while a grim-faced paramedic fitted an oxygen mask. They put her leg in a temporary splint and wound an oversized bandage around her head like an Egyptian mummy.

*

Daniel phoned Anne from the foyer. 'Can you collect Helena? I'm waiting to hear how she is. I'll be late.' He paced back and forth in the waiting room of the Marien Hospital while the nurse in charge stared at him. He sat on his hands on a blue, plastic chair trying to stop them from shaking. When that didn't work, he folded his arms and gripped his fingers around his elbows. His feet were numb in the wet sneakers, so he removed them and placed one on the warm radiator. The nurse shook her head. He ignored her.

As the minutes ticked by, Daniel transfixed his eyes on the wall clock on the opposite sky-blue wall – it was all he could do to distract himself from feeling hopeless, out of control. There was one week before his flight home, six days to convince himself that he needed those papers signed. After thirty-five minutes and twenty seconds, a doctor marched through the clear-plastic doors, surveyed the room and walked over.

'Are you Mr Cohen?' he said, eyes flicking from Daniel to a blue clipboard.

'Yes. I'm Renate's husband.'

The doctor opened a file and said, 'Can you tell me her full name, please?'

'Renate Mayer Cohen,' Daniel said, still sitting on his hot hands.

'I see. You say you are her husband, yet you are English?'

'No. I'm Australian.'

'Do you have any proof of your marriage?' he said, tapping the clipboard with a Parker pen.

'I have papers at her place, yes.'

'You should get them if you want to see her. She's in theatre now.'

'She'll be okay, won't she?' Daniel rose, grimaced and licked his lips.

The doctor hesitated before answering, 'That's all I can tell you now.'

'And you are?' Daniel said.

'Dr Fischer. Chief of Emergency.'

*

When he walked in Anne's front door the first thing he saw was her drawn face. While Anne bathed Helena he gave Anne the news – the accident, her leg, that she was in theatre, that he'd go back after dinner with the marriage papers. Anne just nodded as she prepared the *eintopf pot* stew and spaghetti for dinner.

'They said she had a badly broken femur and was in surgery. That's all they'd tell me until I show them proof that we are married.'

'You still are, aren't you?'

'Yes, I have the papers in my bag. You'll put Helena to bed?'

'Of course.'

*

Daniel waved the yellow envelope at the reception nurse with the starch-stiff face.

'I need to see Dr Fischer.'

'*Ja.* Wait please.'

He sat in the same chair staring at the same clock as if he'd never left. New faces filled the space: a mother rocking a blue-faced baby in her arms, an elderly couple in formal clothes, long tweed coat and matching cap with a bird of prey's feather at an obtuse angle. Daniel paced the room until the old man stared at him for the third time. He looked up as Dr Fischer and another doctor appeared in front of him. The doctor looked at the yellow envelope, opened his hand and Daniel gave him papers to read.

'So, I see you are about to divorce your wife?'

'No, and it's none of your business.' Daniel held his gaze without flinching. The doctor took one step back.

'I see. This is Dr Baeur, staff neurologist.'

They shook hands. 'Come with me please, we can talk in my room.'

'How is my wife? When can I see her?' Daniel paced the room, eyes darting between the two.

'Her broken femur required extensive re-construction. There may be some nerve damage. We won't know that for a few days.' Dr Baeur said.

'But is that all? She'll be okay, yes?'

'Scans have revealed a bleed into her brain. I'm just about to take her back to surgery to fix that.' He leaned forward and his eyebrows drew together.

Daniel stared, hoping for some good news.

The doctors exchanged glances.

'You may as well go home, Mr Cohen. You should be able to see her tomorrow.'

*

He left Anne on the sofa staring vacantly at the TV and plodded up the stairs. He closed the bedroom door, turned on the light and removed the documents from the envelope, arranging them on the bed: the marriage certificate, the divorce papers with their yellow-coloured arrow stickers pointing to blank spaces. Daniel stared at them, frozen to the spot, before reaching down, taking the divorce papers and ripping them to pieces. Gathering the torn remains in a tray, he walked down the stairs and stood before the glowing embers of the *katchelofen*. Opening the metal door, he threw in the pieces of paper, kneeled as if in prayer and started to blow until they flared bright and withered up in flames. Afterwards, he stared at the ash satisfied that nothing remained.

The next day he phoned Alice from the public phone.

'Just letting you know I'm staying here,' he paused, 'Renate has had a bad accident and she will need a lot of care when she's out of hospital.'

'What about the divorce papers?' she said, with a heavy sigh.

'The papers? Sorry, they're gone, I burnt them.' After a longer pause, he heard a faint click in the earpiece.

As he lay on the bed, he remembered what Ilse had said of Renate – *mishpokhe,* family – and realised, without any doubt, that Renate and Helena were the closest thing to real family he'd ever had. Sleep came easier, with the marriage certificate tucked under his pillow. Drifting off to sleep, a smile wound its way across his face as the image of a girl with a limp, whose actions that day seven years ago had sent him halfway across the world to find the family he'd never had.

76

Renate spent four weeks in hospital in plaster as her memory returned, piece by piece. She remembered nothing of the accident, nothing of what came before, just accepted that Daniel was staying and visiting her, as he had every day since. They were inseparable, just as the two crystals were together, nestled against her chest. After the plaster was removed, the physio was relentless; endless hours of treadmill, stretches, water routine until Renate cried, 'When will it end?'

'When you can walk without those,' Daniel said, nodding at the crutches.

Helena began to accept that Mama couldn't play the old games she used to. Daniel stepped in, more and more. After six weeks she was strong enough to come home. Some of her memories had returned – the clock in Prague, the friends from Berlin and another friend whose name she couldn't say. She never mentioned Auschwitz or having been there. Or her father's name. She couldn't understand why Helena didn't call Daniel 'Dada' until Daniel explained it one night. She pulled a face as if pulling wet paper from a blocked toilet.

Spring rains washed the ice from the roads and they went for short rides together, Helena behind Daniel in a bike seat, around the lake, the Orangerie and running into her favourite place, the planetarium. 'Ball, ball.' Helena pointed to the planets. 'No, darling, they are planets. P-l-a-n-e-t-s.' he said.

As spring's thaw turned into summer, Renate was well enough to return to uni. 'We'll have to live in Berlin. I'll contact Asha and see if there's any spare rooms in the squat.'

'Squat?' he said, wrinkling his nose.

'Come on, Daniel, you'll love it! Just like Brisbane!'

*

The next summer, they followed the protests in Leipzig and Dresden as the whole of Germany braced for change. In Berlin, it was all the young people talked about while the older generation watched it unfolding on TV. They moved to a squat two blocks from the Georg von Rauch house and Daniel began volunteering as an English teacher for East German refugees. Renate juggled uni, helping Daniel teach English and Helena celebrated her second birthday with a house party Asha had organised in the old squat. Time dissolved in frantic preparations for an event that would change history forever, if only they knew it that summer. As September turned into October the beech and oak dropped golden reminders of the changes coming. Protests grew in the East, over 70,000 marched in central Leipzig. Hungary flung open its border, Gorbachev, remembering the West's generous offers of help after the Chernobyl disaster promised change. Daniel felt more alive than ever, a bond grew between him, Renate and Helena that couldn't be broken.

Occasionally he thought of Alice, the phone call, and the obvious conclusion that they were never going to end up together – she didn't have the right formula for him, *as that weird Jules used to say. She'll find a partner, I'm sure of that.* At times he thought of the students at Blue Mountain Grammar – but it was mostly a nostalgia for the bush and the birds in the Blue Mountains. Alice's memory would fade away into those locked suitcases where all memories eventually go.

*

In Sydney at a real estate convention Ben and Kate had dragged her to, Alice already had two date offers from successful agents. Kate handed her a Bacardi and coke, turned and winked at a guy walking over. As Alice caught her smirking, Kate mouthed *'wicked'.*

*

One Sunday morning, as they sprawled on the bed eating toast and pancakes, Renate told Daniel of a dream she'd remembered from her time in hospital. 'I dreamed I had a new lover. His name was Paris. He came to me as a poem does, in broken lines and deceit. He told me he loved me and would always be with me but one day he left for another country to fight the Trojans. He said as he was leaving, that he loved a fair maiden, more golden than me. Her name was Helen. My mouth was dry, then I saw two stones come together as one – one blue azurite, the other as green as the rainforest leaves. They merged and we were together. At last.'

'Is that from Greek mythology?'

'Could be, if you believe in dreams.'

*

The young woman unlocked the door with the sign *School Psychologist – Counsellor* and walked in, put her bag next to the desk and switched on the computer. Randwick Girls High was her first appointment. She closed the door on the chatter and din outside, a faint reminder not of who she was but what she'd become. Against the odds, she'd sailed through Uni and been appointed to her first choice, a selective school a world away from where she'd come from – Winburn.

*

The wall came down. Refugees from the East flooded through Berlin. Almost every day, the students doubled in Daniel's classes, now a paying job. Renate finished her thesis and applied for research jobs in Germany, England

340

and Australia. They could afford a small apartment in west Berlin overlooking a park and a lake. Helena started daycare three days a week. She begged Daniel, as he was the softer one, to buy her a piano. One day he came home carrying a long cardboard box with '*Yamaha*' in bold letters. 'Couldn't find a piano, sorry, this will have to do.'

One day just before Christmas, Renate sat Daniel down and held both his hands.

'Before I start my new job, I'd like to take Helena back to Brisbane.'

'Like a holiday? Can we afford it?'

'I still have money from Ulrich.'

'When?'

'How about in two weeks?'

*

Ten days later they said their goodbyes. Renate and Helena gave Anne a final hug.

'Promise we'll be back in three weeks.' She held back tears.

'C'mon, Mama, let's go.'

Renate nodded at Daniel and they left for the drive to Frankfurt. As they drove out of town and reached the freeway south, Renate turned and looked intently at Daniel.

'I've got something to tell you.'

'Sounds ominous. Go on then.'

'Thank you for finding me.'

'You're welcome.' He turned and smiled. 'I always felt bad about leaving a wife stranded in another country.' He looked directly at her face expecting to see a smile. Her brow was wrinkled and her jaw set. 'What is it? Aren't you glad I found you?'

'Of course, and just one other thing.' She hesitated for just a second. 'You're going to be a father.'

341

The End

About the Author

Christopher Williams is a writer an educator living in the mid-north coast of NSW. He is a member of the Hunter Writers Centre and the Australian Society of Authors. When he is not writing, he teaches at a local high school, and writes on his website Wordwheelswrites.com

In the 1980's, he cycled in Japan, Malaysia, Sri Lanka and India, sending back stories to be published in the magazine Freewheeling. When he returned, he began a teaching career in outback NSW, on which the beginning of The Formula of Memory is based.

His recent achievements: The Ice against the Heart, a short story published in the Story Hunters – Anthology 2 (2021), and a poem in the anthology Where the fairy tales go (2023). He has also won two prizes for his poems, including a first prize in a member's competition in 2023.

He began writing his debut novel The Formula of Memory in 2021. The genre is blended socio-historical drama.

He lives with his wife, two children and one grandchild, two cats and two dogs